CHANDOS RING

The *Chandos Ring Cycle:*

Trilogy one
Exodus From Sapiens
includes the following books:

Death Star Earth

I Hear Strange Cries at Jupiter

In My Atom Is Ark

CHANDOS RING

Book Three

IN MY ATOM IS ARK

With Introductory Essay
on New Philosophy:

A NEW THEORY OF POETRY

Mark Chandos

To order additional copies of this book, contact:
Xlibris Corporation
1-888-795-4274
www.Xlibris.com
Orders@Xlibris.com
63666

CONTENTS

Dedicated to the soldiers of our Western Empire.

Only foot soldiers know that they carry
arms to spread the idiom of our poetry.

Summary of philosophic insights of CHANDOS RING

Book Three

Main Thesis:

- *Western scientific, materialist, liberal ideology (modernism) now makes a final movement to total linguistic domination of human life.*

  Each culture that comes into contact with Western idiom is eradicated and replaced with modern Western linguistic codes of information. No alternate human linguistics can resist modernism. Moving now to its final supremacy, modern linguistic idiom is now the only hegemonic interpretation of the human condition. Western liberalism has already transitioned to total control of the human narrative. Modernism is now the agency of surveillance. This is consistent with the aim of any linguistic code to seek hegemonic control of its ideational space. Western scientific, materialist, liberal ideology (modernism) now makes a final movement to total linguistic domination of human life.

Supporting Sub-Thesis:

- *Vernacular speakers, by creating an alternate linguistic codex, deconstruct the monopoly on scientific modernism in order to regain control of the human condition.*

  Modernism is only a linguistic construct. Modernism is a linguistic code that fabricates its own linguistic evidence of excellence. Example: *This year's computers are better than last year's models.* This is typical modernist formula. This is misinformation – newer computers are usually more complicated, more expensive, and more difficult to use. Another myth: *Rational science can solve every human problem.* This is propaganda. In truth, exclusively rational, materialistic machines currently block a more advanced codex of technology. The mind can construct non-material technologies that surpass what material atoms can currently perform with contemporary material and secular constructs. Contemporary, archaic, science is only a degraded language of what is actually possible. How to break modernism's monopoly of linguistic information? The vernacular philosopher counters scientific linguistics with an alternate, more advanced, linguistics of the human condition. Example: Jules Verne made a story of travel to the moon 100 years before there was a scientific linguistic codex to support space travel. The point? The new vernacular storyteller must perform the next human *re-imagination* of future life. Modernism would block the vernacular poet from his central position as *"maker of worlds."* Story Theory counters this paradigm and restores the authority of the epic poet.

- ***Linguistic patterns determine the visible "reality" of consciousness.***

Consciousness, expressed as civilization, is bias. Language informs the expression of this bias. Each linguistic code develops along separate channels of discovery. The linguistic pattern of any high civilization – from the creation epics of ancient Sumer to the Apollo moon landing – directly determines what concepts, or technologies, result from that civilization (human consciousness). Shakespeare's English discovers Hermetic magic; scientific English discovers nuclear warheads and marketable pharmaceuticals. Each linguistic code may only function within the culture that can decipher the respective and highly specific ideation of reality. Elizabethan society could make no sense of rocket science, and modern men could make no sense of Hermetic Renaissance Magic – yet each are products of high human linguistic choice. Without the modern need (or expectation) of machines, any form of technology would seem incomprehensible, unpleasant, and unnecessary for life.

- ***Self-consciousness is a hermetically sealed structure.***

Nothing outside of consciousness can be perceived. No information can be detected in consciousness that is not already contained in consciousness. Therefore, all events within consciousness, as diverse as a human relationship or a snowflake, may only be a mirror of what *already* is encoded into consciousness. A relationship, or even a snowflake, is not a separately existing element – but information already embedded in consciousness. If all possible future human phenomena are already encoded within consciousness, then there is nothing separate from our mental manipulation. Never once has any scientist discovered *something* outside of consciousness. Not once. And if all possible phenomena rest within consciousness – already – then all possible worlds yet to be discovered are already contained in the codices of our mind! If true, then the view of human life is forever altered, and man's vaunted science is only similar to an animal chasing its own tail.

- ***Language mirrors the hermetically sealed structure of consciousness.***

Each linguistic code constructs a human civilization as self-referent superstructure of value – hostile to assault from other linguistic codes. No linguistic pattern (as ideology) can discover, identify, or reform its own linguistic misprision. Linguistically formed ideologies are enforced by a self-referent linguistic code impervious to outside discourse.

- ***Modernism cannot reform modernism.***

The language of secular liberal modernism cannot contradict the self-referent codes of its own linguistic structure. Modernism owns the lexicon of the standards by which correct living is measured. Thus modernism cannot reform modernism anymore than Islam can reform Islam. Each idiom is linguistically self-referent. These civilizations can only be eradicated through a charismatic cyclic economic or ecological collapse.

- ***The purpose of the human mind is not to replicate rationality – but to avoid conventional rationality with alternate imaginative constructs.***

Consciousness is charismatic. Modernism merely makes a rational *representation* of consciousness. Rationality, pointedly, cannot enter other dimensions of information without alteration. Thus, rationality is linguistically crippled. Rationality, as isolated, operates as an ideational prosthetic. All advances of Western men have, in effect, been assaults on the rational and visible spectrum. The oceans were dangerous and unknown – but Western men entered them to make conquest of the globe. Space is dangerous – but Western men enter space to make conquest of consciousness. These achievements are not acts of rationality – nothing was ever assured. Each was an act against conventional rationality.

- *Sentience is evidence of* contact *with an alien entity that is demanding to be searched. A further application of sentience is always required.*

Inexplicably, life challenges every emotion, every relationship with a bias of intention. We attribute the bias enmeshed with life to god, fate, justice, or the influence of the stars. In fact, we do not know the source of charismatic information. It is certainly linguistic. Something intelligent, man, is worked with intelligence. What is the proof of this bias? Life is an entity not stable under the condition of stasis – there is always a necessity for a further application of sentient and emotional life. Life displays a peril that can only be corrected with a *further* application of sentience (prayer, faith, hope) beyond the constructs of a terrestrial, material construct. Consciousness, thus, is evidence of contact with an alien presence. Sentience contains a bias that we have been exploring – linguistically – for millennia. Because we do not know the source of bias in consciousness, we must treat it as an alien force. It can be detected only with linguistics protocols.

- *Modern poetry is irrelevant due to a schism of the modern vernacular.*

The strong poet must use a medium that expresses supremacy. The modern vernacular speaker is unable to speak with supremacy. This is due to the presence of a priestly high language in the culture. The language of high math, quantum physics, and science precludes the vernacular speaker from a discussion of the totality of life. To become a student of these linguistics only results in the student becoming a linguistic follower of these disciplines – thus allowing no hostile or alternate linguistic critique. Therefore the modern poet, speaking a vernacular, is wounded and second-rate. This emotional cognizance has resulted in a failure of poetry since the 1950's.

- *The genetic map of human genome contains the cosmological origins of human consciousness.*

Homo sapiens are a species created from the alteration of the previous humanoid genome. The ancient narrative of the arc of the flood is a "record" of a previous genetic reengineering of the human genetic structure. Noah, it will be remembered, was "perfect in his generations." The ark of the human atom contains numbered elements of life – two by two *(the Double helix, the dividing mitochondria, the electron orbiting the neutron, etc.)*. Therefore, the genetic structure of the human atom contains the complete record of the alien source of human life – and human self-consciousness. Every possible question (and answer) of life is already encoded in the hermetically sealed structure of linguistically organized consciousness. Nothing can be detected that is not linguistically defined. Therefore, all possible realities must *already* be encoded. The atom reflects this *sealed construct* of consciousness. All future discoveries of life are already contained in the human genome. Thus, "In my atom is ark."

- ***The central questions posed by all high civilizations are unanswerable – and remain unanswered until they are superseded as irrelevant linguistic constructs.***

The difficult questions of every civilization are never answered – there is only the linguistic illusion that they may – one day – be answered. In fact, when the future arrives, the burning questions of every civilization are made moot by the newly formed linguistic code of the future human. No civilization survives its own interrogatives. The central myth of Christianity promised the salvation of the soul and the return of Christ. The central myth of science promises a cure to cancer and the discovery of the material "god" particle. None of these questions are ever brought to resolution – the men that posed them merely are supplanted by new faiths and new linguistic civilizations. The questions posed by humans are not answered – they merely become irrelevant.

- ***The human contribution to consciousness is the art of poetry (i.e. classical music, epic poetry).***

Only human poetry/music verifies that humans exist. A machine can translate prose, make a drawing, analyze a design, and make a living clone. No machine, no computer can say what a poem means. Only a man can make a poem. Poetry-making is thus the definition of the human being. Only a human can *compose* and interpret with value an epic poem. Only a human can interpret and compose music of great emotion. Poetry is the human contribution to life. We are the symbol eaters.

- ***No hegemonic ideology can reform itself without dissolution – thus totalitarianism is the only outcome of modernism.***

Any successful linguistic civilization, convinced of its own *necessity*, *exceptionalism*, or *perfection*, ensures that all forms of life (under its control) replicate the same linguistic patterns. No ideology can alter its linguistic formula without losing its self-referent confidence of control. Linguistic modernism, thus, can only produce more modernism. Roman Catholicism can only replicate Roman Catholicism. Communism can only replicate communism, etc. Liberalism, in this protocol – unable to reform itself – must linguistically replicate totalitarian control as ruthlessly as the ideologies of world Catholicism, Fascism and Communism. All ideologies eventually assimilate the profile of their nemesis. Western liberalism must assume a totalitarian surveillance of the population – in order to survive its own inconstancies – and thus, it will be as ruthless as Fascism.

- *Each cosmological age embeds an ideational construct to seize control of sentience.*

In Story Theory, the human mind receives the signals of the twelve constellations. This thesis is verified in the human epic poems written in the age of Taurus, Aries, and Pisces – the only ages of human writing. The pattern is clear and discoverable in epic literature. Taurus, the age of the Bull, emits passion, force and lust (*Gilgamesh, Jason, the Flood*). Aries, the age of the Ram, emits a passion for ruthless law (*Torah, Moses, Solon, Lycurgus, Plato, Socrates, Epicurus, Thales, Aurelius, Rome, etc.*). Pisces, the double fish, emits the trial of brotherly love (*Gospels, romantic poetry, liberalism, United Nations, journalism, etc.*). These are the ages when men wrote epic poems. Each epic poem, including the Gospels (brotherly love) and *Talmud* (law), contains a secret code influenced by the presiding constellation. This thesis is discovered only in this generation – as we just now have assembled the information of past epic poems. Aquarius (c.a. 2100) now embeds a new method of ideation. The fourth age of epic writing is now upon us.

- *Any new linguistic innovation will require a subsequent innovation in human genetics.*

Every advance in linguistics demands a subsequent advance in genetics. The body, as a product of mind, modifies to meet any new innovation in the linguistic code. The material body/world is formed according to the pattern embedded in superstructure of universal *Intelligence*. DNA is a map of intelligent life. Language is thus a second genetics. When human idiom is altered, the human body alters to meet the new ideational condition. One innovation ruthlessly demands another. Our linguistic idiom patterns the human brain and causes the *things* observed – universe, world, bodies, relationships – to be manifested as the linguistic codex dictate. Language gives information of this intelligence embedded in life. The visible structure of universe – as human bodies – mirrors sentience already embedded in the mind. Every event (seeming to appear) in reality, thus, can only be a mirror of what exists already in the mind. Bodies – that is, every happenstance of visible reality – are only linguistic formations.

- **High human sentience has no purpose except Galaxy conquest.**

There is no Earth archeology for the human mind. The human brain is not required for mammal life on Earth. Containing a map of the universe, the human mind is positioned for Galaxy conquest. The human sentient element is a fully empowered agent, independent of the necessity of material causation. The astral mind is the source of all power, and a privileged linguistic pattern is the means to manifest the mind's power.

- **Modernism is a block to a more advanced civilization.**

The Enlightenment experiment has dead lined. Modernism linguistically blocks the information of the human metaphysical component. Modernism privileges only the linguistic spectrum of a dead universe, kinetic robotics, and *rationalized* proliferation as the means to ruthless materialism. Modernism may only preach the terrestrial. Modern science currently blocks more advanced technologies. Thus, as the human mind is in reality and effect astral, modernism must be replaced with a more advanced linguistics.

- **Consciousness is at war.**

The human mind has never been at rest. There is no possibility of stasis in the human mind. Subtracting the white noise of modernism – the false propaganda of peace, advertisements, industrialization, suburbs, political rights, temporary wealth, and electronics – consciousness is revealed to be in a state of war. What business family has maintained its wealth more than a generation? Human sentience is in a state of peril. For political ends, the artificial technologies of modernism attempt to mask the ruthless nature of consciousness. Modern socialism/industrialism attempts to mask the operation of consciousness. Modern linguistics presupposes the expectation of the peaceful proliferation of markets and populations. This is a misreading of consciousness. Each form of conscious life exists in a state of peril. The only proper response to this condition of life is a war of good and evil.

- **Epic poetry contains reliable human information.**

Consciousness is astral and multi-dimensional. The real inhabitants of the universe are the stars. Epic poetry contains information of cosmology

– across eons. Civilizations are based on epic narratives of value. Epic poetry reveals the vital human connection with cosmology – the origin of human consciousness. Science, on the other hand, linguistically manufactures its own self-referent information. The information of science functions within a framework of rationalistic constructs. Being is an astral and charismatic mind – not rational. Thus only epic poetry can address the information of astral archetypes.

- *Modern information is not reliable.*

As a hermetically sealed, self-referent linguistic code, modernism manufactures its own research, evidences, and discoveries of facts. Modernism is an epidemic of false evidence. Modern industrial markets control what information is generated and then privilege the same manufactured data that seems to evidence the superiority of modernism. The answer to any question that is posed by modernism is only an application of more modernism. Therefore any question and answer (as information) that modernism proposes for human life is insidious. Modernism is a self-licking ice cream cone.

- *The aim of any linguistic code is to eradicate all other linguistic patterns.*

Consciousness does not exist without feedback (communication). Thus we say that human consciousness is linguistic construct. How does consciousness operate? Consciousness selects – ruthlessly. Literature (as an expression of consciousness) seeks hegemony. Any hegemonic consciousness (as any linguistic ideology) must eradicate all other interpretations of life. Murder appears not to be a moral consideration in the protocol of consciousness. This can only mean that the bodies that are murdered are not the final form of reality. Real *things* cannot be killed or eradicated. Therefore all that *does* exist is a pattern of communication that makes a privileged selection of bias ruthlessly.

- *All speech is a form of prophesy.*

Modernism denies the legitimacy of prophecy in the modern world. Yet speech, itself, is prophecy. Speech, as text, is a function of making future life forms. Any speech or text that a modern scientist composes is essentially a prophesy of future life forms. Thus prophecy as a function of communication is universally still in effect. Every paper on astronomy, biology, physics, or mathematics, for example, is an attempt at prophecy.

Every word that ever proceeded out of a human mouth is an attempt at prophecy. If all speech is a form of prophecy, then poetry (as high charismatic speech) must preeminently be the medium of prophecy.

- ***The epic trope contains the fossil record of the origin of the astral mind.***

There is no archeology of high human imagination. The origin of the human imagination has no foundation in terrestrial constructs. All our dreams, myths, epics, and prophecies operate from the astral plane of relative cosmology. The five millennia long epic trope confirms the origin of the human mind in a non-terrestrial coordinate. Hercules, Jason, Zeus, Moses, Apollo, Sampson, Gilgamesh exist on no terrestrial coordinate. The epic myths do not concern humans – they concern relative cosmology with an astral location of life from a particular section of the night sky – designated in the star clusters of Orion, Cygnus, and the Sirius system. The human epic trope (our linguistic DNA) contains the fossil record of the origin of the astral mind. All text, all DNA, is a fossil map. Thus we are able to say with concise accuracy, *In my atom is ark.*

- ***The human mind terraforms any astral location in the universe.***

There is no Earth. There is only a human mind that designates – linguistically – a grid coordinate of Earth. If tomorrow there was no Earth, then the mind of man would simply terraform another astral coordinate as a platform to rehearse and enact the bias contained in mental consciousness. We thus make a home for our mind in any coordinate within consciousness. Globular, terrestrial, inhabited Earths are entirely constructs of the astral mind. Until this is fully understood, humans will live as voluntary mental prisoners. *Chandos Ring* shows a way out of this. "*We removed your planet – and then your bones.*"

Philosophy of a Space Faring Civilization

Book Three

A NEW THEORY OF POETRY

It is now known that astrology has provided man with his continuing lingua franca through the centuries. But it is essential to recognize that, in the beginning, astrology presupposed an astronomy. Through the interplay of these two heavenly concepts, the common elements of preliterate knowledge were caught up in bizarre bestiary whose taxonomy has disappeared. With the remnants of the system scattered all over the world, abandoned to the drift of cultures and languages, it is immensely difficult to identify the original themes that have undergone so many sea-changes.

Giorgio de Santillana

And so Gilgamesh rose from his bed
And to his mother, in revealing his dreams, said:
'Mother, I saw in a dream last night
That there were stars in heaven.
And a star descended upon me like unto
The essence of Anu who is god of the firmament.'

The Epic of Gilgamesh

New systems of nature were but new fashions, which would vary in every age; and even those who pretend to demonstrate them from mathematical principles would flourish but a short period of time.

Jonathan Swift

It is not the function of the poet to relate what has happened, but what may happen – what is possible according to the law of probability or necessity.

Aristotle

I hold it that thought can grasp reality, as the ancients dreamed. If you could write it on paper, you can find it in the heavens.

Einstein

PREFACE

Where Is the Essential Information of Life?

There is a secret message so far undetected in epic literature. It is alien. It is a form of life we are only able to decode in the present generation. That, alone, is a fact that should make us pause. Much of the information contained in my narrative makes a claim for originality– if only in the eccentric absence of modernity in my conclusions. This book presents the sudden opening of a hologram. Modernism has mistakenly set aside epic literature as a category lacking vital information of the human life source. Modernism has assumed that ancient poems were separate and individual myths of fantasy – unable to compete with modernism for information – and nearly useless to discover actual facts of human consciousness. As will be illustrated, the opposite is true.

Every epoch of the epic trope has presented men a new structure of life. Consistent with Story Theory (a philosophy explained in volume one), the epic trope's interpretation of life is never contingent upon mammalian archeology – still less, human terrestrial biology. There never will be bones found of Moses, Hercules, Jason, Hector, David, or Jesus. Yet they are real. We have to explain that.

Cosmology, on the other hand, is *always* a part of the epic narrative. We have to explain that – also. So we begin by saying that the poet's work is only marginally related to terrestrial biology. We may observe the biological pattern of life for clues of the *life protocol* – but we will not end up with a single atom of matter – or terrestrial archeology – remaining. We may observe in a mirror the movement of the hunted, yet we wish to engage the hunted – not the mirror. When in decisive contact, we discard the mirror. The terrestrial mirror (our body), therefore, must not be our single interrogative of the life source. It is a dead end. The terrestrial mind – so far misunderstood by humans as the *only* location of the human mind – is contradicted by new evidence. Sentience originates at a stellar coordinate – not on a terrestrial coordinate. The location of the human mind on the astral plane, rather, is our thesis. Life is not matter, nor is it energy. At its basic unit of detection, life is astral information. Epic poems and myths contain the data of this assertion. A new definition of human life is thus explored in this book.

All life gives off feedback. There never has been a living entity, cell, or microbe that did not give off some form of information – some modicum of feedback that falls to a pattern of organized, reliable, and replicable communication. One may label this pattern of communication as *seeking a food source*, or *survival*, or *reproduction*, or *romance*, or *genocide,* or *epic poetry* – but it is a pattern of communicative feedback only found among living things. All living bodies have *some* degree of sentience. *Sentience* may usefully be defined as any entity that gives off feedback.

Only living creatures communicate feedback that falls to a pattern of recognizable intention. Chaos – by definition – does not display any pattern of recognizable intention. Only life performs the oddity of communication with *organized intention*. Therefore, to discover the source of life, we have to understand the nature of communication – as organized intention. What is it about communication that only living things may communicate? How is it possible that communication, itself, is an energy source? What is the *source* of information creatures emit and receive? We might first make an attempt to detect the *bias* of information.

Life has only *one* irreducible fossil pattern. Life gives feedback that is consistent within the code of life that is represented. Feedback always falls to pattern. This pattern takes on the signature elements of perpetuity: it is consistent across a unified field of data; it replicates reliably; it always seeks a position of greater strength. Interestingly these are also exactly the elements found in language. This is the *eternity principle* – only discovered in living organisms – *and* human language. Immediately we arrive at a new definition of life. Life is *a linguistically replicative construct – an ordered communication displaying bias.*

Living feedback is never random. Feedback, as communication, then, clearly reflects a bias of *ordered* protocol embedded in consciousness (life). Feedback is a pattern that expands predictably. Living things not only demonstrate a pattern of replication, but, if observed closely, manifest a clear direction of movement. Life, thus, contains a deep source of intrinsic intention – or *bias*. There is always detectable a movement of bias *towards something* (as opposed to nothing). No one has ever tried to explain this. How do you explain *nothing*? More to the point, how do you explain *something – as opposed to nothing*? It is so difficult that it may be impossible.

This book thereby attempts to make new discoveries with a new method of interrogation. If we wish to understand poetry, then we should understand how communication is intrinsic within life. That must be explained. What is the strange, uncanny bias of information contained within living things? And of the highest order of living things – as the human mind – what is the bias of *our* pattern of information? What is *essential* information? The communications of most men are predicable – only the poet does not expand his pattern of feedback predictably. What does that mean? What is the essential information of human communication – and thus, human consciousness? Merely to proliferate? Or to select? To find this answer is the Holy Grail of a new theory of poetry. This is the purpose of a new inquiry of the epic trope.

Following this interrogative, the purpose of this book is to delineate elements of a new theory of human life – and thus, human poetry. The discovery of new patterns of data within the long history of the epic trope is the contribution of this book. Modernism has mistaken the information embedded within the epic poems – including the *Old* and *New Testaments*. The question is not *"Where is the archeology for all the founding texts of every religion and civilization?"* This is the mistaken interrogative of the modern mind. This is the exact moment that modernism fails the human mind. It is at this moment that modernism misses the entire essence of human consciousness. We live by Story Theory – not by archeology.

The issue, rather, is how texts – that contain no terrestrial archeology – are *still* powerful and endowed with transforming power. How can the story of Moses, Jason, and Christ still be valid – and yet there is no archeology to verify any of the assertions of the epic trope (*Bible*, sacred narrative, myth)? How can texts that contain no terrestrial archeology *still* be operative as exact verifications of the human mind? That is, how can epic texts and myths *still* be actual (real) information of the human condition?

No one has ever attempted this explanation. Humans previously have either referenced *revelation* or *archeology* as their evidence of textual authority. I accept neither as evidence – I make an alternate explanation of the nature of human consciousness. I do not take a position from a foundation of terrestrial revelation or terrestrial archeology. I move the argument to the astral plane. It is the thesis of this book that the human mind has been mistaken as operating and originating from a terrestrial environment. The evidence contained in the greatest epic poems, myths, and religious narrative – just now decoded in our generation – prove otherwise. The fossil record of the human mind is given to us by the uncanny and otherwise unexplainable consistency of cosmological correspondences across the entire scope of epic literature and myth. I have to explain that.

Is Modernism the Final Human Information?

The strong poet is my audience. This book concerns his opportunity for competence. There has never been a sustained narrative directed to the strong poet.

We have the result. Modern poetry is inconsequential and essentially unknown in the West. This is a ridiculous situation for a nation of high idiomatic achievements. Nations of strong poets have always recreated the human mind and skeleton. In consequence of the failure of modern information, the human mind is currently being reconstructed – and thus, the average modern will be likewise concerned with my argument. The epic poems record when the human mind was reconstructed.

Inconceivably (in an epic age), the epic trope has been out of reach of our poets. Events never before witnessed have been compressed into the 20th century. It is a century of epic homicide – an epoch of global war – that still has no epic narrative. A vernacular poet still has to organize the narrative of the century that has just passed. A specialist would only limit the ideascape. There never has been a significant human event that did not find its epic poet.

Yet there are unknown perils. We are still not certain of life. It may be that we have constructed a life form with wars *already* embedded – and *every* human life may face the same wars – the same impassible terrain – the same nemesis. Either way the road is clear ahead. Since, in effect, poetry does not exist in modern societies, and is not missed by the modern, I may recreate a theory of poetry conforming to the idiom of my quest of consciousness.

One thing is certain. A new innovation must be attempted. We are at a linguistic dead end with modernism. After all, what is the final result of life – except we all are compelled to make a discovery of value? Life is nothing if not recognition of a pattern – a structure of value. When first encountered, this new language always appears to be an alien edifice.

A critique of modern poetry is not nostalgia for a previous aesthetic. I do not wish to sell oil lamps to the atomic age. We seek a strong device to explain *sentient phenomena* – but with a new innovation of human life. We seek an alternate voice that we are still able to recognize. Surely this was the original hope of the genre of science fiction – to discover an alternate innovation of human life?

Science fiction, initially attempting to represent the future – is, in effect, a protest against day-to-day modernism. Modernism, in the end, is terminally banal and stultifying – hence the constant need for new technologies to help the modern person to cope with the replicative banality of modern life. All forms of alternate fiction – including body piercing, tattoos and graffiti – are instinctive human protests against the replication and banality of modern life. We all search for new text. Our poets, however, are not only silent about the crisis of modernism – they are missing. There is a lacuna in the linguistic record. A critique will be attempted of this phenomenon. I will move the argument of the human mind to the astral plane.

In the last century, Western men have detected few significant poets. Still fewer are known to a large segment of society. There are no living poets able to tell a powerful human narrative. This is an amazing statistic. How could there exist the concept of a poet that did not sustain a narrative of power? The poets, by definition (in Greek), are *makers of story*. At no point in my fictional essay do I accept that modern poets have simply transformed into television script writers. Poets narrate with strong verse, usually metered. When story tellers transition to exclusively prose, vital charismatic information is lost – of cosmology, of the directional intention of the human life source, and most revealingly, the perspective that situates the human mind as existing, properly as it does, on the astral plane. The prose writer is not inspired – he or she is paid to replicate the age. Modernism in, modernism out. In fact, in the modern prose narrative, vital information of the epic trope is lost. We will explain this thesis.

Historic civilizations are constructs of the narrative of the epic trope. In order to live well, men must make a story of their lives – and this story contains a high construction of value. Seemingly diverse epic texts contain remarkably consistent astral correspondences. This must be explained. It cannot be a random phenomenon. When delineated, astral data combine to operate as a map to the fossil of consciousness. I will show that all forms of human attempts at civilization are products of epic texts. By epic, I include religious myth and scripture. All high Western assertions of value have been made in verse format. This includes the august chronicle of the origin of the Hebrew Covenant, the death of the Lamb of God, and all subsequent Judeo-Christian civilization.

Why epic poetry? If linguistics is the medium of high human achievement, we must define the clarity of the life we seek. The epic *agon* seeks clarity. At some point in our fiction, we must face the controversial question of the *best* and the *beautiful*. This book consequently constructs a new theory of poetry with a wide-ranging interrogation of the soundness of the modernist linguistic superstructure. Since modernism will fail, we must make preparation.

The single product of any civilization is *information*. Unlike prose, poetry detects charismatic information of life. Unlike rational modernism, poetry is able to anticipate and maneuver the irrational. Civilizations fail when they cannot correctly detect information of the future. Consequently, I make a severe test of the reliability of modern information. Ultimately, we will wish to find the origin and purpose of human life. These answers, perhaps, are hidden because the origin of the mind of man is hidden. Answers are still undecoded in the strange and forbidding, the unused ninety-five percent of the human DNA. There is an alternate method. To discover the origin of human life we need only decode the entire record of epic literature. This record contains the catalogue of human origin and purpose. We observe in the epic trope that the same human interrogative is repeated over and over again. The same narrative of stars is repeated. The poets are inexplicably consistent. It is time to assemble the alien record.

Clarity of speech operates as deity. An oracular source of information functions as celestial authority. We know the exact cause of this phenomenon.

Consciousness operates as communication. Where there is clear communication there is a richer opportunity for life. Men have wrung their hands across millennia to discover the location of the soul. We know exactly the answer. The soul is our linguistic construction of consciousness. The soul (as consciousness) is a function of communication. If consciousness is eternal – then so are the protocols of communication. We may explore this insight to build a strong theory of poetry.

What Is the Use of Information?

Life is information. Information, as poetry, represents distinctions between things. Distinctions never disappear. Thus, matter and energy are only products of *distinctive information*. Information is all that survives. A human language never existed that did not give satisfaction of information. Language attempts to represent reality. Blinded by the idol of our speech, we fail to see that our language is conditional. Civilizations never exactly reproduce reality. An assertion of reality is made (with speech) – and this assertion follows a pattern of linguistic modeling. A sharp insight is gained. The strong poet must seize the hour when a national tongue has matured. This moment will always pass for the height of human consciousness. His time is short. If he can complete his insight, he is in the rare position to monument an idiom into perpetuity. The use of information is to make an attack into eternity. I will explain this.

High civilizations are remarkably consistent. Civilizations always pose the same question: *How to seize control of consciousness?* Yet *languages* of civilizations detect different information of this exact interrogation. This book makes a new discovery in literary texts. The universe is made up of packets of information. Matter and energy are only symptoms of information. To discover the origin of life – its purpose – we have to detect the nature of information. This is what poetry performs. My purpose thus comes into focus.

Consequently, this book poses many questions. Can modernism be challenged? Does our civilization *exactly* represent reality? Does Western technology contain philosophical intent and direction? Is modernism the final idiom of Western men? To decide these questions ruthlessly – without the usual veneer of modern prejudice – would be a victory of linguistics.

Paramount to our investigation we must decide a single overarching question. Does poetry contain reliable information? Can this question be avoided? It cannot. If the reader recalls our best poets, he will be reminded that love for that poet was due to the clarity of that poet's information. We do not love poets because they exhibit imaginative fancy. We love poets because they have information of life. Information, then, is the prize – not beauty. Without confidence that poetry contains access to solid information, there is no benefit to build a theory of poetry.

If it cannot be shown that poetry contains reliable human information – then it will be risible to plea for the merits of poetry. No serious person wishes to carry water in a sieve.

The following narrative suggests that modern information is terminal and insidious, that it is slovenly and dishonestly fabricated. In contrast, the information of poetry is permanent. Epic poetry is able to structure the future – because human *reality* is ultimately a linguistic protocol. I do not aim only at a new or curious theory. I show that the epic trope contains the secret information of our origin. How was it concealed so long? Why was it not detected?

Every educated person wishes to experience powerful poetry. Every person of civilized pretension would welcome a strong theory of poetry – and poetry, moreover, that contains permanent and interesting information of the human condition. Does that not include most readers?

To recover poetry in our time will be to recover the origins of the human mind. Where is the locality of the human mind? A strange question, perhaps, as any. First, we must begin to understand the connection between poetry and the human mind. By this protocol we discover the origins of human life itself. I believe that the fossil traces of the origin of human consciousness are embedded in the epic texts – the entire spectrum of epic texts. It is a thesis of this book that this is the first age that the epic poems have been understood and their secrets decoded. Until the quality of human information is explored, we cannot discuss the recovery of poetry in Western society.

CHAPTER ONE

The Perennial Linguistic Equation

An epic poem contains no new information – it contains everything ever known. The epic cycle contains the fossil origin of human life. This means that academic specialists have never understood epic poetry. Academic knowledge is not required for epic composition. No academic ever constructed a successful epic or lyric poem. No academic has united all the epic poems in a narrative to discover what patterns of vital information they harbor.

There is only one indispensable element for the epic trope. It is rage. Knowledge is tertiary. Feeling is assumed. Skill is useful. Yet it is impossible to anticipate the strong poet. No amount of socialized education or government funding can make a strong poet. This is an interesting insight of the human condition. A strong poet cannot be created from a government directive. Only the felicity of a hegemonic language might allow the opportunity for the appearance of an epic poet. He or she is impossible to detect. They appear silent running.

Many persons are found writing lyric poems. They may be passionate, earnest, or more rarely, talented. They are not full of rage. From *Achilles* to *Dante*, from the *Shakespeare poet* to *Milton*, from *Sappho* to *Brontë*, rage is the indispensable element of the epic trope. The causes of rage are clearly stated. The prince has been dispossessed. A religious idiom has been suppressed. A vernacular speaker has been excluded from the intellectual priesthood of her society. A self-referent modernism fabricates unreliable information – and has eradicated the reliable and ancient speech of poetry. These are the causes of honest rage.

In the long count of time, *Homo sapiens* are a linguistic experiment. Civilizations do not exactly reproduce reality – they approximate reality with an idiomatic code. It is for this reason that each human language makes a reality that is alien, even hateful, to other linguistic humans. Every war that has ever been fought is essentially a linguistic assertion. War is language by other means. Every victory of war has been a victory of an idiomatic (linguistic) life view.

Everything a man creates is a *linguistic* device for the struggle of supremacy. Every technological or ideological device operates as a means to *assert* a linguistic reality. Stripping away the artificially biased layers of political ideology, doctrine, faith, culture, technology, and aesthetics, the severe philosopher discovers remaining only a linguistic bias inherent in the human condition. We are farmed with linguistic constructs. Signals are sent out from star clusters. Our prophets are attentive. Stories and epics are the feedback of raging poets signaling that the epochal message was received. With raging heart, the poet perilously climbs up on the rubble of contemporary civilization – gone wrong – to form a linguistic scaffold. Every epic poem struggles to select a new idiom. Until this idiom is found there is no new civilization.

When the eccentricity of the epic poet is first spotted, it is already too late to inquire of the poet's talent and qualifications. Tangentially, we hope he has both. The poet has already surmounted his crisis – he has already found a device to counter the epoch's first instinct – to suppress his audacity. He has already made a calculation for counter-rage. His spleen cannot now be countered with ease. He has already made the race for supremacy.

No modern tracks the location of an epic poet. The meeting is unlooked for. In each case, cited above, a hostile monopoly of contemporary authority has deeply wounded the pride of a strong poet. Because he is unlooked for, the epic poet is able to work undetected. He should be cautious and deliberate. He should show a superior perspective. After all, in each case, the ideological power that caused the hurt to the poet disappeared with time. What always remains, what is forever young, is the vindication of the poet's rage. The epic poet, so recent to his future rumor, so new to a fresh perspective, is the youngest human living. Only stars enjoy a longer rumor.

Epic poetry contains the permanent information of cosmology. Cosmology is the only enduring information of life. Humans give too much primacy to political texts. All governments are self-referent. There is no reliable human government of the *Left* or the *Right*. All modern governments are totalitarian and socialist. Totalitarian control is the goal of every modernist government. Modernism cannot be impeded or reformed. It can only collapse. Modernism has the same disadvantage of monarchy – the prince can only be supplicated or killed. Like a monarchy, modernism is supreme and will suppress all other forms of power.

Story Theory does not select between the *Left* or the *Right*, since both carry the virus of antiquated modernism. *Left* and *Right* – as brackets of Western liberalism – helplessly *advocate* the proliferation of unreliable science and industrial pharmaceuticals. Every act of liberal democracy is enmeshed with hidden compacts, secret payments, and manipulated information. Democracies grope forward into the unknown using the prosthetic device of political bribery. Each party of liberalism takes its bribe from the public treasury. Liberal democracy ensures more debts and an ever-increasing monopoly of information – until there are no more resources to plunder, steal, or distribute – until all other linguistic idioms of life are detected and eradicated.

Liberal institutions are designed to exploit, trade, and disburse resources – more money, more rights, and more goods. When these resources are threatened, liberal democracies must make war. Why? Because when the stream of surplus wealth is interrupted, liberalism collapses. Poor nations are not liberal. Poor nations have nothing to distribute. Liberalism is a construct of expanding wealth and imperial growth – not of a stagnant market. When there is no more public wealth to distribute, liberalism becomes aggressive and totalitarian. Liberalism does not equal poetry. This is a misconception because most modern poets assert liberal ideologies. This has destroyed poetry in our time. Poetry, in fact, is highly prejudiced, selective, and ruthless.

What is the case for poetry, then? Only a human can make or judge the value of a poem. This is permanent information. This is *source* evidence – impervious to any sophistry. Only a human makes a story. This has an exact meaning: *The human singularity is story and poetry.* There can be no human poetry without the agency of story.

I will test this thesis. If successful, I may build a strong theory of poetry. If I fail, there may also be a stronger theory of poetry. Since even by opposing the positions I take, the West will be forced to construct a clearer idea of the information poetry contains.

What is the case for poetry? This is the question I pose in each chapter – until I construct clarity of poetic values. I must begin with the facts of consciousness. The reader will be confronted again and again with the term *linguistics*. Of course, I do not only reference language. I designate as *linguistics* any thought, plan, machine, construct, text or idea that arises from a human brain. This means that *beauty*, *war*, and *murder*, for example, necessarily are forms of linguistics. Why? Because the human brain functions only once a linguistic pattern has structured the brain. Everything a man can see with his eyes, every device made of his hands is directly connected to linguistics.

A high civilization is exactly a linguistic construct. Linguistic civilizations require a base of power. Without *protected* linguistic formations we are faced with linguistic chaos. The first requirement of human language is a *protected* community. The first requirement of a great language is hegemonic superposition. Thus Homo sapiens is a military and linguistic experiment. If he cannot fight and protect his ideational space, he cannot build a code of life. This code of life that is built is exactly a linguistic structure. There is no exception to this rule.

There is a human agency (as story, poetry) only because there is a still *unknown* and *unfinished* consciousness. This will appear as new information to the modern. There is no degree of separation between consciousness and the *feedback* of consciousness. They are exactly connected. For this reason, the definition of *soul* is exactly the *perception* of an unfinished consciousness. This is not a dispersion of *soul*. The sense of consciousness is permanent and eternal. We are presented thus with an opportunity – not a limitation – as it allows the human to construct a *still* unfinished consciousness to fit the conditions of life we seek. This being so, human speech mirrors the bias of consciousness, and thus, the body of human story contains the fossil record of consciousness. This is a discovery encouraged by my choice of interrogation. Thus, yes, human consciousness is a linguistic construct. What human concept of life is not a linguistic construct? This is the case for poetry.

What is our scope? We are interested to find patterns of consciousness in the poetry and the myths of human civilizations. We discover that literature embeds a secret cosmology. This is the perennial philosophy. Therefore we wish to discover the facts, not only of the human consciousness, but the facts of a macro consciousness – outside of our nursery planet. Story Theory confirms it is possible to discover the source and purpose of life. This is a claim that other human philosophies have only made with despair or misprision.

As science has nothing to say about metaphysics, we may proceed with an examination of the *story* Western men have made of their consciousness. There is a record of man's spiritual and metaphysical outline. This fossil record is embedded in human literature. This *ur-story* – the entire outline of the *intent* of human life – is, I believe, clearly delineated in Western literature. While the lyric is interesting, even curious, the ancient epic myths are our principle field of exploration. Human story is the vital feedback of the signals of consciousness. No other linguistic examination can give us a strong theory of poetry – the subject of this book.

In my interrogation of the state of consciousness, I consider the entire record of Western literature as evidence of the intention of consciousness. There are no other reliable tests we can use to test the purpose and intent of consciousness except the patterns made of linguistic sentience – that is, the story men make of their consciousness. Human *story* follows the exact trail of consciousness. As will be seen, these are essentially poetic protocols. There is no evidence of consciousness without linguistic feedback. This is the case for poetry. Therefore, story (poetry) is the fossil singularity of consciousness – not electronic synapses and neurons.

The human brain is a colony of texts. In every endeavor of human life we are left with only one source for all of human events, including every human law, custom, and act: *the story a human has made about his life*. When a human attempts to give an account of his consciousness, even in the first syllables, he transitions immediately to story. No ideology of empiricism, no assertion of modernism, no dogma of Islam can successfully refute this last statement. This is the case for poetry. Can it be sustained?

CHAPTER TWO

The Failure of Modern Information

The bright emitting promise of modern idiom has stumbled at the extremity of its performance. We are not moderns because we are born at a certain time; we are moderns because we are certain that our idiom of life is the most accurate form of accessing information. Modernism, as any age of man, is principally a linguistic coding of human ideation. As any highly developed cultural linguistics, the core linguistic group immediately excludes all foreign linguistic codes and ruthlessly expands its ideational territory. By linguistics, of course, I include all forms of ethical, scientific, technological, and humanistic translation of the phenomena of life. Civilization is an artificial and fragile veneer placed over observable phenomena. Civilization is an *overt idiomatic assertion of reality*. To operate, it must *replicate* and *rule* its own ideational space.

When the linguistically determined human loses confidence that modernism gives reliable information – the modern perspective will disappear in an instant.

After fifty centuries of human writing, no modern text has met or surpassed the information contained in ancient epic poems and myths given to humans by an advanced space faring civilization. Following anthropological contact with the Dogon priests of Africa in the 1930's, researchers confirmed that there was already knowledge of the invisible dwarf star Sirius B – already knowledge, even, of genetics, atomic theory, and quantum mechanics. There is no ordinary way for modern rationality to account for this. To moderns, this is troubling.

According to French anthropologists, Marcel Griaule and Germaine Dieterlen, the Dogon tribe was a cultural people anciently ejected from the lush Nile valley by a newly arrived and advanced form of Homo sapiens. But their exile did not occur before they copied down a pre-literate and symbolic representation of advanced genetics and cosmology of a ruthless and alien high civilization. Dogon myths (lost Egyptian/Sumerian information) assert that our living mineral was created by the Sirius star system. Sirius B, now a white dwarf star, once gave off a supernovae explosion in the pre-history of man. The Dogons say this was the source of all life in our cell of the universe. The remarkable fact is that Sirius B is invisible to the eyes. It is a dwarf star only first detected by modern science in the 1970's. Coupled in binary orbit with Sirius A, Sirius B's implosion injected the particles that constitute life in our region of space. While their book, *Le Renard Pâle*, was only published in French in 1965 (in English 1986), their discovery essentially pioneered the deconstruction of the modern arrogance of information.

The Dogon religious symbology is fossilized evidence of an advanced spacefaring civilization making contact with Earth in pre-literate human times (5000 -3000 B.C.). This was the culture that established (in a few generations) the high civilization (even luxurious) of ancient Egypt and Mesopotamia. The significance for modern arrogance is large. Modern academics and scientists refuse to verify that their highest forms of linguistic science have only begun to approach what was *already* contained in ancient epic poems of pre-literate peoples. Therefore, we possess the first test that modern information is not irreplaceable.

I will outline in this book some previously unknown information contained in ancient epic poetry and myth. It is enough for my present argument to indicate that the anthropological discovery of the Dogon tribe's fossil information is a blow to modern intellectual arrogance. It is a discovery that modern academics have endeavored to deny and to ignore at every juncture – since to acknowledge it would be to discredit the entire edifice of modern arrogance, information, and linguistics. An entire superstructure of a fragile modernism would have to be *linguistically* reconstructed. Since modern academics economically depend upon a monopoly of scientific information, this will never be allowed to happen. A collapse will occur first.

Yet, even if there were no retrieval of the information of the epic and mythic traditions, modern men would already be observed deeply entrenched in a failure of their information. The first sign of the failure of modern information is the disappearance, not only of thousands of animal species and human cultural languages – but the disappearance of Western poetry. Modern ideology is now moving to total eradication of non-modern linguistics.

Why is this a danger? Modernism represents a crisis of accurate and reliable information. A machine cannot detect or judge metaphysics or poetics. A machine cannot anticipate a charismatic arrival – as an extinction event. A machine can only detect patterns of material causation. Thus, the modernist future is a crisis of detection of reality. Until the issue of reliable information is addressed, Western men cannot reconstruct a strong theory of poetry for a future space faring civilization. *Since the purpose of this book is to construct a new theory of poetry, we must discover the linguistic forms of reliable information.* Not only is poetry the most ancient source of reliable cosmology, it is also the agent of a new innovation in human linguistics. Any linguistic genera that can perform anciently and, also, exactly project future ideation, is a supreme linguistic form. *Chandos Ring* explores this opportunity.

Modernism: A Culture of Prosthetics

Civilization is a visual *prosthetics*. Nothing actually exists as any civilization asserts. Consequently, no phenomenon exists as modern civilization portrays it to exist. This means that modernism is a temporary linguistic illusion – as any other. This critique will produce hatred and loathing. How strong is the urge to truth? I suspect it is weak. Story Theory accuses all forms of civilization as misprision. In Story Theory, it is not a question of which civilization is correct – they are all prosthetics – it is a question of which civilization is hegemonic. Though we critique modernism, it is still to that civilization we wish to attach our linguistic superstructure of future men. In the end, we have to reach the stars – and we will ride any beast that can take us there. We will ride a modern, hegemonic English – and fashion it to fit the conditions of voice we seek. This is only what any poet performs.

In the end, all forms of life remain unknown and unknowable. Men still do not understand the origin or purpose of life. To combat this crisis of information, humans construct a linguistically coded civilization of *artificial* value to make sense of their world. Any artificial limb is a prosthetic device. Modernism is above all else a linguistic prosthetics. The hegemonic liberal modernism that we take for granted is actually an attempt to eradicate all *other* forms of human linguistics. No modern will admit this. We simply are not able to observe the ruthlessness of our own linguistic prosthetics. Western men are dangerous and arrogant with linguistic misprision. Western liberalism now enters its final crisis with life. It is a crisis of reliable information.

There can be no theory of poetry that does not also include the linguistic retranslation of information. The human mind may only privilege and value what the acquired linguistic pattern allows into ideation. Nothing clings on the brain until there is a prior linguistic valuation. There is no universe until it is coded with a linguistic codex of *universe*. There is no strong composition of poetry until the mind is mapped for detection of poetic information. Consequently, there can be no strong theory of poetry unless we address, through a severe investigation, the source of reliable linguistic information.

Is it modernism? This book poses a bitter question: *Is modernism the final form of human life?* Though strange to the modern ear, this is the single question of the age. Poverty and injustice will only be addressed by the linguistic code we accept. So the question is not what human evils supposedly exist – the only question is what linguistic code we accept to *detect* and *address* evils. Can modernism detect evil and injustice? No, modernism can only detect and address evil and injustice along a specific (modernist) spectrum. Each language of civilization is a limited construct of what it may detect and address. If this is true, and modernism is not the final form of human life, then the poet may move ahead to the next innovation.

Modernism is a supreme language. The danger of any hegemonic idiom is that it cannot be objectively observed – or escaped. Language, as ideational pattern (math, art, science, economics, any cultural selection), is how a human structures phenomena into a universe of meaning. Without some advanced linguistic form of civilization, life remains unknown and hostile. Without this scaffold of linguistic structure, there is no universe to be understood. Without linguistic formations – a story of life, a story of stars – there cannot be any observation of stars – or life. Phenomena without linguistic structure have no valuation – in fact, they're invisible. Objects without linguistically coded patterns, in effect, do not exist in the human mind.

Moderns are not divided in a racial struggle against other cultures. European ideational supremacy was already accomplished centuries ago. Instead, we assert an aggressive and inescapable modern linguistic liberalism against *all other* forms of linguistic interpretation of life. We export a militant missionary modernism. This modern aggressive linguistics is formulated against the elements, the planets, and all other social life forms. If a cultural nation does not accept modern science and Western industrialized medicine, a silent but deadly crusade is waged against that nation until it renounces its resistance to modernism. Modernism is set to extinguish all other forms of human and biological life. This is a world crisis.

What are the essential modern idioms? They are linguistic forms of academic science, industrial medicine, advertising media, pornography of youth, unconstrained markets, and computerized mathematics. Moderns are additionally recognized with proliferation – proliferation of everything – cities, populations, markets, drugs, laws, disease, etc.. Since modern men are denied their rightful war of good and evil, there is, additionally, the scourge of proliferation on an industrial scale. Above all else, the human must not be denied his war of good and evil. There is no other reason to be human.

Industrial proliferation, advertising media, journalist who exclusively propagate modernist ideology, proliferation of the authority of academics - these are a few of the distinctive elements that structure the Western ideational concept of consciousness. Any nation that replicates these elements – replicates Western linguistic modernism. Thus modern Russia, Japan, *and* China replicate Western idioms of life. Linguistically defined - they are Western ideologies. They speak in the codex of industrial models modernism. They have no choice. China, Japan, Korea, and Russia follow a linguistics (of modernism) developed by the Anglo-Saxon West.

Again I return to the first principle of consciousness. The purpose of consciousness is not to proliferate mindlessly. The purpose of consciousness is to make a selection of the beautiful and the good – no matter the human cost – it does not even matter if the selection of the value of the good and beautiful is even beneficial. Beneficial to whom? The linguistic struggle for the good and the beautiful will winnow any contradictions. We must have our honest war of good and evil. We must discover the value of our mythic code. It is already selected for us – we have to fill out its limits.

The challenge is not to discover a way to ensure more modernism to more people. Such a policy will only lead to the extinction of our original creative mythic code. We would be lost in the count. The challenge is to reduce the white noise of *our* modernism with a severe selection of life forms. This is the narrative and drama of Aquarius.

Again, clarity of expression will substitute for "truth" in any situation. (This is the maxim of politics and advertising). And more than anything else, modern men need a clarity of their position against all other. Only a poem may make this clarity of purpose. Poetry performs *clarity of expression* more than any other art form - and thus poetry is the maker of truth *par excellence*. (Since clarity of expression passes for truth). This is an original cause for *Chandos Ring*. Clarity of purpose is not a quality that modernism will provide – and certainly not without the strong poet. What is the alternative? Should we wait to see where corrupted politicians will lead us? Or the greed of global markets?

No. Modernism would only attempt to obliterate all distinctions in the linguistic body, And to admit all other nations as equal to our high achievement would only obliterate the core of our mythic codex. We would simply become another civilization of Asian, Indian, or African idioms. This is not a racial competition – it is a competition of linguistics. Let me clarify my position. Any skin color that accepts the linguistics of Plato, Homer, Dante, Handel, Beethoven, and the Shakespeare poet is my twin.

The challenge is to make the transition from mere hegemonic modernism to a *Western* space fairing civilization that is able to eradicate all other codices of future Galaxy hegemony – and also keep intact our ancient (and reliable) map of a hegemonistic poetic detection. We must be *the* idiom that names the future – or we must die in a just war of good and evil. *Our* definition of good and evil. Modernism would deny us our rights to a race for supremacy. The Western mind has only one inherent right – a right to a race for supremacy of life forms. By any account, a wildly precarious undertaking. When has Western men not been in this situation?

Only death will separate the modern from his belief in the excellence of modernism. Nothing will convince the modern that his unassailable *modernism* is not the most reliable form of information. Therefore, Homo sapiens must die.

CHAPTER THREE

How Story Theory Operates

Story Theory is a philosophy of the human condition (introduced in volume one). Civilization is a product of Story Theory. Social life is a product of Story Theory. Society is an artificial linguistic construction. Story Theory explains how the mind is linguistically patterned to accept and detect reality of world. Our minds identify structures along an *accepted* linguistic pattern. *Anything* outside the accepted linguistic pattern is *not detected as information*. The language by which a mind is trained determines what that mind *accepts* as reliable information. No human is exempt from a learned and educated linguistic protocol. Story Theory, thus, applies to each person. The linguistically patterned mind is structured to detect and accept as information any phenomena *similarly* coded to match the structure that has already been mapped in the mind. Thus, modernism may only recognize modernism. Science can only verify science. A rationalist can only accept rationality, etc. This is Story Theory.

Let us test this. When a person sets out to buy a certain automobile, one suddenly sees that particular model in the streets wherever one goes. It's not that this model was not there before – they were always there – the eye simply did not detect them previous to your interest (bias). The mind/eye is linguistically activated. We focus the mind linguistically on the make and model of the car we think to purchase. Suddenly we see the model on every street corner. We perform this protocol in every situation of life. It *becomes* our reality. When we have children, we linguistically pattern our mind to detect their welfare and to sense any threat to them. We observe dangers that others ignore who do not have children. It is an involuntary reaction. This protocol so far is logical, reasonable, and involuntary. Let us continue our test.

When in love, we see signs of the beloved. When we are linguistically trained as a dentist, we see signs of poor dental hygiene. It is involuntary. When a human is trained as medical doctor, his mind is trained to detect diseases. It is involuntary.

When we have diabetes, and become experts in the linguistic protocol of the disease, we see the signs of diabetes in others. It is linguistics. When we are learned in taxidermy, we see all bodies in categories of taxidermy. The (linguistically) trained mind has learned a pattern and it expertly detects that pattern in random phenomena – random phenomena other humans may ignore – as they may not have a similarly trained linguistic focus. Other people may not detect as information the data that a specialist may detect as information. In human life, certainly, there is long list of trained human specialties. Each specialty is acquired through linguistic training. That is civilization.

Each of these linguistic protocols is, in effect, Story Theory in miniature. Generally no one objects to these evidences. These are common and verifiable human experiences. They are direct and testable evidences. We may conclude, then, that Story Theory, as a linguistic pattern, is how the human mind works. We have a new perspective by which we may proceed.

Americans have been linguistically trained to recognize and detect modern science, industrialized medicine, pharmaceuticals, youth pornography, democracy, and journalism as reliable information. This is our linguistic training. We recognize this world. These are the exact qualifications for modern life. Being trained to detect a certain pattern of data, our minds are alerted. The mind seeks out linguistic patterns it can associate with normalcy of human life.

Yet there is a difficulty. It is difficult for the modern speaker to believe that modernism, itself, is a trained linguistic pattern. We are so integrated into modernist training from the earliest age that we cannot detect modernism as a separate, and thus artificial, ideology of a linguistic civilization. No civilization exactly reproduces reality – it makes a linguistic representation of reality. The West has had three linguistic shifts – pagan, Christian, and (now) secular science. We may examine them as reference points. When civilizations fail, there is always a new linguistic representation of reality – sometimes surprisingly opposite from the previous civilization. When the Pagan Roman Empire fell, Rome accepted Christian linguistics. Christianity represented a new worldview of humanity. In turn, when Christianity failed, it was because a new generation of men accepted a materialistic, scientific linguistics of human life.

This is why I insist, then, that civilizations do not exactly represent reality – there is only a temporary linguistic code of reality. Modernism conceals this *linguistic* protocol – since we do not suspect that modernism can ever be anything other than *exact* reality. Therefore, there is no *apparent* existential need to challenge modernism. The question does not arise. Westerners believe that modernism is the only way of life *for all of time*. Similarly, the pagan Roman Empire and the Catholic religion also thought their visions of life were eternal representations of life. In fact, each *reality system* was a linguistic civilization that made expert use of a *temporary* use of linguistics. Language only reappears as an artificial construct when it is replaced.

How Do We Detect if Modernism Is a Linguistic Structure?

Modernism operates as a trained language. From the earliest age, the Western child is hermetically sealed within a specific linguistic pattern. It is modernism. A Western citizen, linguistically reinforced with the accepted norms of secular materialism, can only detect as reality data that strictly aligns with scientific modernism. This is how Story Theory operates. This is why persons who join cults and religions appear distasteful to moderns. Modernism proves it is a linguistic code when it detects and expels *alternate* linguistic interpretations of human life. In Europe, American protestant religions are labeled derisively as sects. Linguistic deviancy is immediately detected and appears alarming to modern societies. Disgust and loathing are the usual reactions to any non-standard linguistics.

The modern state would not object to an alternate and rigorous interpretation of life – so long as this remains a privately held faith. The moment a parent – openly practicing faith healing – insist that their sick child need not take modern medicine and should not enter hospitals – the modern instantly recoils. There is an instinctive feeling that some line has been crossed. A line of truth and evil has not been crossed - only a line of linguistic pattering has been violated - modernism. The modern state immediately intervenes – not as only one of many linguistic choices – but as the monopolistic enforcement of the modern secular state. Suddenly modernism proves it is a linguistic code jealous of any other ideational interpretation of life within the social space. Modernism specifically protects itself from aggressive operations of "alternate" linguistic faiths. Modernism is carefully cocooned by a firewall of secular and materialist privilege and education. The moment modern science and medicine are not allowed to reach the children of the social body, the urge of the modern is to immediately intervene and assert the dictates of linguistic modernism. Western governments do not teach faith or religion, they teach math, science, and industrial medicine. Modernism is thus a protected linguistic code. This is how all hegemonic civilizations operate.

The crisis is that the state does not see itself, today, as a linguistic protocol. The modern state will accept any form of belief so long as it does not supersede the actual operation of modernist ritual. These include the right of children to have full access to the scientific education, secular training, and belief in pharmaceutical medicines – modernist doctrines. In our society this has the force of law. This does not seem aggressive to us since we have been trained since youth to accept linguistic and secular modernism as normalcy. Modernism, when challenged, makes the instantaneous transition from an outwardly tolerant linguistic code to totalitarianism. Each civilization contains a linguistic line that cannot be crossed. When you *do* cross it, there is a reflex of urgent revulsion. That is the opportunity to define its central myth.

We detect several correspondences to previous Western civilizations. First, again, we are reminded of the Roman state that tolerated all forms of worship – so long as the central cult of the divine Emperors was honored. The myth of divine Emperors was the central cult of Roman power. This tenant of the Roman political state was not to be negotiated at any cost – the state depended upon this cult to justify the political class. The same can be said for any cult.

Second, we observe how all civilizations appear to make complete linguistic reversal of the previous ideological structure. With early Christianity, the Roman Empire abruptly transitioned from polytheism to monotheism. That is a tectonic shift in linguistic ideology. The monotheistic Catholic Church subsequently eradicated all forms of polytheism. Then, again, in the 18th century, Western men observed a subsequent linguistic shift. With the advent of Enlightenment thought, the secular restructuring of linguistic information has subsequently eradicated all forms of Western theism - including Christianity as a hegemonic ideology. Christianity today is a club of ladies and old gentlemen. Today, we do not look for angels as causation; we look for physics. The point? This illustrates that any alternate linguistic training can pattern the mind to see new categories of information. This is what civilizations do - they make artificial representations of reality.

Ultimately, language is a second genetics. Linguistic usage creates a new species of men – a new set of eyes. A new theory of poetry, the subject of this book, will allow men to supersede modernistic patterns of thought. Language makes the world we see. When you change the language, then you have changed the world liable to observation. Would it not be a victory to see a higher and more advanced form of *Sapiens*? It's a linguistic protocol. It is good to get ahead of any ideological and linguistic transition. It is even better to form it. This is Story Theory.

A new theory of poetry is the most effective means to seize control of a future human consciousness. This is an understatement that has yet to be explored with competence.

CHAPTER FOUR

What Is the Purpose of a New Theory of Poetry?

There is only one purpose for any theory of poetry: *a linguistic seizure of consciousness.* The author does not seek to explain, cajole, convince, or explicate any single poem in his theory of poetry. We do not wish to only make a new poetic structure. We wish to construct a new civilization. The objective of hegemonic information is to *seize*, and after, to explain. Linguistic innovations are measured by their audacity to enchant – not their faculty to be adoptive or merely rational. Audacity gives evidence of strength. Audacity does not appeal to tribal, social, or political bias. Audacity is the means to power. Show me your audacity of story, show me your easy competence of hegemonic expression – this is the victory all poets seek. Only then we may talk about the merits of meter, blank verse, rhyme, or making poems in the form of pyramids. But not with me.

Any linguistic structure that does not allow a poet to have power over consciousness is defective from the poet's perspective. We do not wish to construct a new lyric revival. The subject of the lyric is erotic or sensual opinion. The subject of the epic is *civilization* – the proper behavioral response to life phenomena. Seizure of consciousness, the epic trope, is consequently the only race worth the running. Can the epic goal be sustained?

There has not been a hegemonic theory of poetry in the modern idiom. This is unaccountable. We look for the causes of this phenomenon. There are fewer and fewer strong poets now. There have been few strong poets – as household words – for over one hundred years in the West. There are Rock Stars. There are celebrities. There are few strong poets. There has never been a *universally recognized* strong American poet. At best, Whitman and Dickinson are controversial in their thin achievements. Each desperately needing the support of the relevant progressive – or gender – academic camp to advocate their uneven achievements. Among modern Western societies, there is no pressing interest in the condition of poetry. Among Western academic poets there is only balkanization – biased along predictable political, racial, and gender ideologies. There are no strong vernacular poets. It is for this reason I insist that science represents our *only genre of poetic imagination*. This may surprise the modern reader.

There is not a strong genre of lyric poetry that is able to stand on its own merits in the market – certainly not in the market of authoritative ideas or social prestige. What clarity should we glean from this situation? There can be no theory of poetry unable to isolate clarity of information. Above all else, we must enjoy clarity of information. Clarity of information is the single necessary achievement of any high civilization. After the soldiers and armies of the civilization are dust – the clarity of information of a high hegemonic structure survives. We do not memorialize the plumbing of Egypt, Greece, Rome, or Britain. We remember their poems.

The first worry of a theory of poetry, therefore, is the reliability of information that poetry verifies. Does poetry contain information? If poetry does not contain reliable information – this is a crisis of human ideation – since poetry is the *only* human singularity. These books remind the reader that only a human can write, understand, or judge a poem. That is a singularity. This book – and the poem *Chandos Ring* – races to verify if poetry may contain reliable information. Time is short. The English hegemony may not last until we can sing.

Information is the modern crisis. The modern scientific idiom has failed to achieve clarity of information. The evidences are many. The scientific idiom insists that the material universe is dead and that stars are separate creations from men. This is a mistake. Scientific coding ethically allows modernism to exploit and dismember a thing linguistically nominated as dead – including the entire universe. Modernism is at war with all forms of life it cannot linguistically translate into a material object. In other words, modernism operates as any other form of linguistic ideation. Modernism is not worse than other languages; it is merely hegemonic. Modernism is dangerous since it operates as a monopoly on human ideation.

What is the crisis? Modernism can only *detect* its own linguistic patterns of self-generated information. This is a philological dilemma that cannot be ignored if we aim to build a strong theory of poetry. Though we have clear evidence of the toxicity of science, moderns demand to get more of industrial science – not less of it. This is a stark failure of linguistic information. If phenomena may not be evidenced with specifically *material* causation – then non-material phenomena cannot be detected – cannot even be considered to exist as modern information. Modernism is thus *monolingual*. Western men give the poor nations our science, our industrialized medicine, and our media that *ensure* the hegemony of, and *conversion* to, the material and secular interpretations contained in modernism. Modernism, thus, is a global crisis.

Moderns are willing to fight against any culture that attempts to deny or forbid Western medications – or to challenge scientific authority. We do not go to war for freedom. We are never under attack. Western liberal ideology goes to war to ruthlessly verify the modern idiom. When we observe the starvation of Africa, we do not detect *proliferation* (in a desert) as the root problem – modern men only advocate a further application of modernism to the starving.

We are not at war with Islam; we are at war with its anti-modern linguistics – its poetry of anti-liberalism. Yet we fail to admit this openly. We do not hate Islamic individuals – we hate the medieval linguistics of Islam that would ruthlessly forbid any form of modernism taking hold over their cultures. Sharia law is not hated by Westerns because it is not an effective way to organize societies. It is exact and ruthlessly successful in linguistic Islam. We hate Sharia law because it would permanently exclude any form of modernism in a society under Sharia law. Islam is *acutely* aware that it is in the crosshairs of modernism.

The modern myth assumes that all problems of society may be corrected with a deeper and more rigorous regimen of linguistic modernism. Does modernism contain internal contradictions – even, unsolvable problems? Modernism would answer that, yes, there are problems – but they can be solved by a further application of modernism. Again, a myth.

This is a mistake. Story Theory counters, instead, that the ruthless application of industrial science has allowed the conditions insuring the limit of life on Earth. Modernism, as a remedy to the toxic conditions of modernism, is disastrous. Only science has allowed the over-proliferation of humans that will eradicate life on Earth.

The Western citizen believes that modernism gives the individual freedom. What is freedom itself as a quality? Modern surveillance has already canceled human freedom. Modern freedom is exactly the path of least resistance. I agree there is virtue in a struggle for *actual* freedom – that struggle gives humans their message and nobility. The continued struggle for freedom keeps the human at the leading edge of linguistic innovation. Yes, story originates from the struggle for human freedom. Yet what happens when the human decides that his only chance of freedom is an escape from modernism? Escape from modernism? Is that not a crime of modern heresy? To this, the eavesdropping modern reacts with revulsion and attempts to exclude the foreign opinion that is dangerously inventing a new linguistic pattern of life. Every civilization must come face to face with its own feedback.

The luxury and indolence of a wealthy middle class, the arrogance and stupidity of the rich, the indolence of bored and depressed youths, are a danger to the sentient condition of Western men. Poetry anticipates violent actions. Yet what is modern freedom? Is it not the path of least resistance? What is modern technology if not an entire civilization built on indolence – seeking and accepting the path of least resistance? What is the highest goal of a civilization seeking only more technology? It is the path of least resistance. To flip a switch is far superior to manually digging a ditch – as if the hard toil of digging did not, itself, contain important information. I disavow. Flipping the switch, in contrast, gives no information. Is it possible to have a civilization built on seeking the path of least resistance?

It is possible. Modern information is exactly unreliable because it is obtained following the path of least resistance. Pharmaceuticals are built on the theory of least resistance. Modern health, in the modern view, should not be any more complicated than taking a drug. What is technology if not a firm linguistic insistence of taking the path of least resistance? Modernism is an entire body of linguistically coded nations enamored of the indolence of a socialized entitlement economy – and government-funded access to industrial medicines. The philosophy of solving systemic social problems by the further application (distribution) of Western wealth can last only so long as there is wealth to distribute. There is just one problem. Any condition of wealth is a temporary condition. So the democratic solution is, at best, a temporary solution – as modernism is a temporary condition. The wealth of Western society is now an illusion. Our markets are no longer expanding – they are contracting. Our civilization no longer produces wealth – we currently swim in a sea of debt and sleep upon revolving notes of credit.

Certainly, practically, the benefits of science are many. Yet information of technology is a dangerous human honey pot. The physical sciences have no philosophical component – except to postpone all philosophy. Science eternally feeds the myth of science – that all conclusions may be honorably postponed until science finds the ultimate discoveries – surely in the next year – of the god particle, the elixir of eternal youth, the anti-death drug, the transmutations of base metals into gold – of the next scientific Shangri-la. It is impossible to argue with science in the age of science.

It is hard to argue against working toilets, sewers, running water, electric light, and washing machines. These are the honey pots capturing the soon-to-be killed fly – man. I honor these high achievements. With my praise of toilets and sewers, I make the slight additional comment that – actually, practically, ideationally – there is no high philosophic component to modern hygiene. If hygiene were the only standard of civilization, then we would not let the less-hygienic Plato or Michael Angelo into our house. The clean are not more intelligent than the dirty. Technology does not make a selection of human superiority. Ultimately, cleaning both the good and the evil without regard to the quality of the person, the ethical and philosophic content of technology – is valueless – and merely allows a mindless proliferation of human population.

What is my point? Modern technology – the path of least resistance – becomes the *moral,* the *ethics,* and the *message* of civilization. All philosophy of technology, all sentient selection of ethical modern purpose is delayed to a distant generation that cannot reliably respond to the challenge – the challenge of making a selection.

The question of the value and purpose of our civilization is forever postponed to a future generation that will no longer prize the solutions we now seek. They will have a new linguistic code in that future time. Today the young are already corrupted with the indolence of a civilization that seeks the path of least resistance. This is the philosophic crisis of modernism – never to be resolved by modernism.

What after all is the end product of Western access to technology? It only enables the globe to proliferate without any basis of philosophy – with no severe selection of life – except further proliferation. This works against the principles of Story Theory, where we insist that consciousness is *selection* – not simply mindless proliferation. What part of sentient thought does not contain selection? A hairdresser has to pass a selection process. Yet modern civilization does not privilege the protocol of selection. Modern politics, corrupted with reliance upon a pandering democratic narrative, exclusively advocates mindless proliferation. Democracy can only operate as long as there are expanding markets – that is, jobs and goods to distribute as bribes for votes. The assumption of all democratic strategy is that there will always be expanding Western markets to distribute to mindlessly proliferating populations – populations always demanding more entitlements and more goods. Yet since there are not enough resources or enough wealth for ten billons of people to become middle-class Americans – modern proliferation is the complete absence of philosophy. There is no sentient end goal. Modernism is a virus destroying Earth and all life on Earth.

The danger of materialistic science is that it is impossible to escape the ideational patterns of the linguistics of technology: the path of least resistance. Technology embeds a linguistic pattern. A single message is transmitted: the path of least resistance. We are trapped in the idiomatic machine of high technological dependence and, thus, fixed in ideational confusion. There is a philosophy gap. Technology (as modernism) does not assert a superior human value. Both the good and the bad may acquire technology without selection of any measure of human fitness to receive the goods of civilizations. The human element needs to enter the machines again and seize back the idiomatic control of consciousness. The ultimate theme of these books is: *How may we construct a future idiom to seize control of consciousness – and a form of consciousness, moreover, to suit our purpose of creating a magus civilization?* What is the condition of this civilization? At a minimum, we know that it is a space faring civilization that does not follow the mindlessness of the *path of least resistance.* We know that we must build a civilization that does not elect politicians who promise to vote more entitlements – until there is nothing left to give away. I seek a civilization of ruthless innovators – not a self-satisfied society sustained on the ever-increasing entitlements, apparently, given to anyone wishing such entitlements. How can an entitlement society foster innovation and ruthless audacity? There never was a heroic recovery from self-satisfaction. There never was a further ideational advancement made from indolence.

First, the well-informed modern certainly knows that science is contributing to the end of life on Earth. He knows that species of animals are disappearing daily due to the scientific industrial complex. The modern is confronted daily with advertisements revealing that medical industries have polluted the health of humans – and profited shamelessly from the degradation of human health. The dire written and spoken warnings on modern medicines are so numerous and repetitive that they essentially pass unremarked and unread. This is linguistic mindlessness. Due to a self-referent modernism, we have already arrived at linguistic irrelevance.

The *Advertising Executive* knows that the modern will essentially ignore the dire information of modernism – that is, the amazingly bi-polar modern will ignore the medical warnings on packages. Industrial pharmaceuticals are consumed in toxic abundance – have more warnings posted than a nuclear waste dump – and they are medications, moreover, that have less beneficial effects than a placebo. Yet even observing and hearing clear evidence of a failed presentation of information – the modern will still insist that his linguistic idiom of life – industrial medicine, yellow journalism, and scientific, liberal academic research – is the only privileged form of information. This is a crisis of the modern information. The average modern does still not recognize it. He does not recognize it because the system of information that should warn him is unable to linguistically self-accuse itself.

Civilizations do not exactly reproduce reality. Civilizations can only make a linguistic representation of reality. Modernism, as a linguistic code, is no more an exact copy of reality than that of the Plains Indians or the Mayan civilization. Though significantly different interpretations of reality were made – each cultural representation of *world* made perfect sense to the respective linguistic groups. To people of disparate cultures, only *their own* languages appear to be rational and normative. In Story Theory, all languages are essentially *emotional* copies of reality. Reality is unknown and mysterious. Language struggles to hide this fact.

Just because a symbol is transmitted to the brain – does not mean that the symbol is an exact reproduction of reality. The visible world is only a representation of world. According to this view, we say that civilizations do not exactly reproduce reality. The Western is daily saturated with advertisements of new pharmaceuticals that specifically assert that they are dangerous and have deadly side effects. Then we observe that, despite the dangers of these drugs, the sales of these pharmaceuticals increase daily. What do we say of a civilization that sees its own chaos and is yet unable to retranslate its world? It is a crisis of the modern mind.

There cannot be a strong theory of poetry that does not detect the degradation – the lack of reliability – of modern information. Outside of basic animal instinct, all human ideation is based on a linguistically patterned dimension of value and meaning. This is why there must be a strong theory of poetry – to correct the toxic effects of modern linguistic misprision. Linguistics inform human morals, tastes, behavior, and most radically, even the purpose of stars in the universe. This is Story Theory. When we attempt to give an account of our consciousness, even in the first syllables, we transition immediately to a story of consciousness (poetry). No sophistry can contradict the previous statement. This verifies the necessity of poetry in human society.

The linguistically patterned human mind cannot be separated from the necessity of a strong theory of poetry. Why? Because any form of poetry is a fossil of the human mind. Poetry is a man face to face with the singularity of human consciousness. This is the case for poetry.

Modernism cannot detect non-modernism. A strong poet can only struggle to construct an alternate linguistics of the future. Modernism, dominant and self-referent, does not permit an alternate and alien poetic vision. Hermetically sealed against all other interpretations of life, modernism can only replicate itself. Modernism, to speak crudely, blocks the strong poet who would attempt to construct an alternate, non-modern, non-scientific, vision of future human life. Modernism can only detect and replicate modernism. Math can only detect more math. Churchmen can only argue for more church. Socialists can only demand more socialism. This is the ruthless and severe protocol of linguistic codes.

If modernism does not contain reliable poetic information, the poet struggling to reference only his or her innovative linguistics, consequently, can only oppose modern information. This is what a poet does – he makes a new linguistics – and then, of course, he appears strange, suspicious, and eccentric to modern eyes. Immediately we discover why a child's lemonade stand has more market force than that of a struggling poet. It is clearly understood, at least, that the child is trying to conform to a modern capitalism ethic.

Let us state the case as we know it. Modernism, as any linguistic code, is only a temporary structure that is under continuous pressure of the strong poet to construct the next linguistic innovation – the future of human knowing. That means that modern secular materialism is only a temporary ideational island – a transition point to some other innovation. Modernism may, at times, claim to be exclusively rational – but modernism is still a misreading of reality. Modernism, as civilization, is, after all, only a linguistic code. This is the case for poetry.

With the re-discovery of the cuneiform epics in Mesopotamia, we now know that the modern academic narrative of Western civilization has been misinterpreted. Modern academics have failed to understand the cosmological information contained in the meaning of Greek, Egyptian, Indian, Plains Indian, Mayan, Finnish, Persian, Akkadian and Sumerian myths. If ancient information does not appear as modern and linguistic forms of science or mathematics – then ancient poetic information cannot be detected as valid information. In fact, the ancient poetic scripts must be carefully set aside as suspect data – as a useless, perhaps amusing, myth.

Modernism labels epic poetry as unreliable information. In Story Theory, this is equivalent of one system of mythology calling another system of myth defective. This is equivalent to one form of linguistics seeking to disadvantage an alternate form of linguistics. Ultimately, both linguistic systems – modernism and epic myth – are equally forms of poetry.

The Egyptian, Sumerian, and Greek myths are still unexplored as the verification of deep cosmological information. There is a deep mystery concealed within all epic poetry. We are not sure of the authorship of epic poems. Their origin is essentially unaccountable. We still don't know who wrote the Homeric poems – it certainly was not a figure named Homer. We don't know who wrote the Sumerian epics. We don't know who wrote the Semitic poetry of the Jewish *Talmud*. We don't know who wrote the *Books of Moses* – it certainly was not a man named Moses. We do not know who wrote the *Psalms of King David*. It was not King David. We don't know who wrote the *Songs of Solomon*. It was not a man named Solomon. We don't know who composed the utterly alien epic of *Jason and the Argonauts*. We still do not know who wrote the *Gospels* of Jesus. It was not Matthew, Mark, Luke, or John. It is clear that prior to the modern crisis of intellect, all vital cosmological information was transferred from generation to generation with stories containing poetic patterns of epic ideation. The secret of these riddles remains unexamined. Modern academics, so eager to deconstruct what does not fit into their linguistic pattern, ignore the codes embedded in the epic poems.

If it can be once established that poetry is a medium for information – in fact, deep and comprehensive information – then our book may advance a more radical goal. Until poetry may contain as much authority as the idiom of science, we have no cause for satisfaction.

This, then, is the purpose of a new theory of poetry: to create a new language of future men that have survived modernism.

CHAPTER FIVE

Is There *Ever* a Superiority of Information?

We cannot address a theory of poetry unless we address the problem of information. Any form of linguistic civilization is essentially at war with time to replicate the phenomena of life. The Western liberal idiom – now moving to final hegemonic control of Earth – contains a deep uncharted element of its own chaos. It is the thesis of this volume the liberal idiom is no longer able to anticipate, interpret, or survive charismatic forms of consciousness.

Each age of man has insisted upon the superiority of its information. The Greek poet would not ridicule the oracle of Delphi. The Roman writer would not despise the prophesies of Jupiter Capitalanus. The Medieval priest would not challenge the authority of the Catholic Church. Are these civilizations primitive, or somehow, stupid? No, they were civilizations of high linguistics. Modernism is also a construct of high linguistics.

Moderns exhibit no less certainty in the linguistic bias of their human information. No modern citizen would negotiate his right to advanced secular technologies, industrial medicine, or, in fact, *any* form of the oracle of scientific information. To the modern, even the sound of these terms seems to inspire a certain superiority of insight. The right to maintain a scientific, materialist translation of life operates as *sine qua non* to the modern citizen.

We do not even linguistically bother to point out that *only some* humans believe in material science. We *used* to hear in the 1970's that "some scientists *suggest* that patients must get PSA blood tests" – indicating that this is one human opinion among many. We now say, "the *science* indicates men must get PSA tests." Observe the linguistic shift. Science has made the anthropomorphic transition from mere human opinion to hegemonic and deified idol. Science, as linguistic code, has become unchallenged oracle. A living oracle of hegemony.

Science is no longer one opinion among many educated ideologies – science operates as a living *being* – as an oracle that is no longer even challenged by the modern vernacular speaker. The Gods of Egypt and Greece made a similar anthropomorphic progression from poetic opinion under, for example, the poet *Hesoid* – to the position of hegemonic oracle consulted by serious men setting out to make world conquest – as Alexander the Great consulted the four Oracles of Apollo ruling the Hellenistic world (Didyma, Delphi, Claros, Delos).

Are we certain of the modern insight? To the modern, materialism is not even an idiom to be negotiated. No modern would forgo the belief in technology – nor would he or she renounce the information that is generated via the idiom of electronics, computers, and media. The medium *becomes* the message. Modern information is rooted in the medium of electronic transmission. Yet the danger is ignored by all. If the electronic medium disappears – likewise does the value of information based on that medium. Electronics, science, and medicine cannot be separated from our technological biases of information. The pride and arrogance of modernism is deep. This is our crisis of information. Why? Because the mediums of our modern liberal bias – electronics, instant media, non-local communication, incessant scientific opinions – are as fragile as the gossamer of a wasp's wing. One catastrophic event would wipe out the narrow electronic spectrum of our idiomatic translation of life. All screens will go black and all refrigerators would stop in the industrialized world. Charismatic disasters cannot be anticipated, prepared for, or predicted. No civilization has ever anticipated charismatic disasters. Since no civilization exactly reproduces reality – there is only an *alternate* linguistic copy of reality. This *alternate copy* of reality always fails to see what is coming. In human history, all forms of human revolution or natural catastrophe are charismatic in their origins. As all of history verifies cataclysmic charismatic events, we are certain to immediately feel the crisis of the integrity of modern linguistics.

Consequently, *Chandos Ring* explores the modern misprision of linguistic information. Modernism cannot accuse itself. Ideational ideologies – as modernism – are all built on hermetically sealed, self-referencing linguistic structures. Stalinism is an example here, where the Russian language was changed to enforce a newly invented communist ideology. Western liberalism has similarly modified American English to enforce global liberalism. When the language has been modified to conform to an ideology it is already too late to resist. Linguistic ideologies, once accepted as realty, can only collapse with economic or demographic failure.

If there is no innovation of a new linguistics, then we are unprepared for our crisis of information. Modernism is in the impossible position of refusing to openly declare what is great and beautiful. Never has there been a great civilization that was so afraid to express its linguistic biases with clarity. So deep are our wounded moralities of imperial conquests and racial bigotry, we now are forbidden to exalt our vision of a previously audacious European, mythic, imperial, or, even, Caucasian cultural beauty – since it will certainly offend some previously oppressed group. There is rage from a silenced majority of vernacular Western men that are suppressed in their freedom of audacity. If a poet's expression is not – somehow – multicultural – then it must be suppressed. This affects the strength of poetry in any culture. When audacity dies, poetry dies.

So long as there is suppression of our ancient cultural European linguistic traditions – in effect, an overt political control of our linguistic audacity – there can be no strong theory of poetry. There is no strong poetry in the West because there is fear – we have lost our usual *condition* of audacity to assert our own bias. Poetry is an esthetic bias of beauty. Poetry is not political expression. Modernism operates as prosthetic device that tracks and monitors any assertion of non-liberal speech. The traditional European audacity offends the cultural aesthetics of rising minority groups – now entering the West. What is the result? We are the only high civilization, ever, that is unable to clearly delineate or assert its image of the good and the beautiful. Moderns may speak publicly of only trivial matters –which sport teams they favor, which products they like, etc. This suppression of instinctive joy – a joy of felt superiority – creates fear and loathing in the social body. The disciple of Beethoven and Shakespeare feels suddenly self-conscious in multiculturalism and the ethnic minority is wary of any assertion of specifically Eurocentrist aesthetics. There is only hypocrisy of speech when speech is proscribed.

There can be only fearful, hypocritical poems when poems are written to fit political criteria. Consequently, there can be no new linguistic audacity until there is a theory of poetry that contains a fearless clarity of Western information. This is the thesis of *Chandos Grid*.

When the American soldier travels to Africa, Afghanistan, or Iraq, he or she immediately feels the Western idiomatic translation of life. The entire world exists in crisis either *against* or *for* liberal modernism. Developing nations are either feverishly trying to mimic modernism – or to militantly eradicate it. In stark contrast to less materialistic nations, we feel our expectation of modernism intimately. Modern science, industrial medicine, and advanced technology are structured as linguistic forms of Western human ideation.

How does the modern communicate? With irony and hypocrisy. There is no Western that does not use electronics to access modern information. Computers are now the medium of communicating the high languages of liberalism – scientific/medical/psychological authority. Yet this is essentially a monopoly of information. Only a narrow elite of specialists is conversant with the highest technical reaches of specialized literature or quantum technology. By this protocol of technology, the vernacular speaking masses of moderns are essentially excluded from authoritative expression of the future of human life. Vernacular speaking populations are tributary to a narrow medium of electronically disbursed liberal/scientific information. In effect, science is our single priesthood of linguistic oracle and future prophecy. The vernacular speaking person is not only linguistically, and thus socially, constrained; he is isolated from the secret linguistics of advanced technologies. The status of second-class citizenship directly impinges the audacity of the vernacular speaking Westerner. There cannot be strong poetry without audacity.

In Story Theory, this situation – where only a trained academic, or a scientist, has the right to pronounce the *past*, *present* and *future* form of human life – is a crisis of human ideation. There can be no strong school of poetry so long as the vernacular speaking Western person has no *linguistic* authority. Why is the vernacular important to poets? We all speak in the vernacular. Poetry is the only form of high linguistics that is fundamentally – and permanently – vernacular. The entire spectrum of modern information is consequently a crisis for the vernacular speaker.

The vernacular code has been maligned and reduced to a second-class linguistics. If the highest idioms of specialized languages (quantum mechanics, industrial medicine, and math) are the final source of authoritative expression of human life, then the vernacular speaker no longer is a source of human information at all. This makes the information of the vernacular poet inescapably secondary. The vernacular speaking person's information is tributary – and he is thus *encouraged* to believe in the superiority of academic scientists. Modernism operates as *a faith* – a faith in the validity of modern information.

The modern citizen has only a tangential relation to the secret languages of his culture. The modern exists as a consumer of industrialized information and hegemonic liberal ideology. The modern vernacular speakers – that is, most modern persons – are dependent as a child upon their all-knowing fathers in the scientific community. Modern society is essentially a priesthood/acolyte relationship. Priests descend from on high, via the instantly resourced media, to declare what foods are fit to eat, what behaviors are approved, what medicine we must take without delay. Then science suddenly reverses their oracles in the next decade. Because our faith is great, we accept these wild reversals of doctrine. In effect, we are conditioned with constant and unstoppable messages of secular luxury, liberal capitalistic consumerism, pharmaceutical urgency, and serial pornography. This is the ideational hell of modern and technologically driven liberalism. Access to these elements of modernism is what passes for Western freedom. Modernism is linguistic propaganda – and it is unceasing in its delivery. There is no escape from modernism except by collapse of modernism.

Languages pasteurize populations with a common idiomatic discharge. Linguistic coding does not stop until it has pasteurized the entire spectrum of the linguistic body. Modernism carefully places all vernacular speakers under constant surveillance. Hegemonic liberal linguistic coding will have to continue to make meticulous inventory of our eyes, our biometrics, our genitals, our senses, and then, our minds.

Liberal modernism is the most successful form of linguistic and ideational terror ever devised. Stalinism and Fascism seem amateurish compared to liberal capitalistic modernism. Liberalism cannot even be resisted – as any form of anti-liberal opinion is instantly labeled as a regressive reactionary speech – with horrific tags (as racism) that envelop dissenting opinion in a cocoon of disgust. Liberalism acts as a ruthless anti-body that seals off instantly any virus of *other* that enters the mind of the host. As long as liberalism operates as a totalitarian thought system, there cannot be an authoritative theory of vernacular poetry. Consequently, there must be a new language created – a new linguistic coding – that eliminates the arrogant monopoly of modernism. The first step is to verify that science, as modernism, *itself* is a projection of human poetry. Again, the reader takes a deep breath.

Every great civilization contains high languages that structure and restrain the human emotional charge. Yet when high idioms become so specialized that they transition to secret languages, spoken only by trained elites, the vernacular populations of this culture become alienated. The modern world is famous for its alienated vernacular populations. The evidence of ethnic alienation is omnipresent. The Hip Hop graffiti on the wall of every city in America and Europe verify an attitude of protest – disgust towards established forms of hegemonic modern information. Currently, as I write this, there are riots against Western capitalist modernism in over 250 major cities of the West. Islam already is in revolt. Islam feels and interprets Western liberal linguistic hegemony intimately. It is clear to them that liberal linguistics intends to erase African, Asian, and Arabic patterns of thought and speech. That is what Western men do.

Modernism is now a wounded morality. When the information of secret languages begins to fail, the vernacular speaking populations revolt. The method of revolt always takes the form of a new innovation of linguistic coding. In Story Theory, this revolt – essentially a *re-imagination* of human life – verifies the value of poetry. Currently the idioms preventing the final Western liberal control of human consciousness are: Islam, the Chinese megalith, and African sub-culture (anti-modern urban graffiti, anti-establishment Hip-Hop music, etc.).

The re-imagination of poetry is the subject of these books. So long as poetry operates as if it may ignore the idiom of science, or be in fear of science, then poetry is not a valid idiom. It is wrong for poets to fear or ignore science. Science itself is a form of strong poetry. Already we see the first mistake most persons make about the competitive merits of science and poetry. Poetry is a valid human form of information because human consciousness is never rational, sane, or predictable. Poetry is a valid form of information since human consciousness is charismatic. The idioms of science, medicine, and mathematics are utterly silent on the charismatic structure of consciousness. In the face of charismatic occurrence, modernism is speechless. The linguistic formulas of modernism have no sentient response to immanent charismatic catastrophe. If the future is a charismatic *event*, then why have we chosen modernism as the only accepted speech? Modernism is not able to prepare for what is coming.

The record of humans on earth is a list of charismatic events. We may insist that our responses to charismatic historical events are logical, balanced or controlled – but in reality, each was a moment of crisis. A 6th century Christian Emperor could not have anticipated the sudden uprising of the Arab world by an obscure nomadic people or an even more obscure Mohammed. Islam is a charismatic arrival. No 1st century Roman Emperor could have anticipated the charismatic victory of Christianity in the Roman Empire. No Greek or Roman philosopher could have anticipated the overthrow of the rich Greek Pantheon of gods by an impoverished Jewish sect preaching the kingdom of the poor and humble. Christianity was a charismatic arrival. No pope or theologian could have anticipated obscure alchemists would usher in a world linguistically restructured to serve a world of secular and scientific authority. Scientific materialism is thus a charismatic arrival in an Age of Faith. Can we even limit our examples of charismatic events? What is next?

We wish the poet survives only if his poem contains information.

This is the subject of *Chandos Ring*.

CHAPTER SIX

What Did the Epic Poets Know?

The Greek and Roman gods were emplacements from Egypt. The Greek epic cycles were copies of Sumerian, Indian, and Egyptian poetic lore. The Greek philosophers studied under an Egyptian priest for up to 20 years before they returned to Greece to teach a strange esoteric story tradition that contained advanced math and cosmology. The Mithraic and Elysian mystery cults were emplacements from more ancient Eastern sacred epic literature. As modern scientific idiom has failed to discover the complex intellectual illusions embedded in epic myths – modern academics have ignored them as sources of information. All poetry and myth operates – as the human mind operates – on the ideal astral plane. We now struggle to recover this lost data.

All epic poems are stories of cosmology – and thus, evidence of the astral position of the human mind. We may begin anywhere in the epic trope. The Titan, Cronus (Roman Saturn), ate each of his children to secure his reign – since he was warned that one of his offspring would displace his position in the hierarchy. Mother Gia (Earth), attempting to prevent this disorder, hides the young Zeus (Roman *Jupiter*) in a mountain cave on the island of Crete. The sailors of Crete told Zeus how Cronus ate his brother and sister gods. Zeus went to the mainland and killed Cronus and thereby supplanted him. The myth contains an accurate narrative of ancient astrological information. Science now confirms that the planet Jupiter entered our solar system millennia ago, supplanting Saturn's position – and displaced Saturn to the outer solar system. How did the epic poets gain this information?

No one has ever understood the epics of the Hercules' cycle. It is not a human story. It is archetypical information of the astral plane. It is a horror story of alien bestiary and exact cosmology. If Hercules is seen as a story of heroic humans, we are only confused by the gratuitous murders, pointless bloodshed, and the incomprehensible slaughter of his own family. It is now revealed that the twelve labors of Hercules are encoded representations of the course of the human sun (the human soul) through the twelve signs of the zodiac. The signs of the zodiac associated with the labors of Hercules are easy to identify. His slaughter of the Nemean lion (first labor) is clearly a reference to the passage of the sun through Leo. The Cretan bull was certainly Taurus (seventh labor). Hippolyta, the virgin queen of the Amazons was passage through the constellation of Virgo (ninth labor). The poisonous Hydra (second labor) was Scorpio, and the centaur that completed the death of Hercules was a symbol of the dying (descending) constellation of Sagittarius. We are clearly operating here on the astral plane.

After so many millennia we are still able to follow the cosmology embedded by a higher intelligence. It is remembered that Hercules and Iphicles were twins – yet only one was immortal. Clearly his birth is a symbol of the twin equinoxes. We read the zodiac only by the (immortal) vernal equinox – we ignore the autumnal equinox in regard to the precession of the Zodiac. With the clues of cosmology already detected in the epic narrative, we are alerted that the birth and death of Hercules also represents the two solstices. In Greek times, the summer solstice (Hercules birth) occurred when the sun was positioned in Gemini. The Gemini, of course, were twin brothers, Pollux and Castor – and only Pollux was born immortal. The winter solstice (his death), in Greco-Roman times, took place when the sun was between Capricorn and Sagittarius. And, again, in myth, Hercules died at the descent of the Sagittarius in the night sky.

As if we needed any other confirmation, the protagonists in the heroic narrative are stars – and today they are the names of actual stars and planets – not men, not gods, not monsters. The exact correspondences alert us to the actual *events* of all epic literature: permanent and eternal cosmology. The narrative implies that Hercules was a solar deity – not a human deity. He is associated with the birth and death of light, with the cycle of cosmology, and the labors of the twelve zodiacs. Already there are enough verified astrological precedents to make an interrogative of possible aspects of cosmology embedded in the epic poems and myths. It is a cipher enabling us to decode an entire narrative of alien millennial structures. There are unanticipated benefits. At the end of our inquiry, we discover the source of life itself.

How were the poets of differing ages able to be so consistent in their cosmology? Are epic and mythic poem cycles separate stories written at separate times – and certainly by separate human poets? Or, inexplicably, are they all fragments of a lost superstructure of alien narrative? And, finally, does the totality of this narrative contain the secrets of the origin of human life? The reader will recall my initial comments. An epic poem contains no new information – an epic poem contains everything always known. A statement surely strange by any modern academic assessment – yet somehow this view is beginning to form an outline of meaning.

I now move to Africa and Egypt. The earliest creation stories place reoccurring importance on the numbers two and eight and twelve. The Dogon Tribe of central Africa was once connected with Egyptian culture more than five thousand years ago. In the 1930's, French anthropologists reported that the Dogon Tribe elders told stories exactly describing the function and number of the elemental particles. Their eight ancestors comprised the 7 + 1 elemental waves of potential being – seven waves of matter, the eighth ancestor, as observer, entering the egg of Being, thus making up all created matter. Their symbols indicate exact diagrams of the number and orbits of the atomic structure. Their idea of the emergence of matter in the universe is related to phase transitions, and they know that chromosomes move apart and form spindles during mitosis. Their secret stories (with written symbols) indicated that they understood that sound travels in waves, that they knew the correct counts of elements within each atomic category of matter, that the most basic component of matter is a thread, that this fundamental thread vibrates – and that treads give rise to the four quantum forces. The Dogons further insist that there are 266 elements of matter – moderns are still at 210 and counting. They also state that this region of the galaxy is assigned to the *second world* – and that there is a higher, third world that men struggle to enter.

More startling, the Dogon tribe has ancient knowledge of the Sirius star system – to include the orbits of Sirius A and Sirius B – only recently confirmed by science. They seem to have already known that the dwarf star (Sirius B) is incredibly small and dense – and that Sirius B orbits the larger star, Sirius A. Why is this important? Science did not detect the nearly invisible Sirius B until the 1970's.

There is an overwhelming body of scientific correspondences that show that ancient India and Egypt (and the Dogons) had a knowledge of cosmology, DNA, and quantum mechanics – which were not only unknown, but not even proposed by science – until recently. What is our response to this ancient knowledge? Poetry not only appears to contain information – but it contains the highest form of information.

How did ancients gain this information?

Egypt was also aware of the information of the Sirius twin star system. Further, the Indian Vedic epic poems insist that our sun is also in a twin star system – and that this binary orbit is approx 24,000 years. Only an advanced civilization could discover this information – the time counts are too long for ordinary human lives to observe without advanced instruments.

How did the Egyptians and the Sumerians know of Sirius B – the dark (invisible) dwarf star? The goddess Isis, always in the company of her sister, Nephthys, took on the attributes of the Sirius star system. Isis, who stood for light, represented Sirius A. Nephthys, symbolizing darkness and the invisible (the underworld), stood for Sirius B (the dark dwarf star). Astonishingly, we find the Sirius system poetically evoked in the Egyptian *Book of the Dead*. The god Nephthys is quoted as saying: "I go round about thee to protect thee [Isis] . . . my strength shall be near thee forever." This is a clear statement of the orbit and density of Sirius B. Granted, the modern does not often expect gods to reveal to them exact cosmology. But there it is. It's a question of linguistic bias. Can our minds be opened to information on the astral plane?

The Egyptian Ogdoad pantheon, as the Sumerian Anunnaki, likewise contains eight ancestor gods – again, prefiguring string theory, where *seven* dimensions of potential matter are manifested when modified (formed) by an *eighth* entity (the observer). The eighth ancestor – who is observing the seven quantum waves of potential matter – became the chief creator of the universe. Each living person replicates this protocol of creation. The human, as a sentient observer, conditions the visible apparition of his world experience, by making an observation of the potential ideational state of his or her life. In a remarkable coincidence with quantum theory, the myth is saying that the universe of all material phenomena is created by a direct agency of the *observation* of conscious mind. The educated scientific reader, again, will recall the outlines of string theory and quantum mechanics.

Where did the ancient poets get this information?

Egyptian hieroglyphic language also shows a similar hidden cosmology. We find the word for the god *Ptah*, the creator of men, with the same intertwined snake pattern that we use for our symbol of DNA ⸘. The hieroglyph for the Egyptian word *un* (*to exist*) contains three surprising symbols. Each unavoidably reminds us of elements of modern physics and quantum mechanics. There is a symbol seeming to replicate the orbit of an electron ⚛. Can this be an accident? The next hieroglyph is a wave-like pattern to indicate an electromagnetic force ⌇. Next to the wave-like pattern, there is the symbol of a coiled structure to symbolize the DNA spiral ⸘. These three symbols combine to indicate "existence" – as ⚛⌇⸘. These ancient poetic correspondences of modern scientific information, if accidental, are uncanny. If not accidental then its information.

Most instructive is the Egyptian word for their primary god. The hieroglyph for *Amen*, the god of all of creation, is written with wave-like patterns to indicate: "that which ⸗ draws or weaves ⌇ waves ⌇ into particles ○ in a place ⸙ hidden from ⸙ interference ⸙" (⸗⌇⌇○⸙⸙). This is a poetic representation of god, as *total Being*, and, again, reminds the reader of a textbook statement of quantum mechanics. The hair goes up on the arm when all the elements of myths and gods are pieced together.

What is the importance of this data that is, to many moderns, arcane poetic information? It means the end of the modern world as hegemonic structure. These esoteric forms of information support the thesis that poetry may contain any structure of advanced information. How did ancients gain this information? How did the ancient poets manage their crisis of information? Are we to understand that they practiced, or even understood, quantum mechanics? Not at all - or at most a few priests may have understood the bare outlines of what we, today, call atomic and quantum theory. More radically, I suggest that only today we read these symbols for what they are - they are a map of the physical operation of the material universe. How are we to otherwise account for symbols of atomic orbits, DNA, and photon wave patterns in ancient cultures? Any new theory of poetry must account for these lost symbols in ancient runes. Someone has to face this challenge with maturity.

Chandos Ring attempts to develop and structure this perspective..

CHAPTER SEVEN

What World Does Epic Poetry Address?

An epic poem contains no new information. It contains *all* known information. Correspondingly, all vernacular speakers may recognize the information contained in epic poetry. The epic does not present a newly discovered plot or personality. In an epic poem we instinctively recognize the cultural plots and personalities. The subject of an epic poem is consciousness – how to seize more of life. In the epic trope, there is a super-abundance of value. The poet chases this super-abundance. The poet is a maker seeking a super-abundance of life.

A personality appearing in an epic is something already known for all time. The poet of the Vedic epics did not invent new human personalities – he told the battles of stars for position. The poets of Sumer did not introduce the personality of Gilgamesh. He was known for all time as a "prince" – a star. The poets of "Homer" did not introduce the personality of Achilles, Agamemnon, Hector, or Odysseus. They were known in star myths for all time. *Jason and the Argonauts* were not new personalities. They were stars in the constellation (of Aries). The *Golden Fleece* was the collection of stars of the Ram constellation (Aries). The fifty Argonauts did not even move – they sat on chairs. Just as the fifty Anunnaki of the Sumerian epic poems sat on thrones. These heroes were known for all time – they are stars. Milton did not introduce the personality of Lucifer. He was known for all time – as the fallen luminescence (star).

An epic poem does not contain a mysterious innovation of plot structure. We do not wonder if Gilgamesh will ever gain his quest for immortal life. We know that he will fail. This is how we recognize he contains an eternal message – as all stars embed a high life-giving message. We do not read Homer to discover if it is true that Hector was killed, or if proud Ilium fell. We know that Hector must die. We already know that the source of the poem is the rage of Achilles. We already know the plot before we begin the poem. The Greeks already knew the answer – by heart. We do not breathlessly follow Aeneas to see if he may, somehow, really, found the city of Rome – and thus, the Roman Empire (Aries, rule of law). We know beforehand that Aeneas will carry the fire of the new Aries constellation to heighten the idiom of Rome. He is Aries. We know the *Aeneid* has a prior agenda – but we still read Virgil with interest. Why? Because we know the poet's work contained a linguistic incantation - a healing prophecy - of civilization. This is the essential and exclusive gift of the epic trope - a linguistic incantation of healing information that structures value (that is, manners) from social chaos. After sixty years of civil war, Virgil's civilization was in crisis and chaos. Virgil's epic text gave Rome a myth of recovery. Epic rage engineers the recovery of human life. Every high civilization is based on an epic text. There have been no exceptions to this rule. This is a new insight.

We do not wonder about the theology of Dante – we know he was an exact follower of Orthodoxy and the Catholic Aquinas. We know that he was forced to flee in exile and that he raged against the corruption of the Late Medieval Church. We know he held a raging heart.

We do not wonder if Milton's Lucifer will rebel from God or if Lucifer has a hand in causing Adam to fall. We do not question who should eat the apple of the *Tree of Knowledge*. We know that Eve did it. Everything in an epic poem is already decided – from the beginning. We know that Milton was enraged that the puritan Roundhead revolution failed. He was in rage against the "Romanist" Restoration court culture. We know he had a raging heart.

How, then, can we explain the eternal appeal of the epic form? What does this intend about the information that an epic poem contains? It contains all known information. Only the epic poet is strange. He is full of a purifying rage.

Chandos Ring has an agenda. It enumerates with a hard-fought linguistic code the facts of consciousness – in story. The reader, now familiar with the facts of Story Theory, will find each construct of information monumented for all time in the poem: 1) Consciousness is unfinished. 2) There is nothing outside of consciousness (including death). 3) Everything within consciousness can be modified by the human observer. 4) All speech is a form of prophecy. 5) Consciousness contains an unknown bias (and it selects this bias ruthlessly). The chief proof of Story Theory is portrayed in the poem and remains the solid justification of the epic trope. 6) When a man gives an account of his life, even in the first syllables, he immediately transitions to story. 7) The epic poem is a history of stars – with human agency. 8) An epic poem addresses life on the astral plane. These are the facts of consciousness in Story Theory. They are new.

So long as there are corrupted men, there will be rage. Some imagine that Dante was an orthodox conformist. Instead, we read Dante with a kind of uncanny amazement. Dante had a secret rage to conceal. He hated the hierarchy of the corrupted papacy. Some imagine that Virgil was a paid political conformist. He hated the politics of contemporary Rome. Virgil had a secret rage to conceal.

Some imagine that Milton was a typical Christian polemist. Instead, we read Milton sensing a suppressed rage. He hated the hierarchy of European and Papal monarchy. He was in danger of being arrested for anti-monarchial, anti-orthodox beliefs under Restoration England. We imagine that Shakespeare was an Elizabethan conformist and patriot. Instead, we read Shakespeare with a muted alarm. He had a secret and intimate rage against the Elizabethan political arrangement. He was enraged against a totalitarian political machine – that stole his property and his birthright. All his poems contain only one theme: The prince has been dispossessed. He was ruthlessly dispossessed. All epic poems conceal an idiom of rage.

These are aspects of the epic trope that the modern does not detect.

The epic poet does not incidentally have a talent for epic poems. No one is born to make epic poems. That is an impossible origin. He is usually a lyric poet – turned dark – sometimes bad and forbidding – then releases his charge of joy at the right moment. In every age, the epic poet has suffered bitterly from the loss of *his* world by a monopoly of contemporary and antagonistic power. The epic poet has a secret rage against his time – and he must find an alternate linguistics to expose the secret fullness of his soul. He cannot say openly what the powers of the age would detect. A new idiomatic code is built – merely appearing to the *uninitiated* as high literature. There is no such thing as high literature. There is only high rage.

It is not high literature the epic poet seeks; it is his clarity of rage he must perfect with his device. His message of new cosmology must find its monument of structure. Any poet that *merely* seeks high literature will certainly fail to please, lead, or amaze. The strong poet seeks to channel and divert his rage into power. If power is not felt in his line – he rejects it ruthlessly. It is contempt for his nemesis – the human *powers that be* – that impel his seizure of counter-idiom. Denied of control of his world – he must foster a new world. Every epic poem conceals a correction of ordered world. The villainy within *Chandos Ring* is a privileged nemesis of ideological totalitarianism. The true facts of human life must be shown – and shown with some element of strength. He will stare failure in the face. This is the challenge, and the difficulty, of all epic poets.

An epic poem contains no new information; it contains everything known for all time. The epic poem does not discuss mere human personality; the subject of epic poetry is the cosmology of the stars. This includes events in heaven and hell, above and below the astral plane – dividing the waters (Milky Way) from the heavens. Epic information is gathered outside of Earth – in the wheel of constellations – again, on the astral plane. Epic information includes genetics, hegemonic linguistic codes, and the dark, uncanny, manners of demi-gods. We cannot know the heroes of epic, we cannot interview them, but we recognize them when seen. We know when we are in the bright emitting beam of an epic message.

We know when we are receiving essential information of rage. It is rare in the extreme. It is, in fact, a form of communicating that is essentially alien.

What world does the epic poem address? Only an epic poem verifies that the Earth is not a globe, not a place where insignificant, dirty, miserable humans live. One hundred years of slick advertising and films have misrepresented the human element. The Earth of epic poems is the ideal astral plane – at best, a cosmological coordinate that is continually adjusting to fit the position of constellations. We should not confuse heroes with actual locations on a terrestrial globe. The rare reader will already know (again, the main theme) that since the invention of human writing, there have only been three constellations in the night sky – Taurus, Aries, and Pisces. As will be seen, each of the constellations asserted a particular human message. This will shock the modern reader to his core – yet I will proceed. *Supposed* human heroes – as if someone knew what was *really occurring* in the heavens – are draped in the symbology of the cosmos. Only poetry can provide this insight. The epic astral world is stable. It is reliable.

This is what the truth looks like. *Gilgamesh*, who "stood on the land like a bull," contained the messaged feedback of force and ego of Taurus (the Bull). In this epic, it is illustrated that force alone could not gain possession of eternal life. In the next age, Moses, who came down Mont Sinai adorned with ram horns (!), heralded the message of the Aries constellation. The Ram, of course, is the sign of law-giving Aries. Moses is the lawgiver. It is interesting that at the same period when the Laws of the Hebrew *Talmud* were being finalized in text form, Plato was writing his most fanatical dialogue, *The Laws* (only renamed the *Republic* in our own time). In the same period (Aries), *Lycurgus* and *Solon have* given their laws to Sparta and Athens.

There is the astral aspect of our own dying age. If epic *force (*Taurus), then epic *law* (Aries), could not allow men to gain control of the life force – what is the next constellation? We know Pisces well. Could brotherhood (Pisces) give us larger access to Heaven – consciousness? Already we have learned that epic poetry is based on cosmology. Let us remember the star the Magi followed. Significantly, the very moment the new constellation appeared in the night sky – a savior was born. Do we know his name and deeds? We know him intimately. Christ contained the new message of double fish, the constellation of Pisces. Concise in its poetic elegance, both the Christ message and Pisces are symbolized by the *sign of the fish*. Both born on the same day! Does it seem as if someone – even the *Bible* poet – actually knew what was occurring? As will be asserted later, this is what the truth looks like.

Every epic poem poses the same question. Does human life have value? What is the quality and number of that value? What is the correct behavior towards all other life? May we be astral gods and heroes – or only accidents of biology? Each epic poem has attempted to answer the question: How may we obtain the highest forms of life? The epic poems of the age of Taurus (the bull), tried to seize eternal life with power and force. *Gilgamesh* and *Hector* failed. In the Age of Aries, Moses and Mithras slew the Golden Bulls and tried to seize consciousness with Hebrew *and* Roman law. Jason made a voyage for the Ram's Fleece. They failed to seize control of the life force. If men could not seize immortal life with force (Taurus) or law (Aries) – could it then be taken with love (Pisces)? The constellation and the messenger of the fish (Pisces) preached peace, love, and brotherhood. These are forces permitting unconstrained proliferation of human life. Pisces also failed to perfect consciousness. The planet is now in the brink of destruction due to overpopulation (proliferation). Clearly, it was not enough to only love your brother. Consciousness requires that a severe selection be made.

The modern struggles to give power of information to star constellations – but he begins to see the superstructure of new information. Each constellation left us with the stories and the linguistic codes that engineered man's rise from mammals to demi-gods and heroes of life.

Time is now come full circle. It's always a circle, we discover. *Chandos Ring* heralds the constellation of Aquarius – new in our sky. A message is transmitted with competence. The epic message has nothing to do with the Earth that we know and use as an exploitable acre. The epic poem confirms that the Earth exists wherever men cry and betray. It confirms that all men are connected with the messages of the night sky. Sentient man is an astral and metaphysical coordinate – not to be found on any geographic grid. The mortal human is only tangentially endowed with a body. The human, like the earth, is *actually* an ideal. Only the symbol of a *thing* is permanent. What genre could provide this reliable, and permanent, information?

Only epic poetry could give this information with competence. There is nothing more important to be said about the epic genre than the statements just made. Already we have learned everything we need to know of the epic form. It must be a recognized speech that is used by vernacular men. It must contain astral ideation on many levels – yet able to operate in the same poetic space. It must tell a story of power and discover a unity of national purpose.

An epic poem will insist that there is a hegemonic incantation embedded in a civilization's language – a mythic code. Epic is a language only a few hegemonic idioms have been able to reach. The evidence of an epic poem can only be referenced in the brains of a powerful people that share the same linguistic charge. An epic poem is a people's only connection to the secret cosmologies. It is a brief moment in time when the conditions exist to allow the formation of an epic trope. The subject of an epic poem is cosmology of the true inhabitants of the galaxies – the stars. An epic poem is an astral ideology of men in agnostic struggle to message stars. Poets are at war with their time to herald the message. It is rare.

An epic poem has little to do with the information contained in the plot structure. An epic poem reveals no new information; it contains all information. So why do we read Shakespeare's antiquated, aristocratic English? Because it contains the incantation idiom of self-conscious modernism. That is, he created the modern personality. He presented a new linguistic idiom of human civilization. Shakespeare created the modern introspective: alienated Western man. He formed the modern – stillborn with alchemy, budding science, Western imperialism, and rebellious intent against all previous idols. Shakespeare had only one idol: power in verse. He healed his soul with the highest form of linguistic admonishment in the English language.

The Shakespeare poet constructed an epic device – an epic and historical dramatic scaffold – and constantly revised his works for thirty years until he achieved the mastery of his high idiom. We read the Shakespeare poet to steal a glance on hegemonic seizure of human consciousness. We scan quickly over the plot to find the emitting signals of idiomatic power – five or ten lines at most in each work. Their emitting signals daze the human searcher – man –alone of the creatures of the universe trained to read the signs. Let the plot fall away. The strong poet communicates even when he is not understood. There is time for understanding later. The only subject of the strong poet is astral consciousness. How did he obtain this information? It is unknown. Language becomes oracle.

This is the secret information that has been lost by modernism. This is the cause of the crisis in modern information. This is why modernism is a temporary speech.

There are only a few a strong epic poems in each astrological constellation – a period of approximately 2000 years. We recognize the hinges of ideation – the cycle of constellations. We know the first epic poem contained the message of the Bull (Taurus). This was the first written epic of force and ego – of Gilgamesh, of the wars of the Vedic myths, of the wars of the founding gods of Sumer, the terror of the flood, the rise of Marduk, the tower of Babel, the cosmology of the heavens. Moderns just now may understand their deep message. It is a message that shakes modernism to its core. The mistake that modernism makes is that it can only detect information of the terrestrial. It cannot detect the human mind on the astral plane.

My message is that modernism is only a passing linguistics. My message is that everything that moderns holds dear will be lost in the coming holocaust. We know there was an age of *Gilgamesh* (Taurus) – of force, passion, war – and that was the subject of the first human epics. We know there was an Age of *Moses, Lycurgus, Solon, Plato* – and that they each had an epic message – of laws (Aries). We know there was an age of Christ – and that had an epic message (Pisces) – of brotherhood and proliferation (*Gospels*). Each sign of cosmology contains a message that must be learned with a narration of peril and wonder. Death looms large in the linguistics of each epic message. A crust of tear will form on eyes.

The genre of science fiction has now matured to include every human subject – including past events. *Since science is the central myth of the modern age, we search the narration of science for correspondences to the epic theme.* Science verifies that the modern seeks epic voice. The modern seeks prophesy of future life with unconcealed desperation. The modern recognizes instantly his heroes of the epic trope. There are demi-gods and heroes of science – now deified. We know their names and their stories of meaning.

We know why we follow science with high interest. Science, as poetry, has become anthropomorphic. Science is now an epic message. It has become living oracle. When scientists say that there are *men* in space, what they really mean is that there are *scientists* in space. A linguistic shift has been made and the human landscape is altered – retranslated – forever. Space is now exclusively the scientist's separate idiomatic country where vernacular speakers really don't – exist. And this assertion is true. Thus, we read science with attention, since we feel that science contains the secret language of world dominance in our time.

Yet are modern vernacular men aware that the linguistic shift has accrued? Vernacular men have been eliminated from the future – except as scientists "*in linguistic training.*"

Can this shift of the human condition be denied? Science is our tool of information. What modern would dare to challenge the principles underlying science? His faith is firm. Does the reader see it? This is an epic stance. Science operates exactly as the death of Hector. Troy falls. Noble Hector is dead. The world pivots. Gilgamesh fails to be immortal, Hector is dead, Christ is crucified. Now Aquarius arrives with a new test of consciousness. This is Story Theory.

Science operates as the Exodus of Moses – giving meaning and audacity to national purpose and identity. Science operates as the crucifixion of Christ on the Cross – giving an exact value of mortal life. Each is an epic structure. Therefore the arrogance and crisis of modernism fits the epic trope. The Exodus from Earth is an epic trope. Chandos Ring is well placed.

Science is the greatest epic poem of modern Western men. It is strange that science was not seen before in this light. There is a narrative – the hypothetical supremacy of physical nature as the revelator, the secret oracle, of all Being. The strong poet should both assert and oppose the supremacy of the modern age. It is strange. The poet must build the age and then show its misprision at the crisis of information. There are heroes – Newton, Copernicus, Einstein, and Bohr. There is a tragic death – the destruction of the ecosystems of the Earth – perhaps even *Homo sapiens.* More than any other idiom, science contains the poetic concepts of our time.

Chandos Ring does not mistake the hegemonic information contained in science. Science is the chief protagonist of *Chandos Ring.* Idiomatic science is the bedrock poetic insight of the poem. I take the poetic images of a century of science and build an epic structure. The large moon Europa is increased and made habitable by the machinations of men (exploding the moonlets Thebes and Metis into Europa). An epic poem contains no new information. It contains all information. Jupiter has already been conquered by men in Western literature. Mad scientists in wheelchairs have already transmuted their minds into stronger Jovian bodies (Poul Anderson). Men have already tried to escape Earth for the outer solar system. An epic poem contains no new information. Yet epic language is *altered* speech. Epic idiom is *somehow* more *finished* than other speech. The monumentality of epic statements is strangely pleasing.

How has the poetry of science captured the human mind? As the Shakespeare poet presaged, matter was not real – a dream – utterly under the control of the dreamer. This anticipated the quantum insight. According to quantum theory, matter is not a solid. How may a single element of matter be located in an unknown number of places at the same time? Of course, the atom is now empty. The universe is empty. The visible universe contains only 4% of all matter (or that's the story). Today, the physical component of physical science is not as solid as hoped by the first followers of scientific creeds. We identify an opportunity for a linguistic shift. This is an opportunity of strong poets.

There is only one conclusion to make from this discovery. We are in an age of poems again. Atoms are literature. Photons are syllables that are arraigned by the observer. That is to say, the location of matter in space and time is a subjective interpretation of human observation. Likewise, a poem is a subjective interpretation of human observation. Consciousness, that is, the mind of the sentient observer, creates, influences, directs, and manipulates the visible phenomenon of matter. In Story Theory, the human mind masters the phenomena of matter with the mind's still unknown, still unfinished map of bias. This is possible since the material reality of men is still tentative – still theoretical. This is the information that poetry contains.

Chandos Ring is herald – silent running. The epic arrives – silent running. The stars move in the sky – silent running. All silent arrivals are charismatic. The arrival of any epic is charismatic. *Chandos Ring* does not contain new information. *Chandos Ring* contains all information that is already known – existing permanently on the ideal astral plane – but not yet spoken by fearful vernacular men. *Chandos Ring* restores authority and prestige to the vernacular speaker. Until vernacular speech is enchanted again, my project is incomplete. *Chandos Ring* verifies the human impulse to seize control of consciousness.

Astral man is the world that epic poetry addresses. This may be the information that epic poetry properly contains.

CHAPTER EIGHT

A New Theory of Poetry: Secrets Embedded in Civilizations

The glory of any civilization is the clarity of its information. As we have seen with modern linguistics, it does not matter in the least if it is correct information – at no point in this dimension is there an empirically correct form of information. No civilization exactly reproduces reality – it can only construct a linguistic reality that it can accept. Human consciousness summons and structures its own species of information. What is important is that the integrity of the linguistic tool used is able to build the condition of future transmission of consciousness. Literature seeks the universal message – not the isolated value. Above all else, a context that is ambitious must be seized. This context is the eminence of the American idiom. We are the future. If not us – who? Western civilization must make this race for relevance.

The idiomatic charge of America has always been that American language represents the future of the human condition. There is no other use or purpose for American speech. In the early days of the American Revolution other, established, monarchical nations of Europe never agreed that our democratic experiment was worthy of the future of consciousness. We made it so. We asserted our idiom of future men against peril and hostility. And we have to continue to assert our nation's epic and mythic code. When any civilization is no longer unable (or unwilling) to defend its idiom against encroachment – then that civilization disappears. It is not how we proved we had the correct information – it is how we created the conditions of linguistic civilization that made our information the correct form of future world. We created and met the conditions of our own wish. This is what an epic poem must achieve. The epic poem must discover the secret of the civilization – the idiom of its mythic code.

How did America become associated with the future condition of humanity? It was a linguistic re-imagination of the human experiment. The American idiom was not given to us already fully formed – we forged it deliberately with American use of poetic linguistics. It began with a text – a linguistically biased document (a *Declaration* – a *Constitution*). For a similar cause and necessity, *Chandos Ring* deliberately re-imagines the future human.

It is a thesis of this poem that men will leave Earth one day for the moons of Jupiter. Not a new idea. Yet a new innovation of linguistic information must be forged for this certain eventuality. This has not yet been attempted outside of prose story telling. The banality of prose tells on itself. Our achievement of the seizure of human consciousness – America's achievement of the future – is worthy of a further linguistic translation. This is the premise of the long poem.

There is no large civilization that does not exhibit outwardly its mythic narrative. America did not only possess the material means of future linguistic hegemony – we characterized the future. The mythic code of America is the construction of the future of consciousness. It does not matter that America always succeeds to make the correct future – such a thing does not exist – it only matters that she conceived the future. Hegemonic material means combined with hegemonic texts is the achievement of only the greatest of civilizations. The West has used these linguistic devices since the time of Ur. It is called the epic trope. Modernism is only the latest Western epic linguistic invention. Gilgamesh was the first father of my raging ballad. Science fiction pioneers now lift my high theme.

A Golden Age of civilization is essentially clarity of linguistic information. We read the Shakespearian canon not to get information of the Elizabethan age, but to stand amazed at the use of language as oracle – even when it is not understood. The glory of Western humanism was the ability of our educational systems to access clarity of practical, material, and secular information – of the newly revealed mechanical cosmos. This material focus has allowed us to make the next step of humanity – in spaceships. As long as industrial science was the measure of hegemony, then materialism was a workable model for world domination. When these same sciences and industries, by their side effects, become the means of destroying the entire planet – then it is time to re-address our linguistic translation of human life. It is time to turn a linguistic page. This is the purpose of *Chandos Ring* – a reimagining of national philosophy and purpose.

These books construct a new and controversial theory of poetry. While my approach may often seem a critique of science, this is only because – in Story Theory – modern science *is* a form of poetry. *This is a vital reconstruction of information.* Though my many citations include historical and even cosmological reference, these are to illustrate that poetry includes all of human activity. Why? Poetry is valid for all degrees of human ideation since all activity has been linguistically coded and patterned by a human – including science. Science operates as poetry. It is hard for the unbiased reader to deny this phenomenon. Our world order is erected from our idiomatic linguistic patterns – that is, poetry. Human ideation is a poetic protocol.

The goal of *Chandos Ring* is to recover a theory of poetry that can access the epic trope's *authority of information* for use by all cultural men. Consequently, in Story Theory, there can be no substantial recovery of poetry – as information – that does not reclaim the accuracy of information as attempted by all ancient and modern epic poems. Either the ancient epics told the truth about gods, giants, and teachers of a higher civilization – or they were lies. If it was a lie, then we have to find out why they all told the exact pattern of lies. Why thrones, why pyramid structures, why math, why gods, why temples, why sacrifice, why symbols, why alphabets – why the zodiac as a single code? Was there a previous high civilization that gave us these signs?

The modern poet who does not understand the integrity of information of the epic trope – that is, the myths of cosmological beings – cannot, in my view, give any accurate information with his feeble attempts of modern poetry. Modern academic poets – utterly adrift from any market or public feedback – can only attempt to contribute their microscopic vignettes of balkanized poetic eccentricities. Above all else, poetry is a scaffold of human order. If there is no order, then there is no useful school of poetic achievement. Ordered writing always precedes *ordered* thought. This is Story Theory. Therefore, to reclaim the human effort as poetic, we have to traduce all of science back into its *ur*-strength as a form of human poetic re-imagination of human ideation. To proceed any other way is to remain in separate and balkanized armed camps that tear our civilization apart. There can be no science, no future of man that is not also a poetic revelation – and pronounced as such. When audacious science is seen to be a function of imagination – poetry – there can then be no block to audacious poetry.

My criteria for a theory of poetry will not be complete until I have built the entire underlying scaffolding of *Chandos Ring*. No strong theory of poetic can be substantiated until the entire scope of poetic information is recovered with integrity. The lyric alone cannot inform poetry. This is a pretentious project in its scope – yet it is necessary. Until all of poetry, including the epic form, is recovered as a source of severe information – poetry will only exist as a risible mimic of information in an age of linguistically hegemonic materialism.

What if in the Age of Information – the information is found to be defective? This would be a crisis of large proportions. We are there. The first step is to broadcast early this defective linguistic condition. It is not to be asked why there is a book attempting to recover the story telling genre of the poetic tradition. The question is why there has not been an attempt until now. We must purposely and deliberately ensure that this is still morning in the American idiom.

Second, we have to recover the information of ancient and modern epic form. We must supersede the hopeless modern lyric. Our poets must have a device – a giant superstructure – on which they may build the vitality of their linguistic constructs. It is not only that poets have lost their audacity – I see there is some audacity still. What disables the cry of audacity is the minor and abbreviated structure of the over-worked lyric form. The lyric structure is miniscule for the purpose of large audacity – to encompass a national enterprise. As poets, we have to make a further innovation in modernism. We have to tell a story with solid and vital information.

Modern poetry no longer dares to tell a story. We must verify that poetry is the only permanent form of ideation. Until there is a future explicated with depth and rich characterization –poetry will remain a secondary form of communication. Journalism and academic prose are a self-erasing chalkboard. One official opinion is superseded by another academic opinion – daily – even hourly. We are told each week that the foods the researchers thought were good for us to eat – were in reality not so good to eat. We are admonished to buy new pharmaceuticals – only to be told that these were toxic to the human element. Each academic study strives to make the previous study ridiculous. We recognize our nightmare.

Mass produced medical advertisements tell us that we need new medicines and, bizarrely, in the same instant, we are warned that these new drugs may cause sudden death and rupture of the entire biological organism. This is a form of degraded and bipolar linguistic information. I cannot imagine a more graphic example of the linguistic misprision of our civilization. When the same outrageously contradictory message still does not prevent persons from asking their doctors for these medications – irrationally demanding these dangerous pharmaceuticals – I can give no more accurate instance of a crisis of linguistic information.

On the other hand, we have a choice. Poetic information is solid, unchangeable, repeatable, impossible to erase, and replete with integrity. In fact, the characters memorialized in literature are eternal. There is no opinion, no amount of counter arguments that can change the rage of Achilles. No rewrite or further research can ever change the fixed protocols of literature, poetry, and story. Richard III will always be crying for his horse. And from the beginning of time, Hester Prynne will have already been made to wear the scarlet letter – and Pastor Dimmesdale will be moved to give a full confession. Don Quixote will forever be a crazed romantic knight tilting at windmills. Young Jane Eyre will always exist to love the older master of Thornfield. Miss Havisham, always and forever, will have already been jilted on her wedding day – and she will have worn the same wedding dress for over forty years sitting in her darkened room. Nothing – no power of fusion or economic collapse – no new innovation of deity or philosophy can undo these sources of exact information. This information – of high human story – fixed and permanent, is of more account to Americans than the latest proofs that the universe is expanding – and that it will die with a frozen whimper.

Forever grown men will instantly recognize the bitter pain of Pip's love for cold Estella. Nothing, no physical, nuclear, or quantum force can alter the eternal facts of the poet's linguistic characters permanently residing in Western literature. This is the monumentality of poetic information. After English-speaking men are eradicated from the far galaxy of our linguistic empire – these facts alone will remain to verify there was a high Race of audacious men that first made exodus from Earth. We will be worshipped as a form of divinity by then. It is best to take some time to make our poems now. There will be no other time as the present moment.

Literature is hegemony – and nothing outperforms a human story preserved in poetic idiom. Poetic information is permanent and unassailable. Perhaps for this reason, if a higher civilization would wish to impart the highest forms of knowledge – they would teach men the art of poetry. It is the purview of Story Theory that this protocol has already occurred in the annuals of our genetic makeup. The modern reader will wish to take a deep breath.

It is a sub-thesis of my books that ancient and early modern poetry has been misinterpreted for their secret source of information. As moderns, we don't know who the early poets were. Modern persons really don't believe there is any information contained in the ancient epic form, or even, in early modern epic literature. It is generally an opinion of modern persons that there is no accurate information in modern poetry at all. So we have much to affirm to the modern mind. I must view poetry in the long count of human information. I will take my time to build the superstructure of *Chandos Ring*.

First, a story is told of the mythic narrative of a nation. Every civilization contains a decodable form of mythic narrative. Second, a language is forged that monuments the structure of a future American idiom. It is neither high nor low – it merely strives for enchantment of the idiomatic voice. The speech should be recognized as the speech that Americans might speak.

Though the poem contains elements that allow it to be recognized in the Western tradition, *Chandos Ring* utterly seeks a modern context. It is a future that must certainly come to pass. *Chandos Ring* chases this high adventure.

CHAPTER NINE

A Catechism of Modern Myths

The narrative of science declares that the universe is dead – that it is somehow separate from human consciousness – that it is somehow independent of any supreme intelligence. This is the central myth of modernism. Classical physics has *inferred* the universe of matter, stars, and planets are dead, not intimate to emotional human prognostications – and that they operate in a sphere that is somehow separate from our own condition. This myth is based only on the evidence of linguistics – the poem, the story, the narrative of science. There is no other evidence that the universe is dead. This is only an assertion of a hegemonic class of linguistic men.

The scientific myth now makes a race to become the sole human oracle. How? There is the hope that science will reveal what humanist philosophers have always failed to reproduce – the exact mechanism of reality. Yet what is really occurring here? There is no single reality. We know this. There is only a linguistic reality. By its myth, modernism reveals that it seeks to replace all the oracles of previous literature and religion – based on texts – and texts moreover that could be endlessly argued over. This is the essence of modern intent. Science seeks an *oracle* that permanently *silences* controversy. To eradicate controversy of *reality* would be to ensure absolute and total power. Every hegemony must eradicate a source of controversy.

Civilizations do not seek reality. Civilizations seek exploitation of an idiom. Science does not seek reality – it seeks totalitarian control of a specific (and linguistic) interpretation of reality. The hegemonic power of an oracle, once achieved with strength, will pass for truth and reality any day. This accords with what we know in Story Theory. All linguistic codes seek hegemony and pasteurization of the ideational space. If the universe is dead (silent) and scientists may exclude all other *unqualified* humans from making an interpretation of the oracle (physical reality), they have total linguistic control of human ideation. If the universe is dead, then a single class of men may control and take possession of the dead element. Already we verify that there are only scientists allowed into space. They come on line from time to time, disseminating well-prepared remarks to journalists, to tell us the interpretations of their oracle. Any vernacular challenge draws an attack on any that dare questions the reliability – the oracle – of modern information.

Let us proceed with the science *myth*. Physical matter, dead and separate from human subjectivity, can be empirically observed without any entanglement with human emotion. The myth states that though dead and somehow separate from us, the universe still contains all the secrets we need to further develop the mystery of life. Of course the consistency of this philosophy is not well thought out. It is only an attempt, two hundred years now in progress, to get rid of previous subjective linguistic human interpretations of life. The only way to overcome this modern protocol – the tyranny of linguistic materialism – is to show that the myths of modernism are a very degraded form of information.

I do not wish to disparage science in order to make a theory of poetry. I have only to show that science is, likewise, a form of poetry. I am against the belief that the idiom of science is hostile to poetry. Science is poetry. Only modernism is against the poetic spleen. I have said repeatedly that our greatest American poetic achievements of the last century have been the language of imaginative science. I repeat it again. Science fiction, though now much degraded, is not a mean achievement of prose language. It is a high poetic achievement. Uniquely American and eccentric, *Chandos Ring* is the first epic poem of the genre.

What I contemn is that moderns consider physical matter a privileged and isolated form of ideational reality. Matter is not isolated – the human observer changes, recreates, and structures all visible phenomena. Matter is, then, the mystery - not the soul as consciousness. It is consciousness that controls, alters, selects, and projects the forms of matter. This is what literature, as consciousness, story, poems perform – they change visible life to fit the conditions of life the conscious observer seeks. All human epic symbols are teased and searched for linguistic use as incantation and value. Science is not an empirical reality – it is a poetic *assertion* of empirical reality. Modernism is still utterly inferred. A linguistic superstructure is erected – rationalism – and after severe linguistic training, almost miraculously, a subsequent rationalism is asserted, located, and recognized. Yet material rationalism (as modernism) is still a linguistic superstructure under the intimate influence of consciousness.

Story Theory insists that the imaginative terms of science – as dark matter, Black holes, string theory, quantum mechanics, singularity events, quantum loops, scalar signatures, Z-pinch Auroras, Oort Clouds, event horizons, stacked plasma Toroids, etc. – are the greatest poetic achievements of our time. Each scientific/poetic concept is a linguistic phantasm – a means modern humans have used to authoritatively control and homogenize the universe – poetically. These poetic concepts cannot be proven by any human as empirical information. Quantum loops, scalar signature, and stacked plasma Toroids are not things – they are poetic and subjective interpretations masquerading as privileged reality. No vernacular speaker can verify the existence of any of these poetic concepts of recent science. Moreover, the vernacular speaker lacks the mathematic linguistic training to share the enchanted indulgence of the speculative researcher. This is the ideational – schizoid – premise by which the modern human operates. This is why modernism is in a crisis of its own labyrinth of mythology.

None of the above scientific/poetic concepts can be proven or verified as anything other than an attempt to assert imaginative control of the universe. Literature usually performs this protocol. Literature attempts to represent the *world* as a means to gain ideational control of *world*. This is exactly where modern science and poetry verify they are the same human element. None of these essentially poetic terms should be confused with any actual substance of physical reality.

The dishonesty of modernism is that it attempts to translate physical science as the only oracle of human reality. As shall be shown in these books, in Story Theory, *information* – as any *truth* – is only a linguistic pattern we are trained to see. Justice is a linguistic pattern we accept. Beauty is a linguistic pattern we come to accept. *Reality*, likewise, is a linguistic pattern we accept. There is no actual reality that will be true in ten generations – there is only an interpretation of reality that we recognize at the *present time* – and linguistically determined. Linguistic patterns of idiomatic science are only patterns we have come to *recognize* as authoritative. They are each only possible representations of the human condition.

In Story Theory, science is an assertion of the human poetic nerve. Science is America's greatest imaginative act of poetry. If science itself can be shown to be a poetic achievement, then poetry is restored to its dominant position in human ideation. This is the project of these books. Once science can be placed in its proper perspective of imaginative achievement, we can progress to construct a theory of poetry. There can be no living theory of poetry until poetry has as much ideational value as any other competitive idiom of human life.

There are other myths of modernism to explore. First myth: any problem can be fixed with more technology. Second myth: only persons possessing arcane scientific language may give authoritative opinions on the important questions of the human condition. Third myth: any peer review by academic scientists are sound and authoritative. Fourth myth: any attack on our frail biology can be met with a counter attack of human pharmaceuticals. Fifth myth: medical science will cure every disease – if given enough time. Sixth myth: every person should have the opportunity to be rich – or at least middle class – and this will give them fulfillment and contentment. Seventh myth: if there are horrible consequences of these myths – science will get us through it all. Few moderns will disavow these myths. These are the myths we take to war with us when we subdue nations of other linguistic innovation.

Civilizations and artists exist to test more space and time of human consciousness – more life, more personality. Observing the narrative of the long count, we still confirm the discontent of Gilgamesh. We still want to protest the obstacle to more space and personality. Science does not answer the question of how we may seize more life. Its myths fail to answer what superior form of life should be advocated. Its myths avoid these questions altogether. Thus, I argue that modernism failed to understand the nature of human consciousness.

This book does not intend to recall a pre-modern age. Each human that cries into his pillow can only appeal to an idiom of modern biases. The idiom of our cry will also be in the form of modern speech. It is impossible to appeal to any other perception if I do not confirm the sensibilities of a modern human. According to self-referent modern terminology, it is impossible to even attack modernism. Modernism has built a hermetically sealed linguistic scaffold – a high secret language of science and medicine – that cannot allow a successful attack. Modernism cannot attack itself. Modernism cannot reform modernism. It can only collapse.

The modern myths block a further innovation of the human code. Modernism is an ideology exhibiting idiomatic supremacy. We do not even dare to question the plausibility of industrial medicine, invasive surgical procedures, and the *supposed* proofs of human *reality* by the peer review of unnamed and unknown academic scientists. These are the myths of authoritative actors (academics, medical journals, scientific industrial patents) that generate unreliable, and toxic information.

Modernism is strong. No purpose-made language can accuse itself. No doctor can tell you that medicine is a mistake of reality. This is the conundrum of self-referent linguistics. High languages are hermetically sealed against subversive attack from the outside.

It is impossible to attack the limited idiom of mathematics – using mathematics. It is impossible to verify the abuse of science using the linguistic codes of science. Hegemonic languages are sealed against all attempts at subversive invasion. This is why civilizations cannot change their core myths until they are destroyed with economic or military collapse.

Materialism rests complacent and self-satisfied within its own coordinates of self-reference – its own mythic narrative. Reform of materialism must come from an attack from the inside of this hegemonic worldview. Materialism cannot disprove the merits of materialism. Consequently, any innovative philosophy of consciousness must not merely create a new modernism – it must exhibit a new superstructure of future world. A new language must be formed. *Chandos Ring* explores this insight.

CHAPTER TEN

A World Struggling for Prophesy

Modern rationalism claims it rejects any form of prophecy. This is misinformation. Every word that ever proceeded out of a human mouth is a prophecy. Any speech between family, siblings, children, or spouses is a carefully organized structure that allows a continued future of these relationships. This is a protocol of prophecy. When the hopeful lover speaks, he immediately structures *by communication* the conditions that will bring union with the beloved. This is prophecy. Any businessman immediately transitions his speech to structure the conditions that will ensure success to his goal. This is prophetic speech. Any politician immediately structures the conditions of an issue that will present his speech as the solution – and his own person as the superior candidate for office. All forms of political propaganda are acts of prophecy. We speak in a manner that creates the future. It is a misrepresentation to insist that the modern human does not live, speak, and follow the prophetic protocol of word formations. The future of human linguistics will continue to be prophetic. Modernism mistakes when it publicly disdains the power of prophetic speech. Prophetic speech is *the* human speech. Every human voice is prophetic. This validates poetry as permanent information. The world struggles to prophesy in each breath.

The function of poetry, as the function of speech – is to make future life according to the conditions of consciousness that we seek. Poetry can be defined as speech that transforms phenomena into the conditions of life we seek. My wife's Ukrainian professor of poetry warned his students to be careful what they say in their poem. When you make a deep statement of your life, he said, the poems act as prophesy. Poems are living things connected to *real* life. He said that as a youth he wrote poems about the supposed nobility of poverty and powerlessness, etc. And his whole life he could not escape the deleterious prophecies he made about his life. He remained powerless and poor. Poetry, as speech, is dangerous. Mental ideation, once set in motion, already goes before you to make future world.

It cannot be recalled. Prophecy, as speech, as prayer, constructs future life. Let us rather be kings in our speech.

Who else makes modern prophesies? Scientists. Any speech or text that a modern scientist writes is essentially a prophesy of the future. Every paper on astronomy, biology, physics, or mathematics, for example, is an attempt at prophecy. It is not essential to the scientific – or religious – believer if there is always an accurate prediction. What is important is to know what the audience expects of the clarity of his information. The only requirement of prophesy, after all, is that it is believed to be linguistically sound – that the oracular source is pulsating. It is alive. It is linguistically viral.

How do we verify this thesis? It is easy. If you collected all the science papers together since the 19th century – you would discover that only a few (about one in a thousand) had made somewhat accurate predications (prophetic speech) in physics, biology, and astronomy. This is a mountain of bulk prophecies. Nearly 99% were unsuccessful – and utterly forgotten.

Adam Riess and Brian Schmidt, the scientists leading the searching for the "fate" of the universe (and dark matter) in the last decade, still not finding the information they sought, would habitually look on-line where scientists posted papers. They were looking for the paper that gave them a correct theory of reality to solve the mystery of why the universe contained only 4% of visible matter. Schmidt had searched to see how many scientist's cited their original *dark-energy* research and found three thousand – of which, he says, over 2500 were theories. They all, Schmidt said, were "pretty kooky" – qualifying each, in his opinion, as failed guesses – and now forgotten. The papers they found were not spurious – they were sincere attempts at science operating as prophecy. Schmidt found (in these papers) only unverifiable, unreliable predictions. Each paper attempted to function as science – yet what they produced were merely attempts at prophecy. It is revealing to briefly scan the following titles of papers. The reader will understand why I insist that science is the only school of American poetry.

Tracker Quintessence, Single exp Quintessence, double exp Quintessence, Pseudo-Nambo-Goldstone Boson Quintessence, Holographic dark energy, cosmic strings, cosmic domain walls, axion-photon coupling, phantom dark energy, Cardassian model, brane cosmology (extra-dimension), Van Der Wals Quintessence, Dilation, Generalized Chaplygin gas, Quintessential inflation, Unified Dark matter and Dark energy, superhorizon perturbations, Undulant Universe, various numerology, Quiessence, general oscillatory models, Milne-Born-Infeld model, k-essence, chameleon, k-chameleon, f(R) gravity, perfect fluid dark energy, adiabatic matter creation, varying G etc, scalar-tensor gravity, double scalar field, scalar + spinor, Quintom model, SO(1,1) scalar field, five-dimensional Ricci flat Bouncing cosmology, scaling dark energy, radion, DGP gravity, Gauss-

Bonnet gravity, tachyons, power-law expansion, Phantom k-essence, vector dark energy, Dilatonic ghost condensate dark energy, Quintessential Maldacena-Maoz dark energy, super quintessence, vacuum-driven metamorphosis. (From *The 4 Percent Universe*, Richard Panek, p. 230, 2010).

My point? This is poetry. Science is a form of prophetic poetry. Take your pick of human scientific speech – each, though a *technical failure*, is a *prophesy of world reality*. In Story Theory, a scientific paper (as prophesy) is a perfect example of imaginative poetry – the greatest poetry of the American idiom. These papers represent a struggle for linguistic prophesy as rich as any poetry of our age. This is a high civilization's attempt at hegemonic translation of reality. Every civilization attempts to linguistically seize control of consciousness. There is no other purpose to language. This is a discovery of what we know about science.

Human speech operates on the exact same protocol as prophetic voice – whether the speaker is a scientist, a politician, a hopeful lover, or a poet. We structure the world linguistically to fit the conditions we seek. Moderns do not call their texts or their speech prophesies – but that is how modern speech still operates. They should hear the sound of their voice.

Only look at the universal manners of human speech patterns. We set the conditions for what we speak in the first syllables of the initial greetings of the day – *How are you? – Have a nice day! – Hope you are fine? – Are you well today? – Good day!* By the pattern of our daily greetings, social men wish to set the conditions of beneficial outcomes. When I say good morning to family, bosses, or strangers – I am attempting to get ahead of all prognostications of previous encounters with these humans. This is a protocol of prophecy. We create the world as we speak.

Every human, when he opens his mouth, or writes a sentence, sets the conditions for his own prophesy of the world he seeks. All pre-literate cultures knew this was how speech operated – they declared this openly. At the start of the New Year in ancient cultures, tribal leaders would meet and recite the story of their world – in effect, creating the beneficial conditions for the New Year. Only the artificial edifice of writing cloaks the essential function of speech as prophesy. In fact, with speech we are attempting to get ahead of all possible charismatic actions. We are convinced our speech will go ahead of us and make order from typical chaos. This is the case for poetry.

Can prophecy outclass modernism? Modernism is also a form of prophesy. We live as if our position in the world will be stable and the conditions of modernity will never alter. This is arrogance. The implosion of the modernistic structure has recently begun. We cannot continue to live as if we assume that the conditions of Western wealth and electronic/carbon/economic power will secure us from charismatic world events. We are set for an extinction event.

History has proven that human life is not logical, rational, or predictable. Life is charismatic in nature. And if world events are charismatic, we must have reliable access to accurate charismatic information. This is essentially a justification for the legitimacy and rationality of prophesy. Yet it is enough for my purpose to show how all forms of speech are prophetic in intent. We are all prophets with our own life. Until we recover the prophetic voice, the public mechanism of *speech-as-prophesy*, there cannot be a strong theory of poetry. The first step, in Story Theory, is to acknowledge that a human probes all forms of speech for the outlines of the structure of future consciousness he seeks. And if this protocol is necessary and true, then prophetic poetry is necessary and true.

If life is charismatic – if life cannot be anticipated by a rational liberal linguistic idiom – that is, the rational idiom of science – how shall we construct a future of human space faring civilization? We have to accept the prophetic voices of our linguistic code. Moderns seek out prophetic control of life – but we still claim to deny the use of prophesy as information. This is bi-polar behavior. Ultimately, modern men must face their dichotomy of speech. Humans seek prophecy.

What information is valid? What linguistic interpretation of phenomena is true? What part of life is to be investigated – the physical or the metaphysical? How is the cosmos affected by human prophecy? Does the prophetic observer change the observed? In Story Theory – as life – speech changes the conditions of human consciousness. A single text – the *Declaration of Independence* – made a single nation of many races.

Story Theory insists that ancient epic poems contain reliable information of the human condition. Some modern men do not even realize there is a linguistic controversy at all. This is the crisis of the West – even as Western liberalism moves now to total hegemonic control of the Earth. It is essentially a linguistic crisis of the correct interpretation of consciousness.

Clearly, our consciousness is still unformed – since we do not have absolute answers about the nature of consciousness. The quest for truth is necessarily a linguistic interrogation. This is a discovery of clarity. Only a human has posed the question of truth. The answer of truth is valid only so long as the language that framed it is in a hegemonic super-position. What is truth? Of course, we know the answer. There is only a linguistic construct of truth. We had to make a linguistic representation of truth since we cannot find the final form of consciousness. And until that happens, there can only be linguistic trials. Not to know the exact structure of a *truth* – consciousness – is equivalent to saying the *concept* is still unfinished. I chose to face these questions – since the poet must master the ideational space.

With speech, we structure the future conditions of life that is sought. This is the case for poetry – as found in all prophecy and all science.

CHAPTER ELEVEN

The Struggle for the Great and the Beautiful

There is something the strong poet must face – and modernism blocks the opportunity for an honest discussion. What is the superior human? The question is honest. Art ruthlessly seeks the superior – and that means that there must an enchantment of a particular bias. Every culture, every civilization makes a selection of value and linguistically proliferates the narrative – ruthlessly. In so far as secular modernism recoils from the avocation of any religion – blindly, it also eradicates any chance of high poetic achievement. Both civilization and art are high faiths that select a bias. That bias is explored for enchantment. In any civilization a bias is linguistically selected and ruthlessly teased to high aesthetic purification. This is the epic trope.

Modernism eradicates any non-modern bias. Currently no modern dares to say that a particular type of poetry is better than another – unless they are politically motivated to praise the idiom of a demographic or political minority. The poet is shamed who advocates the superiority of the European linguistic tradition. Never before in human history has the cultural majority in a population selected self-eradication.

My point? Currently poetry is determined by political dialectics. As under Stalinism, political structures block the strong poet. How can there be a strong theory of poetry if the linguistic code does not permit a clear (and audacious) presentation of the *great* and the *beautiful*? For high art to control the educated space, there has to be a bias of culture – not merely an absence of bias (as in multiculturalism). Multiculturalism is propaganda of surrender and social re-engineering of the hegemonic European tradition. Multiculturalism means to eradicate the hegemony of Euro-centralism for – anything else that arises from the ashes of Anglo– Saxon Euro-centralism.

Of course, any judgment of the *great* and the *beautiful* – any projection of future life – are forms of prophecy. Yes, some cultural elements will be disempowered and de-privileged. Any political agency that does not allow for the minority elements to be dis-privileged will block the high linguistic achievement of an advanced civilization. This is the state of modernism.

Bias is the state of consciousness. There never was a form of life that did not give feedback – that is, bias. Bias cannot and should not be eradicated. *Any* speech is biased. *Any* ideational form of interpretation – *any* act of judgment – is an act of poetry making. When we enchant a value and give it form – that is an act of poetry. Poetry, by Greek definition (*poetas*), is the art of making. Poets make the value of life. Yet modern poets are excluded from this ancient protocol. They fail to lead Western societies. Modern poets speak – and are listened to – as children. Yet they are not even children that we like. This is the original rage of these books.

When we form an opinion, a liking, a wish, or a judgment – we are, in effect, making an imaginative retranslation of future human life. A translation is not empirical evidence; a translation is an instantaneous prophetic instinct. Since no man is detached from his bias of intention, we create the structure for the conditions (bias) we seek of life. Ideation is thus a poetic act. What poem of life should we accept as authoritative? To ask this question – signifying that life is still unknown – is to seek a form of reliable prophecy. To have this answer of reliable prophecy is to have the solution of poetry in our time.

Even if we are unable to maintain the European cultural achievement, at least we will demand a theory of poetry that makes a clear statement of the *great* and the *beautiful*. Any sharp declaration of clarity will be a victory. It will be prophetic in its structure of future human ideation. This is the necessary strength of a strong theory of poetry. It will be prophetic in its application. It will make strong poets. It will make stronger readers.

It is an original thesis of these books that the Western tradition is actually an astral and cosmological narrative that is consistent though all of the Western Epic texts from Sumer, to Egypt, from *Homer* to the *Bible*, from the Greek myths to *Hercules*, from *Hermes Trismegistus* to *Jason*, from Isis and Osiris to Jesus and Mary. This device – the discovery – is able to cancel innovations led by political duress and power. The star stories embedded in the epic texts will outlast any number of political catastrophes. The tradition is fixed since the stars are fixed.

We live by a pattern of linguistics. Westerners are modern because they are linguistically trained to perceive life through the prism of technological prosthetics. What is technology – except a pattern of life we accept? What is justice – except a pattern of linguistics we accept? What is truth – except a pattern of linguistic information we accept? What is beauty – except a pattern we accept as beauty? Each culture and each age has its own satisfactory linguistic pattern of truth – of beauty. Each concept of life is a linguistic structure. The modern declaration of the meaning of *truth* and *beauty*, of *great* and *perfect*, must be accounted for. Our *great* and *beautiful* must be faced with honesty. Our *great* and *beautiful* must find a linguistic expression. Yet when modernism speaks it can only detect and repeat clichés of modernism.

Modernism avoids the *great* and the *beautiful* – except accidentally, tangentially – as if making an apology to some group or tribe. Modernism prefers to make *things* (as prosthetics) instead of making clear statements of linguistic purpose. Western modernism intentionally leaves its ideology unclear and unstated. Why? Early modernism was imperialistic and outwardly aggressive. Now, unable to rely any longer on brute force – and the ignorance of the colonist – modernism must, instead, appear as the only *rational* solution of humanity. Western modernism has put its guns away and now achieves its goal of hegemony through control of speech, linguistic shame, and propaganda. Modernism now moves to envelope the globe.

The *subtlety* of the Western message ensures that foreign elements will all the more easily assimilate to modern patterns of Western ideation. A virus is also subtle. A virus enters the body so subtly that we do not know when we have been infected – till it is too late to resist. This reveals modernism as an ideology of linguistic conquest in its core competence. Yet the poet is not content with the unnerving silence about the great and the beautiful – since not to know the great and the beautiful would block poetic audacity to enchantment. *Above all else, the business of poetry is the clarity of the great and the beautiful.* I attack this issue head on.

Each age of man insists upon the accuracy of its information. Each age has a different form of truth and justice. We verify by this protocol that human life is poetically structured. Ultimately, cultural patterns can be traced to a difference in poetics – the poetic re-imagining of the linguistic and ideational landscape. Each language ruthlessly seeks and reveals its own concept of the great and beautiful. Yet the modern age refuses to commit to a strong theory of poetry. In Story Theory this is a mistake. In a mixed democratic culture there is always some group that will claim to be dis-privileged. So be it. Let them be dis-privileged.

We read, and thus know, that every civilization clarified its concept of the *great* and the *beautiful*. This being the case, we should enter this linguistic contest without fear. If men from any age could be interviewed candidly – whether of the archaic, classic, Catholic, Islamic, Enlightened, Atomic, or Medieval age – they would insist that their language of life was superior since their linguistic idiom, alone, was able to discover the true information of life. In the end, it does not matter if they were correct – what matters is that they were faithful to their audacity. They took a stand for *their* great and *their* beautiful. *Advocacy* is the only vital human act.

Hamlet represents modernism since modernism wrings its hands – refusing to clearly state and face *any* vital issue. Of course, we know why. All human issues are linguistically organized and thus you have to choose your bias of linguistic code to solve any human problem. Modernism, politically promising to serve all cultural codes, thus serves none and can address no single overarching problem. Modernism cannot face any vital issue – whether its overpopulation, control of space, religion, cultural aesthetics, or burial rituals. Modernism cowers and refuses to make any list of the great and the beautiful. This is counter to the human instinct. Humans seek a test of power – not a postponement of the human contest with dialectics.

Information is the *ur*-power embedded in any civilization. Are we surprised to find that every advanced linguistic civilization tells a story of its superiority – against all other human interpretations of life? The Greeks, so sure of their linguistic superiority of life, named all others *barbarians*. The British were certain that it was their mission to civilize a world consisting of mostly colored people; they considered their form of *liberal* imperialism *the white man's burden*. This linguistic misprision of ideation is not isolated to the Greek and British Empires. The North Koreans are daily assured that they are racially superior to Westerners. The belligerence of the Japanese prior to WWII was due to a belief that Japanese were racially superior to all Western races. These are merely facts found in history books. Linguistically, then, information – in this case the poetic information of a "supposedly" racial superiority – is imaginatively structured. A human is linguistically patterned to exploit all *others*.

Is Western liberal modernism also a racist ideology? Certainly. Western men (as speakers of modernism) have eradicated indigenous cultures each day the sun rose – for centuries. Linguistically, Western modernism is the most racially arrogant and selective idiom ever constructed by any human civilization. What is our evidence? Any culture that comes into contact with American or European high culture – and mostly this includes brown-skinned nations – is instantaneously and irrevocably transformed to Western idiomatic interpretation of life – called modernism. Whether we reference the Pacific Island peoples or the nations of Japan, Taiwan, Africa, China, or Vietnam – we have colonized every culture with which we have made decisive contact. America used the Pacific Islands as territories for nuclear and biological experiments. We did not ask permission. When the populations became difficult – we moved them to other islands. There are no longer pure Indian tribes in America. Despite their manipulations by white America, so-called Indian tribal leaders each speak English and have European genes. Indian heritage is now only a profitable business model (re. casinos). This is what truth looks like. We colonize and eradicate all other cultural interpretations of life – merely on contact with other global cultures. The Mongol Empire of the 14th century, by contrast, was a mild and moderating force. Modernism exacts total immolation of the cultural root.

If so powerful, why does modern Western society refuse to make a strong theory of poetry that clearly defines the good and the beautiful? Because it does not believe that poetry contains information. Modernism allows each person his interpretation of poetry because modern science considers that poetry contains no vital information. Today, modern poetry is essentially a minor list of harmless demographic opinion. I reply, did Homer contain no vital information? The Greeks thought so. Did the Romans think Virgil contained no information of the *great* and the *beautiful?* For two thousand years, did European men mine the epic stories of the Bible for information of the *great* and the *beautiful?* Modernism rejects the consequence of a strong assertion of the *great* and *beautiful* - since some *voters* or *consumers* will be excluded from the category. Thus linguistic democracy and capitalism blocks all normal opportunities of poetic assertion. What is the use of being a hegemonic power if you cannot assert your idea of the good and the beautiful - in literature? Modernism proscribes a strong theory of poetry asserting the highest and the most beautiful. The lowest and the ugliest will always go on strike to block any such assertion. This is the origin of the rage of *Chandos Ring.*

Literature seeks hegemony. Literature is not a democratic art – we do not choose what we like – we are forcibly trained when young to perceive with a particular idiom. No one is born appreciating high math and the Shakespeare poet's iambic pentameter. No one is born liking beer or Jazz music – these are learned tastes. No one is born understanding the value of pornography – it is a learned taste. No one is born speaking French or English – we are forcibly taught French and English. No one is born finding pleasure in *Milton, Sidney,* or *Dante.* We are forcibly taught the difficult idioms of the high poets. No one is born loving *Homer* or *Virgil* – *Homer* and *Virgil* are acquired idioms. Information – any form of information – is not organic to our life. We manufacture information. We *learn with difficulty* high linguistic idioms – we do not speak high cultural languages organically. Similarly, no person learns to love high English poetry without a severe education in advanced linguistics. No one loves English or Latin poetry unless they also profess an admiration of the racial, cultural, and hegemonic achievements of these civilizations. In any high civilization, a linguistic bias is selected and a careful protective wall is built as cocoon to protect the linguistic bias. Can modernism sustain this construct?

Modernism, as a linguistic structuring of human life, is *hegemon.* Modernism is the most successful linguistic ideology ever devised by the mind of humans. In Story Theory, we observe that each linguistically organized civilization reveals a manic urgency to quickly seize control of the entire ideational space. Language seeks to pasteurize and homogenize the ideational spectrum. War is the forceful pasteurization of foreign linguistic tribes by other means. When we went to war with Japan, what was the result? It was a linguistic transformation. We did not leave behind an organic Japanese element – we did not leave a Japanese civilization – we created a society formed in our own linguistic image – capitalistic, scientific, liberal, democratic – with industrialized medicine and nuclear fission. In short, we created a Japan that we could recognize in our linguistically patterned modern idiom. By 1960, Japan was successfully pasteurized to American modernism. Japan joined the list of Western nations led by American cultural liberal hegemony. China now enters the race to become American. Or can we tell the truth of the matter? I suspect the need for actual truth is weak.

Literature ruthlessly seeks pasteurization and homogenizing of *information*. Linguistic humans pasteurize everything they touch. The linguistic control of human ideation is achieved by the elaborate fabrication of a privileged and enchanted form of information. Any theory of poetry specifically, exactly, ruthlessly privileges and enchants a *particular* linguistic code. This is the cocoon *within* which the strong poet operates. Which demographic or cultural group will be privileged? This is exactly why modernism avoids any strong theory of poetry. In a chaotic democracy, this is a controversial interrogation. Even the greatest poems of one cultural group will somehow, somewhere, appear to dis-privilege another linguistic code.

Yet any hegemonic voice requires just that — a hegemonic control of the ideational space. Language seeks hegemony. We try to infect the integrity of any competitive idiom with our linguistic virus. France has been in a losing contest with American English for decades. The result is already clear. It is America that has the original ideas of modernism — not France. If we cannot overtly make a military conquest, we infect the foreign host with the promising success of our way of life — as modernism promotes by images of consumerism, cinema, fast food, fashion, pornography, and music — each an aspect of the promise of a liberal and Western youth culture.

Today, our modern, secular lifestyle has become the human crisis of Islam — as much as it is in Christianity. Science infected linguistic Catholicism until Catholicism was no longer able to function with linguistic hegemony in the Western nations. Now it is Islam's turn to face modernism. We entered Iraq not to discover weapons of mass destruction — that was pretext. Iraq was a war of choice — not of necessity. We entered Iraq in order to assert our superiority of idiom and to homogenize Islam to Western modes of modern linguistics. Now there is a wild revolution within all Islamic countries — all begun by the aggressive linguistic agency of modernism. As we did with Japan or Vietnam, we go to war to rationalize all nations to our linguistic hegemony. It does not matter who wins the war — it matters who is homogenized to the idiom of the hegemonic power. It does not matter what truth is selected — it matters only what language is used to select truth. This is what truth looks like.

Some say we lost the war in Vietnam. Really? Have you seen modern Vietnam? It is now a modern Western society. It speaks modernism. It is capitalistic, electronic, and connected to the Internet. By any account we won. It is only a matter of time before Western music and Western ideas are active *agents* in every coffee bar, kabob stand, and mosque in the East.

It is our myth that modernism is a linear progression from low to high development. Such a myth is only another static *defense* of the linguistic code. Modernism, as linguistic *device*, is only another idiomatic translation of human consciousness. Linear progression of civilization – i.e. that modernism represents a highpoint – only makes the appeal of modernism all the more difficult to counter. In contradistinction, Story Theory properly observes modernism as only another poetic interpretation of possible human forms of consciousness.

Is modernism the final language of the human race? Can modernism fulfill its desire for prophetic information? This is the question posed by *Chandos Ring*. Moderns act as if modernism is so perfected that it cannot be replaced. Can this be sustained?

In Story Theory, modernism is not essential to human survival. On the contrary, modernism – that is, the linguistic structuring of modernism – is merely a transitional idiom failing to anticipate the next charismatic event that will roll up the civilization like dust in a carpet. Epic poetry is the only idiom flexible enough to accept unexpected and charismatic innovation. And all epic poetry embeds the secret narrative of cosmology.

If human experience of astral information is essentially linguistic and charismatic –then poetry is the human singularity.

This is the case for poetry.

CHAPTER TWELVE

Information Is Charismatic – Not Rational

No agency, no committee, no science faculty, can predict the source, moment, or arrival of information. No historical event, no battle, no attack, no murder, no assassination, no tsunami, no volcanic eruption, no asteroid was ever discovered or anticipated beforehand by a government or academic research committee. Story Theory has accounted for this phenomenon. If information of life is not rational, repeatable, or predictable, then there must be a new language that faces this predicament. If it will be poetry, it will not be modern poetry. There will be a new poetry – only vernacularly related to the modern idiom. Modern linguistics insists that the world is predicable, repeatable, and rational. This is a myth. This attitude, so absurd, reflects the self-referent linguistics of the research laboratory. Truth, in all cases, is a question of the linguistic information we privilege.

The human philosopher, using only logic, linguistic bias, and prose, has never been able to interpret information consistently. Each age differs on the interpretation of the value of life. Each age insists upon a contradictory linguistic idiom of privileged information. The Greeks explained the cosmos by telling stories of the rivalry of the Olympian gods. The Medieval Church (based on Ptolemy) fixed our cosmology on the distinct crystalline spheres of the stars, angels, and seraphim. They were serious in their belief. Modern science insists the universe is dead and all that actually exists is exactly as portrayed in telescopes. Science is serious in this extreme belief. All linguistic codes are extreme. That is why there are armies.

Each civilization's method of information is exactly correct – that is, the language of each culture fits the level of consciousness it seeks. Each culture is self-referent in its linguistic pattern. Each civilization meets the linguistic requirements it seeks. What is Truth? Better to ask what idiom you wish to use. Truth is what we accept as the pattern best matching the cadence of our linguistically formulated ideation of world. I return to the Egyptian hieroglyphic word for truth – "a thing that has been examined or perceived." We *make* ideas true by focusing our mind on it linguistically. Truth is what we agree exists. Truth is what we agree is linguistically sound. You find a pattern that fits your linguistic level. This is Story Theory.

Each linguistic structure of ideation determines what is true to the perceiver. What is justice? It is a linguistically organized pattern we accept. What is truth but a pattern we accept? What is love but a pattern we accept of love that we have already anticipated (in our thought)? What is correct behavior – except a pattern we accept? In Story Theory, poetry is a structured perception created to interpret the charismatic arrival of information of life. This is what a poem performs. This is how truth operates. Truth is a linguistically patterned device.

Information arrives in our dimension as charismatic events – essentially having the origin and energy from a location other than the strictly material Earth. Parents cannot predict, control, or even anticipate their children's character. We do not know the day of our death. We do not know if our love shall be returned. We do not know if our business venture will succeed. Life is determined by charismatic origins. Anciently, it was believed that the stars contained this charismatic information. We have to fully integrate this insight into our thesis.

Consciousness is essentially charismatic and, therefore, the future will also be a charismatic event – arising from a deep and alien source. There must be a language that can accept and adapt to these essential facts of consciousness. In a previous volume, I insisted that if there are multiple dimensions of Being – not only our own – then there also must be a sentient creature to move across this structure of sentience. We know this creature. It is man as *Kosmoautikon*. If life is charismatic in its origin, then there must be a linguistic code that is able to account for charismatic forces. We know this idiom. It is poetry.

Poetry is a language flexible enough to bend to the charismatic forces of human life. Poetry is a language that may operate with oracular structures. Few of us can read with patience or understanding a past age of prose. We read the English prose of the 15th to 19th centuries with pain and difficulty. Yet the best crafted poems of each civilization still contain vital information of any previous human age. A poem contains its own stasis. Each poem is sustained with its own internal correspondences and points of reference. The best poems of every age of man are still – startlingly – accessible. If understood as exact cosmology, even ancient myths are startlingly accessible. Rationalistic prose, on the other hand, from other ages, merely appears to us as risible. Modernism, as prose, stands in line with failed expression – in this case, rationality.

Modernism is a structure that hangs from a gossamer thread. In our crisis of information, how can modernism ensure our progress to the next innovation of charismatic apparition? Modernism – in so far as it rejects the poetic insight – is a failure of human information.

The certainty – the longevity – of linguistic opinion is an illusion. This is why there are military organizations – to ensure that our linguistically coded way of life can survive against all *other* linguistic interpretations of life. Each human cultural perception can be replaced by another linguistic misprision. Linguistic cultures cannot be translated across other linguistic idioms – if attempted, there can only result a misreading of the texts. The people of any failed linguistic code has only the choice to disappear from *world* consciousness – or to be assimilated into another form of consciousness. The linguistic danger is so intimately felt – the security of our linguistic code is so fragile – that we are forced to be an aggressive and militaristic species. There are armies because there is linguistic bias. Linguistic bias and war are exact in profile.

We cannot understand Mayan civilization – which had no texts – any more than we can understand the Islamic civilization – that does have texts. These are both anti-modern interpretations of *world*. Culture *is* language; civilization *is* language. The human orders the information of his eye – with linguistic codes and structures. The infant sees everything (even more than the adult), yet remembers nothing – since his brain is not yet coded with linguistic patterns. When it makes a story of what the eyes see, then he can recall the vision of the eyes. Language is a mnemonic device of human information. Language not only orders the human world – it actually places *things* in the human world. The child does not insist upon the universe – does not even believe there is a universe. The child is given a linguistic device to fit *things* into an unknown, unfinished world. The child is linguistically *instructed* there is a universe of *things*. The child is given a poem called world – and he is trained to accept it as empirical evidence. In truth, it is a linguistic structure – a poem.

As we now recognize in quantum mechanics, the human observer makes a linguistic *projection of world* with every act of judgment – of every mental observation. Not for a moment do *things* exist independently from the linguistically ordered human. Only the linguistically trained adult insists upon the existence (and meaning) of a universe. This point is vital in Story Theory. Human perception is so dependent upon linguistic coding that, without a previously embedded linguistic idiom, the human eye could not function with sentience. Without the sentience provided by an extreme, even obsessive, all-encompassing linguistic bias, we would see the world with cow eyes. The packet of photon waves does not collapse *without* the observation of the linguistically coded human mind. This is not quantum mechanics. Quantum mechanics does not reference the linguistic element of the conscious observer. This phenomenon is more accurately conceptualized as *Story Theory*.

Though presently too deep to retreat from our modern idiom, we are faced with the consequences of our civilization balanced on a precipice. Modernism's high linguistic code, all its vaulted science, has failed to substantiate the solidity of matter. The poetic narrative of matter (science) cannot confirm the intent, momentum, or location of matter (only fragmentally, conditionally). This is equivalent to the Medieval Church having only a *fragmented* explanation of Galileo's observation of the moons of Jupiter. The result? Science no longer can operate as oracle. We already must move ahead with a new linguistics.

With modernism we still cannot determine our position of the grid of sentience. Are we animals or spiritual beings? Is life quickly extinguished – or does it contain a further resource of sentient form? Modernism has no information on these issues. The burnished, godlike sciences cannot find their rotten legs. As the Hebrew god accused the graven gods of the philistines – "their arms and legs do not move" – so we now accuse science: "your eyes misinterpret and your tongue cannot speak." What is the truth? No single specialty of science is able to talk to another specialty – and the vernacular speaker cannot address any scientific specialty with a required audacity. This is cultural madness – bipolar linguistics – psychotic ideation. Secret languages inhibit audacity in others. That is the point of a secret language: to maintain control of ideation. With scientific modernism, the isolation of the vernacular speaker is thus complete.

Science is monopolistic. Artificial strains of industrial, genetic food are within the reach of a single virus. Our water has dried up behind the damned riverbeds. The ten million year underground aquifers are permanently depleted. An argument can be made that science has not improved life on Earth. The single idiom of science has only confirmed the final destruction of all living things. Science, that has manipulated world populations four times beyond what the Earth may support by normal means, only structures a greater holocaust of innocent souls. Are these disasters mere problems to be resolved by an academic community? Of course the answer to any problem posed by modernism – is a further application of modernism. If science has made a miscalculation – then (science will say) we need only to apply more science to the problem. This is the danger of linguistic monopolies. The blind confidence of modern scientific idiom is impenetrable. Modernism is not a true representation of world – it is only a self-referent representation – and this gives modernism the illusion of reliability. It must be clear to the reader at this point that the ideation he accepts as his definition of reality is little more than self-reference of linguistic and visual patterns. I will test this thesis until it is made even clearer.

The modern idiom of life is the most successful ideology of prejudice in the history of the human species. The successful innovation of Western technology has placed all other ideologies of human life in a permanently subordinate, even third-rate, relation. No other idiomatic voice has even managed a partial challenge to modernism. Modernism is hegemon. Each foreign culture that encounters the modern Western life is forever made a colony of the Western modernism.

Yet there is blight in the corn. We have specialized our linguistic tool so opaquely that we can no longer interpret information with confidence. When the secret languages fail, there is a crisis in ideation. Every hegemonic civilization lives off of its secret linguistic codes. The Egyptians used priestly funerary hieroglyphs as a secret language. The Romans used Greek as a secret language – only the Roman elite spoke Greek. The Medieval age used priestly Latin as the secret language of written texts. For over one thousand years, the vernacular laity was never expected to understand the texts or the Latin of the liturgy. For two thousand years the vernacular speakers were intellectually ignored – only the priest could give authoritative prognostications of human life. Yet where are we now? Vernacular moderns are in exactly the same position as the peasants of the Age of Faith. The modern civilization has used high math and scientific medicine as a secret language. How long do we remain spectators?

We have entered another age of magic where exact knowledge is an art – and not a finely tuned measurement. We have entered an age again where knowledge is not *repeatable*. Modern academics, modern science, modern medicine have not established a reliable means of knowing. Each prognostication of science is subsequently reversed in the following decade. Every science is now arbitrary, unsure, indefinite, and unreliable. The mistakes add up. They become wounded moralities.

There are many examples to cite of the inability of moderns to see beyond their own prejudices. How has the modern idiom failed?

We know exactly where modern information has failed.

CHAPTER THIRTEEN

Do Science and Medicine Contain Reliable Information?

To be modern is to be a consumer of scientific and medical information. It is incredible how much medical information the average modern person consumes each year. The advertisements for new medicines are incessant and echo instantly from coast to coast, from Europe to Britain. How sound is the information provided by scientific research and medical opinion? There is not a modern vernacular speaker that does not read or hear of a medical study that is not also certain that he or she has received important information – reliable information – about *real* things. Yet the modern is chasing a linguistic illusion. I do not accuse the modern – we are all moderns. I only show him his predicament.

This brief chapter will illustrate how modern information is biased, corrupted, and impossible to verify. I approach this thesis understanding that the modern does not care if it is shown that his information is unreliable. It changes nothing. He still will seek more modernism. Yet I will proceed with obstinacy. Organized expression comes before organized thought.

Our examples are clear. The contrast of modern scientific prose with epic poetry is dramatic and informative. Strong poetry, as will be seen, reveals information that is repeatable, testable, and permanent – in fact, reliable. The argument will merely amuse the modern ear.

In 2006, a professor of epidemiology at the *School of Medicine of the University of Ioannina* in Greece reported that as much as half of the articles in scientific journals were false, in the sense that independent researchers could not reproduce the same results. The problem is typical of the modern sciences. Scientific literature is corrupt and must rely on self-reference in order to develop the full charge of a scientific article's linguistic authority. There is very little modern medical information that is not directly tied to profit making. That is a biased source.

A growing number of medical journals receive the balance of their income from pharmaceutical advertising. Most medical journals are owned by publishers that also offer marketing services to the pharmaceutical industry. Many of the professional research articles are written by "ghostwriters" hired by the pharmaceutical companies – with instructions to emphasize the benefits of a particular company's drugs. These ghostwriters are paid doctors posing as independent researchers – who then emphasize and tout the benefits of a particular pharmaceutical on the market. This is an exploitation of faith. Medical misinformation takes advantage of the public's fervent belief in medical science – and the complete inability of the vernacular speaker to discern actual medical information from underwritten studies that contain biased, falsified and cherry-picked, information. These medical frauds kill unsuspecting believers and involve billions of dollars of profit for the pharmaceutical industry. These are the first signs of a linguistic monopoly of misinformation.

The most unremarked achievement of modernism is a proliferation of, and a fascination with, diseases. No previous age of man has had a preoccupation, an obsession, or a fascination with disease, as the modern age. Each modern has a special, intimate disease that marks his or her family life. Since the 1950's, there has been an epidemic in mental illnesses in Western countries. There is a reason. Industry has colluded with paid PhDs to exponentially expand the list of syndromes, maladies, and "anxiety disorders." Each new publication of the psychiatric handbooks has consulted with industry to double the number of "disorders" that *usefully* match new drugs that have been patented. This exponentially broadens the consumer base of patients who must turn to industrial pharmaceuticals for the relief of new illnesses – illnesses that did not even exist until there was a drug on the market for these newly manufactured diseases. Robert Whitaker writes in his book, *Anatomy of an Epidemic*:

> "The number of mentally ill has risen dramatically since 1955, and during the past two decades, a period when the prescribing of psychiatric medications has exploded, the number of adults and children disabled by mental illness has risen at a mind-boggling rate. Thus we arrive at an obvious question, even though it is heretical in kind: Could our drug-based paradigm of [medical] care, in some unforeseen way, be fueling this modern day plague?"

As modern Western psychiatry became *exclusively* a drug-solution specialty, the pharmaceutical industry immediately saw the benefits of forming an alliance with the psychiatric profession. Since the 1970's, modern psychiatry began to consider that mental diseases are exclusively attributable to a chemical imbalance in the brain (totally reversing their previous belief in Freudian talk therapy – illustrating the systemic unreliability of science). Suddenly, it is as if the entire evolution of *Homo sapiens* was waiting for modern pharmaceuticals to balance the human brain – since most Westerns at some time are told they have anxiety disorders that require pharmaceuticals to balance their brain chemicals. Modern psychiatry is not reliable truth in action – it is a linguistic monopoly of information in operation.

Psychiatry, of course, is a *linguistic* construct of modernism. Modern psychiatry is, itself, a co-generator of new diseases suggested, codified, and sponsored by pharmaceutical companies to wildly increase their profits. In alliance with pharmaceutical companies, both doctors and industry take advantage of modern man's absolute faith in science in order to invent (linguistically) new categories of illnesses and spend billions in advertisements (again, linguistics) to convince people that they fit the image of the newly "discovered" psychotic illnesses. Westerners, of course, as all humans, feel comforted to know that they have a special disease. They feel that the new diseases make them more human in their uniqueness. They feel less isolated. Having a disease – they are somehow ennobled, somehow better cared for – more able to feel the benefits of their being born as moderns. The result? Humans wish to be – to some degree – sick. There is no other way to explain the phenomenon of persons who now insist righteously that they, also, are sick. Moderns dare you to deny their right to their illnesses.

What are the requirements are for modern illness and their remedies? Industry underwrites enough paid studies, until they get at least two to show positive results to the US Federal Drug Administration (FDA). The proprietary records of the FDA show that drug companies pay for many studies that are negative – until they get at least two that show that the drug marginally outperforms a placebo. This is not empirical science. This is cherry picking of data. In an article reviewing the research of Irving Kirsch, PhD, Marcia Angell states:

> "For obvious reasons, drug companies make very sure that their positive studies are published in medical journals and doctors know about them, while the negative ones often languish unseen within the FDA, which regards them as proprietary and therefore confidential. This practice greatly biases the medical literature, medical education, and treatment decisions." (*NYRB*, June 23, 2011)

She explains that Dr. Kirsch used the Freedom of Information Act to obtain FDA reviews of all studies submitted for the six most widely prescribed anti-depressant drugs between 1987 and 1999 – Prozac, Paxil, Zoloft, Celexa, Serone, and Effexor. She cites Kirsch's findings:

> "Altogether, there were forty-two trials of the six drugs. Most of them were negative. . .The average difference between the drug and the placebo. . .was clinically meaningless. The results

were much the same for all six drugs: they were all equally unimpressive. Yet because the positive studies were exclusively publicized, while the negative ones were hidden, the public and the medical profession came to believe that these drugs were highly effective antidepressants."

More examples of the abuse of data are easy to find. I may choose a well-documented example. If there ever was a moment when the global community needed to verify the reliability of modern information, it was when the World Health Organization (WHO) declared an imminent threat of influenza pandemic in 2009. The deceit involved with this example of modern information, serves as testimony of the fraud mixed up with the production of modern scientific data – as propaganda. Fabricated information in, fabricated information out.

The drug company, Roche, in 2009, benefited by scaring the Western nations into buying large quantities of their drug *Tamiflu* to prevent influenza pandemic – an epidemic that never occurred. In May 2009, Roy Anderson, a well-known British epidemiologist, advising both the British government and the World Health Organization (WHO), warned on BBC radio that *Tamiflu* and *Relenza* alone might prevent a pandemic every bit as horrific as the 1918 influenza. A month later, WHO declared an influenza "pandemic emergency." It was later revealed that Roy Anderson was receiving nearly $200,000 a year from Roche, the maker of these drugs. Governments all over the world spent billions on buying this medication – based on *information* that was later discovered to be unreliable, biased, and corrupted.

Another *NYRB* researcher, Helen Epstein, who uncovered the facts listed above, presents information to indicate that the drug was not even proven to be helpful to persons with influenza – in fact, the drug was the direct cause of deaths. The entire system of scientific information is riddled with conflicts of interests and a biased sifting of available case studies – to select just the right information that companies needed to promote their product. She found that it was clear that the companies (Roche and GlaxoSmithKline) paid researchers to privilege certain studies over others, stating that "the person reporting the statistics might select for publication only those trials showing that the test drug has a positive effect, while suppressing the findings of the others."

After her investigation, she became convinced that most medical journals were liable to conflicts of interest – and that all the rapidly proliferating professional journals and organizations were funded by industry to front studies that could promote the supposed benefits of a new drug. Of course the drugs that were advocated were only new drugs that could be patented by a single company to exploit for profits. *But first* the linguistic narrative of a disease has to be built. The data supporting any new drug has to be contrived. A complicated thicket of *ostensibly* independent studies had to be manufactured by industry to document the public need of a new medication, and then, they present their new drug patent as the solution to this new human crisis. Thus both the new disease (usually simply a new name for an old illness) and the solution were manufactured as *information* that would induce a fearful public of the need to buy a new product. This corrupt production of scientific information is widespread in the West. She comments:

> "Conflicts of interest plague American Health agencies too. One member of the WHO's Emergency Committee was Nancy Cox, head of the influenza Division at the US Centers for Disease Control (CDC), whose lab receives grants from the International Federation of Pharmaceutical Manufacturer's Association (IFPMA) of which Roche and GlaxoSmithKline are members [both pharmaceutical manufacturers of Tamiflu and Relenza]. I was surprised to learn that a US government agency, which issues policy recommendations to state, federal and international health authorities, could receive money from an organization supported by industries that stood to profit from those recommendations. A recent CDC guidance document issued by the influenza division, listing Cox as director on the first page, ignores the Cochrane group's concerns, claiming that clinical trials show Tamiflu is effective against severe influenza complications and is not associated with neuropsychiatric side effects."

Western governments were advised with corrupted modern information. *Of course* the company producing the drug ignored the other research trials that showed that *Tamiflu* patients jumped out of windows, walked in front of passing traffic, and have died with respiratory complications after taking the drug. (My text scans an *NYRB* article, *Beware the Drug Companies*, May 12, 2011, by Helen Epstein.)

With any scientific journal, we are instantaneously confronted with the signature constructs of fabricated modern information. From these short excerpts we learn of medical journals, professional associations, and government agencies that authoritatively promote and disseminate modern scientific information. Medical journals are modern inventions made to manufacture and endorse scientific information to a vernacular speaking public – usually for the monetary benefit of advertisers and industry. These modern elements have proliferated exponentially in the past one hundred years – exactly the age of unreliable ads as information.

Medical journals serve to push some medical research ahead of other researchers who do not have the backing of large pharmaceutical interests. If the modern vernacular reader could see a list of these journals and professional medical organizations – he or she would not only be astounded – they are numbered in the thousands – but the reader would begin to suspect that there is another agenda in operation – and not a careful search for unbiased information.

Each new medical patent is so *controversial* in its *supposed* effects that it requires a separate professional body to front the information – in order to shelter under the appearance of impartial research. Well-known in academic/industrial circles, these professional journals and medical associations proliferate for every form of science that is tied to a need to promote and sell a particular product of the medical and pharmaceutical industry. They are not for the public consumption. Costing as much as $40,000 for a single year's subscription – they are intended only for giant university libraries – also supported and subsidized by pharmaceutical industries. We are alerted immediately that there is something wrong. The average yearly subscription cost of a journal of literature, philosophy, or religion is only $250. What is going on?

First, this illustrates that modernism considers that science is the only reliable form of information – such a sacred form of information, moreover, that not a single specialized discovery can be missed, no matter how small – no matter how corrupted and self-referent. This shows the deep entrenchment of modern belief in science. In fact, the corruption of information is *irrelevant*. It makes no difference if we can show that journals are self-generating, self-referent, and corrupted profit models. It makes no difference if we can show the biased nature of the information that is presented in journals at astronomical costs. Moderns are convinced that their well-being, even the possibility of a future, is dependent upon access to unreliable scientific data. It is a linguistic honey trap. It is a high church.

Second, we can see by the price disparity for literary and religious journals that one kind of modern information is privileged over another at a disproportionate rate. The inference? Poetry has no information of life. Science contains serious information of life. Modernism so earnestly believes in the reliability of scientific research, that it is willing to be exploited by science publishers that operate as monopolies of the information. Savvy publishers have diagnosed the insidiousness of modernism and have built a self-generating, self-referent information machine to feed the virulent virus of modernism. Realizing the myopic need of modern universities (universities are only successful if they generate ever more competitive modern science), publishers have found a way to exponentially leverage the needs of the addled addict – modern academia.

When any privileged sector of human endeavor is feverishly sought, talked up, and hyper promoted, humans lose their grip on reality – a dangerous bubble is formed that can burst at any moment. The information of modernism is not what it is represented to be. Modernism is a linguistic bubble, every bit as prone to deflate and harm society as any financial bubble that innocent people have been persuaded to invest all their savings in.

Modernism is all smoke and mirrors. The fact that medical journals can charge $40,000 per annual subscription – one year, perhaps six issues – tells the reader everything he needs to know about the linguistic health of modernism. In effect, this phenomena is in no way different than how rich men of the medieval period were convinced to give their fortunes to a monastery that would say prayers for the dead sinner throughout eternity. Today, modern secularists would consider a monastery a total waste of money. No. It was a choice of information privileged. The Medieval Church also claimed a monopoly over information – the information of the soul.

This phenomenon should not only appear as a large waste of money to the modern – it should alert the reader that modernism is exploiting a monopoly over linguistic control of the human ideational space. Medical journals exploit the willingness of vernacular moderns to privilege self-referent and self-generating scientific information. The corruption of modern information is registered by a recent article in the *Scientific American* (June, 2011), stating, "False positives and exaggerated results in peer-reviewed scientific studies have reached epidemic proportions in recent years." The article continues:

> "The problem is rampant in economics, the social sciences and even the natural sciences, but it is particularly egregious in biomedicine. Many studies that claim some drug treatment is beneficial have turned out not to be true. We need only to look to conflicting findings about beta-carotene, vitamin E, hormone treatment, Vioxx and Avandia. Even when effects are genuine, their true magnitude is often smaller than originally claimed.
>
> The problem begins with the public's rising expectations of science. Being human, scientists are tempted to show that they know more than they do. The number of investigators – and the number of experiments, observations and analyses they produce – has increased exponentially in many fields, but adequate safeguards against bias are lacking. Research is fragmented, competition is fierce and emphasis is often given to single studies instead of the big picture.
>
> Much research is conducted for reasons other than the pursuit of truth. Conflicts of interest abound, and they influence outcomes. In health care, research is often performed at the behest of companies that have a large financial stake in the results. Even for academics, success often hinges on publishing positive findings. The oligopoly of high-impact journals also has a distorting effect on funding, academic careers and market

shares. Industry tailors research agendas to suit its needs, which also shapes academic priorities, journal revenue and even public funding." (*An Epidemic of False Claims*, Scientific American, June, 2011)

Billions of dollars are involved with the correct presentation of medical information in "professional" journals and medical organizations. Doctors are solicited and generously paid – what amounts to a bribe for using their name on a ghostwritten article (using information specifically supplied by the industry hoping to enjoy the profits). The proliferation of medical journals and medical associations continue unabated only because modern information is deeply conflicted and in need of self-generating authoritative entities to manage all the misinformation of the modern scientific-capitalistic idiom.

In many cases, the protocol operates as follows. Professional medical "associations" are ostensibly established to promote excellence in a particular field of medical science. In fact, these supposedly independent research associations are paid *fronts* where willing doctors are lavishly paid to promote *selected* information, data, and studies (provided by the industries themselves). Modern science journals and professional associations exist to serve an important function – to self-generate an exploitable monopoly of information.

Readers familiar with Story Theory, already recognize the function these "associations" serve. The numerous medical journals and associations operate as the self-referent points on the grid of a hermetically sealed, self-reinforcing, linguistic system. Medical journals are used to manufacture information to fit a society already prepared to digest the linguistics of modernity.

How serious is the modern proliferation of new diseases? Every few years a new psychiatric manual is issued, called *Diagnostic and Statistical Manual of Mental Disorders* (DSM). Each DSM published exponentially finds new mental "diseases" – from 182 diagnosis with DSM II (1968), to 265 with DSM III, and finally to 365 "diseases" with DSM-IV in 2000. Of course the main charge of these psychiatric "bibles" is to insist that more and more persons must seek out the industrial pharmaceuticals to balance the chemicals in their brain – that more and more of modern society must enter the linguistic control of science and industrialized medicine. Of course, investigators have discovered the agendas behind these publications.

Of the 170 contributors to the recent DSM-IV, ninety-five had financial connections to drug companies. Dr. Roger Whitaker, cited above, shows that the pharmaceutical cocktails are more dangerous than the supposed original illness. Powerful negative side effects emerge from initial proscribed drug cocktails (as many as six at one time). As antipsychotics cause side effects that resemble Parkinson's disease, the episodes of proscribed drug mania usually lead to a further diagnosis of "bipolar disorder" and an additional prescription for "mood stabilizers." This allows a proliferation of even more disease. It is dangerous to even attempt to go off the pharmaceuticals. The symptoms produced by withdrawing psychoactive drugs are often confused with relapses of the original "disorder," which lead psychiatrist to resume drug treatment at ever higher doses. What is the point? Psychiatry reveals that it is a self-generated system of *mis*-information. Modernism can only infer that it needs more modernism.

It was announced this week (*Reuters news, Kate Kelland* - Sept 4, 2011) by the European College of Neuropsychopharmacology that nearly 40% of all Europeans have some form of mental disease and must seek treatment (a cocktail of pharmaceuticals) at the youngest age possible. Forty percent – and growing (it was 27% in 2005)! Surely this is either an inescapable condemnation of modern life (modernism makes humans sick) or a verification of the profit-driven unreliability of modern science – or that humans were *always* sick and only by the grace of modern techniques has science verified correctly that most people are diseased and in need of pharmaceutical cocktails at the earliest age! Either way, my point is made. Modernism cannot reform modernism. It can only be eradicated or de-mystified.

With industrialized medicines, modernism, in effect, creates the linguistics of a crisis, then presents the manufactured *solution* as a justification of the high level of modern ideological information. Of course, the implication is that science is correct information and we need more science. Every linguistic system thus appears – to itself – as the *only reliable* human solution – that is, to those speaking and living within the linguistic system of self-referent and self-manufactured modernism. In truth, this is all fraud. What is actually occurring is that a linguistic system is privileged in society (in this case, scientific materialism) and a corrupt, profit-driven bias is used to manufacture information that *appears* to meet the conditions set by the same self-referencing linguistic system. This is the crisis of modern information.

Most sources of authoritative modern information can be traced to large and well-funded institutions, with prestigious titles – ostensibly established as independent and unbiased sources of information. These are the *beautiful* and *good* faces of modernism – repeat with colorful graphics, rich facades, and elegant surroundings. They are, in fact, created to manufacture the information the industry needs to convince a materialist, secular, and vernacular speaking (but faithful) public that they have an immediate need of new drugs.

I can give another example known to all readers.

In the last twenty years, industry associations and medical journals have promoted an entire family of drugs, called *statins*. Billions of dollars were spent in advertising campaigns and *selected* medical studies to convince doctors and patients that taking statins is the only effective means of preventing an early death or stroke from the ill effects of the build-up of cholesterol in the arteries.

We can say much about this. First, it does not take much research to reveal that statins are no more effective than natural remedies that already exist in nature. Any doctor will tell you that niacin, seaweed, garlic and a balanced diet, to name only four natural substances, more effectively reduce cholesterol – and without any dangerous side effects. What is the offending element of these natural substances? Simply this: there is no profit. Nature cannot be *patented* by any pharmaceutical industry for massive profits. Therefore both the emergency – the danger of dying from blocked arteries – and the pharmaceutical product – statins – had to be carefully packaged as vital modern information. It was fraudulent information.

The campaign for statins was a multi-decade, multi-billion dollar public crusade specifically designed to manufacture modern information. Statins not only have the slight disadvantage that they are not any better than natural products already mentioned – but that they create painful muscle reactions, harm the liver – and most alarmingly – are not necessary at all. The result? All the medical studies that claim to privilege the benefits of statins – like the *Tamiflu* previously discussed – are unreliable in their means of modern information.

The final insult of modern information is to be told (this year, 2011) that all the studies indicating that cholesterol was the chief cause of heart attacks – were, in fact, also fraudulent. The studies promoting the danger of cholesterol were – now we are told – biased. They were the result of choosing some test trials over others that showed that groups with high cholesterol had no greater incidence of heart attacks than many other possible human factors.

For the person alerted to linguistic pattern recognition (as in Story Theory), the evidence of the failure of modern information is everywhere visible. Westerners have been told for years that *free radicals* (a purely poetic term) are the cause of cancers. There have been billions of dollars spent in advertising industrial pharmaceuticals to encourage people to take medications that prevent *free radicals*. The truth? This year it was announced in several medical journals that a reexamination of the evidence indicates that *free radicals* are, in fact, necessary to prevent most cancers.

My thesis has gained some definition. The science community controls and manufactures a monopoly of linguistic secret information to their own advantage, just as a Catholic hierarchy controlled a monopoly of information coded with a secret language during the Medieval Age. In the Age of Faith, a worldly sinner could look forward to going to Hell. This was information that was *serious* to the medieval mind. For prestige and money, the Roman Church gave rich medieval sinners a way out of their dilemma – they gave men false information of forgiveness of sins – in return for large donations of money. The corruption of information could only operate so long as the Roman Church maintained a monopolistic control of *human information* with the device of a secret language of High Latin (non-vernacular speech). The new tyranny is modernism. It cannot be overlooked that science, as the Roman Church before it, claims to speak as the single interpretation of *world*. Every academic institution checks for scientific orthodoxy.

Medical journals, professional foundations, and universities now perform exactly the same protocol – they insist on a form of privileged information that the modern cannot live without – medical research, industrial pharmaceuticals, and especially, the authority of the doctor's learning and the sacred character of the information contained in his secret language. Like the medieval Church, modern doctors compete for massive amounts of money and social prestige. As the Latin Church exploited the fearful authority of its information, modern science now ruthlessly exploits the serious nature of privileged information – to generate employment, immense profits, and most assuredly, to maintain hegemonic authority over the interpretation of reality – that is, the *information* of reality. We have not even discussed the uncontrolled rise in medical treatments and "advanced" industrial medical procedures.

Where does it all end? It does not end. No self-referent linguistic code can reform itself. Scientists will reply instantaneously that they only need more time and more funding and they will discover the solution to every ill known to man. This is the modern myth that we have all been indoctrinated with. It is a lie – not a myth. Modernism, as any linguistic code, can only reply that it needs more applications of modernism. Modernism cannot reform modernism. Modernism can only be superseded by a further innovation of linguistic patterning. What is needed is not more modernism – but a new linguistic idiom of human life..

I remind the reader that our interest is the solidity, reliability, and integrity of modern information – to construct a strong theory of poetry. I have not chosen these examples randomly. One was the dangerous threat of global pandemic. Surely that was a moment that modern information should prove itself reliable?

Another example is the most prevalent pharmaceutical marketed in my generation. Again, this was a moment when truth was demanded of modernism. The fear, and prevention, of heart disease was the greatest campaign of mass public information in my generation. If we may find any single moment to assess the reliability of modern information, surely these two moments should be our test case. While these are only a few examples of the failure of modern information, they exist in symbiotic paring at the moment when the entire globe was in desperate need of accurate information. Having suffered the betrayal of modern information in the moments of human extremity, how can modern information, in so far as all modernity shares the same self-referent and corrupted protocol, ever again have human allegiance?

We see that profit interest can buy souls (under medievalism) and generate biased medical information (under modernism). Can poetry also be corrupted with money? We are certain of our response. It is revealing. It is impossible to improve the quality of poetry by the application of money, profit, or selfish interests.

What may we say about the reliability of poetry? Poetry cannot be bought. When poetry is bought, when it is purchased to please the vanity of an industrial patron, or any patron at all, it is painfully bad. Poetry is never made to order. The poet cannot even make a living wage from strong poetry. No poet laureate ever made a decent poem during the period that he was heralded as the nation's official poet.

Poetry that is promoted in journals of poetry – as humble as they may seem – or as sincere – cannot produce, induce, or discover a single strong poet. Few bother to buy slim journals of modern poetry. Few believe there will be any source of information revealed in a journal of modern poetry. So how could money influence the information of poetry? Every source of funding for poets, every hapless DEA grant, has always failed to discover or foster the talent of a strong poet. Money, politics, and the lure of prizes cannot corrupt poetry.

No modern government agency, no matter how well intentioned, can make a nation of strong poets – even as much as it has tried – no matter how many grants or dubious awards (public or private) are presented. My proof? Not a single winner of the annual Yale Poets Contest, beginning in the 1950's, has ever risen to national, international, or even local prominence in poetry. That's a lot of winners – sixty. Not a single strong poet? Then it is only linguistic liberalism that is being supported, subsidized, and honored with these prizes.

Money, authority, or favoritism cannot influence the true information of poetry. Poetry is more reliable as a medium of information. Poetry cannot be bought. Yet when the strong poet is found, his information is not only reliable, it is permanent, and the pleasure of the poet is repeatable and testable. The Sumerian poet of *Gilgamesh* is still searching among the gods to discover if his humanity may yet gain immortally. We are still that generation of Hebrews that left out of Egypt. The human condition, as portrayed by the first poets, has not changed.

Older, even ancient, strong lyric poems are *still* strong lyric poems. Ancient epic poems *still* contain permanent information of the cosmology of the human condition. As I write this sentence, Macbeth has still been edged on by his wife to murder the king in his sleep. Lady Macbeth still wipes the spots of blood from her perfumed hand. Nothing can change the permanence of the reliability of poetic information. The rage of Achilles is still as deep. The bright emitting brow of noble Hector is still bright, noble, and still the hero is winning our heart – even so much as we know that he will die. Hector's death contains emotional information that is still operable on the astral plane. This is the point. That was his message, in his death. So important is Hector's death in Western history that we do not even record Achilles' death. The epic reliably discharges human information. No hate for the enemy, no contempt for the victim.

CHAPTER FOURTEEN

Poetry Operates on the Astral Plane

We wish the poet survives only if his poem contains information. Modern science insists that the only valid form of information is that which is material, testable, and repeatable. Can science sustain its own test? Can it give reliable information of our solar system? It cannot. Ancient epic and mythic poetry of many cultures verifies that we are in a binary solar system. We are circling around a distant sister star still undetected by modern science. The point? Poetry sustains reliable information across the eons. Science denies any information that does not fit in the modern narrative. Science, deeply invested in terrestrial life, is unable to detect that the human mind operates on the astral plane. We must escape earth, therefore, before we can build our brave and beautiful machines.

Physics is in crisis. Matter, so long the idol of the secular materialist, is now discovered to be essentially empty – *of matter*. Matter, in fact, exists as a product of ideation – that is, consciousness – as predicted by poetic texts. In quantum mechanics (to simplify in vernacular), the observation of a conscious observer collapses the wave packet of a photon (particle of matter) into a position on the visible grid. This is a protocol that requires a conscious observer. The point? Consciousness is the underlying substance of all physical and metaphysical phenomena. This is the greatest discovery of modern times. Yet poetry already made this assertion five millennia ago. The human mind does not exist in the terrestrial plane. The human mind operates on the astral plane. We verify this protocol in every dream.

After investing two centuries into developing the subject of the physical world into a high linguistic form, we now confirm that matter is essentially a linguistic pattern of ideation. That is, the observer changes the observed. The observer changes matter *merely by the act of possessing consciousness.* This is the insight we seek. Consciousness is the quintessential element – not the element of matter. Matter is subsidiary to consciousness – a *symptom* of consciousness. For this reason we insist that the universe will not be understood until consciousness is understood.

The West has yet to fully develop the implications of quantum mechanics. There is no philosophy, no theory of poetry that accounts for the emptiness of matter. Quantum physicists have, in the final analysis, undermined the solidity of materialism itself. We are not in a physical struggle to discover something that is separate from human consciousness. We are in a *linguistic* struggle to structure the world we experience – the universe. Then we must assert this linguistic code over all other codes – or be lost. We must be ruthless and audacious.

The physicist Anton Zeilinger has discovered, independently of Story Theory, that it is no longer plausible to make an absolute distinction between the *experimenter* (the human) and the *physical matter* under experimental study. The need of the observer – his question, his goal, his high ambition, his level of linguistics, in fact, controls the result of the observation:

> "One may be attempted to assume that whenever we ask questions of nature, of the world outside, there is a reality existing independently of what can be said about it. We will now claim that such a position is void of any meaning. It is obvious that any property or feature of reality "out there" can only be based on information we receive. There cannot be any statement whatsoever about the world or about reality that is not based on such information. It therefore follows that the concept of a reality without at least the ability in principle to make statements about it to obtain information about its features is devoid of any possibility of confirmation or proof. This implies that the distinction between information, that is knowledge, and reality is devoid of any meaning."

This is an excellent introduction to Story Theory. We cannot observe an observation, we cannot even qualify that we have detected it – unless we have first made a story – a context – with which to proceed with the act of observation. If scientists (as above) are brave enough to take away the independence, the solidness of material phenomena, how much more should we be brave as poets to test the solidity of human consciousness – the power of mental ideation? Mental processes cannot be located as points in physical matter, neither in the brain as neurons nor in laboratories. So where does the mental process exist? All that exists "out there" is the *story* men make. This is where matter appears – where we summon to our vision with sentience – call it story, purpose, intent, ambition, need, desire, wish, dream, hope, love – or fixed determination. We summon matter – as we summon world. We summon lovers – as we summon our enemy. As we discover in Story Theory, we are as responsible for the creation of our world as it is responsible for creating us. This is what truth looks like.

Of course, in some areas of space, as in our own field of gravity, science is able to make practical use of scientific theorems. In some conditions, when gravity and electromagnetic forces are balanced – initially – there is often favorable and practical results. Some science – as some garage tools – bear repeatable, predictable results. Yet in other parts of space, there is another form of physics – and not only in *Black Holes*, etc. How can we discount the mind as the place where an alternate physics assembles? Of course the mind/soul is the source of all ideation – and matter follows the path of our ideation. The observer always changes the observed. Even medical science is forced to use a placebo in all medical trails – since the mind is actually the sole competitor to the drugs. In most studies medical researchers find that a placebo often gives a more favorable result than an actual drug.

At the very large and very small scale of matter, something strange begins to happen. At the very large (Dwarf stars, Back Holes, etc.) scale there is a singularity. At the very small scale there is a singularity. At the quantum scale matter resists most forms of quotidian definition – the photon cannot be reliably located *and* its motion fixed – unless there is first a human observer – with a sentient mind that makes a selection, a collapse of the photon wave packet – to fix the location of the photon. In this way, in each discipline of science, we observe that science itself is no longer testable or repeatable. Medical studies reverse and change from decade to decade – from biased study to biased study. Truth depends who is paying for the research.

Each week we are told that medical studies of ten or twenty years previous were found to be biased – that "reliable" science gave us unreliable information. So many example lay at hand. For many years we were told repeatedly and vehemently that a high cholesterol count would lead to an early death from heart congestion. We reviewed in the last chapter that these studies were unfounded, that as many persons died of heart failure with low cholesterol, and the studies were skewed to promote the mass marketing of pharmaceutical statins. No need to repeat the list of examples I cited. In far too many cases, then, science cannot meet its own test of reliability of information. Science is still an emotional medium and biased by emotional practitioners – and ruled by the protocol of Story Theory. Every observation is rounded with – a story. This annuls any claim to empirical information.

And poetry? How often has poetry been honored for its reliability of information? Poetry's quality of reliability – that is, poetry's repeatability of emotional and informational charge – its testability to communicate information – is seldom remarked as the principle of its strength. Yet reliability is poetry's principle singularity. Poetry, as literature, as myth, as anecdote, exists as the most repeatable and testable means of communicating solid information of the human condition. Not a single story or myth of ancient times has altered its message.

We still quote the parables of Socrates and Jesse (the Golden Rule, etc.) as the basis of Western ethics and justice. Almost casually, we are startled to observe the eternal reliability of poetry. The cosmos was reliably mapped by ancient epic poems. Egyptian religious poetry already detected the Sirius star system – and the invisible Sirius B. We still ponder the irrational Anger of Achilles. The noble soul of dying Hector never fails to reeducate the human condition. The *Twelve Labors of Hercules* is a star narrative of zodiac cosmologies (more later). We are still that generation making Exodus from Egypt. Each story of the Western canon is repeatable from generation to generation – and contains the same emotional charge of information to each generation of listeners.

Chaucer, though his English is archaic, still communicates the conditions of human life in the 14th century. Any poet who is able to still make us laugh and smile with interest after five centuries is propagating reliable human information from generation to generation. Does science tell us anything reliable from the 14th century? Nothing. The 13th century B.C.? Nothing. We are even advised that Newton's 17th century's science has been helplessly superseded by 20th century science. Yet Chaucer's information remains reliable and repeatable. The Shakespeare poet's information is still reliable about the human condition. The red stain of murder and ambition is still on the white hand of *Lady Macbeth. Falstaff* is still boasting acts beyond his courage. Hamlet has information of his father's murderer from beyond this dimension.

The literary theorist Michael Riffaterre shares my view that poetry outlives the language of its own time and civilization. He stresses that a poem "is so well built and rests upon so many intricate relationships that it is relatively impervious to change and deterioration of the linguistic code." Science *does* attempt to operate as a poem – it attempts to fix their achievement into a hermetically sealed, self-referent linguistic matrix. How does this operate? The self-referent linguistic code of science *pre-ordains* that the hypothesis of science will meet the test of science – since the evidence sought was already sustained in the language used by the scientist. Yet any theory of science can be superseded and made worthless. No scientist will even deny this. A story cannot be superseded and made worthless. But a new story (as poetry) does not erase or diminish the value and enchantment of a previous poet's work. The comedy of *Falstaff* does not erase the comedy of the *Wife of Bath*. This is the ideational distinction between the linguistics of science and poetry. Poetry will win out every time. Without the illusion of a electronic world, science has no permanent meaning.

The *Theory of Relativity*, for instance, is actually a hermetically sealed linguistic experiment. Why? No vernacular human can explain, test, verify, or prove any practical information from Einstein's theory. It's linguistics. So what is the value of this transmission of information? Surely it must be a very low grade of information – if the average human cannot understand it. Only specialized persons sharing Einstein's *exact hermetically specialized language* seem to find any relevant information in his theories. This protocol fits exactly with Story Theory: i.e. that the linguistic code defines, values, and constructs visible human *"reality."* The rest of us honor Einstein, as we are taught to honor all unknowable gods – blindly. Additionally, we have the evidence of Einstein himself, who doubted the reliability of his own information when he denied – absolutely refused to credit – the implications of quantum mechanics. He said that God does not throw dice.

The discovery of the last century was not only the splitting of the atom; rather it was that poetry contains the secret of the exact cosmology of the stars. We say it is secret only because the epic trope is thought to contain stories of human heroes – not stars. This is a misreading. The ancient Sumerian cuneiform texts were finally translated in the 1950's. There we learned that early epic poems contain astrological information. From the beginning of the human condition, human myths have represented cosmological references. The Sumerian gods told an uncanny story of the arrival of superior beings on Earth. Distant stars, still unseen by the human eye, were already charted and spoken about (Sirius B). Advanced telescopes are only now seeing some of these bodies – stars commonly spoken of in the ancient city of Ur.

The poets of Mesopotamia, of the city of Nippur, of Ur, of Sippon told of the violent rearrangement of planets in our solar system. The Egyptians and Dogons had knowledge of *Sirius* A and Sirius B. Where did they get this accurate information? We do not know. We only know that poetry was the preserver of this (until now) unobservable information. These epic poems contained the genealogical origins of humans, stars, and planets. Before the discovery of the cuneiform tablets in the deserts of Mesopotamia (1860's), the modern would have never suspected that epic poems contained reliable information. It is a discovery never properly explained in the classroom. The record of the first epics – only fully published in the 1970's – still remains to be explicated in their full scope. This book could have only been written now.

There is evidence in India. Indian Vedic epic cycles told of impossible combat between gods in the Heavens. There is evidence in Anatolia. Assyrian epics told the violent story of Marduk's dismemberment of Tiamat (early Earth). We now know the Earth was dismembered to make our moon. The Egyptian gods, clearly related to Sumerian antecedents, similarly represented secret cosmological data of a more advanced, non-humanoid narrative. Moreover, the highly evolved poetic epic texts of Egypt and Sumer, with no prior antecedents for poetic writing, appeared in the space of a few generations. Humanoid creatures lived for over one million years – and writing suddenly appeared only in the last few moments of this time scale – with no prior antecedents! What should we make of this recent and sudden appearance of epic literature – a sophisticated narrative embedded with consistent cosmology across a spectrum? We have no choice. We have to consider that poetry contains information of a genetic and cultural intervention by other entities – whether humanoid, mechanical, or stellar. This is information that modern science cannot assimilate without reformation.

It is a sub-thesis of this book that it is not only possible that poetry has contained the highest forms of knowledge – but poetry has preserved this foundation of knowledge across the longest time period of the human era. Not only do the early epic poems surprisingly contain complete cosmological information, not only do they contain an understanding of genetics, but data of the wave function of quantum mechanics. They contain the names and agendas of the first founders of human knowledge – all etched in thousands of cuneiform scripts of poetry.

We are only at the beginning of what we know about the epic trope. Yet we know more than any other age. We are surprised to discover the astral references consistent throughout the epic trope. How did the poets all meet and then agree to embed secret information of cosmology? They posed the same interrogative. How do we get more life – more time, more personality? They exactly reproduced message of the cosmology of their times.

Knowledge is tertiary. What actually would we do with knowledge? The wish for complete and final knowledge is, in the end, a death wish. We would still need to make a rigorous selection of life. Our concern is the reliability of poetry. The bare outlines of the message contained in the early epics verify that the information is astral – and only tangentially human. It will, however, be an important discovery if we can verify that poetry contains more information – and information over a greater eon of time – of the human condition than any other linguistic medium.

We do not specifically seek knowledge – again, after all, what would we do with it? We seek the medium along which all feedback of life runs. We seek the process by which feedback operates. This will lead us directly to the life source. That is a discovery, perhaps, of the first order – outclassing any contemnor search for the secret information of common particles. If it is discovered that matter is subject to consciousness – then it is useless to only make interrogatives into matter exclusively. This is my thesis.

There can be no corrected theory of poetry until it is established that epic form not only contains information of importance – that it is not only able to preserve this information across eons – but that it moves across distant galaxies. That would be a discovery of considerable interest. This would illustrate our thesis that sentience is alien contact. This would verify that our mind – so far from operating only from a terrestrial or global environment – functions on the astral plane. And it always has. *Chandos Ring* introduces the structure of this message.

CHAPTER FIFTEEN

Is Modernism the Final Human Idiom?

Modern arrogance is so great that no one has addressed this question. The interrogative does not once arise in social or political conversation. Every modern living assumes that modernism is the highest and final interpretation of reality. This is our crisis of information.

Civilizations do not exist because nations have control of material resources; civilizations exist because they contain a superior hegemonic source of information. The brilliance of Greece continued even after it lost economic hegemony and suffered conquest by the less developed Romans. China always had access to the same human and material resources they have today. Yet China did not have the high kinetic curiosity, the aggressive technical information of the European. Linguistic control of material consciousness (technology, science) has made the West kinetically dangerous. The indigent cultures of Japan, Korea, Vietnam, Taiwan, and China are now undermined as their societies have renounced their own ideational systems of fashion, education, and traditionalism – merely to become powerful influential colonies of Western idiomatic modernism.

Poetry, as myth, homogenizes ideation. Literature seeks hegemon. Yet in the struggle of hegemonic control, something strange always happens. Ideologies always take on the aggressive characteristics of competitive ideologies. Democratic Athens became the hegemonic tyrant of the *Delian League*. Republican Rome became Imperial Rome. Revolutionary France became an empire of tyranny under a tyrant (Napoleon). Communist Russia had to quickly move to totalitarianism to protect its *people's revolution* from the subversion by predatory Western democracies. Mao transformed from benevolent people's leader to totalitarian dictator – and murdered millions of his own people.

American liberalism will not avoid its totalitarian metamorphous.

Western linguistic structure is so technical, so specialized, that the only way other nations may compete with our civilization is to speak with our same linguistic codes of modernism – science, industrial medicine, aerospace, digital military forces, and genetics. Not a single one of these innovations are a result of Asian linguistics. Asia is a Western colony as America is still a colony of European linguistics.

The West is linguistic construct – not a geographic coordinate. The West exists, as the human mind exists – on the astral plane. Even if America may disappear tomorrow, and China should become the linguistic world hegemony – then China would be the leader of the Western pattern of ideation. China has all the linguistic codes to be the carrier of Western civilization. The ideational patterns between modern Asia and the modern West are replicative – not innovative. China has already been colonized by our idiomatic vision of human life. Western modernism is already that far advanced. The West makes ideas, and the rest of the world replicates our patents at the lowest labor cost. At the present moment, Asia replicates Western patents on technology. Any talk of the merit of diversity of world cultures is either political propaganda or harmless utopia. This book is written to ensure this dichotomy persists.

At first, the philosopher will consider that the Western idiom is well placed in the world to advance to completion our total hegemonic control of human consciousness. I suggest that we have not accounted for the charismatic event that is certain to arrive.

Story Theory critically identifies the limited constructs of modernism. There is an element of chaos in all great civilizations. Civilizations collapse when they can no longer explain new sources of information. According to the epic poetry of Ur and Nippur, the crisis of Mesopotamia was when the Sumerian gods could not explain the devastation of their cities by pestilence, radiation clouds, and the invasion of the stranger. The Inca/Aztec civilization could not explain the superior information of the Spanish conquest. The Plains Indians could not have anticipated the British, French, and German invasion of the North American continent. Entire civilizations collapse in one generation. Linguistic modernism, singly reliant upon a stable electric grid, will collapse rapidly. The future landscape is a mountain of useless and blank computer screens. Modernism is not the final human linguistics. There will be another.

Civilization Caught Accessing Wrong Information

All civilizations fall with an implosion of the linguistic code. Deeply involved in the misprisions of its own ancient aurora of information, the Roman Church unluckily pinned its prestige on the (incorrect) doctrine of the Earth as the center of the solar system. This was fatal. It broke the linguistic illusion. A hegemonic worldview was caught accessing the wrong information. Gentlemen with telescopes? How could there be a challenge from this quarter?

What will now break the linguistic illusion of modernity? I am certain that it will be an unexpected and charismatic event. To keep the leadership of the human condition, we must supersede modernism. Western civilization must not be caught accessing the wrong information. *Chandos Ring* attempts to over-reach modern misprision. If not this text – then which?

The fall of civilizations is a linguistic protocol. Wealth, education, or intelligence cannot out-live a failure of linguistic control. Expectation of intelligence and wealth will fail human kind in every test of life. Intelligence is only a promise of arrogance. Wealth and material resources were not able to preserve the Catholic worldview. It was a linguistic problem. The hegemonic Catholic Church could no longer access the correct information of human reality. How could the Church guarantee eternal life if they could not give accurate information of the cosmos – so easy to confirm with a handheld telescope? A prosthetic device, the telescope, eradicated the entire Catholic worldview. Can modernism assume that it will always be able to explain every charismatic event? No civilization can survive accessing the wrong information. No one sees what is coming.

The problem with any age is that it must be addressed with its own idiomatic voice – and thus, already our modern idiom tilts to insubstantial verification. If we had met in a room in the 13th century, we would have to use language that assumed there were angels and saints dancing past the doorposts. If we meet in the 21st century, our language would be imbued with the certainty that, in a medical emergency, a man would be attached to machines for survival. A call would be made to a complete stranger – then, again, to an ambulance driver – and then again to another stranger – a white-smocked priest of surgical and material fanaticism. All manner of tubes would enter by body without hesitation. This would transpire with same fanatical certainty of the medieval man's certainty of guardian angels protecting our souls. Significant to our emphasis – that is, the linguistic protocol – each code utterly excludes the possibility of the other.

The difference of civilizations is linguistic. Modern behaviors would terrify the person from the 13th century – he would react with fear and loathing to witness the modern response to medical crisis. Any foreign linguistic idiom creates fear and loathing in an established linguistic tradition. Again, the question is not what is truth; the question is what linguistic tradition is hegemonic and in ascendancy. All human behavior and practice is a linguistically directed phenomenon.

And you – the modern? What if my reply was for me to reach for a small book and with the aid of one line from this book, a poetic image really, I could reverse the broken and bleeding element? What if I could enter another dimension of life? What if I could push away any supposed disease? You – as modern – would recoil with fear and loathing of my idiomatic translation of human life. You would not even want to hear the details of any possible benefits - you would not want to make a trail of the new linguistics - you would only want to reach for your phone and call the police. Yet this is exactly the prognostication of future human consciousness. Modernism will be supplanted by a new linguistic code.

What lesson do we take from past civilizations? Do we assume that modernism is the last idiom of human life? Is this even a serious question? Who would take this position? Either the arrogant or the wealthy – surely. Will there always be a Western expectation of wealth – to bolster our linguistic audacities? Or will unanticipated charismatic forces arise (as they always arise) to challenge the static condition of any hegemonic power? I wish to move ahead of the problem itself. I want to discover a language that will already place myself on a further level of discovery in consciousness. I want to eradicate modern medical tyranny – with a higher idiom.

Is poetry the highest linguistic idiom? Do we dare answer in the affirmative? Then it must seek all knowledge. Poetry must not limit its theme. It must be able to move seamlessly between lyric and epic formations, between technology and medicine. Seeking hegemonic control of the ideational space, poetry must encompass all of knowing – including, as we have seen, advanced cosmology, genetics, space travel, and nuclear fusion. Poetry, observed in the long count, has been the only medium that has proven able to contain all human knowledge – even the knowledge of the ancient genealogy of the stars. The record of the ancient Sumerian and Egyptian creation myths contains the entire history of the cosmos – including the origin of the physical world and human kind. It's a question of the means to access reliable and long-term information. It is not science – science changes it opinion daily. Permanent speech is poetry.

I don't wish to make a next step – I want to make a farther, deeper strike of ore – to the furthest ideational position I can reach in this dimension. The modern use of scientific technology as the oracle of information is insidious and soon to collapse. The crisis of every civilization is the reliability of its information.

CHAPTER SIXTEEN

An Oddity of Nature: Sentience Is Alien Contact

The human brain is an alien element in mammal life. The human brain is over-engineered to fit the environmental condition of Earth. The human brain is not required for human evolution. The human uses only five percent of his available DNA data. Clearly, the human brain is an advanced storage structure from outside our solar system. There is no previous precedent – in Earth's history – for our mind. After so many animal evolutions, how is it that there should appear only one animal with self-consciousness – with no regard, moreover, for the necessity of self-consciousness? God is hidden because the origin of the mind of man is hidden. Unlocking the unused DNA code will reveal the origin of human consciousness.

Darwinism fails miserably to account for the human brain. There can be no evolutionary explanation for a self-conscious sentience in a single short life span. An educated human with a short life span may only *begin* to make use of a *high* sentience after a lifetime of mental practice. Most human brains are not used at all – and none has ever been used its full potential. Thus, given the single life span – especially the pre-modern brevity of life – there is, in effect, no opportunity for the use of self-consciousness. Even after the application of earnest diligence – after the most stressful periods of study and problem solving – all a human can claim is to be is an absolute beginner. Darwin is shamed in his explanation of the evolution of human life.

There is an insight here. If we do not fit the surroundings of a creature of Earth – then our consciousness must originate from a separately located environment. There must be an alternate source – and purpose – of high sentience. The human consciousness is an alien element that was grafted on to physical nature from another construction of life. High sentience (self-consciousness) is not an expected faculty in a creature made to be extinguished at death. High sentience is more likely embedded with eternal requirements. In a brief life span high linguistic sentience is evolutionarily useless. Therefore, sentience is misunderstood in its physical location. The human mind is not located where evolutionary science would seem desperate to place us. The archeological and logical links are all missing. In Story Theory, if there are alternate dimensions of Being, then there must be a creature that is able to move across the sentient branes. High sentience performs this protocol. So we are the alien element of Earth. Sentience is alien contact.

The materialist observes the dead body and infers the end of all form of life. How accurate is this information? Should the mind of man be limited to a mortal existence – because the linguistics of science requires this conclusion? There is other data that is overlooked and ignored by rational methods of verification. The modern conclusion is made because the materialist separates himself from the observation of nature – acting as an independent agent. Yet if we are already a part of eternal communication – how do we observe the longevity of consciousness? It is impossible – unless there is information passed down to us from texts – or we decipher the ninety-five percent of unmapped data in the human DNA. All we have is text.

Certainly, sentience is strange. Nothing – not even life and death can occur outside of consciousness. That alone is very strange. It's a vital clue of the nature of consciousness. Death and life *both* occur within consciousness. If death did not occur within consciousness, then we would have no cognizance of death. Since death occurs solidly within consciousness, we verify that death contains information. Everything within consciousness contains a feedback of information. The only sign of life is *feedback* – and if death gives feedback – then death contains information. Both life and death are equally tools of communication. To insist that death is a distinct condition from life is a linguistic illusion.

If death is firmly located within consciousness, then we have communication across the sentient spectrum. I may address the dead since they contain information. What language should I use? Of course, we know the answer. Poetry alone has addressed the information that the dead have mined. In our myths and epic poems, the poets have inscribed a true history of the cosmos. Nothing has changed in the cosmos to make any story of cosmology less true.

The elemental propagation of life contains essential signs of sentient feedback. Thus information cannot be separated from evidence of life. Quantum theory *proves* that there is an essential link between the apparition of material phenomena and the *necessary* application of sentient observation. Yet the dialectics of *imperative materialism* denies that the human is connected to the observation of matter. The ultimate expression of quantum theory is that there is no universe of material phenomena until a man arrives *en scène* with his fully sentient condition. Why?

Because the entire known universe is already replicated in the human DNA. There are as many neurons in the brain as there are active star systems in a galaxy.

We have no other *inference* of the existence of *universe*. Only a human has made this claim. The animals and plants do not infer a universe. The only verification of the existence of universe is the repetitive and constant poetic *declarations* of *universe* from sentient humans. The universe is a myth of modernism. Before modernism, there were stars – but no universe. The recent universe is an invention of modernism.

Only a human has *inferred* the stars to consist of a *universe of matter*. Only a human has postulated the eternal phenomena of life. How should we not then consider the universe – that is, all observable phenomena – utterly a fiction of humans? This must be examined with some care. It is the thesis of this book that the universe is a human construct – a human poem. Actually, there is no such thing as a strictly material universe – and we know the composition of universe appears to change its linguistic structure from century to century. Why does its outline change? Because it is a human *alone* that defines, describes, and retranslates the universe.

Is life a fiction? Certainly it is a fictional text. We treat it as a fiction. We replicate life in our texts as a substance that cannot be verified or replicated with any other reliability – except as text, story, or poem. Each human story, report, or sign of life is contradictory; each human story is unrepeatable. Consciousness is thus still unfinished. And if unfinished, it can be modified.

Every deviancy from the norm is a protest against the mortal body – against modernism, against scientific humanism – against the limitations of the given description of reality. Modernism is opposed by the vernacular of the rebel, the protester, and the prisoner as hero – the killer who is sympathetic, the revolutionary, and the escape artist – the deviant with a fanatical insistence of the alternate interpretation. The anti-modern signal is pulsed, received, and retransmitted. Modernism has proliferated the deviant forms of linguistic protest. This is text no different than any other attempt at human text. A story is told. A revelation is at hand.

There is something in the human psyche not well with the modern body. The modern interpretation of the body has failed – and there is a protest – linguistic or otherwise. There is a protest against the interpretation of the mortal frame. It is not without significance that an entire generation has a fascination with tattoos, body piercing, multiple skin implants, suspension piercing, plastic reconstruction – in fact, any form of alternate reconfiguration of the body. The first pattern to observe is that there is never an end of the alterations – it is seldom just one tattoo, or one piercing. The skin becomes a temple-text of multiple chapters – each a significant communication. The average citizen does not closely track the phenomena of deviant expression. They should. It is prophecy of a future mode of life. It is a deep literature. It is not yet acknowledged how deep and how far deviant transmutation has multiplied and proliferated in modern societies. Yet there is information in the reconstruction of the body as text. There is information as feedback. In Story Theory we recognize the body as text. It is a text that prophesies that the modern world will disappear – that is a temporary representation. The body is only a text of alternate eternity. It is a firm statement not to define humans by a mortal body. The well-tattooed body is an alternate humanity.

Only modernity insists that man lives a short time and then is extinct. The rest of us must make texts of high protest – tattoos of rage and escape – piercing, disfigurements, and reconstructions of the skin that step outside of the structures of the modern homogeneity. The strong poet will make an epic poem of this rage. He will tattoo his mind on the fabric of future human skins. The body, as text, as speech, verifies the power and eternity of life. Any force that encounters a strict limitation of the eternity of life must be mocked, stepped around, superseded – shocked into new horizon. The modern needs only to look outside their window. They will see a protest against a self-satisfied modernism.

No two persons may give the same account of a complicated issue. No one chooses the same tattoos. No one selects the same body piercing. We are all infallible liars. This verifies the soundness of poetry that treats each person as forever individual and unique. No one person has ever been able to replicate the life of another person. Each is a separate story.

The human is like one of ten witnesses to a large, complex accident, and each gives a differing account of what happened in plain sight to all. Or did it? Each novel, each nation, each culture, each language, each poem insists upon a differing quality of life – each verifies a more unique outcome. The *outcome, or product,* of witness is always linguistically organized. We prove that human life is a fiction since few humans will agree on the nature and significance of the material universe, the metaphysical universe, or, even, the gossamer meaning of a modern work of art. A modern artist has one message – "*Do not assume that all men must be modern – do not homogenize, do not capture our essence in the horrible beauty of your cities, machines and appliances.*" Modern art uses prosthetics more exclusively than any other age of Western art. Why? Modern artists use prosthetics to illustrate and ridicule the *use* of modern prosthetics as oracles. Every machine, every media, every technology is a prosthetics that attempts to replicate exponentially modern human information. It is a brilliant technique – and never fully recognized. The human will resist definition with every syllable, every paint stroke of protest.

If the universe cannot be universally verified, then it must be categorized as a form of fiction – in fact, a poem. There is no world until a man appears with a sentience designed to observe, translate, and designate world. This makes the unfixed, unfinished universe potentially strange in the extreme – liable to transform at any moment into a new vision of life. So we say that sentience is strange. We say it is alien since no human has ever seized control of sentience. Shakespeare and some other epic poets have come very close – but *somehow* they appeared and disappeared with no biography – no clear location on the sentient grid. Not even a single handwritten manuscript survives. This is strange. This is a clue that has not been explored.

We face a second problem with sentience. Can sentient consciousness be extinguished? No part of physical phenomenon is immune from sentience. There is always feedback in any form of life. Death has feedback. If sentience is viewed as a coil of feedback, then there is never an event of extinguishment along the entire structure of the coil. If we are already in movement within the coil, how can we waste time debating how to enter the *coil* of *sentience* a second time - supposedly after the death experience? This gives us evidence of a new fact of being. We are acting as a committee of persons who, already sitting in a room, are debating violently the best means to reenter the room. We are already in the room of Being – yet by questioning the finality of human death – we are asking to reenter the room (of life) again. This is a failure of philosophical perception.

High sentience is not a requirement in the evolution of a life form designed to be extinguished. So men cannot be explained away with evolutionary prosthetics. If we were to be extinguished – that is, taken from the room (or condition) of consciousness – then there would be no cause or requirement for high forms of communicative sentience. On the other hand, if we come and go along the coil of sentient life, then we may keep intact the high energy of the fully sentient condition. This protocol verifies both the *eternity principle* and the necessary element of *feedback* in all forms of high sentience. No data, no text is lost along this coil.

Each of us is proof of a wild and potent high imaginative sentience. What then should we perform with our high linguistic patterns – that is to say, our linguistic choices? Poetry is exclusively the value of linguistic choice. We privilege information along the linguistic coil; we select linguistic patterns along the grid of the sentient coil. This is as much to say that there cannot be life without a necessary form of communication. And what is communication except a form of poetry? We begin now to earnestly build a new theory of poetry.

Why is poetry important to us in Story Theory? Because men pose poetic questions of life. Is consciousness extinguishable or is it a condition without beginning or end? These are questions allowed only by the constructs of our linguistically patterned ideation! The condition of eternity is not an actual issue within consciousness. Eternity is human worry. To even pose these questions is similar to imagine a group of persons, who, *already* having entered *the room* of consciousness, set about to argue passionately *how they may enter the room*. Linguistically, there is no answer to this debate – since even by *posing* the question – that is, partaking of a state of self-consciousness – proves we already entered the room. This is the solution to the linguistic question of the nature of consciousness. We pose questions: *Is there a god? Is life eternal? Are there souls?* Yet these are questions that are formed by only the ideational structures of languages (poetry).

There can never be a linguistically empirical response to an interrogative that is formed by an *opposite* linguistic structure – as subjective emotion. The question of a soul is not a scientific question – so why would we expect a scientifically patterned answer? Why? Because modernism confuses linguistic science to be a *complete* representation of life. Life is still a poetic construct. In Story Theory, there can *only* be poetic responses to poetic questions.

We certainly do not know every aspect of consciousness – but we still seem nevertheless to be operating efficiently *within* consciousness. If we still love, and wonder, and question, and feel, and search – it's clear we can still operate within consciousness without knowing every aspect of consciousness. We may not know everything about gravity – yet we live by gravity. We may not know all there is to know about love – yet we live by diverse poetic theories of love. Of course, gravity and love are weak forces in our dimension – so we may be tempted to think that consciousness is also weak in our present dimension. I counter that it is only a matter of focus. The rumor of consciousness is only as wide as our linguistic structure allows. We freeze our mental states with poor linguistic constructs. When we construct the linguistic question – "*Is there a god?*" – we halt the god process. To name a god is to die with this god. We are frozen in time and ideation by naming our gods. By such linguistics – "*Who is the great god?*" – we are merely insisting to know every aspect of consciousness. This is a linguistically imposed criterion – and this linguistically imposed interrogative does not take into consideration any *actual* operating principle of consciousness. Thus we say that no linguistic civilization can ever answer the questions posed by the same civilization. Linguistics in, linguistics out. This is Story Theory.

Consciousness does not need the structure of linguistic criteria – as "*Is there a god?*" – to operate efficiently. God, after all, still unknown, is essentially a function of a human interrogative. We are still able to love, to feel, to wonder, and to search – better – by not having a clear answer to this imposed interrogative. To know if there is a god should not even be a goal, since we are certain that we have all the elements we need to expand our position from the perspective of *being in the room of expansive consciousness* – already. We have already entered the room (of consciousness).

What, then, is sentience? We know it as the condition of self-consciousness. Yet, we have to look hard to see it exactly. We struggle incessantly with linguistic bias to make a value of life – to form the still unformed cosmic consciousness. This is essentially a poetic function. All forms of life give off feedback imbued with a strange unknown bias. Space and time are already known to be malleable – as Einstein insisted. Accepted. Story Theory insists that all objects within consciousness can be manipulated (volume one). Poetry attempts the modification of the observed. Poetry demands the modification of the observed. Can the scientist make a similar demand?

The pattern of our consciousness, therefore, may be manipulated. Let us take this construct to its logical extremity. In effect, if you insist that your consciousness is eternal – then you create this reality of eternity in your apparition *within* Being. From this observation, we conclude there can be no form of sentience unless it is generated by our own minds – our own assertion of sentience. *Something* is demanding to be manipulated – to be worked – to be verified – with a still unknown bias. This charismatic form of sentience is unknowable – except that it exerts bias. Yet the bias of sentience must be a *communication* from a position of strength and permanence. And, if it is a communication, then, control of consciousness is within our reach. Since men are the supreme agents of communication (story) then all men are potentially epic poets. This is the case for poetry.

Human consciousness, then, is a communication. There is no form of life that does not consist of a communication of information. Human sentience must contain feedback – or there is no detection, no definition of life. Already this tells us much about the nature of consciousness. There must be a division of the substance of consciousness – since a *solid whole* cannot communicate with only itself – there must be at least two to make a communication. Every god of text needs his fallen angels to speak with. So there are separate entities. Men and stars take on this *apparatus of separate syllables of a single phrase.*

Being therefore must be a coil, connected, yet able to transmutate across equal and opposite sentient positions along the structure of life. We do not see all the integral components of sentience. We do not see the origin of gravity or love – yet we communicate with gravity and love. The coil seeks diversity ruthlessly – yet unified. Why? Because a value is required to be selected. An uncanny unity – in this case, conscious life – must divide in order to make sentient feedback to its component parts. Yet to maintain its unity, conscious life operates as a coil – separate at a distance and degree – yet allowing feedback and communication. Communication across the gird remains perfect, round, and just.

The communication, the sentient feedback, is the only actual manifestation of the permanence of the life source. Poetry connects, and reconnects – moves and prefigures – the differing degrees along the sentient coil. All speech is prophecy that can read the signals emitted across the other points of the coil. This is the mechanics of prophecy and poetry.

Sentience is a circuit that is racing through its notionally *spaced* coil to replicate its first source of energy. Sentience is consequently a layered division within the unified field of life. Knowing this, we make a new discovery. Sentience is evidence of *contact* with an alien entity that is demanding to be named. Something is teased; something is worked; something cannot be left alone. Sentience is evidence of contact with an alien presence. Sentience, itself, contains the alien, unknown, unfinished bias that we have been desperately trying to explore for millennia. All we have to do is to follow the fossil runes left for us embedded in the linguistic codes of the epic trope.

We already are arrived at our position of supremacy. We have entered the room. Are we secure in our position of supremacy? This response may certainly be conditioned by the clarity of our positions – the audacity of our linguistic goal. Language, alone, is our opportunity to manifest our supremacy by the assertion of supremacy. Consciousness is not a thing – it is a condition that we assert and demonstrate. Therefore, it is important that we assert and demonstrate a new linguistic consciousness according to the results that we seek. This is how poets and scientists work – they assert and demonstrate according to the result of consciousness that they seek.

Once in possession of a clear demonstration of a principle of consciousness, we can exploit our sentient feedback to seize control of consciousness itself – *no matter what is asserted against our position*. If it is suggested within consciousness that we are challenged – by adversities, disease, and death – it is clear that we may make an *equally potent* counter-assertion to support our well being. So long as we are *authorized* to give feedback, we *can* also deny a given condition of Being or assert an alternate condition of Being. The very fact that the human condition requires our manipulation of the unknown bias inherent in consciousness – indicates we have already made contact with the alien element of our consciousness. We are authorized to be in the room.

CHAPTER SEVENTEEN

The Alien Bias Embedded in Consciousness

There is a problem with human information. Information of *reality* is not human. Un-encoded information is alarming to human societies. Information *appears* – initially – not to contain human structure. Raw phenomena of life – that is, unpatterned information, unselected information – is alien information. Raw information is so alarming – so unusable – that only an intense investment of linguistic training allows humans to make intelligibility of life phenomena – through a restructuring of phenomena. A Bible, a text, an epic narrative – even a constitution – is required before a human can proceed to build a life of any meaning. Homer's *Iliad* gave a structure of value to Greek civilization. The entire universe has to be linguistically reconstructed to make any sense at all to the human brain.

The necessary human linguistic organization contains its own misprision. The essential difficulty is that pre-coding all perception with human linguistic patterns, human information is irretrievably biased. In other words, information of life cannot be empirically evaluated at all. Humans have so specialized in their necessary linguistic coding that if the human race would ever receive new or unanticipated information of the nature of Being – this new information would be greeted with hostility, incarceration, terror, or more likely, dismissed as nonsense.

In an age of pre-technology, in ancient India, for instance, the sudden appearance of a spaceship would be interpreted as a god on a flying carpet – as we see in ancient Indian Vedic epic poems. Linguistically, it would be impossible for a person of that time to accurately give a representation of the meaning or composition of the spaceship. Likewise, in an age of linguistically hegemonic science, any *actual* faith healing, any evidence of spiritual or charismatic power – which occurs daily in the human condition – is immediately dismissed as religious mania, as a mirage, as a cult, as an *unknown entity* – an event alien to modern linguistic formulation. The modern human, the result of linguistic training, essentially a strict materialist sensibility, could allow of no reality other than direct material or physical causation. The result? The modern world cannot explain or even acknowledge charismatic appearance of consciousness, sudden artistic insights, or even the rise of unforeseen charismatic leaders that change the course of human life. For this reason, modern information is arbitrary and conditional. The best definition we can make of human information is that a *poetic interpretation* is made with the *prevailing* linguistic coding. Thus, all information is poetic. Science and modernism, then, are forms of poetry.

When has it ever been different with human civilizations? Consequently, to a world looking for reliable evidence of *actual facts of Being*, modern information is useless. Information merely becomes what the prevailing linguistic pattern may accept. Modern justice, for example, is only a pattern that modern linguistic ideology can accept. Truth is only a pattern we accept within a narrative of a previously constructed story of human life. If the information (of life) does not fit our pattern of linguistic ideology – then this information is rejected harshly. Information, therefore, immediately takes the form of propaganda. Information, as a poetic protocol, becomes a function of Story Theory. How? Raw information is made to fit in a narrative of a previously constructed story. We will never find evidence of consciousness that does not require a human interpretation – an immediate and instantaneous transition to story.

In fact, raw information never reaches consciousness. The mind, as ego, makes a poetic interpretation of raw information – every time. What reaches the bedrock of human consciousness is a poem – an interpretation of raw, alien information. A child given a strange unknown object will endlessly tease it linguistically to make it fit into the child's world. The toy picked up from the carpet is not a toy car – it is the world's fastest racecar driven by the boy in a dangerous race. A doll that has lost its hair is not damaged – it is a doll that is in the hospital. The story process is instinctive and continues eternally. The child makes a story of an object and only then can an object fit in the world as *object*. A story must be made to construct a human link to any phenomenon in life. This human need is the justification for the protocol of poetry.

Yet there is peril. The human translation of information into story is a very dangerous protocol of sentience. It is essential that the poem we make of information does not destroy our being. Most humans, not understanding the translation of information, give full scope to their fears and misprision – leading to certain ideational destruction. We all know of persons who totally (and tragically) identify with the negative elements of their life. Nothing is more subversive to human life than when a stranger (doctor) tells us we have a disease that will kill us – and believing the language the doctor speaks, we accept the sentence of our death. Like the child, we make a story in our minds of the deleterious causation of the disease – we allow it to fit within our fear - until it is a story we feel we have no choice but to accept. The signature of modernism is above all else a total belief/fear of all forms of disease. We never get news of the failure of modern medicine – only the dubious success stories. Incessant daily advertisements inform the public that they will certainly have the disease advertised. We never get the information that any attack on our life source is an attack that can be countered. Thus vital information is suppressed. This is the major discovery of Story Theory: All linguistic and "*material*" challenges can be met with an opposite linguistic counter-attack – a further resort to sentience. It is a power that is neglected. This is exactly the failure of modernism. We are blocked by an idol (of linguistic modernism).

High Sentience Without Power Has No Value

It is a thesis of this book that high sentience has no purpose except as a source of power. It is a power essentially unexplored. Modernism attempts to disparage the power of the human metaphysical component. Modernism places power only in technologies, engines, formulae, kinetics, and money. Modernism, for example, displays revulsion and loathing when confronted with the sudden healing of diseases by purely mental protocols. This is because modernism, as a secular material ideology, does not privilege the linguistics of metaphysics. Non-material healing methods are a foreign dialect that engenders only fear and loathing. Linguistic modernism can only privilege the linguistic protocol of strict material causation. Again and again, I am asked: *Where is your machine that proves Story Theory?* This is the idiomatic demand of modernism – it wants and demands a machine. There must be a material *lever* or *prosthesis* involved with any modern construct – or it is not information to modern men. Modernism operates as if the power of mental agency is secondary in the expansion of human life. We need a machine to live. Where is your machine?

I disagree. My reading of Western literature indicates that the balance of opinion is on the side of poetic imagination over the evidence of strict (and recent) material supremacy. There was not even science before there was a story of imaginative alchemy. Alchemy is not a science; alchemy is a coded philosophy of metaphysics. Alchemy was a secret linguistic code of cosmology. Alchemy is essentially a mythic exploration of the secret (Hermetic) powers embedded in stars and elements. Alchemy, as the epic trope, is an emplacement of an astral religious interpretation. The chemists, the forerunners of scientists, began their hypothesis from this mythic exploration of Hermetic (astral) metaphysical formulas.

Technology was pre-imagined by literature. There was no space travel before the novels of Jules Vern. It is impossible that there were rockets to the Moon *before* there was a century of poetic imagination of travel to the Moon with rockets. *Literature* was the causation of a space faring civilization – not science. Science fiction came before science fact. Jules Verne first wrote of moon travel in 1870's – and the landing on the Moon did not *follow* until 100 years later. This evidence – of the necessity of imaginative literature (poetry) – contradicts the arrogant supremacy of strict material causation. Today, we cannot return to the moon since we still do not have stories that necessitate our return to the moon. Story Theory comes into outline.

Story Theory privileges the separate and independent ideational power of the human mind. In Story Theory, the human mind is a fully empowered agent, independent of the necessity of material causation. The mind is the source of all actual power – and linguistics is the means to release the mind's power. The world we experience is transformed by mental constructs, where the human is preeminently induced to re-imagine his world. In this perspective, the scientists, the architects, the engineers, the blacksmiths, the metal workers, the surgeons and the dentists – are only tributary human elements to the original imaginative and poetic source of human power. High sentience has no value if it does also not embed power. Poetry has no value if it does not contain a power that is felt and observed. There is no value of deity (life) without access to power. In so far as modernism denies the power of metaphysical imagination, it denies the human singularity. Any strong theory of poetry must correct the misuse of human faculties. Again, the main theme of *Chandos Ring*.

The belief of scientific medicine (as a linguistic idiom) is so great in the modern world that it is able both to heal and to kill. Yet it is *the mental* protocol that heals – not a causation of chemicals or surgery that is active (these are usually agents only of well-known and harmful *side effects*). Those who have seen the dehumanizing effect of modern medicine know exactly what I mean. Most moderns are not face to face with the madness of modern medicine until it is too late. Modern medicine creates as much disease as it claims to correct. Most surgeries are unnecessary and are profit-driven – leaving the human maimed, morally defeated, prostrate, and unable to make a strong moral counter-attack. Death sentences (of newly manufactured modern diseases) are delivered daily. The pharmaceutical industry daily finds new diseases to name and rename, so men will multiply their subscription to more industrial pharmaceuticals. Linguistics in, linguistics out.

New mental defenses must be also developed to counter the malignant suggestions of modern industrial medicine. It is not only the corruption of the interest of profit we accuse. It is not only the use of secret, unknown linguistics we accuse. The chief disability that is promoted is that industrial medicines rely upon a specifically material causation. A belief in strict material causation blocks all further human sentient development. The overwhelming faith and belief in "material causation" tend to cancel the efficacious potency of the original human mental power. This protocol attempts to cancel the power embedded in sentience – the proven power to overcome all crises, all malignance – by our further resort to superior mental and spiritual information. The linguistics of spiritual and metaphysical healing is not only proscribed in academic institutions – they are attacked and ridiculed. This is a crisis of modern information.

It is interesting to observe the contradictory language used by scientists to describe persons who inexplicably survive their confirmed diagnoses of terminal diseases. They disavow, insisting that it is mere speculation to attribute the patient's survival to any non-material source. This is a modern myth – and it is a complete abrogation of sentience. In truth, considering the hermetically sealed linguistic idiom of material science, it is impossible for science to explain how some people overcome their diagnosis of inoperable cancers. Spiritual healing is unintelligible data that is not recognized or processed by modern linguistics. It fits no linguistic pattern of secular materialism. This is the danger inherent in modern linguistics. If we cannot rely singly upon our mental and spiritual resources, we are that much less human. The machine makes the human mind into a machine. Modernism can only detect modernism. Becoming a material machine, we are less able to confront the charismatic nature of life.

The truth? In truth, each man only follows the logic of the language they use.

In Story Theory, the linguistic idiom the human accepts *equals* the power of life he accepts. If consciousness is beyond rational causation – then rationality is a faulted construct to explain the source and purpose of life. If this is true, then only poetry may be the medium that can translate charismatic events. Despite the propaganda embedded in the idiom of academic materialism, high human sentience (that is, the state of being self-conscious) is not of earth or fit to earth environment. The mammal body of man should never be confused with the otherworldly activity of the human mind. Who will deny that the human mind does not formulate, detect, and seek otherworldly activity?

If god (life) is unknown, it is because the mind of man is unknown. For this reason we say that human consciousness has an alien source.

CHAPTER EIGHTEEN

Our Minds Already Contain the Universe of Alien Phenomena

What does a strong line of poetry perform? Try to describe it. Is it only pleasure – or is there a vital element of life information that is decoded? Can the authority of a linguistic phrase create the condition of consciousness that it seeks? This is a proof of poetry. Only if such a statement is true can there be a strong theory of poetry. How else should we judge the success of a poem? If a poet cannot achieve the condition of consciousness that the poet seeks, his or her production of reality contains no information of the structure of life. If the poet achieves the condition of consciousness he seeks – then necessarily this new construction must be a modification of any previous (or given) human reality. And if consciousness can be modified, altered, reconstructed – then consciousness is still unfinished – and thus liable to seizure by a new idiom of life. There can be a new theory of poetry if consciousness can discover a new innovation of life. Thus, we say that poetry makes new life – new consciousness – possible.

We see that humans respond exactly to the linguistic speech of contemporary authority. Television, film, and prose exclusively replicate modern linguistics. Modernism in, modernism out. We are seldom surprised about the information we see in modern media and print. There is a reason for this. Modern men can only detect modern linguistics. This is why most of the information contained in these books appears, initially, hostile and aggressive. In truth, it is just new and unmodern.

No human wishes to be placed in disadvantageous relation to life. Yet this is exactly where modernism would attempt to fix us – dependant solely upon industrial materialism. Any arrival of malicious information (as disease) should engender a further emotional and intellectual development – not a stunned acceptance of an unfavorable position on the station of sentience (human life). When challenged by a peril of life, we must be free to make a further resort to consciousness to overcome that obstacle. We read with instruction and pleasure the message of the epic trope: *No problem, no horror, no attack on the human condition is outside the competence of consciousness.* This is the *heroic* act. If Story Theory has a crusading message, this is it.

Is conscious sentience dependent upon physical causation or upon mental manipulation? This is the controversy that places all our information in wild suspension. If sentience is a protocol of a strictly physical causation – then let us make plans for extinction now. Extinction is an ancient and honorable argument for this prospective. Let us drink and be happy for tomorrow we die. Yet it is the thesis of these books that there is no part of the human condition that is not susceptible to mental prerogative. Everything within consciousness can be manipulated by the sentient observer. I will try to make the case for this aspect of Story Theory.

It is impossible to discover consciousness outside of consciousness. This is the solid foundation of any competent philosophy of the human condition. This is a first clue that consciousness is a hermetically sealed, self-replicating organism. At an extremity of our prognostication, what does this discovery mean? Just this: The furthest Black Hole that can be charted is already contained in our mind. The furthest, still undiscovered cloud of nebula is already located within our consciousness. All still undiscovered planets are already located within our hermetically sealed consciousness. This is a radical and new statement in philosophy. It is not correct to say that stars in the universe are still undiscovered. Any uncharted cosmology is not "undiscovered" – it is only accurate to say that data still remains *unnarrated*.

According to Story Theory, there are no *things* – there are only *narrations* of things. All cosmologies – as assertions of new observations of science – are not discoveries – they are rather newly formulated narrations of value. What is our proof? If phenomena were not already contained in consciousness – then how could we make a sentient detection of phenomena? It is impossible. We build a linguistic supposition that a phenomenon may be new – but in reality it is only a newly constructed *narration* of linguistic value. *All* of life is *already* contained within the information of life (DNA). What part of your universe cannot be encompassed by the imagination? Not a single particle. Perhaps the ultimate thesis of Story Theory now begins to come into view.

We have had many universes. We had Ptolemy's universe, then Newton's, then Einstein's – and now String Theory. According to Story Theory, no phenomena are replicable since each manifestation of phenomena – each theory of universe (reality) – is a product of a human's one-time narrative. Is it not strange that each narrative of universe is incompatible with the previous narrative of the universe – that Ptolemy's universe cannot mix with Newton's – that Newton's text of reality cannot mix with quantum mechanic's protocol of reality, etc.? Each is mutually exclusive. That is because they are separate *narrations* already existing within consciousness. Any other way of explaining the cosmology of the universe would be to make the assumption that an object existed outside of human consciousness and magically entered our *dimension* – as a *deus ex machina* – complete with its own text and its own narrative. This never once happened – men had to be already on the scene – to make the narration and give a vision of value of universe. *Men with the same linguistic proofs may only see a single proof of universe.* This is a maxim. Stars do not suddenly appear – they were always in man's mind – firmly lodged within consciousness. Thus we say there is no great poem that does not move towards a cosmology.

Only humans may observe formations of objects. Only humans give narrations of value to objects. This alone should tip us off to the ideational process active in the representation of any *proposed* human reality. Consciousness, though unfinished, still in solution, is a sealed system. Everything we become conscious of *already* existed inside of consciousness. Man is the agency, the acidic element that settles the solution of consciousness – to fit the state of consciousness we seek. This, of course, is a new, even alternate linguistics. For this reason we say, in Story Theory, that the universe will not be understood until consciousness is understood. It is alarmingly simple. It also engenders hostility in the modern. They see no machine.

Humans are able to understand, or "chart," phenomena only as a function of sentience. Consequently, in the very moment of a *supposed* discovery – the moment of an *asserted discovery* – we have *already* named the observed phenomena and given a context for the same phenomena – a narrative – a story containing value. Thus the objects forming in the eyes are linguistically pre-structured and formulated. This is a new philosophical construct in Story Theory. The universe is formed and structured only as human consciousness *previously* organizes and patterns the contextual matter of the universe. Phenomena *within* universe are recognized *only* as humans linguistically formulate the structure of "out there." In other words, only the human mind poses the question: *Out there!* In the animal kingdom "out there" does not exist.

Only a human makes the assertion of an outside universe. This is a linguistic illusion. *"Out there"* does not exist – except as a linguistic assertion. Only the story-making mind formulates universe. Berkeley (d. 1753) was initially the human pioneer in this idiom. But the good bishop was in the awkward position of balancing dishes on a stick for Christian orthodoxy. European Christianity never practiced or accepted his ideas of the mind's supreme control of all human phenomena. He was ignored. Only the contextual superstructure of Story Theory insists upon the mind as the primary source of all evidence of the senses. It is not enough to assert the minds primacy for all visible sensation – there has to be a map – a superstructure of linguistics – to make it applicable for use – as a complete system.

A Further Resort to Sentience

Consciousness is first contact with a still unnarrated alien element. Human symbols are the single agency of recognizing a structure of value of consciousness. First, we say that the universe will not be understood until consciousness is understood. Second, we confirm by this statement that the required interpretation of physical matter (as ideationally observed) is essentially a poetic function. The fundamental singularity of men, then, is that they make a poetic transformation of phenomena by means of linguistics. This allows a degree of authority and primacy to any strong theory of poetry. We can modify our sentient condition by making a further resort to sentience. We can conform our use of linguistics to meet the desired conditions of our conscious state. Language is not only a second genetics – it is a second physics. This verifies the necessary *informational process* of poetry.

This is a perspective portending greater ideational freedom. This discovery is good news – it means we are potentially able to restructure consciousness. To restructure a thing – is to seize control of a thing. This discovery signifies that with the innovative (and audacious) structuring of our sentience we may seize control of Being. Life itself is under our sentient pressure. For the first time we may understand why the *Old Testament* epic poem insists that we "take dominion" of the world. We know the reason why. The universe will not be understood until consciousness is understood. A new theory of poetry must account for this discovery.

It is impossible to discover any object or phenomenon independent of sentient consciousness. So impossible is this action, so remote from human experience, that the first human to achieve such a breakthrough would be a god – and not a man.

We have said (alas, many times) that scientists perform as poets. This statement only *appears* to be radical to the modern. A poet performs the same function as the scientist – exactly. A Romantic makes a poem of a *particular hypothesis* of love, and the *exact hypothesis* of love appears that the Romantic seeks. He usually marries it. A businessman makes a plan of wealth, and that plan of wealth appears. A general makes a plan of war, and the plan of war appears. Lovers, poets, generals, and businessmen may fail many times before they arrive at the value of consciousness they seek. Failure is part of the linguistic protocol. My proof? Look how long scientists have been struggling to piece together a poem of reliable universe – and it stubbornly remains unreliable, unquantifiable – yet they persist in the poem of universe. Poets still try to make a unified theory of love – and the project is frankly hopeless. We cannot discover the exact source of love any more than we can find the exact source of gravity. If honest, it is the language of the scientist's love of his poem of cosmos – not so much the god of the cosmos. They love the poetry of the cosmos. They see that each star contains a unique fingerprint – a separate story and message. This is the love of the cosmologist. If he were severely honest, the scientist would reveal that, at the end, the universe is a linguistic phenomenon. This is the evidence of the primacy of poetry.

How poetic is our ideation? If the reader needs reminding, we still suffer from the poetic *theory* of the age of Romanticism – utterly dreamed up and linguistically coded by Romantic poets. We still suffer from the alien constructs of Romanticism. Romanticism is a closed linguistic system that does not account for its own misprision of enchantment – its own chaos. As any sealed linguistic code, Romanticism is self-referent. Romanticism cannot reform Romanticism – just as modernism cannot reform modernism – since both are self-referent linguistic constructions. Romanticism never actually works in real life – but it is still idealistically believed and honored in wasted lives. No one has ever survived a *romantic state*. This is because Romanticism was an artificial creation. Yet this is the power of poetry – as science is a power of poetry that now rules our world by linguistic precept and authority. Science is merely another romantic state of consciousness created by the poets of science. Science is the last romantic poem. Again, the reader will take a deep breath.

Story Theory verifies that there are no facts observable outside of consciousness. This is not a limit – this is an exponential expansion of universe. For the first time it is revealed that the universe – seemingly inferred to be so strange and distant – is really our *intimate, all-too-near universe*. The possibilities are exponential. Are we still constructing consciousness? Yes. We prove that consciousness is still unfinished (re. volume one). Then we may still lay down new uncanny structures within consciousness. It is morning in the mind.

Scientists violate this principle when they *presume* to observe a star, a comet, an atomic particle, etc. as something *outside* of our own consciousness. They are mistaken. The stars, comets, photons, electrons they observe are *utterly* under the control of human mental calculations – under the linguistic coding of the sentient observer. Anyone who has looked deeply into the implications of quantum mechanics cannot but conclude that science itself has confirmed the agency of the conscious mind – over *everything*! For the universe to *exist* and to *operate* an observer is required. Thus, significantly, the universe is a poetic construct.

It is the discovery of Story Theory that everything within consciousness can be manipulated by a further resource to the sentient condition. If we can see a star in space, or a troubled relationship, or a condition of the body, then these phenomena are *already* within our consciousness. Any otherwise, if any object were outside of consciousness, such an object could not be detected with our consciousness. Thus, objects of any structure cannot be perceived unless it is by the act of our interpretive – and linguistically patterned – consciousness. If the object observed – any visible or imagined object – is within our consciousness, then it can *subsequently* be modified to suit the conditions of linguistic application. This is *modification* of sentience (life) by a further resort to sentient intention (life). In this insight, it is verified that life is not an independent or self sustained entity.

Life is dependent upon the further *application* of life. Yet this step is always omitted. Humans make the mistake of assuming that life is already complete and self-sustained and there is no need for a further – and organized – application of the consciousness. Story Theory identifies this lost protocol. In all cases, our modifications of sentience (life) are effective only after a further application of intention – of sorrow, of rage, of joy, of passion. The cry of a prayer or poem is powerful.

Consciousness is a sealed cosmology. If there are no independent phenomena to observe – if every object is under the influence and translation of a story-making human mind – then empirical science cannot exist as a separate discipline of human knowing. Scientism, as romanticism, as Fascism, as racism, is a poetic assertion of human information. Scientism is not empirical, objective information at all. Consequently, any claim to any independently existing observed phenomenon, any supposed new discovery that is external of human consciousness, is a poetic representation of fact – a narrative of someone's text – a form of literature.

If the still unknown – that is, the still *un-narrated* – phenomena within consciousness appear, we make a narration to fit the conditions of our consciousness – every time. Consciousness is first contact with the still undiscovered alien element.

We know that poetry seeks alien contact. When the strong poet achieves his mastery, all the clues of alien contact are evident, both to the poet and the surprised reader. All strong poetry is the presentation of the *strange* we are able to detect. The strong poet is not satisfied with a sentimental replication of previous beauty – there is something far more uncanny desired. The poet is not at rest until his idiom, somehow, has performed the miraculous. What is the condition of the miracle? It is when the poet has reproduced a new dimension of strange ideation – uncanny, unexplained in its origin or its arrival. It is a strange new voice of power. The alien, unknown element is still not fully detected; yet it is reachable by the human poet. This is the source of the poet's power.

The poet seeks the strange. And this is a clue of the origin of the human mind. The miracle of the poet's detection of the *strange* is understood when we discover that the strange, so alien, so unexpected – is still immediately recognized and embraced. This proves that the *supposedly* unknown alien element is still intimate, as if it was placed in consciousness for our discovery. The discovery of what? Future human life – since we can recognize the immediate attraction of the strange. When the poem's beauty is strange and suddenly idiomatic, the poet knows he has found an important divergence of the linguistic route. It is a direct path to the origin of the human mind.

It is one thing to write poetry. It is another thing indeed to compel attention to what you write. Modern poetry does not compel the attention of the modern public. It is the thesis of these books that modern poetry fails because the modern poet does not find a language to tell a story of new human life, that he or she does not discover the strange alien element of information. Modern poets fail because they do not detect strange, unmodern information – the strange rune that fascinates – as it compels you to give up faith in your normal, conventional life.

To perform this great and difficult work, that is, *to compel attention*, the poet must forgo the lyric form, since in no other way can the modern poet outreach the tired limits of his own insignificant personality. This is exactly the mistake that is made. The modern lyric form must be largely abandoned for a time. It may be reinvented at another time and by a more advanced human. But the modern lyric is dead. It contains neither information for contemporary humans nor any innovation of future speech.

If modern poetry does find a marginal market, it is a market for tawdry biography. We don't read Sylvia Plaith's poetry, we read about her melodrama. If poetry is to reach beyond biography, as most modern poets are remembered for some biographic scandal, then it must recover the power to tell a story. But it won't be with the self-absorbed lyric form. We do not love poets who make a fruitless, desperate search for some scrap of meaning, some single syllable of value in the modern poet's life – where there is none. To compel attention, the poet might better wish to tell a story and invent a strange new linguistic idiom, at times jarring, at times uneven, with which to portray that strange, yet recognizable world. It is an argument made in *Chandos Ring*.

Much has been made of the term *inspiration*. Any inspiration must still be imbedded in the consciousness. An inspiration is an influence that is self-contained and circles in upon itself. This a perfect description of the linguistic prism – language is self-contained and circles in upon itself. When a poet insists he has been inspired, he has only found an idol to obsessively serve. It is usually an object of Eros (lyric) or rage (epic). Inspiration is the expertise of the poet – every poet understands his inspiration. His conscious observation is so strong that he alters the observed. Yet the linguistic result of inspiration is so strange, so unlike the personality of the poet, so unlike the everyday human, that it has been previously and euphemistically attributed to a detached muse. This is merely a rumor circling around a rumor. In fact, this discovery of strange idiom is the code embedded in consciousness to make a further enchantment of the life source.

Life (consciousness, god) is essentially strange – and we have to continually reorganize life according to the population of our strong poets. That is, we must poetically retranslate, re-code the newly arrived information to our idiom. Poetry contains the information of how this alien consciousness operates. Any negative human condition may be countered with an opposing resort to human sentience. Poetry, as any healing process of the soul, is a further resort to the information that arrives from sentience. There must be a reply – and not only the reply of the coward. We seek a feedback of courage and audacity. A further resort to sentience is a resort to an alternate physics. Until this is understood, then my idea of poetry will not be understood.

Poetry is the strange prefigured. Poetry is idiomatic information resting unfinished in somatic prescience. This sentence is the entire text of a new theory of poetry.

How else may we understand the verse, "And if they should drink any deadly thing, it should not hurt them?" This is strange. This statement of epic poetry is initially counter-intuitive – until it is realized that it represents our *only* salvation from the dire predicament of modern information. What does poetry insist upon if not an appeal to an alternate physics? Human life demands *in every instant* a further resort to *alternate* sentience. What is a crisis, except a need for *alternate* information? What is a severe illness, if not a need for a further resort to *alternate* and more potent information? Any peril of the human condition – and the perils are loud, jarring, and many – is a wild search for still unknown information – information, moreover, as a new radical solution. In every case, it will be discovered that the *solution* has a linguistic structure. Therefore, human life demands a poetic translation in every human event.

This is very strange. It means that poetry is a reliable place of human sanctuary. It means that sentience is contact with an extra-terrestrial intelligence. Poetry is contact with the message of the stars. The alien element – life yet so distant and uncharted – is still lodged intimately in our receiving faculties. All alien contact is exactly structured *within* consciousness. Thus we ourselves will determine, summon, and formulate future contact with alien life.

At that time we will discover we resemble them.

CHAPTER NINETEEN

Experimental Applications of Story Theory

Which interpretation of the universe will the future poet construct? Based on past revolutions of the perspective of the universe, it is certain that it will appear wildly different than the conjectures of the present day. Reality is a movable feast. In quantum theory, as poetry, the physical matter of which the terrestrial earth consists cannot be verified as existing or being located in space at all. In quantum physics, the *necessary* interpretation is made when the human observer collapses the wave function into a single point and fixes its sudden position. In other words, a human observer modified the observed with the entanglement of his mind. One conclusion is made. Whether you are a materialist, a scientist, an agnostic, or a spiritualist – a sentient *interpretation* of phenomena is required to be made by the sentient perceiver. Either way, I can proceed with a verification of the primacy of the poetic structure of reality.

Science, by application of the new discoveries of Story Theory, becomes a poem made by poetic humans – a form of literature. What does this mean? The meaning is that we can seize control of still unfinished consciousness – that is, life itself. The meaning is that we can make a new theory of poetry. This new theory of poetry may heal the long schism between vernacular and scientific languages. Both perspectives of Being (scientific and vernacular) are human poems – both are a hypothesis of human linguistic coding. We take information – and recode it linguistically to our purpose. This is the protocol of Story Theory active in every human brain.

The unavoidable element of consciousness is that the observer must make a translation of what he *presumes* he sees or knows. *Therefore*, it is impossible for the human – even the human scientist – not to operate as a poet. The reader cannot forbear to make a translation – a judgment – of the validity of the visible world of phenomena. In both classical and quantum physics, then, an *interpretation* is unavoidable. Any act of human *interpretation* is an immediate and unavoidable transition to Story Theory. Moreover, unlike the crisis present in contemporary physics, Story Theory is a unified theory since both large and small phenomena (in Story Theory) are subject to modification by the observer. Contemporary physics insists upon *separate* laws of physics for very large and very small things. Story Theory includes *everything* in the purview of the human perceiver. This is vital information for a new theory of poetry.

The newly perceived protocols of Story Theory answer the question of how humans have been able to perform supernatural acts – the healing of terminal cancers, the recovery from horrific medical diagnoses, the revival of success for certain failure, the overcoming of impossible adversity, the discovery of new forms of Being. These are not supernatural miracles. Phenomena occur *within* consciousness. All phenomena – both the apparent terror of crisis and the miracle of solution – have sentient components. Both the terror and the miracle of any human situation are utterly elements of sentience. They are both located *within* consciousness. They need to be faced with courage, decision and audacity necessary to make a reconstruction. According to Story Theory, the human has the linguistic ability to deny or accept any desired state of consciousness. There is a physics that seems to be controlled by atomic theory. We are well versed in this everyday physics of solid matter. Then there is a *second physics* that seems to be controlled by the human mind. What choice of physics – as information – should we trust?

When confronted with the terror of a supposedly physical manifestation, we should make a further resort to sentience (consciousness). Moderns fail to do this. This is a serious miscalculation. Any disease or physical manifestation is under the control of consciousness. There is no other way to observe a disease or a healing except by *sentience*. A human observes a crisis by his sentient faculties. Instead of surrendering to the fearful consequence of what, after all, is only a linguistic formation (physical matter) – a *further resort to sentience is available.* A doubling down, as it were, is the key to apparent miracle events (i.e. non-physical causation). A further resort to linguistically determined consciousness operates as a second physics. Therefore the terror experienced in sentience is a membrane consciously connected to the observed sentient solution – all within a sealed organism of consciousness. A healing of terminal cancer may certainly seem a heroic achievement of the manipulation of consciousness. But it is in no way a miracle – it is only a further resort to an alternate linguistics – an alternate physics. Linguistics is merely a manipulation of consciousness. With Story Theory we attempt to master this protocol.

We each modify consciousness to fit the conditions of life we seek. There is no other explanation of the purpose of human life – we attempt to linguistically manipulate the conditions of life to fit our ideal of life. Only close observation and practical experience gives sufficient mastery to the protocol. Life is just long enough to learn to manipulate consciousness. So long as the sentient solution is as real as the sentient terror (no matter how real the peril may seem *at first*), the entire protocol is resolved within the sealed coil of sentient consciousness. It is impossible to escape this logic if we remember the maxim of conscious observation – that *the conscious observer changes the observed*. This is a fixed law, and it contains the force of any affirmation we need to make a resort to a further (and heroic) use of sentient formation. Thus, consciousness is an epic trope.

According to Story Theory, no phenomena may occur outside of sentient perception. By this logic we test that the use of an opposing application of consciousness may counter any challenge arising inside of consciousness. Any application of thought, fear, or alarm may be modified in turn by an opposing application of consciousness – by whatever force we are pleased to call it. It's a sealed system of sentient recognition. Sentience is hegemon.

Healing of cancers without medicines, surviving falls without parachutes, etc., may certainly be called heroic recoveries – but in Story Theory they are not miraculous acts of a supposed deity operating outside of physical reality. Resolutions – that is, solutions to any human crisis or disability – are already contained within the sealed hermetic structure of still unlimited, still unfinished consciousness.

If a human detects a problem with sentient perception, then in turn, a further sentient observation is equally able to recover a solution – no matter how desperate – by the same protocol. Sentience is a sealed, hermetic linguistic coil. This is important, since, if there is a problem identified by sentience – then the solution is also a resort to sentience. That is to say, all problems and solutions are mental constructs – all within our control. Science ignores this protocol, and, when a cancer appears, it is considered to be something like a bizarre crisis of material failure and must be attacked with material constructs – such as heroic surgeries or toxic pharmaceuticals. Yet all of life calls out for a further resort to *sentience* – not a resource to matter. This is the lesson of human life that Homo sapiens have never learned. The genes of Homo sapiens must be improved again. This is the story line of *Chandos Ring*.

Story Theory asserts the observation that the bias in consciousness moves toward the light – not the darkness. We know this since all literature moves toward the light. Human life seeks *something* as opposed to *nothing*. We seek light – not extinction. Our only proof for this assertion is the experience that when men strive for honest actions – just acts – they are empowered with uncanny strength. Health appears able to make a claim for justice *of health*. Life appears able to make a claim for the justice *of life*. Nothing can resist a well-argued appeal to justice – not for long. Yet who makes the cry of justice? We turn to lawyers and medical doctors when we seek health and justice. So our health and justice are degraded, and thus, we are not, ourselves, the agents of health and justice. This is not a correct response to the sentient life that we insist that we love so well. We ignore the greater part of sentient life. Only a few are awake to full human sentience.

This is not such a radical concept. What, after all, is our life except a sentient *imagining* of each day and each event? What part of our life is not exactly, precisely, immediately tied to our sentient reflex? When do we not imagine the life we wish to have? Do we not keep the image of the life we imagine before our eyes continually? Is not imagination, itself, an appeal to sentience? What is love, or Eros, except that it is heightened by our sentient reaction to our imagination? We do not live only in the first instance of love – we imagine loving before we experience love. In fact, many persons would insist that sexuality, beauty, and romance are *utterly* an imaginative stimulant. Sex is in the mind. Romance is in the mind. Success is in the mind. Defeat is in the mind. Health is in the mind. Is it so radical to insist that pain, or harmful crisis, or death are merely an additional application of sentience – and thus, able to be countered by an opposite assertion of sentient intent? Theses protocols are tested daily. Each human works a lifetime to modify his life to fit the level of consciousness he seeks. All the power of the universe is on the side of the practitioner of sentience. We are already authorized to be here. Life is a powerful position. We are well placed to take dominion.

The critic will note that I have not advocated any national god or advanced the denomination of any established religion – *nor* do I deny any agency of deity. The attitude of the human operator is important. If you intend to accept only the negative sentence of peril – the one-sided prognosis of disease, for example – what is the use of your fully sentient mind? The power and effect of the mind is lost – with surrender. If, on the other hand, you intend to counter any peril with a recovery of sentient power – then I suggest this is the proper intention of human sentience. If you have great emotion at the outset of a crisis, you will need to summon an equally powerful effort of emotion (of calm, of confidence in the reversal of malicious formations) to counter the original undesired condition. Sentience in; sentience out.

The human crisis and the human solution are manifestations of the same theorem principled in sentience. Only the refusal of the active mind to employ this insight may block the satisfactory working of the equation. Certainly, the mastery of sentience by the human mind may be a limiting factor – but we do not refuse to learn Japanese or Russian only because it requires mastery of a new alphabet. We fortify ourselves with the passion to learn difficult tongues. The potentiality to seize control of a still unfinished consciousness was always there. Any product of sentient registry can be met with an opposite assertion of sentient registry.

The opportunity to live beyond the body and operate as a god ("*made in His likeness*") was always felt intuitively – only because it was actually a skill set embedded in consciousness. Every challenging life experience we survive reinforces the protocol of heroic solutions. Reconstruction of human life is the only way to escape from a previous linguistic predicament. The epic trope reorders human life along new superstructures of ideation. We live by sacred texts and precepts, by stories that invite application. Each of us makes a story of the experience of peril in life. Therefore, we say that human life follows an epic trope.

We have our proof. The question centers on the relevance of our honesty. Every person who is told he or she has a serious medical condition knows exactly why he or she has arrived at that condition. Every person told he has lung cancer or throat cancer knows exactly what has caused that cancer. Every person that receives a court judgment knows exactly why he has been judged. Everyone who is accused knows exactly why he is accused. People in a bad relationship at home or at work know exactly why they suffer from the relationship. Every person that has lost a relationship knows exactly why he or she has been left behind. Everything we need to know – the cause of the crisis and the solution of the crisis – is already contained within a self-sealed consciousness. There are no magical arrivals of information from *outside* of consciousness. We have the facts of consciousness always before us. We are only too dishonest – too much like children – to admit responsibility for the facts of our consciousness. We want the state, doctors, courts to care for us – to pick up the pieces of our lives.

Modern men simply refuse to turn and face the painful and frightening elements of our responsibilities of consciousness. We prefer to hire strangers to do the mental battle for us – and this protocol has its own destructive message. We may deny the justice of sentience, yet, when we are alone in our thoughts, we know exactly how we reached a chaotic place of consciousness. Like love and death, life is a question of courage. We have to take dominion.

One needs only to enter into the act of life to test this thesis – that each person struggles to modify consciousness to fit the conditions of life he seeks. We receive feedback from life and we make a counter response. Some surrender at the first sentence of horror and peril. Some wrestle with the predicament of life endlessly until a value is demonstrated – until a recovery is made with power. What interpretation shall you make of your own experience of life? Does the reader not observe that he or she steps closer to heroic recovery in each moment of sentient life? Or do we retreat into death?

This supremely human interrogation is the origin of the epic trope. If any alien civilization might have ever farmed the earth, they would prize only one product of the human mind. It would not be high technology – they have that already. They would wish only to harvest our epic story (poem); they would ask for our Beethoven. *Only* humans could innovate consciousness in this direction. All else would be as dross to them.

CHAPTER TWENTY

Two Failed Questions of Modernism

There is one generous salvation embedded in human linguistics. All questions posed by men are essentially moot. That is, there is no fixed or eternal reality perceived by humans. Reality, in the end, is only a linguistic illusion. Every civilization is only a linguistic representation of reality. Every human question forever unanswerable by speech will become irrelevant by the next idiomatic innovation of speech. When the human language changes – as with the rise of new civilizations – so do the questions posed by the *previous* interrogative human. The medieval church, for example, could not resolve the question of the precise composition of paradise or how the stellar bodies were exactly organized – as they could not resolve why the planet Jupiter had four large moons. These questions became irrelevant when the *civilization* of Scholastic Catholicism was replaced with the *civilization* of modern secular materialism. With the victory of a secular civilization (linguistic modernism), the question of angels, souls, and moons were no longer in a crisis of information. The interrogative of angels, souls, and stars was re-configured with a new linguistic context. But is modernism any more reliable? Is it correct in its representation of reality? Is modernism correct for all time? If not, *then what will replace modernism?* If something *will* – then my case is made – and we may already subsume modernism with innovation. *World* is a linguistic *and* prosthetic superstructure.

What happened that allowed modernism to represent *world*? A linguistic revolution was constructed. A new linguistic civilization was formed – and the new linguistics (of modernism) made the questions of the older civilization (of Scholastic Catholicism) seem nonsensical. Why is this historical linguistic transition important to observe? Because the same revolution awaits *our* civilization.

No civilization answers the questions it poses. Previous questions are simply replaced with new unanswerable human questions. In the epic trope, it is not important that we know the name of god – to know the name of god is impossible.

It is only important that we search for the value of a missing god. This is the human situation. By this protocol, at least, we retrace the origin of our mind – and thus the origin of human life itself. This is the use of Story Theory.

Scientists have convinced their followers that, being a material construct, the universe is a dead thing. If science proved there were four large moons, and that there was a heliacal solar system – then that ended the linguistic authority of Catholic theology (based on Ptolemy's seven crystalline spheres). No one looked to the Church any more for reliable information of modernism. There was a new materialistic language created to answer a new set of questions: *What is the secret of matter and how do we exploit more of it?* After the next linguistic revolution, modernism will be seen as equally risible, odd, and unreliable. So we move ahead to our goal.

This is how Story Theory operates. There is no *exact* verification of the human condition. There is only an accepted linguistic pattern that is self-referent, allowing men to act as if all their questions are answered – or are soon to be answered. There are thus many myths that arise out of the human predicament. What else then is real except our narratives – our myths? The ancient myth of the *Chosen People* is a linguistic construct – one still fought over in the streets today in Palestine. The 600 laws of Moses would verify – by 600 separate *linguistic* compacts in *Leviticus* – that the Hebrews were the chosen people. This is a linguistic construct. The modern myth of science, likewise, is a linguistic construct. Science is supposedly – shortly – nearly – soon – if only given enough time – about to answer all the questions of modernism. The Christian myth was a linguistic construct. Christ was always to return in his power to judge the good and evil – his parables of severe authority confirmed the Second Coming – linguistically. The point? Every high civilization linguistically proclaims the imminent substantiation of all *information*. Each system contains its own self-referent linguistics. Every civilization is inherently insidious.

The difficult questions of every civilization are never answered – there is only the linguistic illusion that they may – one day – be answered. In fact, when the future arrives, the burning questions of every civilization are made irrelevant by the newly formed linguistic code of the subsequent generation. Why should we assume that modernism is exempt from this movable feast? We know the truth. A civilization's highest terror, hope, and preoccupations are made irrelevant and replaced by a subsequent pattern, a subsequent innovation in linguistics. To the severe philosopher, so anxious to solve present human preoccupations, it is breathtaking to make this discovery. There is no way out except by death or a strong narrative – a text of power.

Modernism fails to answer two questions that men have always posed in their literature. The first: How may we obtain more life? The second: What form of human life is superior?

Modernism no longer has the courage to address these human interrogatives.

How can there be a strong theory of poetry that fails to address these questions? These questions accuse modernism.

First, modernism rejects the investigation of any form of life that does not contain a corporal and secular body. Thus, modern men scorn any form of prophecy as solid information. Second, the dialectics of a racially mixed democracy forbids any opinion that seems to disparage another culture. Thus, modern men cannot assert with audacity their cultural idiom to the full extent of our wish. White men must curb their cultural enthusiasm – or be attacked. The hypocrisy of these positions is profound. In truth, we all feel our own culture is superior to all other linguistic tribes. In truth, we all search for evidence of spiritually constructed eternal life and feel it instinctively. Despite the alternate propaganda of modernism, all men seek prophecy. When the most ridiculed soothsayer looks into a man's palm and says, "I see your life . . ." – at that moment the silence of the room is profound, as all humans turn their attention to the prognostication. Modernism is not honest speech. Modernism forces men to speak in a way that does not imitate actual human thoughts. Thus, modernism must be an agent of surveillance and censorship.

These are the two questions that cannot be addressed with competence by contemporary speech: What is the best life form and who are the beautiful? Is the spiritual form of man the most beautiful – do we construct our value of life to prepare for eternity – or is it our goal merely to increase the mortal lifespan of the physical body for the greatest number possible? We know the answer – and thus this is a dilemma important to the poetry makers. We are no longer allowed to promote specifically the excellence of English – or especially the Anglo-Saxon perspective of literature – we are compelled to allow other demographic bodies to assert their ethnic and ideological languages. Modern speech seeks to proscribe public discussions of spiritual matters – but actively protects and encourages a discussion of the scientific methods of getting a few more years out of the human body. A strong theory of poetry would block the political compunction of modernism. Why? Since organized writing always precedes organized action, we must decide what is the superior form of poetry. We must decide if modern poetry contains reliable information. Ultimately, this will not be resolved without war and cataclysm. An entire civilization must disappear and be linguistically reorganized. This is work of the epic trope.

The deserts of ancient Sumer contained the clues we sought. With the discovery and full translation of the ancient cuneiform tablets in the 1970s, suddenly speculative thinkers and poets were able to assemble the information contained in the first epic poems. We trace our evidences back to the question posed by Gilgamesh. This earliest human epic poem was the first human textual linguistics. What was the intention of the first epic poets? To know this is important, since we wish to identify the epic spleen.

Each epic poet seeks only one question: *How do we identify and celebrate the best and the beautiful?* That is, *What is the value of human life?* The epic trope has only one narrative: *How do the best men ensure and verify more life, more personality – more space, more time?* Not all men – only the *best* men surely.

Who makes this choice – of the best manners of the best men? It has nothing to do with actual truth. How could there be an empirical verification of the best men? Impossible. So it must be an assertion of audacity – specifically a poetic assertion of audacity. Strong poets need to be free to achieve this audacity of expression. This is how great civilizations operate – they control the ideational space and assert their representation of beauty. Modernism blocks this freedom – specifically, by insisting that all values are equal – and thus there is no value. The result? The idea of the great and noble achievement of the European civilization, for example, becomes forbidden speech. This is the crisis of Western men of European descent and allegiance.

Every civilization has attempted to answer the epic question of Gilgamesh: *I am a prince of men – therefore, how may I obtain more of life?* Gilgamesh did not ask how may all his people gain immortal life – only himself. *Achilles, Aeneas, Jason, Odysseus, Dante* did not look for the salvation of all men - only the salvation of select co-peers. This makes the blood of modern men run cold with surprise and confusion. The principle modern myth is that 10 billion humans may be chosen people (middle class). There will be war and cataclysm over this myth.

There is more. I have discovered a hidden narrative pattern in the epic poems. Each age of text was influenced by the star constellations – directly, overtly, literally. The careful poet will scan immediately the connection between the presiding constellation – Taurus, Aries, Pisces – and the method by which the interrogative of *"more of life"* is achieved in the epic narratives. In the age of Taurus (the bull), Gilgamesh tried to gain immortal life by force. In the age of Aries (the ram), Hebrews, Spartans, Greeks, and Romans tried to secure the supremacy over other peoples by the observation of strict laws. In the age of Pisces (the fish), the text of Jesus announced that immortal life was to be gained by grace (proliferation). This is the treasure codex of epochal communication – the key that may be used to measure all the human texts from the earliest days. How can we gain the supremacy of life – by force, by laws, by love, or, now, (under Aquarius) by selection? The poet immediately is able to line up the texts with their epochs and the surprising position of the constellations. A pattern suddenly comes into view.

Alerted, suddenly we ask: What new constellation just now appears in the night sky?

What do men want? Modernism endlessly rings its hands over this interrogative. The answer is easy to list. We want more space, more time, more personality – more life. We do not want to understand the supposed final form that consciousness has already taken. This is a prospect of terror. What if life has taken a form we cannot accept? No. We want to seize a *still unformed* consciousness to fit a condition of life we seek. All humans attempt to modify life to fit the condition of life they seek. Every human. No exception. At some level this will appear a new discovery. Yet it is an ancient and – necessarily – an ancient linguistic process. We want life to be monumental and replete with a meaning that we can affirm linguistically (art, beauty, song, architecture, story) and enjoy seamlessly – without abridgement or chaos.

Is this goal realistic – or even sound? This is a question no human idiom could give an uncontroversial answer to – so subsequent human civilizations always changed the dialectics. No age of man finds its final answer to the question posed. All man can do is make a myth of his desire. Wish is an act of poetry. Then, of course, we are back to the requirement for a strong theory of poetry. This is the epic cycle: *How to seize (and thus modify) the life force?*

Modernism has framed questions that can no longer be answered by the idiom of liberal materialism. We have isolated two of these unanswered questions. There are more. We have asked, as all moderns have asked: *Who is free (that is, who is selected)? Is it any people possessing a constitution that protects human rights – or is it any people who manage to keep the government from intruding in their lives? Is it only those people best able to access industrial medicines? Are those people most free who possess technology?* Modernism is unable to give an answer to these questions since it has already lost control of the subject – of the meaning of freedom. Every modern is under twenty-four-hour surveillance. Due to the rise of intrusive technologies, the quality of freedom no longer has a possible definition. Freedom is moot. Thus, there needs to be a new civilization – and a new linguistics – to account for this seismic shift.

Technology has made the meaning of *modern* freedom as useless as science had previously made the Medieval Church useless to Western men. Technology is essentially useless as information. Technology is unable to answer the questions posed by the charismatic appearance of new, unforeseen structures. It is now irrelevant to ask who may be free. We are all under precise and intimate surveillance of technology. Only in space may we now seek sanctuary from totalitarian control. We must hide in the hidden cavities of the universe to secure ourselves from the surveillance of the modern idiom. Then we are faced with the horrible contradiction that we must take our machines with us.

As technology allows continual tracking of the human in every sphere of modern life, how can men under *intimate* surveillance be considered free? Why even bother to pose the question? What has occurred? Modernism has been supplanted by a new linguistic idiom; modernism is no longer able to control information or answer questions the modern civilization poses. Technology (linguistics) makes all previous questions of modernism moot. We do not know who shall now be free, or rich, or favored, or well-contented. Technology (as any self-referent linguistics) has only one response to all human questions: we need more technology. How will the human survive this linguistic holocaust? What lies at the end of the road?

Do we recognize the linguistic pattern? Technology has now become a self-sealed linguistic echo chamber. We have seen this before. This was exactly the linguistic formula of Catholicism. Every answer of the medieval Age of Faith, every question that could be posed by the Catholic theology could also be answered by Catholic theology. Medieval theology had only one response to human questions: to apply more Church theology.

In our own lifetime we recall the answers of modernism. Every question posed by modernism could be answered only with the need for a further application of modernism. Modern societies have only one answer to world problems – *more modernism*. Even today, we don't see the problems of the world in an unbiased light – we see only answers that can be supplied by modernism. We do not feel that African societies are evil or corrupted. We do not clearly see that nations who overpopulate their natural resources should be proscribed. We only consider that they need more industrial medications. More pills. More genetic crops. More industrialism. More science. More television. More hygiene. In short, *more modernism*. Yet each of these utterly mistakes the actual conditions of chaos in Africa – or Bangladesh, or India, or Pakistan – or Earth. The evil is *proliferation* in deserts – not the failure to obtain modernism.

Not once in modern dialectics do we discuss the injustice and chaos of the proliferation of impoverished lands. We refuse to accuse the poor and indigent of mindless proliferation. Why? Because we refuse to face the issue of consciousness itself. Consciousness selects. This message frightens the modern today – at the setting of the age of Pisces. The age that struggled for brotherhood and freedom (Pisces 0-2100 A.D) was large and terrible in its contradictions. Now a ruthless scythe arrives at our station – the Age of Aquarius. Consciousness abhors mindless, helpless, blameless proliferation. What modern would even dare to address the issue of selection outside of the linguistics of modernism? What demagogue of democratic counselors would dare allow a speech intending severe selection? Not a single Western leader has even the courage to accuse modernism of containing unreliable information. Consciousness, as love, as death, as life, first demands courage. Modernism has no moral courage. When a selection of life is cried out for – what is superior, what is best, what view of life is to be privileged? Moderns will turn away in horror. They will look for their democratic demagogues for protection. Their time is short. Let us hope they die well.

What form of human life is superior? It is a stunning and refreshing interrogative. It is as fresh as the small rain from a spring sky. What civilization is superior to all others? What form of life can we advocate over other forms of life? After WWII - after the Holocaust - it is a question that is forbidden in modern dialectics – but it is still a living interrogative in the heart of every child of the Age of Aquarius. It is hidden but present. It is the secret interrogative on the minds of all men. Unanswered for so long, it will burst with rage. That these questions are forbidden in public spaces only verifies their true source of emotional power. The Best will not be mocked.

We have found the dark, rotten core of modernism. It cannot advocate what is superior in men – only what is superior in machines. This is the key deficit of modern dialectics – as exposed by Story Theory. There cannot be a strong theory of poetry until we resolve the issue of what form of human life, what form of human idiomatic gesture, is to be advocated as superior. As we have seen, this is a trope of the epic cycle. Yet this is a question that makes the modern linguist cringe and look about the room in horror. Germany, Britain, Russia, and American genocide of brown peoples has forever disallowed Western modernism to address which form of human life is superior. Any further selection by Western men – any further reduction of Earth populations to fit the conditions we seek – has been proscribed under liberal and dialectic modernism. We have become a victim of our own liberal propaganda. This holocaust mentality has forever shamed the West from any critical use of its faculty of severe judgment. The grim and precisely documented murders of Hitler and Stalin, of American, French, Belgian, and British Imperialists in the 19th century, have made Western modernism a wounded morality that may only justify its hegemony with a promise of ethnic proliferation. The West now follows *exclusively* the single remaining, still bright and burnished idiom – the untarnished hope and promise of technology. It is only a new holocaust.

So, as moderns, we align ourselves with hypocrisy. Modernism scrupulously avoids the very questions modern humans want answers to: *What form of life is superior? What form of life should be selected above other forms of life? What is the best form of human – and who are our worthy co-peers? What is the highest form of language these men should have?* If these questions cannot be addressed, much less answered – then we are mindless robots – merely proliferating, merely breathing. This mentality has a direct influence on our educators, poets, and intelligencia. Can professors of modern poetry pose their question of what form of poetry is superior? No. Any assertion of superiority can be proscribed with the modern slurs of imperialism or racism. Modernism therefore cannot decide this critical issue. It is a state of madness, chaos, and hypocrisy. Rather, we should be strong. We should be ruthless.

So we arrive at the core problem of a strong theory of poetry – modernism (as a surveilling, monitoring, intrusive, political correctness) can neither pose the question of what *is superior*, nor cite a strong example of what is superior. Therefore, modernism cancels itself from the discussion of a strong theory of poetry.

Chandos Ring attempts to move ahead of modernism to make a new linguistic coding of the poetic medium. Organized writing comes before organized action. Poetry is selection. The question is – who may decide what is superior?

CHAPTER TWENTY-ONE

What Do We Say to the Dead?

I had to ask about death. I could not find its information at the crossroads. I could not discover its meaning from the stranger on television. I could not locate a reliable account of death in the suburbs of a thousand American cities. Death seemed to be everywhere, but there was no language to describe death. Everyone I know had an experience of death. Yet it was muted, smothered with pillows and electric wires. When asked about death, men were silent – almost ashamed. The citizens' experience of death was muted, secondhand – and, moreover, the recent dead were never exact in their information or location.

We ask the dead to show us their hands. They are sooty from other dimensions. We say to the dead that we have read their poem of value. We would tell them that their message of death still remains within our consciousness – whether the dead be our fathers or our brothers of the first epic poems – *Gilgamesh, Hector, Moses, Hercules, Thoth, Osiris, Orpheus, or Jason*. There is always the matter of our own response; it may be given in any human century – as the constellations have no expiration of the epic trope. We find we have much to say to the dead. Our hearts are full. We write new texts. We name new planets and new worlds.

We give, in return, our response – our own poem of value – yet one that must *approach* and *envelop* the high idiom of the dead. We must speak honestly to those writers we have murdered with our text, or those poets who have died in our heart – even to those weak poets who have peacefully departed this dimension. We have so much to say that was previously unsaid. What would they say if they returned to us? It would be an epic sentence. What if they reply that they never died – that nothing happened at all – that even now they are in the same grid of consciousness? Never for a moment did we correctly honor the living. The living died neglected and ignored by our speech – so how can we reliably honor the dead? We cannot.

Every god has died at some point in his education. The dead have not been addressed responsibly in modern generations. Sobriety and patience is demanded. For generations, men in the West have murdered and taken joy in death and, yet, still have concealed their *linguist eloquence* towards death. Ezra Pound did not have an epic spleen. Eliot did not begin or finish his epic poem. It is strange that the greatest century of murder and horror lacks an epic poet that could possibly begin to endow Western death with information. How could so many deaths pass without a clearly delineated epic information? Modern deaths still appear to be worthless – containing no valuable information.

The last answer that we should give was that the dead simply died. Never for a moment does a person simply die. Death is loud – it cannot be missed. There was a much deeper significance to the act of death. All death is deliberate. It was deeply pondered over the time span of many, many years. Consciousness is exactly structured with a beginning, middle, and end. Consciousness reflects a necessary sequence of story – with a beginning, middle, and end. So how do we approach this truth? We honor births, as if they are some achievement. We honor activity. We celebrate promotions at work; we honor a man at retirement. Yet death is ignored by the modern acolyte. There is a truth to be told about the death of these 20th century millions – yet it has not been made – because the poetry has not been made. Modern poets have therefore failed the dead. Why?

Moderns ignore death, not because they are ignorant. Moderns mistake death because they mistake life. Moderns who value exclusively material life can only afford to be angered by death. The Greeks made the same mistake – to them also there was nothing after death. Yet Greek rationality did not preserve them from a rapid extinction – by their own hands.

To the modern, death does not contain information – only a construct to be avoided at all cost. Moderns ignore death because of death's mistaken remoteness to human communication. This shows a poor judgment of perception. This proves there is a scarcity of poets to translate the information of death. Moderns ignore death since we are certain that death does not negotiate, that there is no purpose to communicate with death. Since death is so strong, so set on its ancient reputation of strength – death does not need our insight. This is not a correct view.

The truth is, each of us desperately negotiates with death. Each of us works to build a good death. We pray to the god of death for enlightenments. Exactly as life – we work to make a better form of its expression. Death is like love – we work to possess the highest form of its expression. Is the emotion of love so different than death? Love (we feel) is weak and needs every human thought, every poem, and every song. Death needs nothing? No, death also needs every human thought, poem, and song. Our ignorance is strange. Our civilization is stranger.

Does Death Contain Information?

Does life occur *within* consciousness? It is an important question. If life occurs *within* consciousness, then life can be modified to meet the conditions of consciousness. According to Story Theory, since all observable phenomena are arraigned, identified, and valued by linguistic sentience, the same observed phenomena might be subsequently modified by linguistics. Life, occurring within consciousness, is a property that is arraigned, identified, and subsequently modified by the perceiver. Death, equally detected by consciousness, can be modified by the observer.

Does death occur within consciousness? Again, it is not a spurious interrogative. We must verify our parameters of ideation. Yes. Like life, only the sentient human perceives death. No other creature perceives death. The consequence is elegant and pure. If the sentient perceiver can modify life – he may also modify death. Sentience occurs within consciousness. Death is a form of sentience – we *do* perceive and form an opinion of death with sentient observation. We have previously said that the definition of life is an entity that gives feedback – with intention. The feedback of life is recognized since the feedback *always* takes the form of a pattern that is detected. Thus life, in all its forms, is a protocol of communication. Death also falls to a linguistic pattern that is detected. Death is a form of communication. A text.

For the first time in Western philosophy, it is verified that death – philosophically – linguistically – is a pattern of linguistics *within* consciousness. Death, as life, then, is utterly under the control and manipulation of linguistic consciousness. The sentient outcome depends on the translation we make of our life and our death. Thus, both life and death are exclusively epic tropes. If life and death is essentially a form of communication, then poetry is the singularity of feedback of life and death experience.

We are certain that our literature insists that *life* contains value. Every story of Western civilization confirms that life has information. Every poem exhibits towards life a source of biased value. It is impossible to discover a poem that is indifferent to life. We thus confirm that life contains information. Does death also contain information? A quick scan of Western literature verifies that death, as life, occurs within consciousness. Death is located securely next to the living in every story, history, and poem. So death must also be linguistically manipulated for information. Objects within consciousness are linguistically scanned by humans for meaning, transformation, and leverage. Death thus must contain information. The epic trope records this information.

We look again at every Western story and myth. Yes, there is a pattern that emerges. We see there is death in every story and myth. We observe there is an expectation of information in a man's death. There is an answer of the value of life in a human's death. There is a summary of judgment. There is a deep introspection of the reach of life into death – as portrayed in our literature and theater.

We know exactly what the message of death is. The message of death is that you must learn to master something. No human master ever once feared or felt the pain of death. He has only had to master the anticipation – the narrative – of death. But are we not faced with the same challenge of life – that we face the challenge to master the narrative of life? Thus both life and death are the same linguistic protocol. Life and death have only one theme – *master something*. And, at once, we see the difficulty modern humans have with death. The modern is incapable of mastering *anything*. Yet this incapacity of mastery, in effect, draws and summons an ever-greater measure of death in the 21st century. Death will have its message heard. The history of the twentieth century was a history of persons searching for mastery of a subject – and failing to master anything. The implication of the epic trope also enjoins the same message: master your life. This is what epic characters prove – if they master their life, their deaths contain information. What is the severe ethic of the epic poem? Mortal life is not the important element. A man's body is not the single vital element. Mastery is the only vital issue of life and death. It is only important that life has been mastered with a further resource to consciousness – whether this be an act of courage, faith, or sacrifice. Mastery is the subject of the epic trope. Did the epic hero master his life? It is irrelevant if he kept his body and life in good working condition. The question is how a human should master his life. What else is signified in the epic trope? A human sacrifice is made to achieve a state of mastery – or to prove a mastery over the human condition. And this discourse – this communication – builds linguistic consciousness to fit the conditions of life we seek. This is information that an epic poem properly contains.

Epic poetry has only one idea, and it speaks only to the mastery of each nation: no hate for the enemy; no contempt for the vanquished. The epic poem wishes to honor this perspective.

Death demands a deep draw of breath into the well of life. Ancient poets always had to stop their narrative and consult with the dead. Did they do this because they knew that the dead had no part of life? No. They believed that the dead had information to relate to the living. Homer, Virgil, and Dante spoke with the dead in their epic poems – and they had much yet to tell. Clearly the modern person has unreliable information on the quality of death. In *Chandos Ring*, the dead are consulted for the conduct of life.

We have to ask again. Does the death of Jesus contain information? It appears to some that his death is the only vital information about the Christ figure. Does the death of Socrates contain information? It contains a profound sentiment of his total information. Does the death of Boethius contain information? Likewise. Do the deaths of Catholic saints contain their significant information? Yes, some would insist that the deaths of saints were a significant narrative of their value of life. Of Hamlet, of Caesar, of Pompey, of Alexander, of Richard III, of Ophelia, of Mark Anthony, of Cleopatra? Death appears to be very eloquent. Did the entire world not wait to hear of the death of Hitler? That was information of victory and release for an entire generation of men and women. Hitler is still the most dramatic and decisive human of the 20th century. The Hitler narrative is the single most referent text in modernism. All stories of heroic value are measured against the backdrop of one man's audacity. If one made a graph of the narrative of television, books, and cinema of the last one hundred years, there is only one figure that defines the values of Western civilization. The entire 20th century – its values, treaties, alliances, wars, technology, and murder – is defined by the passion towards, and recoil from, the life and death of one man. This is information that is not yet accounted for by Western liberalism. Perhaps best positioned to judge Hitler's achievements, Stalin was obsessed with the death of Hitler – even after the death of Hitler. What did he know? Inexplicably, modern men are still obsessed with the death of Hitler – even after the death of Hitler. If modernism denies this as information, how can we trust a modern academic's account of the 20th century? What new information did Hitler embody? Only evil? Modern men still reference him for information.

The modern is so unprepared in his narrative of a good death – a death that contains information – that he avoids the subject altogether. It is even necessary to eradicate coffins. Cremation is now the norm – suddenly – overnight. How did this tectonic shift happen unnoticed – in one generation? This transformation of the most important custom of the dead – coffin burial – has passed to another idiom. It happened in the dark of the night. This sort of death – as cremation – is a quick and meaningless transformation of the body to an urn of ashes.

The subject of poetry is death. Why? Poetry must be eloquent with death – since death, as life, contains information – and information, moreover that demands mastery. Without a narrative of the calculation of death, modern life looses any information it might have contained. My poem contains information because I address the dead. We must summon the wisdom of poems since without poems we never say the right things to the departed. Without poetry we cannot detect the charismatic apparition of human life at the astral or mythic plane. We do not even admit that the dead have departed with high sentience and continue to live by the majesty of the deep significance of their death. We cannot even find the words to morn with competence. The poets of death are not called for in the modern world. We consequently never empty our spleen of mourning. We only retain the brief and undigested black bile of writing the final checks. We recoil from the abbreviation of dead men, cut short in their narrative of deep feeling. The modern rituals of death are not constructed to contain vital speech. Yet we know the opposite is true. Every person we love is heightened by the death.

Even the stranger, even the unloved, even the evil men are made into objects of information of wonder by the manner of their death. We don't even begin to see or to love the dead until they enter their high station. We do not contemplate life at all until there is the message of death. So clearly we confirm the dead contain a high station. Why does modernism defy this information?

I have much to say to the dead. So much has for too long been omitted from my memorandum. By my own death, I intend to critique all other dead. I intend to make them suffer by comparison. In my poem, I am more kind; I give each character a death that contains a value of information. In my poem, the dead return to give accounts of the value of life. The dead see things differently. They make protests – but they are reasonable. The living are too myopic, too passionate about things of little importance. We don't even wish to speak with our modern neighbors – so why do we pretend that the living person, alone, contains high information? The dead know what is important. The dead tell us that we refused the cup of blood that draws. We act as if we don't understand the message – but we know exactly what they refer to. They see a far perspective. What is information if not perspective? So I address the dead in my poem. I desperately need their information. I am partial and poorly constructed. I ask for their eyes.

Death has information that is passed down from generation to generation. Why does modernism insist to rob the human idiom of the majestic canon of death? Because modernism is, itself, a form of death. Modernism destroys languages, cultures, and species of wondrous animals. Modernism is a continual mourning for *all* the departed tones of the linguistic human codes. The chief characteristic of modernism is its nostalgic mourning for everything lost. Modernism, in the final analysis, is the Age of Nostalgia. The information of the stars – lost. The wonder of life – lost. The information of epic poems – lost. The living Earth – lost. The certain knowledge of the afterlife – lost. *Chandos Ring* inserts the meaning of death into the post-modern world beyond the funeral pyres of Earth. Death will not return in all its majesty until all the populations of the Homo sapiens are eradicated by their lack of reliable information of the value of life. Homo sapiens must die. *Chandos Ring* is a funeral text.

We can discuss related patterns of the human perception of death. We already know when archeologists and anthropologists wish to know about the lives of ancient people – the *entire* ancient civilization reveals its value of life through the treatment of the dead – especially in the treatment of burial tombs. These deaths still contain eloquence. Thus the treatment of the human value of life corresponds directly to the treatment of the human value of the death narrative. This is clear information.

Is it possible to modify death? It seems to the uninitiated that we cannot influence the sobriety of death. To us, death is a drunkard – somehow outside of influence. No use to speak with it. This is a horrible misreading. Death is as much about sentient control as life is. Still, because we have no strong poets, we do not trust the information of modern death. Yet I know the truth. Modern humans still seek to insert a silent negotiation with death. I observe we still attempt to delay our death in every moment. We prolong our death for hours and even years beyond its ripeness. We consume enormous numbers of pills; we undergo invasive surgeries to buy a few months of time. We place ourselves (as if it is our right!) on the industrial hospital *machine* to avoid the consequences of a frank, face to face discussion with death. When death comes to tell us its mystery, when it arrives to finally ask for eyes, we are already drunk on a cocktail of drugs.

In each culture the story of death is altered, different, opposed. If each culture's treatment and narrative of death may be so diverse, then this proves that death is liable to modification. This proves that death is a movable text – that is it not fixed, but only requires some linguistic mastery. The method of this *modification* is a further resort to sentient innovation. To accept death does not mean we may not intend to modify its narrative to our advantage. We accept death because it contains undiscovered information of life.

Every god has died at some point in his education. Every mythology contains a story of decent into the underworld. Every god, every religion, every human contains a story of death. No exception. Who then will suggest that death is not continually modified to fit the condition of consciousness that we seek? Then death is a form of mastery – as any other construct of consciousness. That is as much to say, death, as life, is represented as a linguistic poem – a narrative with value. This cannot be ignored in a strong Theory of Poetry, since any honest theory must insist that all aspects of human life are linguistically hammered into a fist of text.

CHAPTER TWENTY-TWO

What Happens Inside of Language?

Literature is an expression of hegemon. Literature does not only convey information. Literature makes an idiomatic discovery of human life. This idiomatic discovery (of the nature of life) represents a perspective that no other language pattern would have detected. Thus literature (story, language) carries this unique and idiomatic discovery of life to war against all other discoveries of human life. What does this mean? The future of human consciousness is under the compulsion of the ideology that controls linguistic structure. Whatever linguistic *causation* (of reality) we accept is the hegemon we accept. Poetry is consequently dangerous and serious. Story Theory, as practiced in literature and politics, is ideational control of human minds by linguistic coding. As every language seeks a further innovation of ideational control, so literature is an expression of hegemony. This concept will become clearer as my text matures.

There is no form of literature, no linguistic code, which does not operate as a virus. Each linguistic pattern ruthlessly homogenizes and pasteurizes the host to fit the pattern of the linguistic idiom. Each cultural idiom contains its own mythic code, its own direction of movement, and its own signature of destiny. This is information passed over only with consequence. The choices made by Shakespeare, a single operator, created the future Western human personality. It takes a moment to fully realize this statement. A *single* operator can create the entire future of the human race – by a powerful reconstruction of future linguistics.

No separate idiom wishes to share with another linguistic idiom. It's not even possible. No proud Arabic, Russian, or French speaker can long tolerate the assumption of the universality of modern hegemonic English. Due to a previous strength or isolation, Arabic, Russian, and French operated as supreme languages (in their spheres) before the modern Anglo-Saxon hegemony. Islamic nations have no compunction to eradicate non-Arabic speaking humans. The French and

Russian nations make it a policy to undermine Anglo-Saxon hegemony. These are linguistic necessities – not political necessities.

There is no epic poetry that does not originate from a highly developed idiom. English is currently the supreme medium of human communication. It dominates all other forms of global expression. English is the *lingua franca* of global business, aviation, science, medicine – in fact any specialized form of militant modernism. There may be persons that call themselves poets in obscure languages – but in so far as their idiom is not sought by all other nations as information – what they express is local *dialect* – a patois. Only a hegemonic language can truly function as the audacious language of the hegemonic poet. No language has achieved hegemonic status that did not already achieve an exquisite level of ideational expression. English is the supreme device of Western men. Yet a modern epic poem in English has not been attempted on a galactic scale.

Can American English support an epic theme? First, all civilizations operate on the founding myths of epic texts. No exception. If American English is a hegemonic form of expression, if American history contains an epic event, if America is the inventor of the future, then we must answer in the affirmative. Yes, Western modernity contains an epic event. There will be an Exodus of Earth. Yes, our English is able to bear the structure of an epic poem. The state of contemporary English is stark and pure. It is uncluttered with **bric-à-brac**. English is strong. The nation is strong. We are only at our crisis. Every hero is verified at his crisis.

The first principle of a new theory of poetry insists that – to be vital – poetry must still be the medium for storytelling. This opinion is a new concept in a modern American poetic theory. It is so long neglected as to be forgotten. It has not even occurred to modern poets to advance such an opinion. How can the necessity of poetry to carry and construct a story be overlooked in the last century of Western poetry? It astonishes the educated mind. How did no academic uncover this lacuna in American Letters? The information of academia is thus tertiary and secondary.

Prior to English, other Western languages were hegemonic – certainly French, Latin, and Greek. They are presently giant memorials to previous Western hegemonic control of human ideation. The globe was seized with Greek, Latin, and Hebrew men. The Chinese have stayed within their borders since the 1430's. Previous to my generation, few persons were considered to be educated until they were read in the literature and languages of the French, the Latin, and the Greek poets. Why? What form of information did the hegemonic languages include? The answer to the men of that age would have been that it contains the information of everything of first-class importance – laws, manners, history, politics, and poetry.

Since Anglo-Saxon science uses the languages of Latin and Greek – it is clear that English still contains all Western information. The lesson is critical. No language should be used for the epic structure that does not contain all of the human information of the civilization. English meets these criteria. It is a global hegemony and it contains the information of all human manners and all human knowledge. Moreover, English is the language used by the nation that created the future – America. English is the original language of the genre (*and* the technology) of Science Fiction. Either way I can proceed with my project. A moment waits to be seized.

Literature may avoid the status of local opinion by following the armies of the hegemon – thus becoming the linguistic medium of all authoritative means of information. Even after the Romans conquered Greece, Greek was still used as the language of authority, philosophy, and oracle. When a language is developed with a high perfection due to the *space and time* won by the hegemonic power – this idiom becomes the standard for all further forms of human life. This muscular linguistic agency becomes more powerful than any favorable gene, more selective than any form of biological selection, more sustaining than any mineral or natural resource. Language selects. Consciousness selects. What is the lesson here? Hegemonic voice operates as a virus that strengthens its host and eliminates all foreign linguistic microorganisms. Poetry is thus a second genetics.

The reader may pause to consult the pattern of cultural control imposed by all great powers. We still have our worlds torn apart with the conflicts of the hegemonic linguistic cults of Hebrew, Latin, Greek, and Arabic poetry – that is, Christianity, Judaism, and Islam. Religious strife is not the strife between individuals – religious strife is due to opposing linguistic patterns of life. Language is genetic warfare by other means. *Chandos Ring* explores this horror. The modern world completely ignores the role of linguistic codes in warfare. This is a crisis of the modern, who will be eradicated by linguistic and genetic competition. The struggle has already commenced on the globe. There will never be peace until all men read the same poetry.

Story Theory identifies the mechanism of control of the human mind with the hegemonistic immolation of the minority languages – and thus, the eradication of the *patois*. We see the same agency active in music. Each idiom of music is also a linguistic code, has a particular pattern that clashes in a hostile manner with all other forms of music. *Mozart* does not mix with *Jazz*. American *Country Music* does not mix with *Hip Hop*, etc. Language functions with extreme prejudice. Music, as any language, is hermetically sealed against all *other* idiomatic forms. English, as one example, is antagonistic with Chinese ideation. Language, literature, poetry, and music can only strive for hegemony – there is not even a choice in the matter. Language, literature, poetry and music contain the ideational genealogy, the vital information of the genetic idiom of the human host. This is not survival of the fittest – it is the ruthless survival of an asserted superior human code. When a poet succeeds to become the measure of what is human – he seizes control of the pattern of human consciousness. His linguistic pattern is now the only future pattern of the human idiom of sentience. Poetry is that serious. Like DNA, poetry contains vital information of the human host. Poetry not only recreates the past – its hegemonic charge powerfully forges the future. The Greek and Hebrew languages created the Western human. Shakespeare (and the *King James Bible*) created the modern human personality. Who will wish to argue this?

Story Theory operates as means of ideational control by the hegemonic pattern. When a man's poetry, that is, his language, originates from a particular linguistic idiom – he has already surrendered his mind to that idiom. Any form of surrender is a powerful and monumental event. The reader may test this theory with the observation of either the Western scientist or the Islamic acolyte. Each, though utterly at odds to the other's world view, are merely following the idiomatic patterns dictated by the training embedded in their chosen high – and severe – linguistic structure of ideation. English and Arabic ideations are at war – not individuals. Science and Islam are opposite forms of poetry – the minds of each have surrendered to the patterns of different ideational poetry. There is a fierce war for the future currently underway between these two linguistic codes. We already know the outcome.

Will Liberal Ideology Force Us to Renounce Our High Idiom?

Because of our struggle with the racial ideologies of Japan, Korea, Russia and Germany, modern men have renounced the purpose of Western civilization: *to seize control of human life*. We have consequently, that is, linguistically, renounced our ability – openly, overtly, graphically – to make a severe selection of what form of human life is to be advocated – over all other life forms. Western men do not *discuss* racism – it is to be avoided at all costs. Why? Because we are afraid to reveal true instincts. This breeds hypocrisy of expression. We only make the accusation of racism in order to silence the speech of our ideological enemies – so great is our fear of our racial instincts. The white man of European extraction is constantly surveilled for any signs of overt racism. All humans are racists – whether in honest spleen or while over-reacting in recoil from the guilt of racism. Thus, conservatives and liberals are both racist. I accuse both of linguistic cowardice.

Liberalism is not a philosophy at all. Liberalism is intellectual surrender to materialism. Current liberal ideology strictly avoids any confrontation with foreign ideational structures. We are the only world power that ever agreed to self-destruct. We are victim of our own success against totalitarian governments that made a ruthless and hysterical race to selection. Our revulsion of Stalin/

Hitler has created a linguistics of liberal pacifism. Hitler lost – and the Western World lost its linguistic audacity. The Western human lost his right to wage his war of good and evil. Above all else a human civilization must be allowed it's war of good and evil.

After the defeat of Hitlerism, Germany cannot even field a single combat troop outside of its borders – according to its own constitution! That is surrender from the outset. The West lost the struggle of WWII since we cannot even use our own idiom now to make a severe selection of ideational space. Presently, our philosophy of selection is crippled – no severe selection of consciousness is made with liberalism. Liberalism (both republican and democrat) merely argues over the ruins of Western Civilization – to whom should we give the material remains. Liberalism now transitions to socialism as a political means to avoid all forms of courage and inequalities. All people are to be made equally non-entities. Current liberalism in no way differs from socialism – both are entitlement cultures.

If you have a theory of human superiority – then share it – that we may test it. Why speak like a coward, without attempting to verify what you are really feeling in your heart? This is the insidious pattern of modernism – it makes men linguistic cowards. Speak with honesty.

Story Theory verifies that the racism of skin color is only an aesthetic response – not an actual value. We don't need to die for aesthetics. Yet we do affirm that our linguistic codes – our actual patterns of our way of life – may certainly be defended to the last breath and last weapon at our disposal. We defend our linguistic heritage – built up over centuries of homogenous ideation – not mere color tones of skin. We accept that future humans are brown.

Any man that loves the language of Shakespeare, Milton, and Dunn is my fellow citizen. As Isocrates said of the Greeks, and I validate for clarity of my racial position, "The people we call Greeks are those who speak the same linguistic codes as ours, not the same blood." I confirm this perspective. I am a linguistic being – not a racial being. Language is my house of being – not the color of my skin. My idiom *may* be eternal. My bloodline, in contradistinction, can change in one brief and flippant accident of procreation. The concern of these books is to advance the interest of the linguistic code – not to advance the claims of any superiority of race. Anyone who makes a prediction of the genetic code in five centuries will only be setting himself up for ridicule. I only want to advocate the possibility of human language at that futurity.

Western men, though faulted with modernism, certainly wish to advocate their idiom of life. Without actually making the declaration – in our hearts we truly feel that our way of life is superior. We thus hide behind the excuse of *freedom to all*, when we take arms to eradicate all non-liberal ideologies. *Freedom*, of course, is an euphemism. What we actually mean is *freedom to be modern* – freedom to be Western. What we are really doing is asserting our superior view of idiomatic life over lesser linguistic codes. Yet we fear to say as much openly – as if we should be ashamed of having a highly selective form of consciousness.

Consciousness selects ruthlessly. Language selects. In so far as the modern cannot express his urge to hegemony openly – then the modern is disadvantaged in his struggle. Any man who is not free to dominate his fellow human is not human. This is a statement only audacious in its honesty. The man who is prevented from being fully human – and the human was made to be superior over his competitors – that crippled man, I insist, is only an animal in a zoo. By making this statement, I only sacrifice decorum for integrity of expression.

The reader sees at once the Western dilemma. Can Western liberal ideology – our fear to express our superiority openly – convince us to renounce our hegemonic struggle? Can a hegemonic language be successful if it is no longer dangerous? The French example gives us pause. In a single century from 1900 until 2000, the French language descended from a summit of the highest language of civilization to being just another regional European tongue. The French poet, once the very measure of how poetry should be expressed, has descended to the level of a minor and irrelevant curiosity. No one today can list the name of a living French poet. The modern lyric form that the French poet used is now risible, contains no information, and cannot be distinguished from prose. This is a linguistic crisis of the greatest magnitude. It is a national humiliation, moreover, I wish to avoid with American audacity.

The central necessity for my work is the dangerous confusion of the Western genius. Not only do we exhibit a crisis of linguistic information – a debilitating schism where we hide our true intentions with timid euphemisms – the West suffers from a *philosophy gap*. What is freedom? No one knows. What is the best? No one knows. What is the pest poetry? No one knows. What type of man is the happy man? No one can say. What future do we wish to build? Only more proliferation? No one can answer. When you cannot speak what you think, when you can't explain the meaning of your words – this is the utter failure of intellectual philosophy. What shall correct this lacuna of modern Western intellectual competence? We have already stated that modernism cannot reform modernism. What then? Let us construct a fearless theory of poetry. It will embed a new perspective of human life. It will be brave. Let us not be afraid to advocate what is superior – even if we must give up modernism to do so.

Secular liberalism (*that is*, both Republican and Democratic versions of liberal ideology) is based on unconstrained markets, conspicuous consumption, serial pornography, and the arrogance of material science – these forces now represent wounded moralities and can no longer hold a civilization together. So now the transition to socialism seems to be a panacea. At best these forces can allow proliferation until the political, social, and ecological systems of Earth collapse. There will never be ten billion middle-class consumers. The Earth cannot sustain that monstrosity. There will be no reformation of modernism by the forces of modernism – there can only be collapse of modernism (and Earth).

A new idiom will survive the ashes. It will be an idiom far in advance of modernism. The danger is that we do not allow the collapse of the traditional Western idiom along with the collapse of modernism. Currently, only modernism ensures the West enjoys linguistic invulnerability. The globe still believes it needs modernism – Western modernism. Yet once modernism is revealed to contain unreliable information – once our reserve currency collapses – nothing will attract other powers to assimilate our idiom. That will be the age of large war.

Until then, the West must proliferate modernism ruthlessly. There is no alternative. Until we possess the means to escape our atmosphere on a grand scale, we must dominate the future of global life – by war or by cultural linguistics (that is, patents). Yet ideological liberalism will forbear to take the appropriate actions of audacity. In its debilitated state, the central intellectual core of Western liberalism only provides, in the end, for an uncritical propagation of life. Western liberalism does not contain a selective judgment of a final product, or value, of human life – except the goal of unconstrained proliferation. Life for life's sake makes a poor philosophic goal – what is the end game? Ten billion humans? One hundred billion? Where is the human mind that selects? We are cowards if we do not demand our war of good and evil. It will be a climatic holocaust of languages.

So afraid are we of reproducing any severity of selection resembling the political systems led by a Hitler or a Stalin – that we have avoided all philosophical constraints (selections) of our social definition of political liberty. We ruthlessly avoid the question of what life is superior. We have linguistically castrated ourselves from detecting the idiomatic curse we have created in our ideology. We have thrown the baby out with the bath water. To avoid a certain class of totalitarian evil, we forfeit the right to assert any form of national or linguistic excellence over other forms of ideation – including our avowed enemies. This is strange. This is not an assertion of Western ideals – this is not fair play – this is not tolerance. This is surrender.

Liberalism, then, in effect, is fear and loathing of our own achievement. This is the crisis of the West. Both Republican marauders and Democratic socialists are scientific materialists – both are moderns moving to exploit modern conditions to their own army of ideational followers. Neither the left nor right can govern without expanding government control and spending every last resource. Democracy is governance by spending and distributing resources to their constituents. This is a policy of governance ensuring collapse of the state. When resources run out there is no democracy – there is only war. Political modernism is a colony of vicious ants that intend to pick the skeleton of Earth clean. No nation and no culture will survive the holocaust of modernism.

Story Theory exposes linguistic modernism. My advocacy of the Western idiom does not preclude a ruthless critique of the philosophy of my civilization. I assert the superiority of Western civilization, our intellectual achievement over all other forms of life. Though I critique linguistic modernism, I only intend to supersede it with a more reliable Western idiom. Let the consequence be what they may – as a final act of desperation, I speak with the audacity of my ruthless ancestors. I severely criticize Western modernism only to correct our lives enough to allow a strong theory of poetry. I do not disavow the Western experiment. I only prepare for the next evolution of Western hegemony. I even state our goal: the conquest of the galaxies with English speaking civilization. I do not care who is offended by my audacity.

It is not decorum to insist that modern men are cowards. There are many that are still brave. Yet the phenomenon of Western pacifism is seldom perused in print. Of course we wish to have our idiom of life triumphant over other forms of life. Of course we intend to keep our linguistic heritage secure for future Western generations. Of course we want to make the future in our image. Of course we do not want our children's children to speak an Asiatic or Arabic language – and learn to hate our ancestors. This is only minimal honesty. But can we still afford the luxury of honesty? Should a free people hide their real thoughts as secrets?

CHAPTER TWENTY-THREE

All Literature Contains a Secret

For the first time in human writing we can view the epic poems of all ages with a cosmological template. It has never been done before. To do so reveals an unsuspected message. We discover across the entire spectrum of epic poems that the epic trope contains an embedded secret. Apart from the generosity of the assertion, we can point to substantial evidence of cosmological correspondence. At this point in my fiction, the reader encounters a virginal category of information. There is a phenomenon evident in literature that has passed unremarked in academic accounts of human writing. This should be accounted for.

How do we discover the secret embedded in epic poems? We may use three classic interrogatives to discover the alien element of information embedded in the epic trope. We may decide to examine epic literature for archeology, for location, and for time. Each method of interrogative – of archeology, of location, of time – will reveal that the epic trope has no specifically human origin – but shockingly, uncannily – only correspondences of cosmology. What does the linguistic explorer discover? Each time we will discover that the story and characters of the body of great epic literature tell histories of the original life source – of stars – not of human interaction on a terrestrial grid coordinate – and not on a human time scale.

The Western epic poems uncannily correspond exactly with the constellations that gave them their signal messages. Taurus, the age of the bull, emits passion, force, and lust. Aries, the age of the ram, asserts an obsession for ruthless law. Pisces, the double fish, demands the trial of brotherly love (proliferation). Each period of epic literature (including the Bible narrative) contains a unity and consistency of cosmology decoded only in this generation. The clues now fall together in a mosaic that was always before our eyes – but overlooked as ornament of fantasy.

I will make a review of these texts that will serve as our principle data for the thesis. Each age of Western man has produced texts that were consistent in their correlation of cosmology. There is no usual way to account for this. The cosmology of the last six thousand years is well known. The Age of the Taurus constellation (1800-3800 B.C.) illustrated the passionate and forceful heroes of *Gilgamesh*. The Greek poems are more ancient than their written codex. *Hercules*, *Odysseus* and *Achilles* are each Greek heroes of the late Age of Taurus (though not encoded into Greek until a later period when Greek writing was invented). In astrological literature, Taurus is a beast of force and passion. The epic heroes of this Age (Taurus, 1800-2800 B.C.) were heroes of force and passion. In the Iliad, we recognize the ancient Achaeans as men of the last age of Taurus. They still believed they could seize immortality (more of life) by passion and force (epic battles).

The subsequent Age of Aries was equally consistent in its message. In the Constellation of Aries (1800 – 0 B.C.), the heroes, Moses, Lycurgus, Solon and Plato, promulgated laws – not justification of life by passion or force. This is an ideation shift that cannot be ignored. The only method of discovery is to decipher the cosmological references embedded in the poems. It is not without coincidence that the ram of Aries stands for the force of law. Subsequently we discover the clues of Aries in the poem of this period – especially the Books of *Moses, Deuteronomy, Leviticus*, as well as Virgil's *Aeneid*, and the oddity of *Jason and the Argonauts*. I will explore the signs encoded in these poems.

After the setting of Aries in the night sky, there is a new transition at the year 0 B.C. In the subsequent age of cosmology, Pisces (0 – 2200 A.D.), laws are rejected as means of human salvation. In three cosmological transitions, we clearly detect a pattern that comes into view. It is curious that the sign of Pisces is a double fish and not a single fish. In astrological texts, the double fish is a symbol of proliferation (fish multiply and school together in large groups). An outline of cosmology is generous with benefits in a review of the epic trope (especially the *Bible* as epic poem). The first miracle of Christ, the multiplication of the loaves and fishes, is a miracle of proliferation. Again, an overt sign.

The point made – and briefly mentioned previously – is that each age of epic texts contains heroic narratives of persons and agents that have no archeology. Where is the archeology of human texts? It is missing. The bones of Hector, Gilgamesh, Telemachus, Jesus, Isaiah, David, Moses, Abraham, Jason, and Hercules cannot be found. They will never be found. What we thus discover is that epic literature does not discuss humans – they are a discussion of values of life – and life, moreover, that mirrors consistent cosmology. The story-structure of the epic poems mirrors the message of the constellations in the night sky. Not only do the epic heroes portray characteristics of the astrological age, the epic texts embed symbology exactly matching the star constellation when the poem was composed. These symbols are not spurious; they are intimately connected to the hero. How can it be that star constellations inspire poets to craft messages of the nature of consciousness? It is uncannily consistent. Though eccentric to the modern ear, we may still proceed with the evidence. The modern will suggest that this thesis is not rational? Perhaps we should show care. The influence of the stars is only surprising to the modern. As we shall see, rationally, the stars are the most ancient linguistic code of human information. There is a deep rationality to all poems of cosmology.

As initially rehearsed in an early chapter, it is now revealed that the twelve labors of Hercules are encoded representations of the course of the human sun (the human soul) through the twelve signs of the zodiac. The signs of the zodiac associated with the labors of Hercules are easy to identify. His slaughter of the Nemean lion (first labor) is clearly a reference to the passage of the sun through Leo. The Cretan bull was certainly Taurus (seventh labor). Hippolyta, the virgin queen of the Amazons was passage through the constellation of Virgo (ninth labor). The poisonous Hydra (second labor) was Scorpio, and the centaur that completed the death of Hercules was a symbol of the dying (descending) constellation of Sagittarius. We are clearly operating here on the astral plane. These are not miracles of coincidence. These are narratives of cosmology. Again, for whom? Only star men tell stories of the stars.

We go deeper. In the Age of Taurus, the lawless and passionate Gilgamesh (and his city) worshiped the bull. In the Age of Aries, Moses steps down from Mt. Sinai with ram's horns (and laws). Moses is enraged that the Hebrews still persist in worshipping the previous constellation of the Bull (the *Golden Calf*). The ram's head adorns the boat of Jason, the hero of *Jason and the Argonauts*. The fifty Argonauts are never mentioned as moving, living men, but are fixed rowers in the boat of the sky – that is, they are from the Argos cluster in the Aries constellation.

We may also review the epic religious texts. The god Mithras, the god of Roman soldiers, is identified with Aries – and he is portrayed slaying the bull of (descending) Taurus. The next cosmological age is signaled when the Magi follow the star to the birthplace of Christ. The Magi, whoever they are – and we are not certain at all of their biology – are followers of cosmology. It is clearly intended by the poet of the *Gospels* that we identify the birth of the Pisces constellation with the birth of the new message of Christ – and the travel of the star worshippers (the Magi) to witness the birth of Christ at the conjunction of Jupiter and Saturn (the "new" star). Why? As if this was not a clue overt enough, we observe that the symbol for Christ – the fish – was also the symbol of Pisces. When we hear talk of Magi, we are instantly alerted. The message was the *star* – not the infant. By any account, these are overt astrological correspondences.

I include as epic trope the narratives of the *Bible*, the *Talmud*, *Mithras*, and the *Koran*. These are poems of the epic trope. Each contains stories and parables of life and death – and cosmology. There is a pattern in the epic texts that can be represented as a coded conversation of secret cosmology. These texts include the

Western Bible, but also, the Torah (*Laws*), the Egyptian *Book of the Dead*, *Jason and the Argonauts*, *Aesop's Fables*, *Hesiod*, the *Orphic* texts, Homer, Plato's Laws, as well as the Norse, Persian, and Indian epic cycles. There is only one way to characterize the origin and source of these uncanny and un-human epic texts. These poems are each narratives that became structures of entire civilizations. They contain essentially extraterrestrial and cosmological information. These texts are star matter. Thus, my interest is in the epic form. Each epic follows the cosmology corresponding to the period of composition.

The lyric does not interest our interrogation. Why not the lyric? The lyric contains few consistencies across all the epochs of human writing – and less cosmology. The lyric celebrates the erotic spleen. The lyric wishes to boast - or to complain. Certainly, to boast and to complain is a specifically human behavior we can recognize. The epic heroes do not complain; they only wish to kill, to establish laws, and to die with a certain value. The lyric avoids this alien eschatology all together. Terrestrial humans want to live and to fornicate. The epic agent strangely wants to burst by following a pattern of cosmology. The lyric does not conceal its erotic sentiment. Eros is replicated in the lyric – endlessly. It does not advance. Opposed, the cosmology of epic poems always advances. The epic demands a further resort to the peril of consciousness – even a heroic sacrifice. The lyric often attempts to mimic the epic – yet it is usually when the lyric poet insists that men should be prepared to die for Eros. It is a hard argument to sell – and there are few takers. The erotic spleen is perhaps sharpened and certainly ennobled by the lyric. The modern lyric trope is overused and exists only as a wounded structure.

More significant to our theme, societies of men justify and organize their life by the structures of the epic trope. The Greek lived according to the precepts of Homer – not Sappho. Virgil was the authority of a thousand years of European Latin culture – not Catullus. The Western world has followed every theme contained in the epic poems of the Western *Bible* – not the lyric poems of the Earl of Rochester. Few scholars would deny the *Talmud* and *Torah* did not function as the principle epic poems of all Hebrew civilization – including modern Anglo-Saxon civilization. The West has teased the Judeo-Christian epic texts to exhaustion. The Greeks teased the text of Homer to exhaustion. The Romans and monks teased Virgil to exhaustion. The Islamic people have teased the Koran to exhaustion. Can we detect a pattern here of treatment of epic texts? In contrast, the lyric is only topically felt by civilizations and honored more with temperance than passion. Any charismatic arrival of the epic trope, in contrast, is revolutionary. National epics – including the *Iliad, Aeneid, Talmud, Koran,* and the *Bible* – have served as the structure of future civilizations. It is an assertion that, even for the modern scholar, is impossible to counter.

Immediately we ask – why? What is so different about the epic trope? Where is the *location* and the *time* of the events portrayed in the Bible and other epic literature? With wild open eyes we finally come to realize that there is no earthly, terrestrial time or place in the epic poems. There is only the astral time and location of the zodiac – from our relative *ideational* position to the zodiac!

How can the constellations rationally influence the epic poets? To the rational mind, stellar influence is not evident. The richness of the epic trope is often in what is not said – except by implication. That is very strange. How can there be an effect of communication that leaves no fossil of communication? An epic begins from nowhere – in *medias res* – as if it had no Earthly location. The epic event has no previous genealogy – as if the poet and the characters were also not of this world. We are reminded of the *Magi* and the *Argonauts* – *of Beowulf* and *Grendel* – *of Moses* and *David* – *of Abraham* and *Jesus*. Where did they come from? They arrive from no *Earthly* grid coordinate. Moses (the only epic agent that has a hopeless attempt at genealogy) came floating down a river - like the god Osiris!

Stranger still, there are no bones, nor archeology of the epic poets. We cannot find them. And stranger still, the epic poets somehow found a way to agree on the same quests: *How do men gain more fullness of life? How to seize greatness (immortality)? What is the value of human life?* How do diverse epochs produce poems asking the same questions? How did they use exclusively the cosmology of their night sky? Did the poets meet in order to conspire together? No. We are certain they never met. Clearly there is an underlying stratum of consciousness that has so far passed undetected in epic literature. There is something strange about this.

We are not sure of the biology of the epic poets. We have no artifacts of their actual mortality – and less of their biography. Yet they were uncannily consistent in their correspondences. Each epic poet, as each religion, as each civilization, has posed the same question: *How may man acquire, win, or ensure more life – more personality – more time, more space?* It is not glory or heroism that is explored in the epic trope. This is a modern dispersion. Essentially, what the epic poet explores is the means to seize more of life. Gods advise the human protagonists, the heroes attack demons, they enter the underworld to consult with the dead, they suffer peril, they meet with bloody ends. What actually is happening in an epic poem? It is a heroic search for more life – immortality – more time, more space. *Gilgamesh* was the first to seek more of life than he already possessed. The question remains unresolved with any satisfaction. The epic quest continues. We know this is true since even modern men still desire more than they possess.

It is the thesis of these books that the ancient epic poems and myths were never understood – even by ancient people – until our own time at the beginning of the 21st century. That is a tall statement. Can it be sustained? Only at the present day does the strong poet see all the elements of the epic trope in the full relief of millennial message. Only now can we tease the ancient cuneiform texts of their full cargo of alien information. It is certain that there must be an alternate interpretation of human history. This new interpretation of humanity is a perspective that undermines the arrogance of all modern assertions. Our only choice of understanding is to move ahead and examine the information that was possibly pre-positioned for our astonishment and discovery. But why now? What is so special about this time in the human era? With the completion of the Age of Pisces, Aquarius portends to be a ruthless age of selection.

A deeper perspective is now sought to support the thesis. It is astonishing to the modern to discover that each constellation in the night sky – Taurus, Aries, Pisces – has generated a series of epochal texts – exactly consistent with a specific bias – and containing their own space and time. Each poses a differing approach to the *same* questions. How do we ensure ever-greater expansion of life? How do we ensure the seizure of more consciousness – by passion, by laws, or by brotherhood?

The modern reader will correctly hesitate. He will not wish to acknowledge any realistic connection between cosmology and human life. To do so would not fit into modern linguistics of rationality – of normal physical causation. Of course, if honest, the truth is that the modern still does not know the origin of matter. Matter, in fact, may be far stranger than mere physical causation. Matter may only be a tangential symptom of consciousness.

Of course, the modern is unfamiliar with the ancient consistency of the epic trope. He is unused to either overt textual rigor, ancient myth, or astral symbology. My response is that entire civilizations follow the structures and dictates of the linguistic code embedded in the epic trope – whether a poem, a *Bible*, a religious narrative, a constitution, or a political narrative. Civilizations follow the message of the epic star-runners. They seem to be familiar with poetry. The modern, even if ostensibly indifferent to a previous age of cosmology, may follow our discussion with interest. Aquarius, the constellation just now rising, presents a new message.

After the review of each interrogative – of archeology, of location, and of time – we are faced with the same conclusions of the origin of epic texts. We are in a position to make a final review of our thesis. There are inexplicable clues, so unnecessary to the narratives under consideration, that they could only have been pre-positioned for discovery by a later generation that would recognize the signatures.

In the first age of epic poets, during the constellation of Taurus, *Gilgamesh* sought to gain immortal life by force – to force the gods to give him their gift of immortality. It is not without significance that *Gilgamesh* is said, "to stand like a bull on the Earth." Immediately clues are signaled. He tried to seize immortality by violence. Force is an act of animal *passion* without regard to *law* or *brotherhood*. Reading the clues of correspondence to the Taurus constellation, we know enough to look for cosmological signatures in the subsequent patterns of epic poetry.

In the succeeding constellation of Aries, Moses, Mithras, Jason, Solon, Lycurgus, Romulus, and Plato sought to frame human immortality by making laws. In each case, their epic narratives of *lawmaking* are inexplicably embedded with signatures of the ram – as a sign of the Aries constellation. Law, as a means to more life, was an alternate approach to the same question sought by all men – how to win the condition of being long-lived, special, exclusive, chosen – immortal. The narratives of Moses, Mithras, Jason, Solon, Lycurgus, and Plato were products of the age of the ram (Aries). Our theme (and surprise) is deepened when we observe – in exactly the same astral age – Mahavira and Buddha in India, Lao-tze and Confucius in China, Jeremiah and the Second Isaiah in Judea and Zarathustra in Persia. There never was such an age of human laws – and their epic narratives each contained symbology of the ram constellation.

Moses is cited as returning from Mt. Sinai bearing ram's horns (and laws); he is furious that the Hebrews still persist in worshipping the Golden Bull (of Taurus). This clue in the texts of Moses is inexplicable. How is it necessary to the Hebrew covenant with Yahweh that Moses wears ram's horns after his encounter with Yahweh? It is unnecessary to the narrative. Why does the poet add this material if not to make and overt signature of cosmology? All epic poems operate with similar clues of cosmology. Every one. We are reading the signals of the Zodiac.

We can now take a final perspective of other epic narratives of the age of Aries. Mithras, the leading religion of the Late Roman Empire, is portrayed as slaying the bull (of Taurus) and pointing to the rising of Aries. Images of Mithras are accompanied by two torch-bearers on either side of the bull, Cautes with his torch pointing up (towards rising Aries) and Cautopates with his torch pointing down (towards descending Taurus). The Roman epic poet, Statius, described Mithras as one who "twists the unruly horns beneath the rocks of a Persian cave". The connection between the religion of Roman soldiers and the constellation of Aries – of Mithras who turns the wheel of stars from his cave – is clear to the epic poet. This movement is nothing less than the procession of the equinoxes! Mithras was the first *overt*, and *named*, star runner we are able to identify in literature. We are interested in the taxonomy of a new class of beings – *star runners*. To the human, this is a new uncanny being. We will see more of their genealogy in *Chandos Ring*.

Rome was an empire built on laws. Rome was the image of the Aries constellation *par excellence*. The laws of *Moses* (Leviticus), Plato (*Laws*), Lycurgus of Sparta, Solon of Greece, and the Senators of the Roman Republic are familiar to the average reader – roughly bracketing the epoch of Aries. The lawgivers are known and require little explication – undeniable in their sudden appearance *only* in the Age of the Aries. These are too many heroic lawgivers to ignore as coincidence. We now examine a more obscure epic text of the Aries constellation.

No ancient or modern has ever understood the epic poem *Jason and the*

Argonauts. It cannot be understood with a normal human perspective. No one knows the origin of the poem. No one knows the author of the poem – and no candidate has even been suggested with substantive biology. It is an alien document. It was a poem of cosmological information. The reader by this point will not be surprised that Jason's ship bore the masthead of a ram (Aries); his fifty *Argonauts* were individual stars – sitting in a boat of stars (the Argos cluster). Jason's quest was to chase the *Golden Fleece* (the rising constellation of Aries). Why was a ram's fleece important? Why is cosmology always present? The poem's goal was a map of cosmology. Why? Was a map of cosmology important to the humans of the day? If not, then to whom?

Jason, *already* in a boat of stars, chases *another* group of stars across the sky – the *Pleiades*. This is an exact description of a star map. All constellations can be described as chasing the previous constellation out of the night sky. This is a central text that alerts us to consider that all the great epic cycles were secret maps of cosmology. We are not on Earth. We are in another part of the universe. We are being spoken to from the astral plane. This is a clue of the origin of men. The mind of men, the epic poems teach, is not a terrestrial organ – it functions on the astral plane.

Many examples from Greek myth illustrate this thesis. Hercules is not a terrestrial human acting in stories of a terrestrial earth. His uncanny twelve labors are a recitation of the zodiac. The myth of Europa's lust for Jupiter was not an explanation of the lust of a woman (who climbed into a wooden cow to mate with Zeus (Jupiter) in the form of a Bull). No. This is a narrative of cosmology where it is explanted that the moon of Europa is caught up in the attraction of gravity with the planet Jupiter. (And this myth was constructed two millennia before Jupiter's moons were detected by Western men – again, a clue to what we are dealing with here.) Earlier, I cited the example where Coronus (Saturn) was supplanted by his son Zeus (Jupiter). Jupiter entered our solar system from another location. The epic myths, then, contain data of unknown cosmology. Epic myths are maps of cosmology.

Again and again, from narratives of ancient Egypt and Sumer, to the poems of ancient Greece and India, we are alerted to certain regions of space – the Orion Belt, the Pleiades, the Sirius star system. There is a secret message.

An important question arises. Why? To whom was this cosmology so important? Not the humans of the period. No contemporary age ever understood the actual message of their epic poems. There must be an alien source of obsession with the retrograde movement of star constellations and the strange inhuman bestiary they contained. Only star men would tell stories of the stars. We now look for star-runners to tell us what we want to know.

What is stranger to realize – we are just able to understand all of this. If we can recognize the cosmological signatures, there must be a connection between our minds and the source of this alien information. An embedded clue is never emplaced unless there is an emitting and receiving intelligence for detection. This generation, as will be seen, is the receiving intelligence.

Let us leave *Jason* and the Age of Aries. The reader is now face to face with his own night sky. The Age of Pisces, just now passing away in the night sky, allows us a further resort to exactness. After men failed to gain immortal life by passion and force under Taurus (*Gilgamesh, Achilles, Hercules*) – or by use of laws (*Moses, Lycurgus, Plato, Solon*) under Aries – suddenly, charismatically – a new approach towards immortality was breached in the year zero of our era. The timing was exact and revealing in this case. At the very moment the Pisces constellation appeared in the night sky, the *Gospel poets* composed the birth of the Christ message. Again, we recall the alien interjection of the *unnecessary* narrative of the three *Magi* following the new star in the night sky (Pisces). A heavy-handed clue.

Only pausing slightly to remark the exactness of the coincidence, we note that the epic interrogative – the quest for more of life – was still unchanged with the Pisces narrative. We know it well by now. *How do we seize eternal life? More personality? More space? More time?* Always the same epic quest. What is the value of life? How to seize it? What is the secret of consciousness that is embedded in the repetition of this quest? We might ignore that a single epic narrative posed the exact questions – but every single epic poem? We have to think.

In epic narratives, we are given generous clues of cosmology. The epic poet consistently makes an attributive acknowledgement of the previous constellation. *Jason's* boat, with its sculpted prow of the (rising Aries) ram's head, contains the fifty *Argonauts* (the Pleiades of Taurus) beneath the deck as rowers. Taurus was descending below the equinox – that is, Taurus was being chased (by *Aries/Jason*) out of the night sky (and thus, astral influence). Moses, wearing ram's horns, executes three thousand Hebrews still worshiping the old god of the Age of Taurus (the *Golden Calf*). These are heavy-handed clues indeed. There is more. The poet of the *Gospels* also took the trouble to make a reference to previous age of the ram (law): "*I came not to destroy the law, but to fulfill the law.*" Again, a clue of Aries. Paul, speaking of the Christ message, says, "*For what the law could not do, in that it was weak through the flesh, God sending his own Son . . .etc.*" It can be argued that the entire *Gospel* was a discourse between the failed attempt of a previous age of laws (Hebraic laws) and the new message of proliferation (Pisces) that overreaches all law. It is not only God's son that arrives – it was cosmology newly arrived in the night sky.

As stated, it is conclusive evidence to observe that the age of Christ *and* the Constellation of Pisces were both identified by the same sign of the fish. Why was this deemed necessary? The sign of the double fish, of course, symbolizes proliferation (brotherhood, love of other). Fish proliferate and multiply mindlessly.

Their mindlessness is justified by an appeal to brotherhood – they swim in schools together – they move and feel together as a body. They darken the seas.

Who considered it important to give Christ the same astrological symbol as the new star of Pisces – the sign of the fish? Because there was a geometric theorem represented by overlapping ovals? No – this would be irrelevant to the men of the age. In fact, the symbol of the fish was not immediately apparent – it was a poetic reconstruction of the story of Jesus. The double fish only first appeared as the symbol of Christ in Rome in the 2nd century A.D. Only the poets of the 2nd century Christ narrative deemed it important – just as the poet of the books of Moses thought it was important to embed cosmological signatures of the ram. How? None of the epic poets – texts upon which entire separate Western civilizations were constructed – ever met. And why was it important? Important to whom? In the end, a case can be made for an alien source of information. A pattern of extraterrestrial life is detected.

The truth is generous in its conclusions. Only today can we assemble all the clues of cosmology found in the epic poems – including the newly discovered Sumerian cuneiform epics. We now understand that each epochal epic poet left signs of the contemporary constellation embedded in every poem! Was it a sign that *Christ, Moses, Abraham, Noah, Enoch, Jason, Orpheus, Hercules, Buddha, Mahavira, Lao-tze, Zarathustra* and *Mithras* were supernatural creatures? Certainly. They had no biology. Were they star-runners? For what other cause are they consistently symbolized with star signatures and exact cosmology? This is the secret that epic poems contain.

Christ's first miracle was the multiplication of the loaves and fishes. In this light, the miracles of *Christ* were not specifically miracles of religion – they were miracles of proliferation – and specifically proliferation as a signature of the Pisces constellation. Consequently, the modern epic poet may likewise follow the signature of a pattern of cosmology. He finds more than he dares to think possible. How could so many epic poets agree, as a committee might agree, on placing clues of cosmology in each epic narrative? Though we still do not know their biographies, we know that if they were humans, then they could never have met to compare notes. We are, tangentially, certain that they lived at different human epochs. Or did they? What force of intelligence holds these poems together? Was it necessary for *Moses, Jason,* and *Mithras* to bear on their persons the ram horns of the age of Aries? Was it necessary for *Gilgamesh* to be adorned with the symbols of the bull under the sign of Taurus? Was it important to ensure that Christ was represented by the exact astrological symbol of Pisces? Are the characters of *Gilgamesh, Abraham, Moses, Noah, Hercules, Achilles, Jason,* and *Christ* actually stars? We certainly cannot find their antecedents in other humans we know. We are not certain of their biology at all. The bones are missing. These are solid questions.

This is the thesis we have labored to establish (with honest recitation). Clues of exact cosmology are pre-positioned in epic texts of diverse periods. So consistent is the message of cosmology, we are not willing to believe they are accidents. It is clear, moreover, that the cosmology of the poems was never understood by the people of the time that the poems and myths were written. They are clues that could only be decoded and understood at a later time. Our time. From the *Torah* to the *Bible*, from *Homer* to the *Gospels*, no group of texts has engendered more scholarly research and commentary. Yet not a single word about the *total* unity of cosmological reference to the constellations – across all epic texts – is found by any academic commentator prior to this generation. This, perhaps, may qualify as new information.

Why did we need this information – and how is it only pieced together in our age? It is based on close observation of the epic structure. Astrology is the oldest human science – that is, if by science we mean astrology gives data that is coded by humans, gives reliable linguistic valuation, and enjoys consistent human interest. The language of astrology is the most ancient form of human speech. Yet, a final question. Where did we get the exactitude of the zodiac bestiary? How are they consistent in divergent cultures? Because all of earth life was encoded from another location.

Certainly, the preceding hypothesis is distinctly unmodern in its superstructure. Yet it is possible that this is what truth looks like. Every age of epic poetry follows cosmology. If true, we are compelled to investigate the connection. Any strong theory of poetry must account for this information – just now discovered at the dawning of the Age of Aquarius. This is the secret that literature contains.

No one in power ever anticipates the new charismatic message. Only the epic poet performs this function. Whether he is the poet of a *Bible*, a mythic narrative, or a long narrative poem. A story of cosmology is told with authority. We do not know where the parables of Christ came from. They are charismatic in their origin and power. We don't know where Aesop Fables came from. We do not know where the twelve labors of Hercules came from. We do not know the uncanny source of poetic authority – we only know there is a linguistic code and it is connected to cosmology. This is a victory of original information.

Chandos Ring introduces a new constellation in the heavens. The constellation of Aquarius, now just entering the night sky, portends a new message. What is the secret of its message? We will have to understand the astrology of Aquarius to answer that question. *Aaron, Talon, Cheda, Black Terry*, and *Wakeda*, the characters of *Chandos Ring*, meet the constellation of Aquarius – and linguistically code the new message of future men. We know for certain that the Age of Pisces (brotherhood, proliferation), is over. Already we see the empty churches of European capitals. Christ, the double fish, is no longer followed in the West. The great cathedrals in Europe are museums. Western men do not turn to their churches in crisis – they turn to their doctors. Christianity is a shadow of its former *linguistic* power. In *Chandos Ring,* a new human language (that mirrors the protocols of cosmology) now privileges a severe selection of ideation. This is the last days of an entire epoch. Western modernism will not survive the arrival of the *Water Carrier.* I tell the narrative of the Aquarius constellation.

Before his final madness, Wittgenstein said, "We make to ourselves pictures of facts [stories]." This is consistent with the principles of Story Theory. Western men have made factual gods from texts arraigned by cosmology. Abraham (and thus, the Hebrews) never existed in archeology – they are fabrications of an epic poet. The Canaanites simply *became* the Hebrew people as the *Books of David* and *Moses* were written. A new poem, a new people. Organized writing always comes before organized thought. The *Bible* is an example of a strong theory of epic poetry. We have lived twenty-five hundred years by a stitched quilt of epic poems!

If true, what power on earth could compare to the skill of the poet? These are the linguistic myths: We are the chosen people of Yahweh. We are defined by the Laws of Moses. We are citizens of Rome. We are followers of Christ. We possess the inalienable Rights of Man. Science can explain and cure every evil. America is the only indispensable nation. These are poetic assertions of the epic trope – as embodied in subsequent Western civilizations. Each represents a narrative of national civilization. They are long lived. Each is a linguistic myth that has been asserted with a hidden cosmology. Each myth is certainly true as men live by the assertion that they are true. How can anyone say that Christ is not Christ if there is 2000 years of an assertion of the fact? Of course it was true to the Western men of the last 2000 years. That's how truth operates – with the assertion of a narrative. Now, we move ahead to the next heroic assertion of the human.

There are no human facts. Humans linguistically *assert* facts. There are only facts of relative cosmology. No civilization exactly reproduces reality. All a civilization can do is to assert a narrative of artificial reality. Our proof? No linguistic outsider will agree that the Hebrews, or the Romans, or the Greeks, or the Americans were a chosen people. Only these peoples have made an epic narrative of their own exception. The Arabic-speaking people will not allow that modern Americans or the Hebrews (for example) are chosen people. Still less will the Russians or the Chinese honor our assertion that we are a superior nation. Only we who believe in these poetic narratives will enforce this assertion of our mythic code. To be an elect, to be a chosen people, is a high poetic aspiration. It is a quality not bestowed – but linguistically claimed. Then enforced – with determination, control of resources, and blood.

Humans do not follow the supposed rationality of Being – they follow the picture – the story – they make of the facts. Most humans are essentially slaves – to advertisements, desires, addictions, fashions, and emotional obsessions. Yet Western humans still insist that they are free. This protocol is not rational

– freedom is only a protocol of linguistics. Let us, then, follow this pattern we have learned of the linguistic transitions embedded in the cosmos. Let us look into the night sky for a pattern of human sentience. It is distinctly unmodern, yet generous with benefits and solutions.

An outlander, a star runner, makes an assertion of power: The Water Carrier makes a new selection of life. It is an Exodus from Sapiens.

CHAPTER TWENTY-FOUR

Why Is There Poetry?

Why is poetry a valid form of human information? Because there is no externally existing fact about our life outside of our asserted narrative of life. Not even matter can be proven to exist. Matter –as *world* – is a mutable category within a still not understood method of perception. This makes us creatures – not of physical matter – but of story.

Further, we don't know where our Western mind originated. It is a mystery. There is no archeology for the Western mind. There is no previous biology, no previous archeology for the human mind. Consciousness, it is proven, then, has elements alien to mere physical causation. Seminal poetic texts cannot confirm their supposed human originators.

We don't know who wrote the Orpheus poems – it wasn't a man named Orpheus. We don't know who wrote the Homeric poems – it was not a man named Homer. We don't know who wrote *Hesiod* – it was not a sheepherder named Hesiod. We don't know who wrote the *Vedic* epic poems. We don't know who wrote the *Books of Moses* – it is certain it was not a man named Moses. We don't know who wrote the *Song of Solomon* – it was not King Solomon. We don't know who wrote the *Psalms of David* – it was certainly not the murderer King David. No one has ever confirmed the archeology of any of these epic texts. We don't know who wrote *Matthew, Mark, Luke,* and *John* – it wasn't these gentlemen. We don't know who wrote any of the many first human epic poems of Sumer. We don't know who wrote the epic of *Gilgamesh*. We don't know who wrote the epic of *Jason and the Argonauts*. We don't know who or what is exactly in pursuit of the *Golden Fleece*. We don't know who wrote the *Sonnets*, *The Tempest*, or *Hamlet* – it certainly was not a bag goods salesman.

My point? Epic poetry is alien information. All poetry originates in cosmology. There is something alien and nonlinear about human consciousness. It comes and goes – it rises and disappears – as on a wheel. It reminds the philosopher of quantum mechanics – where the photon (according to quantum theory) comes and goes as the observer modifies his observation. It is clear we don't even know where Homo sapiens came from – it certainly is not the DNA belonging to Neanderthal man. I find these deep mysteries a significant clue about the veracity, the accuracy, of our modern assumptions of civilization. So many unexplored clues may yet be conjured from our epic poems. I hope my point is clear. Consciousness is revealing that it is still unformed – unfinished. We are absolute beginners. It is still morning in the mind.

There is poetry since we have no evidence of the nature of our existence. All we can substantiate about consciousness is that it contains a strongly prejudicial bias – every other supposed *fact* is opinion and story – it is literature – it is pulp fiction. It is Story Theory. To even make the assertion that you are alive, even this tentative first attempt of fact is a prejudice about what you are – it is a story you have made. With the first syllables of a narrative of your consciousness you immediately transition to story. This is a fact so easily verified, so basic in its construction, that no speech of modernism can contradict the first principle of Story Theory.

Who told you that you are alive? You are the only creature in the universe that makes a story of consciousness – as a form of life. What if consciousness is only a virus that has escaped the crib of other forms of being? In truth, there is no independent verification of your human *construction* of life! And if so, how can scientists claim to make independent verifications of any material proofs - if they cannot even obtain independent verification of human life itself? According to materialism, the human mind is a singularity – that is, we cannot verify of what the human mind consists? Why did early men build temples oriented towards strange unknown cosmology? Why build temples at all? Why water Baptism? Why invent poetry? Why give stories to the constellations? Why favor one type of men over others? Why do we favor one kind of beauty over others? Why do we always fear to tell the truth? Our fellow creatures are disqualified as objective observers – since they merely have the same virus!

No, you gained your ideology of life from another man's text. I am certain that you were told that you are alive. Where was the necessity for this declaration? It seems suspiciously shrill. Is there some evidence, some fact, outside of consciousness that confirmed you are alive? That is impossible. What is there that exists *outside* of consciousness? If there is *something*, tell me how you know it? You cannot. Therefore, your condition of being alive is merely a rumor, a strong suggestion you have heard. I am certain that your *condition of life* is a story you have read – and believed. How does it end? It has an epic explication – not a lyric footnote.

You don't actually know who you are, since your consciousness may as well be only an illusion, or a dream, or a virus. We may as certainly be at the center of the Black Hole, as standing in the Garden of Eden, or living in the New Jerusalem, or struggling for freedom inside the dark, alienated heart of modernism. None of these epic poems exist on earth. We are living lives within epic poems on the astral plane. Which is more real? Can you verify the difference? You cannot.

Modernism is what we say it is – as the Black Hole is what we say it is. Your belief of world has either come from a *text of faith* or a *text of science*. Both are inescapably poems. In Story Theory, each is a poetic text. Is one text really different from the other? Is one *linguistic code* – one linguistic assertion – better than another? You have proof? No, since all texts are poems of bias. We do not know the source of bias contained in consciousness. Therefore, men can only make a poem of their consciousness. This is why there is poetry. Epic poetry is the supreme human feedback – since it best represents the human protocol of ideation. Epic poetry detects charismatic arrival of information (of life). Every civilization is based on an epic text/hero/myth.

This book is a complete reassessment of human consciousness. A dispassionate view of the evidence may suggest that the bias of human consciousness is possibly dangerous to all *other* life forms. It is true – humans are attempting to destroy all other life forms to fit the conditions of their own alien sentience. It is happening all around us. Humans that use linguistic codes seek hegemonic expression. This means that language and men – virulently proliferating with linguistic devices (as modernism) – are dangerous in the extreme. Danger cannot be separated from linguistic patterns. Self-referent modernism *obscures* the hurt of modernism. Men are more exclusively involved in deceit, betrayal, and murder – even as they become more civilized.

Life contains menace. Peril is the only condition of men. Murder and death are embedded in every Western text. This cannot be an accident of spleen of the writer. Murder is strong statement of text. Death is an element of chaos that we have not fully delineated. This is not wise, since death, as life, is firmly positioned within consciousness – and thus, death is liable to be changed by the sentience of the observer. We have to carefully watch our concept of *death*. Most of us fail to survive our own pronouncements, our own representations of death. In truth, each of us has exactly trimmed and ordered our own deaths. When it arrives, each man intimately recognizes his own death.

There is poetry because there is unresolved chaos in the human condition – and modernism cannot fix it. Consciousness is at war – and no propaganda of a prosthetics of peace can fix it. There is a direct line from the first written texts of *Gilgamesh* to the mass death machine of the atomic bomb and quantum mechanics (as linguistics). Gilgamesh had to break into the guarded spaceport to attempt to wrest control of the machine of consciousness – guarded by the alien god. The record is very exact in this respect. The first poetry contained uncanny information – and it is still not fully digested. The complaint made by the first epic poem was that there was something wrong with human life – it had a strong element of chaos – and Gilgamesh cited his passionate protest. He did not know yet the secret that consciousness was still unfinished – so he went away hopeless. Only now with Story Theory do we know how to seize control of consciousness. *Chandos Ring* stumbles upon it. But first, the modern idiom must be shamed into non-operation. Then, a new ear may hear the emitting pulse.

There is poetry because there is death. Death is a large issue with Homo sapiens. Consciousness of death is our signature rune. Our stories do not tell of life – far from it – the central player of all Western literature is death. To prove to other men that he was alive, Pompey inscribed on his temple to Minerva (62 BC) that he defeated, killed, and enslaved 12,183,000 men in his life. Look again at that number. At the end of his Gallic Wars, alone, Julius Caesar estimated proudly that he killed 1,192,000 men in battle. Look again at the number. His civilian casualties were not even listed. Caesars' work in Gaul was a series of mass extinctions. Using the code of genocide, men wish to verify that their consciousness was a fact. Is there genocide in our own time? We have a clue that consciousness seeks its own severe conditions.

Yet why was murder a means to verify their excellence? Was it for the same reason that mass murder was so often resorted to in the 20th century? Is murder the highest art of human consciousness? We must test this theory. History seems to support the thesis. I have estimated over 13,000 genocides and/or extinctions in my career as a scholar of the Western canon. Clearly, the Roman leaders were searching the strongest form of language to validate and verify the from of their consciousness. Murder is what Western men do. Perhaps the question is – can we do murder better? Like death, moderns appear to recoil form murder with insensibility. Yet modernism is the most capable and effective mechanics of murder ever invented. Let's be clear. Murder is another form of human linguistics. The atomic bomb is a monument to high human linguistic codes. It is a poem of high clarity. The human code is germane to all forms of eradication. Any theory of poetry must account for this element.

There is poetry because the acts of men are inexplicable. The case can be made from the human record that if you were not of the murdering class, then you were of the secondary class of slaves. Is it any different today? Our leaders lie to us with contempt once they gain power. Beloved leaders as Mohammed, Hitler, Stalin, Mao, and Pol Pot have murdered over 200 million people to verify their consciousness. They each advanced a text – a book – as acts of hegemonic struggle against other. All books are linguistic warfare against previous men – against alternate linguistic control of human life. Linguistics is deadly. Every war is a war of textual genome.

Linguistic motivation is the key to all human acts. The goal of the last century's murdering regimes was to seize the hegemonic language of modernity from the West. Stalin, Pol Pot, and Mao sought to counter Western capitalistic, linguistic men – by eradication of modern men (the overpopulated, capitalistic, metropolis, information culture). They lost the struggle for hegemony. Modernism survived the contest with socialized ideology. Just.

Yet they lost to a modernism that is unable to reform its own toxic waste. The liberal West won the Cold War – now there is no longer a competitive world power able to make an *alternate* modernism. All men that advocate genocides are, in effect, grammarians – they wish to eradicate another man's linguistics. Stalin failed; Hitler failed; Pol Pot failed – though they murdered millions. Modernism will survive so long as there are large urban cities. Russia did not defeat Hitler; the city of Stalingrad defeated Hitler. Even Mao failed – because there were great cities in China. Today, China has a linguistically capitalistic form of government. There is only a Western modernism – and it is globally hegemonic. It is a temporary construct. Modernism can survive so long as the giant cities survive.

What shall our victorious modern liberal idiom now make of the life on Earth? It will murder billions. In the space of my generation, over 60% of human languages have become extinct. Industrialization and human proliferation, empowered by science, now ensure the extinctions of entire species – daily. What does it mean if animal species disappear more rapidly now, under liberal scientific modernism, than under all murdering dictators of the past? It means that *death* is what linguistically superior humans perform. We eradicate what does not fit into the conditions we seek of consciousness. Modernism, as any text, is murder by other means.

What if it should once enter our lexicon that the Earth is fatally over-crowded and must – for the sake of life – be selected to size? That would be a new human idiom. It would be opposite from the faith of modern proliferation – for the sake of proliferation. What if murder becomes a linguistic expression of morality on an industrial scale? What if our final entry into space will not be achieved until there has been a complete eradication of the populations of Earth? Will the political class currently in control of modern technology always be in control of modern technology? It seems naive in the extreme to make this assumption. What if there is (another) economic collapse – and another Hitler rises to popular enthusiasm again? The nightmare of liberalism is a Hitler with nuclear weapons. Therefore, liberal ideology will use this excuse to move to final ideological control of all human culture and all human societies. This is the excuse that will be made. There will always be an excuse to surrender freedom of speech and movement – for a propaganda of greater security and protection. Like a monarch, a hegemonic power can only be accommodated or, alternately, eradicated. Resistance is fatal so long as the hegemon has the power to control all ideational space.

We cannot rest assured that kind and tolerant minds will use the modernism in a beneficial manner. Beneficial to whom? My fellow townsman, President Truman, dropped the atomic bomb and killed 250,000 in one hour – yet we were under no imminent threat – we were just tired of war. Democracy is therefore no sanctuary from mass murder. Democracy will kill with advocacy given the slightest encouragement. Democracy, alone, has used the atomic bomb. Democracy is as murderous as any tyranny. The democratic Greeks exterminated each other in three centuries. Democracy stands in line with Pot Pol.

There is poetry because there are unanswerable questions. Consciousness is essentially charismatic because consciousness is still unfinished, incomplete (a discovery of Story Theory). These are the questions we are faced with when we wish to discover the linguistic bias contained in consciousness. We cannot escape – or competently anticipate – the charismatic tangents of sentience. Charismatic reality is always running down rabbit holes. *No subsequent civilization has ever detected the civilization that immediately replaced it.* That says a lot about the charismatic structure of consciousness. Asserting that life should be stable, humans make a counter prosthetics. We make linguistic patterns of modernism to ensure the stasis of the modern perspective. Yet this makes us into machines. Will we be reduced to Replicants? Are we at that station now?

Consciousness makes a selection of life forms – *no matter what* are the negative consequences to populations not selected for life. This is what happens within consciousness – selection. A severe judgment is made each moment of sentient consciousness. Why have we not faced these facts before? Murder, as selection, is a thoroughly human protocol. The historian of human murder must assemble unaccountable and irrational mountains of cognitive evidences. Who could make the accounting with competence? This is why there is still no high philosopher of murder.

Is consciousness beneficial to all forms of life – or is there a rigorous selection made? Is consciousness suited for proliferation? No. There is clearly a rigorous selection made. If a rigorous selection is made of the living – then who performs this selection of bias? Is the recent significant rise in human murder merely a reaction to an increase of over-populated cities? Then, as the planet becomes more populated, the exterminations will only have a tendency to continue. I conclude it is time to make a radical reassessment of what value humans place on consciousness. We will have to accept the protocol of consciousness – or disappear ourselves. Consequently, we may be surprised to see consciousness in a new and unsettling perspective. All the previous assumptions of human nature have utterly failed us. We must begin our assessment anew. Consciousness is not mere proliferation. Consciousness selects – ruthlessly.

How can consciousness – and the uncanny source of bias in consciousness – be approached? What language should we use to access the information of a hermetically sealed and self-referent consciousness? It takes a lot of care. It takes deliberation. It takes a lifetime of study of symbols. Poetry, alone, exists as the human singularity. Therefore, humans are not confined exclusively to a rational choice of action. This discovery is a victory, not a regression.

The rational element has always been misunderstood. Rationality is a linguistics used to quantify our dreams. Dreams always *precede* rationality. Rationality is only a tangential tool to be used *after* the original inspiration of life. Rationality is not an original life message – it comes *after* the life message is signaled. Dreams, inspirations, prophecy are the human element. That human who does not set out to fulfill his dreams – though dreams may be an impossible reach of the imagination – is, in large respect, not human. So this is a clue we have discovered about human consciousness. We persist with a small lamp of story to light our way against peril and adversity. The human is irrational. Only robots omit the function of dreams. Every love is a prayer of courage. Every child is prophecy of courage. Every poem is a prayer for courage. Only men can interpret a poem. Only a machine is exclusively rational – because a machine has no quality of courage. Courage may supersede rationality on every occasion. This is the message of the epic poem.

There is poetry because we ruthlessly reject rational life. We don't embrace everyday reality – we avoid it at all cost. Humans have made vital discoveries of life – that is, from their imaginative (and courageous) choice to deny normal, visible reality. We deny that our failures are permanent. We deny that our work is useless – though we clearly undertake worthless projects. We deny that our mistakes are final evidence of our Being. The philosopher therefore must consider the role of irrational poetry in the human condition. Because we deny visible and rational realities, I confirm by this action there is a bias contained in sentient consciousness. The human is well placed to make conquest of the galaxies.

If all phenomena can be viewed as information that is arraigned or summoned to appear on a screen, as a holograph, then all we have to do is to master the way the mind summons information. In Story Theory, and as quantum theory suggests, material objects are closer to holograms in the mind – not actual solid *things*. This is the first step in the stations to seize control of unfinished consciousness. Just to admit that consciousness (life) can still be structured to our will is a complete victory – a new innovation of the human condition.

How solid are the conditions of our mortal state? It is ridiculously fragile. Our mortal state, as a quantum construct, is only as solid as our consciousness – our belief *within* consciousness – permits. If a man experiences the challenge of a material sickness, he has another choice above and beyond the faith of medical science – above and beyond acceptance of the visible, even rational, spectrum. He may make a further resort to sentience. Who told you that a cancer should kill you? At what moment did you accept this logic? That was a moment you built your coffin. Even now doctors are telling us that, based on their trials, it does not matter what a human does – it does not matter what medical procedure he accepts – it *matters* what he thinks about his condition of health. The trained mind can *always* obtain the time and space, the location of the *information* of our well-being – in the protected dimension where the experience of our well-being is still intact.

This is not a form of magic; this is not positive thinking; this is the trained mind in action. This is an overt act of a further resort to conscious manipulation of life. This is not merely the act of faith; this is the act of a mind fully engaged with all the powers available to it. If, due to sentience, we are informed of a condition of life, we may, likewise, make a further resort to sentience to alter the condition of that life if it may seem to harm us. When this mechanism in sentient consciousness is fully understood, then all the other questions of the material body will also be understood. According to Story Theory, there is no justification for men to exist if it is not, in some degree, a project to seize control of consciousness. Peril and sickness are only the first trial of the human project. What must survive – what always scurvies – is the *process* of life you have chosen to use as your idiom of life. It is the process of life we must win – not mortality.

What do we seek in our new idiom? After the next genealogical advance of Homo sapiens there will be a new creature and a new mind. We seek the condition of the human *magus* – the human that reconstructs the conditions of consciousness at will. The magus personality, the end state of a future *Homo faustus*, is able to reorganize consciousness to fit the conditions of consciousness he seeks. Until then, we wear the blinders of our limited investigation of life –I mean, our limited materialist linguistics. All the beautiful machines that we seek will no longer be blocked by modernism, materialism, and aggressive secularism.

Before then, there must be a transformation of human linguistics. A new linguistic code is equivalent to a new genetic code. If modernism is not the final human idiom, then we may already move ahead of a failed linguistic pattern. Our goal in life is not to be modern; our goal is to gain control of our consciousness. When we arrive at our end state, we will not be asked for our modernism. We will be asked for our eyes.

Men do not struggle for power; they struggle for language of what may be. Men struggle for a wider narrative of enchantment. The concept of power has no meaning at all. Power explains, nor reveals, anything – except that it contains a linguistic bias. We may as well say that men seek joy. Again, we don't know what this means. We reveal that men seek a hegemonic discovery of language. Therefore any power of poetry will be located in a theory of poetry that may advocate a severe selection of life forms. As long as we cannot define (or explain) the terms, human *power* or human *joy*, then consciousness is still unknown – and unfinished.

How can we encompass the truth of the matter? Consciousness is largely a killing machine – a machine that eradicates, crushes, and grinds mortal bodies. Consciousness, historically, has no existential difficulty with the murder of mortal bodies. This clearly shows that mortality is a temporary condition – and not a real substance. Essentially all religious and political ideologies are forms of murder and justification of murder. The Jews murdered the Canaanites with Yahweh looking on with approval. In fact, it was Yahweh's idea. This tells us everything we need to know about supremacy of the mortal state. It is not made for supremacy. It is a conditional courage. It is a peril to be faced. Morality is a moveable feast. There has never been a morality that was not subsequently reversed – by a linguistic bias, prejudice or agenda. There never was a god that was not made by a poet – then superseded by a poet. That tells us everything we need to know about poetry. This tells us why there is poetry.

There is poetry because Cain murdered Able. All new discoveries of men are deeply drenched in murder. From Cortez's gold to Einstein's atom – each discovery only leads to murder – a selection of life forms. What does this signify about consciousness? Clearly a severe selection is made with any new discovery. We are now far from the idea that *love* is the single force contained in Being. Consciousness is dangerous in the extreme. The Age of Pisces – the double fish – is disappearing from the night sky. Love and toleration (Pisces) are a wounded text – a veneer– we place over a murderous form of consciousness.

There is poetry because we do not detect the original source of life. We bravely make up names of worlds. We try to build a life on literary texts – as world. Poetry is nothing if not a naming of worlds. To name the world is to possess the world. The future linguistic choice will be a poem as rich as science – as rich as the faiths of Abraham.

The language of this poem is the Manhattan Project of the 21st century.

CHAPTER TWENTY-FIVE

The Irrelevance of Modern Poetry

What serious person will deny that poetry is irrelevant to modern Western societies? Modern poetry is unloved, not because it lacks acolytes – there are a surprising number of Western people who still write and give their opinion of poetry. Modern poetry has no prestige because it has no modern authority – that is, poetry is not the chosen medium of information of modernism. Anciently, poetry was loved because it contained superior human information. Does this mean that poetry is permanently defective, passé – in fact, unmodern? It will take a rugged honesty to address these questions.

We have already rehearsed all the reasons why poetry is so crippled that a new theory of poetry is demanded. Modern poets *use* poetry as a form of individual and confessional journalism. They do not write poetry assuming that it must be a strong narrative that lives forever in human ideation. Poetry, to moderns, more closely resembles a hobby. And it has assumed the aesthetics of a hobby. Our proof? Without a vibrant market for poetry it is impossible to distinguish important poets from – any poet. In modernism, anyone's practice of poetry contains as much value as another person's practice of poetry. Society no longer makes anymore a distinction between poets – than they do between home pottery makers. Each, apparently, has equal value. This is as much to say that poetry no longer gives vital information. Thus we observe that modern poetry replicates the aesthetics of a *hobby*. Poetry just does not matter to the modern Western. It is one of the unspoken mysteries of our civilization.

We don't know what day this fatal transition was made. . . sometime in the 1950's I suppose. It happened unnoticed. There was no announcement in the newspapers that modern poetry was only a hobby – a pastime of dilatants. Not a single winner of the Yale poetry contest (since 1952) has ever become known to American households. At the end of the 20th century, the use of the adjective "great" or "superior" before the name of a poet (even a single poem) was risible.

Such a phrasing is simply meaningless – in the same way that a certain Mr. X could be called the most superior stamp collector. It is linguistically risible to say there is a great poet, a superior poem - as much as it is to say there is a great stamp collector. Under modernism, a great poet or a great stamp collector is equally risible - or alternately, indefensible. Only stamp collectors recognize other stamp collectors. And this is exactly where poets are in modern society. Today, only poets give recognition to other poets. It simply does not matter to modern society who is the best stamp collector – or the best poet. Subsequently, consequently, there is no longer a need or an expectation for a great poet in society – unless it was to honor the perspective of a demographic class that fit into the narrative of modernism. An unknown minority woman, for instance, could be declared the greatest poet (a typical modern political maneuver) – and then, modern academic critics were simply dared to challenge this assertion. Of course, there was only silence – since the threat of social retribution was implied in the assertion. This act is poetry in the service of politics. The hegemonic social narrative makes an assertion of audacity – and threatens to monitor who does not fall into line with the assertion. This is the state of *play* in contemporary poetry. There does not exist an independent arbitrator of poetic merit because there is not an independent (and public) market for poetry. Why?

We know exactly what modern poetry cannot do. It has not maintained its ancient prestige in our civilization. Poetry has not attempted to address (or monument) the last 100 years of Western scientific imagination. Murder and science are the principle human events of the last century. Modern poets do not address either. Modern poets do not address science – they do not act if science exits – yet science is the greatest imaginative achievement of our century.

This is the issue. Poetry no longer dares to tell a story. When the element of story is removed – the human element is removed. Lemonade stands contain more vital modern information than modern prose poems. No one fails to be charmed by a small child selling lemonade. It is a sight that makes any adult stop and wonder. On the other hand, no one is charmed by modern poems. No one reads or buys modern poems. Why?

Poetry has failed to contain the human *information* of story. Human story is now exclusively portrayed in film, novels, or television, but not in poetry. Modern poets do not have the confidence or audacity to use poetry as the medium to tell a story with character, depth, or intense scope. Therefore, modern poetry is no longer practiced as a vital art.

Our proofs are already well rehearsed. There is no current market for modern poetry. No American may live exclusively from the craft of modern poetry. No man on the street can name a living poet. What kind of poets are those who tolerate this condition? Is it possible that humans, the language-makers, do not even recognize their unique singularity – telling stories with poems? This, then, is the *first* symptom of the failure of poetry in our time – the failure of the confidence of the modern poet to tell a story – an extended human narrative of power and significance.

The *second* symptom of modern poetry is more intimate. Modern poetry is weak because there is a schism in vernacular English. This volume shall discover the alienation of the Western vernacular. In volume two I showed that the sign of all great poetry is the confidence and audacity in the voice of the poet. This confidence and audacity of a poet is gone. Modern poets, at best, are tentative and minor. They are so unsure of their art that they have ceased to give a narration of men. Modern poets no longer enumerate narratives of human character – with a beginning, a middle, and an end. Poetry cannot sustain a substantial narrative. Poetry can't tell a story in the modern idiom. Why did they lose their courage?

I have shown that scientific materialism is based on poetic belief. I have shown that science contains unreliable information, and that all modern faiths are temporary. Thus, I establish that science has no lasting authority over the narrative of our creation. Yet the authority of scientific hegemony has sucked all the air – and confidence – out of the Western cultural space. This is a mistake. According to Story Theory, science operates exactly as poetic speech. Yet modern poets, spectacularly, *fail* to include in their poems a linguistic investigation of modern science. This is a shocking and revealing lacuna in modern poetry. How can modern poets claim to reflect modern men – when they avoid all narration of modern America's greatest linguistic innovation – science? Not only do they ignore science – they mistakenly fear it.

Modern poets are afraid of the secret language of science. So Story Theory, as presented in these volumes, races to heal this schism in our cultural space. What is remarkable is that no one – no poet, no philosopher – has addressed this issue. How is it possible that the schism has not been recognized before? We know exactly why. For the same reason that modern men don't care if stamp collectors are in crisis. To modern men, poetry is a hobby. It is not essential.

We have to see what science is - in its constitutional parts and structure. When closely examined as a series of linguistic assertions - science immediately degrades. Science is a linguistic protocol. Full stop. Civilization is a linguistic protocol. Full stop. Modern science is a language, as any other, that seeks hegemonic control over the ideational human landscape. To say that science has any referent authority other than its linguistic achievement is only to construct a false idol out of the scientific community. Science is not the final reality – it is a linguistic assertion of reality. Science is a poem we have made of the modern language of the universe – that's all there is to it. As any language, science is temporal and liable to change its value at any moment. Science is not a fixed star – any more than Christianity was a fixed star. Both are susceptible to a further linguistic innovation. Both are wounded moralities.

In the poem of science, men have decreed the universe is made up of dead matter – and matter, moreover, is somehow separate from human consciousness. We have rehearsed this point beyond the patience of the reader – only because this is the key that unravels the entire modernist structure. The misprision of materialism calls for a strong and clarifying counter-argument. This book was written not only to present notes of the poem – but also to counter insidious *word*-philosophers as Bertrand Russell. There are many founding "charters" of materialism – when the concept of the human – as a being with a soul – changed to that of a mortal with a physical brain. I present one. The following is Russell's summation of the dark human condition in 1912 – when materialist academic culture first made it's race to hegemony:

> "That man is the product of causes which had no prevision of
> the ends they were achieving; that his origin, his growth, his
> hopes and fears, his loves and his beliefs are but the outcome
> of accidental collocations of atoms; . . . that all the labors of
> the ages, all the devotion, all the inspiration, all the noonday
> brightness of human genius, are destined to extinction in the
> vast death of the solar system, and that the whole of man's
> achievement must inevitably be buried beneath the debris of a
> universe in ruins – all these things, if not quite beyond dispute,
> are nearly certain. Brief and powerless is man's life; on him and
> all his race the slow, sure doom falls pitiless and dark. Blind to
> good and evil, reckless of destruction, omnipotent matter rolls
> on its relentless way."

This is the kernel of modern linguistics – isn't it? This is the suspicion lodged within the modern mind. This is the central philosophy of modernism. The treatise that cannot give a response to Russell's essential ideology of modernism – need not pretend to philosophy. Not only is Russell's worldview impoverished in its selection of data – it is aggressively prejudiced. Not only is his prophesy of modernism insidious, it makes the *magus* human cringe with disgust. How many moderns were undone by this narrow selection of data? It is a poem of pure ideational construction – that is, it is a poem of hate against any life that cannot be controlled, exploited, and dissected by the accepted clichés of rationalism – that is, secular, capitalistic, scientific linguistics. Russell's paragraph is a prose poem of messianic and missionary zeal – a call for rationalized self-elimination of the Western heritage. Subsequent quantum physics and String Theory confine Russell's prose to the dead letter office. The universe is a selection of linguistics. It contains no archeology of scientific origin or stasis.

This is what the rationalist does not suspect: the universe is a linguistic construct. The universe changes as the language of a hegemonic civilization changes. The epic trope records this ideational shift. It is a shift that exactly mirrors cosmology. Newton's laws of an inanimate, dead universe have long been exposed by Einstein to be wrong. Newton was actually an alchemist and a follower of Renaissance Hermetic astrology (unknown to the modern public). Today, the classical physics of Newton are passé. His physics do not operate at the very small scale. Newton's universe, as Einstein's, as Ptolemy's are now linguistically exposed as only one of many poems of reality of universe – among others. In one hundred years, there will be a new universe – and a new linguistics to form the structure of this still unknown universe. In Story Theory, there are many poems of "universe reality."

Though perhaps interesting as speculation, Einstein's universe, as Newton's, is essentially irrelevant to average humans living their mundane lives. No one needs Newton, or Ptolemy, or Einstein to live a good life. Einstein's ideas are thus a form of poetic and imaginative excess – soon to be outclassed by further interpretations of phenomena. Quantum mechanics, in turn, exposed Einstein's universe, to be a conditional construct. Quantum mechanics proved that matter was not even where the math predicted it should appear. Small objects had a separate reality apart from large objects. The observer changes the objects he observes. Thus, in effect, the observer *makes* world. The point? There is no *single, fixed* universe. It is only a linguistic construct. Thus there is no room for the arrogance of modern materialists such as Russell.

So, why is poetry supreme? Since there are no eternal facts, no fixed universe existing outside of human poetic belief, poetry is a human tool of meaning. As we make story, we make our own construction of logic and self-referent reason. We assemble, in effect, our own *Higgs Boson* (the supposed missing element that explains how *empty matter* has visible mass). This much we can predict. When found, the Higgs Boson will be an element that is under the control of the self-conscious observer. So what is vial about its discovery? The conscious mind will still be the central element of ideation. That is, we mentally create our own mass that is observed and assembled on to our ideational screen (the mind) – in effect, as a hologram – by the architecture of our language. Our minds are entangled with other *suggested* forms of ideation. The world we perceive not only *appears* – it *appears* to fit the conditions of consciousness that our minds were trained to perceive. This is how the human lives his life – he linguistically organizes his reality in a way that achieves comprehension. There is no human exception to this protocol.

There is poetry since humans are not formed by "outside" realities. We construct an *internal universe* of causation to justify our own actions of irrationality. This makes us all poets. We create all dimensions – all perceived space and time – with our poem of life. Our poem of space and time has a beginning, a middle, and an end.

When the modern poet attempts a poem about the slow debilitation of his or her father's disease, for example, he is not using an audacious language of dominion. Instead, the poet is using a language that is subdued and intimidated by the scientific logic of the disease. Any belief in a process of disease is but a short step from making that disease an idol of ideational power. Material logic is a tyrant that attempts to force you to its rules. Any logic of disease firmly held in the mind may be manifested on the body. In this way, by this insidious protocol, the modern poet is utterly intimidated by the linguistics of material disease process. After all, if modernism is an accepted speech, how else should the modern poet speak? Of course, he thinks he should speak modernism - with all the horrible logic of modernism.

Initial Conclusions of a Poetic Theory Can Be Made

For our desired construction of a strong theory of poetry, our way has become clearer. To summarize our argument thus far, we have the facts that must inform a linguistic representation of human consciousness.

First, we have seen that modern information is corrupt and unreliable. Second, the epic trope embeds poetry that contains reliable forms of accurate information of life. Thirdly, science is the highest form of *poetry* in our generation – and should be celebrated as such. Fourthly, if science is only a form of high poetry, there no longer need exist a schism between the vernacular speaker and the priestly secret language of science. Fifthly, all forms of speech are methods of prophesy. Sixthly, no civilization exactly reproduces reality. Each civilization enthusiastically privileges a specific, and selected, ideational linguistics – in exclusion to all other idioms. The power structure of civilization is always corrupt and accumulates wounded moralities. Therefore, we may at any moment make a further innovation of linguistic reality. In light of these facts (Story Theory), there is no impediment to the confidence of strong vernacular poets.

The strong poet must combat the civilization that would make his voice secondary. In modernism, the emphasis is not on the audacity of a vernacular language, but the feeling that the human is *subdued* and utterly dependent upon the modernism's *secret* language, that is, the hegemony of political and rationalistic determination. Modernism, as materialism, mathematics, technology, medical descriptions of disease, etc. – are only linguistic constructs.

This, then, is my critique of modern poetry. The modern poet does not dare to change the formula of modernism with innovation. The modern poet is manically satisfied with modernism – even as much as modernism reduces the poet's vernacular to a nonentity. Modernism cannot reform modernism. The strong poet can change the linguistic construct of his civilization by an opposite, and further resort to linguistics reconstruction. What else is the competence of a poet?

The modern poet fails to disentangle his poetic craft from his social defeat – his schism – of language. If he cannot dissect a complicated mathematical equation, if he does not use footnotes, should he thereby allow that his vernacular is somehow second-rate, until his thought – even his language – expresses his second-rate condition? No. Poets should write as if they are billionaires. Intimidated daily by the linguistic structures of science and medicine, the modern poet is not free in his own imagination, and his language reflects his position of curtailment. For this reason, we see that vernacular English has become, somehow, second-rate. This is why our poets are silent and our language is alienated from human audacity. This is why the time has come for a new theory of poetry.

Poetry should be unlike a prose report. Prose contains an expected and scheduled language. Yet poetry's independence is based firmly on audacity and confidence of language. If the poetic language used is not audaciously independent – then it is not poetry – it is prose. When the vernacular loses its audacity, its sudden innovation, its confidence, its natural enchantment, then the poet cannot operate in society as a force of independent value.

The first image we have of any great poet is his audacity and confidence. It does not matter if you prefer classic French, Italian, or English poets to modern American poets. Whether we wish to reference Villon or Rabelais, Whitman or Shakespeare, Donne or Blake, Milton or Marlow – the first evidence we are in the presence of a great poet is his or her clear, and refreshing, voice of audacity and confidence. (I do not speak of a false confidence that is not supported with merit). If there is no startling, strange appearance of new powers of audacious language, then we do not credit the poet for any achievement in poetry. We pass on with indifference. *Chandos Ring* faces the challenge of the secret language with an audacity that acknowledges no superiority of secret or scientific languages. Can it be sustained? My eyes meet yours as the question forms.

CHAPTER TWENTY-SIX

The Alienation of American Speech

There is a blight in modern speech. Modern psychiatry, literature, and film have attested to the alienation of Western men. It is the theme of all academic Western literature since World War II. Yet never could they discover the actual locality of Western man's alienation. It is a linguistic alienation. Vernacular men are alienated in the modern world because the vernacular speaker is relegated to irrelevant conversation. There is a schism in Western language.

It is the thesis of these volumes that men depend on language for the construct of their ideational experience of world. That is to say, our human power is based on our linguistic power. The unity of language in a culture directly influences the unity of the human being, as well as the possibility of high poetry in the culture. Poets don't search Being for regular life; we search Being for an alternate discovery of audacity. Artists do not seek everyday life; everyday life should be avoided as a plague. Poets do not seek linguistic realism; they seek linguistic power. The poet seeks the opportunity of audacity. The poet chases the utterly strange – yet recognized.

The West suffers from a schism of human language. Since the invention of advanced calculus (17th century), there has been a new audacious language of men. Milton was the last poet not subdued by the presence of a higher, *secret* language in his culture. With Newton, suddenly, there was a class of Westerners that used a language that to other men seemed impenetrable – and somehow superior. Math, as any linguistic cult, is an alternate exploration of reality. Languages reconstruct the human mind – never the same in any epoch. The practical use of this scientific language, operating as a new genetics, transformed the human mind from his former mental state. Astrophysics and, most recently, quantum physics are math dependant languages, which have given us all our modern technologies. From the chaotic human perspective, technologies, working toilets, and machines appear to *linguistically* resemble perfection! As a result, vernacular speakers – those who do not make specialized advancements in technology – lost the prestige of verbal expression. That is, vernacular men lost the authority to speak about the constructs most appropriate, and thus important, to humans. Subsequently, the math specialists (alienated alchemists as *Dee* and *Newton*) successfully transformed the world with *symbols*. The modern mind was thus a poetic reconstruction.

Eventually, insidiously, silently, the vernacular speakers began to feel they possessed a second-hand linguistic mentality. Modern poets, of course using only the vernacular, feel this second-rate condition intimately. If the poet's business is the audacity of language, how may he or she perform this audacity using a second-hand, degraded linguistic tool – the vernacular? The scope of the modern poet's work is fixed to purely *subjective* fields of knowing – the erotic, the romantic, the sentimental, the fictional, the esoteric, etc. Insidiously, today, the most common subject of modern poets is the melodramatic agony of someone that has a disease. How many Western poets in five thousand years have made the subject of their poems a disease? Only the modern poet has done so. This is the modern poet's *niche* – to show his awe of the modern *disease codex*. He calculates that only a codex of modernism (the wounded gravitas of disease) might gain the respected attention of the modern. Modernism can only detect modernism.

In what age can the poet, alone of all craftsmen, *not* make a living of his craft? Only in the modern age. The language and authority of scientific terminology have excluded the possibility of a living, enchanted universe. Therefore the poet, insisting upon the audacity of an enchanted human universe, becomes a risible prophet – at best, a guide for children and impoverished liberals. A well-tuned toilet has only one modern message: the poet's performance has no information. Yet, this crisis raises the possibility of a new theory of poetry.

This is the point. Vernacular speaking men, in so far as they are story-makers, have lost the means to contribute, as a source of authority, to the modern worldview. The vernacular speaker has thus lost the future. That certainly includes most of us. Not confident that they carry the prestige of human discovery, the vernacular speakers have lost the *indispensable* skill of poetic innovation. I speak of the innovations of discovering a new brane of consciousness. All mythic and epic literature tells a story of the cosmos. Epic poetry contains information of the nature and construction of the cosmos. Yet to the modern, this is only white noise.

Though misinterpreted by the incredulous modern academic, it is now clear that the Vedic epics, the Egyptian *Book of the Dead*, the Sumerian creation epics, the Greek epic myths, *Jason and the Argonauts*, and nearly all of Hebrew *Genesis* are stories containing star genealogies. The *New Testament*, as epic narrative, is no exception to our thesis.

Each epoch of zodiac constellation told the story and message of a hero. Gilgamesh/Prometheus, living under the constellation of the bull (Taurus), attempted to steal eternal life from the gods. These cultures, likewise, worshipped the Golden Bull. In the next age, Jason and Moses wore the ram's horns (or ram's fleece) and gave new laws under the constellation of Aries. Moses specifically forbade the former worship of the golden calf (Taurus). The sign of the fish symbolized Jesus, who sought to improve the laws of Moses with the innovation of brotherly love (Pisces/proliferation). At his birth, the *new* star that appeared in the sky was the constellation of Pisces – the sign of the fish. The reader is now familiar with the mechanics of this thesis. The epic trope follows the cosmology of constellations. Yet the point to be refined is that poetry is able to contain and impart the future history of the universe. Each age of the sky embeds a new linguistic idiom.

Modern poets have lost the audacity of star cosmologies. I attempt to illuminate the powerful device embedded in epic cosmology. This does not mean we have to be mathematicians – only that we understand the interpretations made by the stars. They are incantations of probity – and they are oracular in nature. Initially, the message of the new constellation (Aquarius) will be loathsome and rejected by moderns – just as Prometheus (Taurus), Moses, (Aries) and Christ (Pisces) were loathsome and initially rejected. Prometheus has his liver eaten each day – as punishment. Jesus was crucified. Moses (Aries) was not even allowed to see the new Promised Land. This is the fate of the herald. We must burst on contact.

If modern poets have forgotten the communication of the stars, there must be a new theory of poetry that teaches them the sky's cosmologies. *Chandos Ring* is the medium. To the Greeks, the art of poetry was the embedded art of numbers. Until the Age of Johnson, poems were as equally enumerated as *numbers*. Modern poets do not understand their connections to numbers. Modern poets are unable to compete with the math speakers, since they have lost the confidence of their own superiority of ordered idiom. So poets withdrew from the humiliation of not knowing the secret language. Of course, they also withdrew from the modern world. The modern poets, forgetting their connection to stars, constellations, and numbers, gradually lost their audacity just as an educated Western elite began to use calculus to conquer the known world in the late 17th century. The final victory of this modern language was the discovery of the practical use, and thus, the hegemony of industrial mathematics in the 20th century.

A Dark Age is not due to a lack of resources. A Dark Age is due to the schism of language in the human society. After the fall of the Roman Empire, Latin was no longer the vernacular lingua franca, still less, Greek. The Roman and Greek worlds – worlds defined by Latin and Greek – were lost to a society now linguistically divided. German tribes brought in many competitive languages that utterly confused the literate achievement of men in late Roman society. Late Roman writing has consequently the reputation of being a Silver Age of literature.

Latin was only preserved as a unity of cultural ideation under the Roman Church. Guarded behind their high walls, monks kept alive the poetry of the high secret language (Latin). Since all other vernacular men were either illiterate or bound by the violence of the age into slavery, there was no possibility for language to remain unified as a proud and confident literature. Without their unity of language, medieval poets, also suffering a schism of vernacular, could produce no text to assert their unity of free movement in the imagination. Until the rise of vernacular authority, in the 14th century, the authority of priestly languages effectively intimidated all forms of early vernacular. Only in the 14th century do we find vernacular poets – Chaucer in England, Dante in Italy, or the troubadours in Southern France.

The Latin language of the Church was so remote to the common man that the non-Latin speaking populace lived in a separate, alienated world from the priestly class – the class, moreover, who exclusively interpreted the texts, verified the cause of the plagues, the failure of the weather, or, in fact, any human phenomenon. The illiterate vernacular had no voice – and thus, no audacity – in medieval culture. The voice of medieval authority remained with the priests that spoke a magical and forbidden *high* language. The vernacular speakers were alienated from a world where they had no text and waited for the divine judgment, as outlined in the fatalistic narratives conceived by a linguistically insane and confused St. Augustine.

So far from understanding the language of the literate class, the medieval illiterate did not even listen to the meaning of the priest's words at all. We call it a Dark Age when words do not share cultural unity – when they have no effective meaning. We already see the signs of a Dark Age in our time. When modern medical advertisements warn that new pharmaceuticals will possibly kill, cripple, or maim you – and yet *the public ignores this dire language* – we may confirm we live in a dark age where the words do not have meaning. This is proof that modernism's secret language has already begun to fail – as direct information.

A Dark Age is a schism of language. In effect, the modern is in a similar position to the peasant attending a Latin mass of the 10th century church. Today, we don't understand the mathematics behind the scientists' declarations, but we give scientists complete authority over our lives. This is utterly astonishing – a direct confirmation of Story Theory. Modernism is a form of medievalism – another Age of Faith. Moderns live by faith – not by reason. The opinion of the scientist – no matter how humble the scientist – has more value than the opinion of the highest vernacular speaker. And though the value of the scientific information is proven worthless by the findings of the next generation of scientists, we overlook, even forgive, the patently false prognostications of science. That is a protocol of Dark Age – when unreliable information is accepted as the norm. Science has never predicted the next human crisis.

There is only one remedy to a schism of modern vernacular speech. The vernacular speaker has to make a larger innovation of information than is possible by the (now exposed) corruption of *modern* secret languages. Either there must be a charismatic collapse of modernism (due to natural disaster *and* economic failure) – or the vernacular speaker must be enchanted again with his audacity. Either way I can proceed with *Chandos Ring*. I am set to discover the message of the new constellation now rising in cosmology.

If we doubt the agency of language for the health and strength of the human organism, we may observe what developed in the European nations at the beginning of the Renaissance. The Italian poets gained their voice only as the vernacular took its place as the vehicle for authority in a newly emerged middle-class revolution in Florence. The vernacular poets of the 14th century made an audacious protest against the dominant influence of the Latin speaking Church. Of course, nationalists, as the troubadours, had to undermine the authority of the Church to assert their *alternate* linguistics. Luther and English dramatists *had* to attack the hegemonic Roman Church to recover the use of vernacular German and English in the 16th century. Only in the Renaissance did vernacular German, French, and English language gain unity, confidence, and audacity. It was exactly at this moment that the great epic poems of Dante, Chaucer, Shakespeare, Spencer and Milton achieved their high voice of audacity. These vernacular recoveries healed the language schism of their lands. Now we must do the same in our cultural spacescape. I take the galaxy as my territory of audacity.

The English made an audacious act. By the 1560's, the English Protestants banned the Latin language from their churches and, at this very moment, great English poets suddenly appeared – apparently from nowhere. Great English poets, as Watt, "Shake-speare", Sydney, Spenser, and Marlowe suddenly appeared in one generation – as well as the eternal English of the *King James Bible*. These vernacular innovations could not happen in Northern Europe until the protestant movement *disenchanted* the Latin of the discredited Catholic Church. The hatred and suspicion of Roman Latinists came *before* the resurgence of the vernacular poets of Europe. The suspicion and dislike of modern information must likewise be experienced before the vernacular speaker can find the audacity to re-enchant vernacular speech.

Was the rise of strong vernacular poets merely an accident? Let's observe the timing. In the decades just before Elizabeth I, the monasteries were disbanded and the Latin mass was forbidden in England. This had an immediate effect on the confidence of the English vernacular. Clearly, the very moment the schism of priestly language was overcome by the vernacular poets, a single language restored pride and confidence in the audacity – and centrality – of the vernacular. And they immediately showed this attitude in their audacious works – the stories of new modern men. Who can deny that the most noteworthy distinction of a Dante or a Marlow was their aggressive audacity? Neither Dante's *Inferno* nor Marlow's *Faust* were products of indecision, trepidation, or hesitancy. They above all were audacious poets, and they aimed at hegemony – they did not seek a second-place prize with another entity of influence. There would have never been a Shakespeare poet without the wild audacity of Marlow. The Shakespeare poet never recovered from his own ideational competition with Marlow.

My point is easy to anticipate. Let us now reclaim our own age. The preceding clearly places in perspective the alienation of today's modern poets. We may observe how modern men suffer from a feeling, a profound instinct, of alienation of their social language. Modern common language, vernacular English, has lost nearly all its authority and confidence. After 100 years of unparalleled scientific discovery, led by the use of scientific languages, everyday vernacular English is, somehow, second-class – even archaic. It is scientific mathematics and quantum physics that are now entrusted with the discovery of new worlds and new technologies. Until *Chandos Ring*, no poet ever dared to find the audacity, the poetry, to embrace modern technology and the machines of space travel. Why did it take so long to give a vernacular response to the secret priesthood of modernism?

Every Age of Poetry Represents a Vernacular Recovery

The vernacular has failed and recovered in every age. Not only in Renaissance Italy or England do we have to look for the sudden rediscovery of a unified, audacious language. In Greece, the late formation of the Greek alphabet made possible the Golden Age of Pericles. For the first time outside of oral culture, Greek writers were able to codify the discovery of their linguistic freedom from the anthropomorphic oral tradition. This made the Greeks new men.

Bookish men did not compose the *Iliad*. Homer is an older oral epic tradition (from the Age of Taurus – only written down in the Age of Aries.) Plato – who possessed a mastery of the new alphabet – resented the influence of the archaic Homer. Over one third of the *Iliad* and *Odyssey* is composed of verses repeated elsewhere in the poems. In the first twenty-five lines of the *Iliad* there are twenty-five mnemonic phrases. To the new literate men of 5th century Athens, Homer was nauseating. For the first time, humans sought *specifically* linguistic innovation (writing) as a way of seeing the universe. They became Western men.

This individual power – the newly free power of an individual poet – or philosopher – represented the modern *innovation* of Western men. Suddenly we had Sophocles, Plato, Socrates, Sappho, Aeschylus, and Euripides – writers of a newly discovered audacity of idiomatic control of ideation. With the magical alphabet, language became self-referent. Writing a text encouraged the *old* universe to conform to the *new* text. When has it been otherwise? With a magical form of writing, Western man became individually self-referent in his or her audacity. This audacity required a freedom and a sense of mastery over the poet's own world. Thus the poet's freedom of innovation became the freedom of the individual that subsequently characterized the Western human. No other civilization developed so obsessively the freedom of the individual power. This was a vernacular recovery.

What modern poet feels himself to be the master in his culture? Few. There must be a new recovery of literate audacity. So the reader may see the scope of my work.

If the language you or your peers use is not the language which, also, is the means for the discovery of the good things of life – if the tongue you speak is not allowed to address the highest gods, if the tongue you speak is clearly outclassed by another worldview, then there is a profound and deeply felt schism in the language we experience.

So how should we proceed? Our poems should discover an alternate source of ideation that *outclasses* modern dialectics. When this new tongue is formed, it will make men and machines of uncanny new structure.

This is the end game of *Chandos Ring*.

CHAPTER TWENTY-SEVEN

The Language of the Beautiful Machine

We are all moderns. We want a beautiful machine. We all look for the next beautiful machine of high construct. Above all else, the modern needs a machine to verify the linguistic superiority of his civilization. There is nothing left to verify his high excellence – or his salvation. His linguistic gods are all gone. His ethics and morality are gone. So we need Big Medicine. Where do we get this Big Medicine? From the interrogative of a human *incantation*. There never was a beautiful machine that did not originate in a *single linguistic phrase*. The future beautiful human machines will arise from a similar innovation of linguistics. And, as ever, this is the ultimate case for poetry as information. Poetry is *Big Medicine*.

Every language, every culture, seeks a *Big Medicine*. The Plains Indians had a Big Medicine. Egypt had a Big Medicine. Modernism has a Big Medicine – it is the machine. It is the pharmaceutical factory. The machines are made to fit into a narrow, self-referent medical establishment. Modernism's Big Medicine can be industrialized and proliferated on a missionary scale. These are the linguistic excellences of modern idiom. How much longer?

Whenever challenged, the modern will demand to see the machine that can arise from our strange *new* idiom. *Poet, where is your beautiful machine? Can your machine compare to our high constructs of multiple levers?* Of course they are right to do so – what other language should modernism speak? I do not want to berate modern linguistics – we all want a beautiful machine. I only want a device to supersede modern men. Modernism may only form questions based on the self-referent linguistics of (exclusively) secular materialism. We don't expect anything else from modern speech. The problem is this. Any self-referent linguistics is essentially a circle. At some point the innovation and discovery of any particular linguistic code will fail into non-entity. The Chinese and Indian linguistic codes prove this. They both kept their languages free from outside invaders and impurities. They reached a certain level of technical expertise – and then froze in their tracks. They turned inward to survive. Western men still look outward to survive. There has not been an original text, technology, or conceptional idea out of China or India for over eight hundred years. That is not a stumble – not even a dark age. That is a complete collapse. Will we also exhaust the possibilities of secular materialism and, refusing innovation, turn inward? If we do so, we will not be the linguistic code that makes conquest of the universe. *Chandos Ring* makes an opposite assertion.

Each civilization, cocooned in the arrogance of its deep linguistic misprision demands the same challenge to every new form of civilization: *Can you show us an excellence greater than our high construct?* So sure of their excellence, dying civilizations seldom bother to pause and record the reply. Paganism never anticipated that the uneducated Jesus could threaten the shining high construct of literature and philosophy of the Greek/Latin civilization. Yet their world was eradicated. The Roman Catholic Church, ensconced in its wealth and arrogance, never anticipated that the new language of (amateur) science would utterly eradicate the beauty and power (and wealth) of its dead god on a cross. Yet their world was eradicated. Science, securely embedded within the greatest linguistic movement ever seen by man, cannot even begin to imagine how any other idiom of life can equal the beautiful (and useful) machines of modernism. Where to even start? It is not even comprehensible by modernism.

It is easy to turn the question of the machine on its head. If we interviewed Galileo or Newton in the 17th century, we would exactly confirm that early science had no concept (yet) of the jet engine or the atomic bomb. They could have rightly replied that the practical application of any idiom must be developed over centuries – as the Greek, the Roman, and the Christian Church developed their linguistics in the first centuries of their early development. I caution the reader, therefore. Story Theory cannot be discounted because we currently cannot point to our beautiful machines. There will be beautiful machines. They will cross the galaxy with strength.

Dying civilizations have never made the correct prediction of the next worldview. Modernism does not see what is coming to eradicate it. Previously, Christianity could only detect constructs of Christianity. Greek paganism could only detect Greek philosophy. Modernism, now, can only detect modernism. This is what the truth looks like. This is the function of the poet: *to tell the truth of the next world*.

We may not build strange new machines of alternate beauty (and function) until our idiom of beauty transitions to a new innovation. Then we are back to the competence and opportunity of the strong poet. Only the strong poet dares to make a new innovation in the language. All machines begin with a bias embedded in the linguistic codes. Is there any other reason to be a poet? In effect, by creating new languages, the poet builds new machines of future wonder and power. The strong poet is taxidermic since he makes a new skeleton. This is a perspective never explored before in philosophy. It's new. It is the poet that reconstructs the human skeleton. It is the poet that will remove the planet earth and our terrestrial bones. The hardness of bones will always follow the location of the human mind. If we locate the human mind at its astral coordinate – we will lose our terrestrial ligaments. We will terraform a new man.

We become writers not because we have some special talent; we become writers because of our agonistic struggle with the fame of other great writers. Men become writers because their hearts are full – and they will not be displaced. Yet it is not enough to only have a full heart. Many people on death row have a heart that is full.

Poetry, itself, is very strange. The consciousness of the poet exhibits a powerful jealously of text. We wrestle with the influence of the poems we love. Every writer we love must also be displaced. Thus, talent is useless without the rage of ambition. We want to take back our text from previous men who have written the text of our Being. So the desire comes first, not the talent. Only after decisive engagement of the human will, does talent, luck, or device come into play. Yes, we hope that the angry poet has talent. We only survive if we find a message and a new idiom to kill the writers we love.

Science fiction gives the poet a new device and a new context to discover the innovative linguistic limits of human consciousness. Science fiction still allows a super-abundance in the modern tongue. As science fiction is positioned as a harmless fantasy, it is not subsequently monitored by the powers of modern orthodoxy. Only poets and stars have a status that cannot be displaced by another change in the firmament. Everything else degrades into extinction. That is a strong statement – can it be sustained? We will have to speak to the dead.

Writers do not struggle to discover their message; there are too many. We struggle to edit and to connect our message to beautiful new machines of our idiom. We take our place in Being through our own agonistic battle to control the human text. This *agon* exhausts. Yet, in this struggle nothing *real* is ever lost, and much is gained. We discover the next high construct – the beautiful machine of the next high civilization. With this next machine we wish to explore consciousness and to take dominion of the galaxy. Why? Because, in the end, it is the constellation of stars that contains the actual movements in the universe of men. Poets are antennae to all stations alert.

All the sciences degrade into pasteurized crafts. Once, the Bronze Age metal workers were the greatest magicians and scientists – then, with time, they became blacksmiths who shod horses. Once, the alchemists discovered the secrets of human knowledge – then, with time, they became local pharmacists. Atomic and quantum science will take the same path into the language of common avocations.

We want the practical benefits of science, as we want better clothing against the wind, as we want a lever to move the moons – as we value sound toothpaste.

But do we want science to stand astride us as an idol that drowns out the other gods lurking in the personality of Being? It is a thesis of these books that only the language of poetry will permit man to survive past his own scientific insight. So what is the proper function of the human animal? What skill do men exhibit – in contradistinction to all other life? What is our singularity? Is it merely to make a larger lever to proliferate the Earth? Is it only to find a more perfected pill? Is it our goal to find ways to sustain ever-greater cities and ever-greater human populations? Is it to be the last problem solver on a dying planet of proliferation? We know the answer. The Age of Aquarius is an age of anti-proliferation. It is an age of selection.

I shall not make technology my adversary. The next linguistic code will subsume technology as the Roman Empire subsumed Greek philosophy. We will turn the river of modern technology to our own purpose. We only wish to gain linguistic control of technology subordinate to our purpose of seizing control of consciousness. We need linguistic competence to build spaceships. We still need iron to shod horses. Yet when the science becomes a god and stifles with scorn all other enchanted values of life – then I have to fight this idol. The language of the beautiful machine will homogenize the language of the human host – every time. Beauty is terrible. Beauty sucks up all the air in the room. The beauty of science diminishes all other sound, all other forms of representation. The code of technology must be used – but cocooned.

The Shakespeare poet discovered a horrible machine. Its great beauty made his new linguistic devise terrible. The felicity of the Shakespeare poet only weakens the poets that study him – they know his influence will eclipse their new voice. Any strong poetry must aim to supplant all other forms of poetry. The poetry of Shakespeare eradicates all other forms of poetry in English. Any poet worthy of the name must perform the same alchemy – that is, to transmute vernacular into cosmic gold. The modern poet is challenged! He has to overreach the powerful images of science, Shake-speare, and the dead universe of modern information. That is a large undertaking. What chance does the modern poet have with these adversaries? He has a small chance. So it is a moment of individual audacity. I pause to give the modern poet a poem that contains story. I leave behind a new theory of poetry that may be consulted with curiosity.

Beauty, like great art, presents a great danger to all *other* life. Beauty makes all other forms of life – all other language – second-rate. Great linguistic and imaginative science makes average poetry appear to be empty of information. This is the fault of the average modern poet – who has recoiled, speechless, from the prestige of linguistic science. Every great art makes all other arts, somehow, second-rate. The Rock'n Roll music video makes the church choir seem a second-rate activity. The success of NASA has made all amateur rocket enthusiasts second-rate hobbyists. In his *Civilization: A New History of the Western World,* Roger Osborne believes that the West has always, at its own cost, made toxic idols out of our desire to discover the limits of human achievement. Osborne, speaking here of artistic triumph, explains the terrible price Western men pay for their great imaginative achievements:

> "Once the high artistic element has been separated out from any activity, whatever remains risks being devalued as mechanical and even contemptible...This legacy has not simply divided "low art" from "high art", but has decreased the possibility of artistic achievement in everyday life... Artisans may take pride in their work but they must know that it is always somehow second-rate. When the artist is removed from society and made into a special person, the artist within each of us begins to die."

I believe his view can explain the dangers of *any* idolatry. Regarding science, I may add this sentence: *When the scientist is removed from society and made into a special person, the scientist within each of us begins to die.* That is to say that today, when a non-academic vernacular speaker, no matter how well read he is, or otherwise talented, dares to engage in scientific and cosmological issues of the day – and what issues are not? – his competence is somehow second-rate. Vernacular language is forbidden to address the ultimate meanings of science. The vernacular speaker should not discuss the meaning, in print, of quantum mechanics, String Theory, etc. – since these are the purview of scientists who exclusively *own* this linguistic code – as a monopoly. This represents a schism in world. This is the modern vernacular peril.

Modern science has crossed the line – since it is now an idol with its own priestly class and a secret, priestly language (mathematic equations). If the poet should attempt a high theme in the vernacular language, he appears somehow contemptible. He has no beautiful machine – no device – to counter the prestige of modern science.

This is exactly the position I have selected for a cunning victory. I may enter undetected. Previous to *Chandos Ring,* modern poetry has recoiled with fear and loathing to embrace the linguistic achievement of science. Yet, divested of its idol and prestige, the highest linguistic science is revealed only as another poetic achievement. If not, there is danger of science becoming an idol that will permanently eradicate the human element. Who does not see that if left unconstrained, the ideal human form of scientific rationalism is the *Replicant* – not the fallible human? The language of scientific authority, as any form of exalted beauty, denies all other possibility of authority. Every language seeks hegemony over the ideation host. The logic of the modern machine leads directly to the gas oven of the Holocaust. Every beauty intends to kill all other.

I challenge the presumption of modernism. The educated vernacular speaker may as well discuss the implications of cosmology and quantum theory without being a mathematician, as much as we certainly discuss the possibility of life after death without being a priest. As poets, we must face and challenge the source of the alienation of our language – the public degradation of the value of our human information. This is the issue of this book.

The dogma of the materialists contains the following narrative: In order to maintain life we must preserve our material bodies and the Earth – there is no information apart from our bodies and the material elements. Is this correct? This perspective places the human mind exclusively on the terrestrial plane. It is exactly wrong. I refuse to make an idol out of the material element. The modern has already decided that his body, alone, is what defines the human condition. And if our bodies are the only standard of what makes a human – how can any of us survive our youth with any dignity or hope of recovery of the human element? Only at the astral coordinate can the human mind have eternal power and wisdom. This is our home.

An Old Man's Shoe

How can we display the fault of modernism in one symbol? It easily falls to hand. Under a secular modernism that honors only sensuality and youth, how can an old man's shoe, discarded in a corner, ever have value? It cannot. Wisdom is not a quality of modern information. So much information of life is lost when human age is devalued – and only youth is privileged. This image of the value of an old man's shoe, poetically, is able to condemn the entire structure of modernity. The human of age, degraded by the modern experience, recognizes the truth of the image at once. Under modernism, the body that is aged is a linguistic condition that cannot be recovered with information of vital power. How sound, then, is the humanity of the materialist? The only chance, thus, for dignity of the human mind is to surpass the body *as an illusion*. The human must be reconstructed on the ideal astral plane – not the physical plane. And only cosmology gives data of the spiritual component of sentient life.

Is there evidence for a pattern of reality in the stars? Yes, and we may discuss the observed patterns – whether it is with astrology, cosmology, quantum mechanics, or astronomy. Cosmology is a more accurate model of freedom. Can the vernacular speaker speak with authority of the cosmos? Yes. The average educated American today has as much information of astronomy as Galileo and Newton – and do we not have better telescopes? Galileo made a contribution of *science narrative* with less technological competence. With a poorly constructed telescope, he was in a position to make an opinion of the order of the stars. I see that stars burn and that they collide. I see that stars orbit and that their orbits give and partake of influences. I understand that in my atom there is an orbit that exactly mimics the trajectories of the objects that orbit the Black Holes. I see that they burst on contact. If stars are the evidence of material life, then are the patterns of the stars not also elements of human spiritual composition? Can I not suppose that small planets may be terra-formed into large planets more suitable for life? Any science fiction hero gives me an opportunity to make my case. Who can disprove the ultimate ideational goal of science fiction? Not the scientist – he has been shackled by academic tenure.

The point is this. Vernacular speakers are not in ideational control of their world. Lets imagine the scene as follows. This is the situation at the present day. An assembly of the most trusted men of judgment convenes to discuss a world crisis. Suddenly, a scientist knocks on the door of the assembly room and sends in this message to the chief wise man: "We have made new calculations on the duration of the eclipse. Use this information in your deliberations." The wise man says, "Thank you – please be available when we need more technical information." This process is acceptable to the vernacular speaker. We want scientific information. We even want timely and exact technology. We want wisdom. But this is not our situation at all.

Instead, the situation Western men actually face is similar to the following portrayal. There is an assembly of all scientific *Nobel Laureates* in a room to decide the future of mankind. A vernacular speaker knocks on the door saying he has a new idea that the men of science have overlooked. The academic asks, "Are you a journalist?" The man replies, no. The academic tells the man, "When we know your fate, we will let you know – in our terms." Then the door is slammed. *This* is the situation of modernist information. *This* is the agon of the modern poet.

Science has come full circle. Originally Francis Bacon said in his *New Order* that there had to be an alternate way of knowing *information*, since his contemporaries were all under the *idol* of Christian theology. The physical sciences subsequently created scientific language to eradicate the *idol* of religion – since it was an *idol* of religion that blocked an understanding of an exclusively material causation of phenomena. Now that science has successfully eradicated the *revelatory* idol of religion, it has civilization all to itself. This has only made a new tyranny. Modern linguistics forbids any attack on the idol of science. Mankind is strangled by a new idol. We need a new Francis Bacon and a fresh projection of a *New Order*. An idol must be killed.

Science does not act as a useful adjunct of wisdom – it acts as the only *source* of corrupted oracular information. We all agree that scientists and academics have useful data. We all want washing machines and reliable measurements to make spaceships. The crisis is that the academic, industrial, scientific, medical megalith has control over *all* human information. Science is not an open exchange of ideas. Only a linguistic replication of science idiom is allowed. We all understand what an academic tenure committee is. No academic may achieve tenure until he demonstrates that he has read the relevant texts of modernism and can reliably replicate the dialectics of scientific materialism. Can this be denied? Science is a materialistic ideology that jealously guards its power and intervenes to assert its control over ideation.

The most recent narrative of science is that the *Big Bang* is the source of all possible life. Excellent. Yet that makes no difference at all to the metaphysical condition of men. *The Big Bang* is interpreted in a way that is counter to the linguistics we seek. Surely, if nothing else, the Big Bang means that the stars are connected to men – since men are the only creatures of intelligent life. Thus the Big Bang should be evidence of consciousness – and not only of matter. Matter is certainly only a *symptom of conscious perception* (Story Theory). Yet, this is exactly the position that science does not take. So we are offended by the myth of the Big Bang – it misses the point of our interrogation completely. The search for the Higgs Boson – also misses the point entirely. Each only celebrates – each only is willing to detect – a construct declaring the origin of matter. Is the Big Bang all there ever was to the question of life? What was before the *Big Bang*? No answer. What comes after the universe passes away? No answer. So a human must intervene with his own deep, if vernacular, poetic discoveries of consciousness. Yet this is not accepted by modernism – not as information. A strong poet is thus looked for to remake the skeleton of the human mind – to reassemble the broken pieces. We need a great unifier – not another specialist. This *unifier* will need all information as his handmaiden.

How can science continue to posit that highly sentient and self-conscious humans are somehow separate from all other forms of creation? It is incredible that scientists continue to make this mistake. It is certainly due to an ideological bias of a linguistic prejudice – a materialism that wishes to maintain its modern supremacy as *the only* linguistic idiom. Is it true that we must hold on to our rotting bodies until the last possible breath? How could science mistake this crucial interpretation of life? Life has death, danger, and violence. Science cannot prevent any of these – so let our mind master these perils. Man is in a superposition to any violent act. The idea of man, his self-conscious information, is eternal and not subject to violent happenstance. There are many ideational folds where his information is still active and has viability. We must burst to show what value we verify. We must endow our death with information again.

In literature and myth all gods and heroes burst. How do we know that the stars are our gods and heroes? We can read the ancient epic poems that told the truth of the origins of men. Why do moderns so persistently disbelieve stories of mythic value? It is because modernism has a horror of bursting. After the event of bursting (as death, as sacrifice) there would be no more modern information. If science cannot detect spiritual information, then it cannot rule this space. Science must disenchant any space it cannot rule. The intent is clear. The purpose of modernism is to maintain a prestige of materialist information against all other forms of life. It is a church.

Scientists are speechless with the charismatic origin of consciousness. And yet science would preclude the poets from the discourse of human life – *even* so much as science admits it cannot explain consciousness. How then should we trust science with the human element? We cannot. We must make a counter-language and a counter-world.

Only poetry can make charismatic detection. A machine can perform every function of man – yet a machine cannot understand a poem. Therefore we have found what is unique to our Being. It is poetry. Armed with this discovery, we have work to do. We must re-enchant the vernacular English language. *Chandos Ring* insists upon the consequence of this insight.

CHAPTER TWENTY-EIGHT

Will Western Liberal Ideology Transition to Tyranny?

All ideologies take on the darkness of their enemy's political system. There never has been an exception. Can Western liberal democracy avoid the usual fate of all human ideologies?

Religions, philosophies, and ideological parties do not fail because they are poor interpretations of human life. They fail because their idiom accumulates wounded moralities. Communism did not fail because of the supposed rational projections of Karl Marx; communism failed because of Joseph Stalin's untold murders. Communism, counter to their own propaganda, replicated the aggressive morality of imperialist nations. There was no liberation of the proletariat under communism – there was only a replacement of an high linguistic Western aristocracy with the brutality of a select gang of uneducated murderers. It was the communist system itself that excelled at oppressing, exploiting and enslaving its own people.

Ideologies fail when they take on the very beliefs and practices of their counter-ideology – as all great movements do. Catholicism, the Church of the otherworldly – the Church of anti-Caesar – performed the same idiomatic transformation. The Catholic Church replicated exactly the ideology of the worldly, material, secular Roman state it was fighting. So far from rejecting materialism and overcoming all forms of disease and death with faith – the Catholic Church, in the modern period, has accepted every precept of pagan, worldly, and secular materialism. Christ commanded men to reject the world. Christ never once asked the name or prognosis of a material disease. In Christ's clear message, disease, as an ideational formula, was entirely the same construct from small itch to malignant cancer – disease was the logic of the world of material flesh. Modernism utterly rejects this premise. Disease is the central fascination – the obsession and fear – of modern men. There are few modern cinematic drama's that do not include a battle with a medical diagnosis of disease in the narrative. Medical diseases, and the drama of diseases, are a key signature of the modern mind. The logic of disease reinforces the linguistic structure of materialism. It gives an opportunity to show the prestige of medical-industrial hegemony – and the majestic authority of the medical profession. The detection of disease is the *lingua franca* of modern speech. All modern men recognize the linguistic code.

Today, the Catholic Church never insists that a sick person should omit to go to the hospital. The linguistic reversal is breathtaking. The Church has utterly surrendered to the logic of material causation that so disgusted its dear master. It is strange that the followers of Christ omit to follow the precepts of Christ. This is a profound idiomatic surrender to secular and material pressure to conform. This is how Story Theory evaluates all institutions: *follow the trail of linguistic duress*. It is for this reason that Western liberalism will become its opposite – that is, with social pressure to exact conformity, liberalism will become an all-pervasive tyranny. In the Dark Ages, it was the glory of the monarch's prerogative that allowed the logic of the tyranny of the prince. Under modernism, it is corporate greed that insists the entire social system is under hegemonic control of linguistic consumerism (advertising).

We may list many world ideologies that made a similar linguistic transition when they fell into crisis. The French Revolution immediately comes to mind. So disgusted with the monarchy, democratic French revolutionaries proclaimed *liberty, equality,* and *brotherhood.* The leaders quickly set about to murder their own revolutionaries and were finally led by Napoleon to make conquest against all the non-French world – again, in the name of *liberty, equality*, and *brotherhood.* In fact, Napoleon made himself king and established a dynastic empire. This, of course, is exactly the mirror image of the monarchial system his revolution intended to destroy. Like other revolutions (as Christianity and Communism), the French Revolution subsumed the image of tyranny that it initially revolted from. Today, the modern socialist police state of France still uses the propaganda of its failed Revolution. An educated (and Christian) French aristocratic caste was replaced by a class of secular politicians operating by bribery, corruption, and police surveillance. The exact method of government as the monarchy it replaced with such high linguistic ideals.

What is the point of these examples of high linguistic ideologies? Western liberalism will follow a similar pattern of reverse transformation of its linguistic code. Liberalism (modernism), the greatest totalitarian ideology the earth has ever seen, will follow the same devolution as did communism, Catholicism and French republicanism – into the image of their nemeses. It is already becoming evident that Western liberalism, so long the enemy of all totalitarian ideologies, the champion of freedom, now takes on the dialectics of totalitarianism. As liberal ideology makes its final movements for world hegemony, it will be forced to develop an rigid linguistic code, a liberal *dialectic*, to keep its propaganda of modernism unchallenged – yet insisting that you may only be free, or have rights, or be protected, or get welfare – so long as you accept the tenants of secular materialism, industrial pharmaceuticals, and allow science to continue to operate as oracle. You must, above all, consent to be monitored by a police state to ensure you are following the linguistic dictates of modernism. In effect, to have the questionable goods of capitalism, you must ensure to the state the faithful use of the linguistic codes of modernism. As under Stalinism, you may have the benefits of communist "goods" (a job, a flat) only when you followed the linguistic dialectics of communism. To control social linguistics is to control how the mind structures ideation. Totalitarianism is the future of Western liberal institutions. It will lead to the finale wars of destruction of the Earth.

Each religion, as each ideology, is supported by the integrity sustained by its own self-referent linguistic code. Since each ideology is linguistically self-referent, it is impossible that they may restructure their own ideation to meet the conditions of a new form of consciousness. Religions fail when their human practitioners – through a long record of murders, injustices, lost battles, and treachery – acquire wounded moralities. Every civilization, no matter how successful, cannot avoid the slow acquisition of wounded moralities. Today, the Catholic Church is known not only for its previous failure to anticipate the future hegemonic idiom of science – but under modernist dialectics, it is exclusively remembered for pogroms against the Jews, the discrimination against women, the execution of Giordano Bruno, and the abuse of young boys. These wounded moralities gut the creditability of the Church's linguistic code. Each ideology acquires wounded moralities from which there is no possibility of linguistic recovery. The Catholic Church survived every charismatic event in the last 2000 years. Yet it could not survive the dialectical restructuring performed by the instant surveillance of modern journalism. Every Church, every ideology, is a secret linguistic structure. It must be guarded.

The Church may have survived the attacks of Medieval Islam, but it could not survive modern journalistic propaganda. Modern forms of Christianity are consequently not positioned well for even marginal control of the minds of modern men. Modern men do not judge the Church on the merits of its spiritual claims – they judge the Church on its accumulation of wounded moralities. The pattern of dissipated linguistic inertia, once started, cannot be linguistically reversed. A wounded morality – as a linguistic code – is unable to recover the enchantment of its original message. No exceptions.

We recognize now that the previous human century took physical matter too seriously. It is one thing to make use of the physical environment – it is quite another to make materialism the only linguistic source of human information. Physical matter has assumed *mythic* proportions – true to secular materialism's creation as a ruthless linguistic trope (science). There has always been a body of human opinion that has vigorously denied the permanent reality of matter. As with Bishop Berkeley, I make a severe protest against the misprision of materialism. From Berkeley to Blake, from Nietzsche to Chandos, from Giordano Bruno to Yeats, there have been incisive attacks against Western materialism. Christianity could be dismantled only because it accumulated an abundance of wounded linguistic moralities. Now modernism will fail on exactly the same model of an accumulation of wounded moralities. The attack begins with *Chandos Ring*, where modernism is exposed for its lack of reliable information.

The materialist presumption in the West is all-engrossing. We do not know what aspect of modernism will snap first. It will be a charismatic event that suddenly exposes the unreliable foundations of modernistic assumptions. There is nothing more perfect than a laptop computer – until there are no electrical power grids or there are no servers to connect to. Then the modernistic idiom is exposed to be razor thin. At that time, soon to arrive, the symbol of modernism will be mountains of blank screens that will never emit or receive any form of information of life. So we build a strong theory of poetry for the future crisis.

What does the poet do today? He begins by telling the truth. He gives reliable information. He avoids all dissembling. He makes no apology for secular materialism. Atoms are not independent, self-contained units of matter. Atoms exist only *inside* of consciousness. There are no atoms *outside* of consciousness. Matter is thus totally dependent upon another dimension of energy – human consciousness – the power of the observant and linguistic mind. In Story Theory, matter is a conditional, tentative concept – and is liable to run down rabbit holes into other dimensions.

Nothing is so great a terror as when men lose the foundations of their secure world. When the world is not perfect, men rise to make perfect stories. String Theory is a leap of the human imagination – and shares with poetry the imagination's attempt to bring equilibrium to the human mind. Poetry alone is able to reliably explore tangential dimensions of ideational value – often in a single page or stanza. Poetry is compressible to incredible densities of ideation. Poetry can outclass both prose and computer code for brevity and conciseness. The poetic phrase, *unfinished consciousness* (as only one example), alone, is able to give information that could fill a book – just from its implications. If there is a creature able to move across the multi-dimensional branes of Being, then there must also be an instantaneous linguistic code that facilitates this movement. Poetry contains this code.

As men can only perceive poems from a state of consciousness, human reality *itself* essentially remains a language problem. The visible spectrum can only be a poem. Human reality is the result of a competition of linguistic ideas. Reality has nothing to do with supposed *empirical data* outside of sentient human manipulation. Men are what they focus on – that is the law contained in consciousness. That is Story Theory. All that a man can tell you of his life is the story that he or she has heard in a lifetime of competitive stories. And all that a man can repeat from all of these projections and assertions – are the poetic stories they believed.

Story Theory attempts to integrate quantum mechanics into a theory of poetry– a new translation – a revised *poem* of world. My aim is a form of information that would privilege the poet as much as the mathematician. There is room for both in the wide galaxies. If poets and mathematicians may have the same imagination of information – then they might also have the same authority of information. Of course we must honor science – but we must honor science as our greatest poetry. This heals the schism of modern speech and allows the poet his audacity.

This is the aim of Story Theory – to allow poets to have the same authority of information as the scientist. *Of course* scientists operate exactly as poets. *Of course* scientists construct a newly revised translation of *world,* in each decade. *Of course* scientists first have a story of what they search for – and *of course* they find exactly the evidence they were already looking for. This is exactly the poet's protocol.

There is nothing so rare in the universe as a strong poet. This is strange. It appears at first unaccountable. If the poetic instinct is so prevalent, so basically human, how can strong poets be so rare? It is useless for us to say that until one hundred years ago poets were the celebrities of society. And it is useless to claim that, yes, you know of one or two living poets that have managed to get published – or won some questionable prize. It does not matter. If they exist, they are unknown to the average Western citizen. If they are unknown, then they have no power to pattern the modern world. I have traveled the world for thirty years and never could I discover a Western person that might name a living American or European poet. That's a hurt of misery for a young person wishing to become a poet. What chance does he or she have?

Still, people confirm to me that the poetic instinct is present. I am willing to believe. My heart is full. The *Internet* is overwhelmed with persons trying to spread the passion for poetry. Yet all efforts hit a glass ceiling of wide popular indifference. Moderns want information that is vital and represents the future of life – not the past. We do not wish to sell a gas lamp to the modern electric consumer. So we wish to linguistically preach the beautiful machines of a space faring civilization – machines that allow us to linguistically levitate immense bodies and to instantaneously travel across the galaxy. Every idiom has its beautiful machine.

Chandos Ring explores this possibility.

CHAPTER TWENTY-NINE

Consciousness and the Superposition of Men

The rage that is building against modernism is now reaching sobriety. The broken families. The lost generations. The dead universe. The toxic and corrupted industrial medicines. The genetic manipulation of food. The over-proliferation of men and cities. The extinction of millions of forest species. The permanent draining of world aquifers. The false idol of material wealth. The insidious propaganda of advertisements. The degradation of poetry. The ignorance of the protocol of consciousness. All these failures of modern information will find retribution in a future space faring civilization. What language shall be used to monument the discoveries of the new idiom of life? The poet must move ahead of all raging complexities. He must tell the truth of the epic trope. How? He must center himself on the actual protocols of consciousness. He must advocate the superposition of men – as the supreme observer.

Whenever the human has been able to imagine his position as the center of the universe, he has excelled in poetry and philosophy. At the height of Athens' power, Protagoras insisted that man was the measure of all things. This was the first step towards the *magus personality* of the West. From that moment, men boldly set out to seize control of global consciousness. Similarly, the Renaissance placed men uniquely at the center of Being – as the measure of all things. Marlow and the Shakespeare poet (De Vere) placed men at the center of all phenomena. The benefit of this perspective was the necessary courage of imagination allowing the discovery of new innovation of life.

Each time we lose the perspective of the human's central importance, we descend into dark ages of fear, self-loathing, and crass materialism. Ideation is essentially a courage. Life cannot be advanced without courage. A man cannot live well or die well without courage. If we think we are mice, then we consume as mice. If men think they are nearer to gods and heroes, then they live larger than life and sacrifice every comfort to prove their status as divine creatures. The reader will decide for himself which path has more merit.

The truth looks like this. Men make a story of life and follow its linguistic superstructure. Humans create the universe with their mind. There is no evidence to be discovered before the arrival of the sentient mind. The observer must arrive before the observed object can reveal its supposed substance. The object could have only had its source originally in the human mind – so what object is there that must be new and undiscovered? This is the contradictory relationship between the scientific hypothesis and the charismatic human mind.

Our brains contain exactly as many neurons as there are stars in a galaxy. This is not coincidental. How could such fantastically large numbers be exact matches – in two *apparently* different phenomena? The pattern seems to be pervasive. Recent photos of all the galaxies of the cosmos exactly resemble the network of neurons and their connectors in the brain. The answer is that the mind and the universe are the same co-dependent phenomena. The materialist refutes the connection. The scientist insists that there is some empirical *stuff* separately existing from, and outside of, the human mind. Story Theory counters this perspective, insisting that matter is continuously under manipulation of the consciousness of the human observer. The universe is a map of the structure of the human brain.

Since he is human, the scientist cannot avoid a necessary *and* prior act of story making. The observer must always arrive *before* the observation. This is a fact of consciousness ignored with peril. Yet, this protocol is *specifically* ignored by modern science. No man discovers in a vacuum. He has to first conceive – in his mind – of what he must discover. This connection cannot be argued away. Scientists perform Story Theory in advance – then they deny it.

The universe will not be understood until human consciousness is understood. Consequently, men are still at the center of this universe. The superposition of men is still a front-loaded ingredient of sentience.

The mind of a human is in a super- position. That is, we are not dependant only upon exclusively a material manifestation of matter to have a manifestation of Being. We compel the *truth* we seek to match the conditions required by the universe we create in our minds. Trials of medicine have discovered exactly the connection between our minds and the health of the body. Health – and illness – is largely influenced by the human consciousness. Not a new idea. In Story Theory, the observer can manipulate anything within consciousness. This is why modern clinical researchers have to use *placeboes* in their trials of human medicine. The actual agency of the industrial chemical is slight – in comparison with the *juggernaut* causation of the human mind. The mind must, in effect, be tricked, blocked, before scientist's can perceive any independent benefit of a chemical prescription. Then they proceed to pick and choose the data they are seeking. Then they have to use advertising to make people think they are sick.

Even when the chemical makes a response – it still cannot be denied that the mind was sentient of the outcome desired by the researcher. Socrates said that a disease could be healed if the sick ate a leaf of a certain plant *and* special words were pronounced at the same time. Then he adds: "The leaf alone does nothing." Story Theory is very old. The story telling observer changes the observed. The patient's mind does not operate in vacuum – it is entangled – it is connected to the desired outcome already (or the feared outcome). All sentient minds are entangled with each other. And the universe we observe is entangled with our minds.

Man Is Still the Center of the Universe

A strong theory of poetry privileges the position of the poetry-makers – perhaps not a surprise. There is no other place for humans to stand – since everything that appears – including all other life – appears from human consciousness. That places our minds in the first position of ideation. The reader may experiment with this concept at his leisure. What is there that exists outside of consciousness? If there is something, tell me how you know it? You are aware of things only from the source of your consciousness. Therefore, the phenomena that scientists pretend to study are not somehow *independent* from humans – objects are not magically self-existing – or hanging in the heavens (as if lost). Rather, all phenomena that we observe originate from the protocol of human consciousness. There is no other place for things to appear. In Story Theory, humans are the central sentient observer. The self-conscious mind is the center of all possible worlds. In such a scenario (if understood fully,) there cannot be an extinction of consciousness – since how could consciousness make its own extinction? It is impossible.

If the visible spectrum is dependent upon recognition and arrangement by the human mind, we may plausibly insist that the human mind is the center of world ideation. Quantum theory verifies that the mere observation *by* the human mind changes the matter being observed. We now know that this protocol of manifestation of phenomena (quantum mechanics) operates at the micro and macro dimension. Until this central relationship is understood in practice, consciousness will remain a mystery.

In Story Theory, the fact that there is an infinite number of dimensions is not an agency that lessens the human super-position. This fact *confirms* the superposition of men. We are the only consistent form of consciousness across any numeration of possible dimensions. We are not in competition with other beings that own these worlds; we, ourselves, are *that* sentient DNA that owns, operates, and moves across worlds. According to our epic literature, it was required of man that he take dominion of worlds – that is, that we order and fit consciousness to the conditions of life we seek. We were given freedom to seek widely and with free choice. I exercise free choice by seeking, in this book, a further resort to consciousness. We are *the* creatures able to move across other dimensions. In effect, we are only traveling in our brain. The human brain, finally, is the epic genre. We are all text-makers within consciousness. The reader will complain with justice that he has heard this argument at least once. Yet I am willing to err on the side of impatience, until I am satisfied I have reconstructed his mind to understand my thesis.

There is nothing that exists outside of consciousness – not men, not planets, not photons, not aliens, not galaxies, not scary monsters. And everything within consciousness can be manipulated, imagined, translated, and represented by linguistic transformation. This discovery, if applied, changes everything a man has ever thought about his visible world. With this knowledge, all moralities will be instantaneously reassessed. There will be a new idiom to meet the challenge of a strange new morality.

This book insists that we are not cowering accidents of Being, nor are we reduced to insignificance by the supposed immensity of other phenomena. As all phenomena, ultimately, are in the mind – it is irrelevant if we are challenged by mild itch or a virulent cancer. They are all mental and emotional constructs of observational bias – and thus, manipulation. Mortal phenomena are all under the suzerainty of the human operator. We are the creatures that make use of ideation to order our environment. With our sentient mind, we claim not only this Galaxy, but all dimensions within the folds of Being. We are able to pass straight through the machine, past the factories of heat, and reassemble the information, the story of our Being in other dimensions. We build a great house.

CHAPTER THIRTY

What Conclusions Come Into View?

I have posed and answered many questions that modern writers have avoided to address. This means that many unmodern statements will cross this page. If I posed a linguistic hypothesis, I am certain that I would find the evidence I was seeking to fit the condition of the hypothesis. This protocol ensures that my linguistic structure is essentially self-referent. This fact, then, will serve both as an insight and – a warning. Yet the linguistic human has no choice but to proceed. A man must be able to discover the very thing he was made to perceive. Anything else is linguistic brick-a-brack. Our language is evidence of the understanding we are fit to perceive. That understanding, alone, is a victory.

This book has made new discoveries. Only in this generation – after the recovery of the ancient epics of Mesopotamia – can we make an informed investigation of the epic trope. Only now may we understand the epic trope in its full intricacy. The epic trope contains a pattern of star maps. Epic literature (including religious texts, national narratives, and all ancient myth) is actually a medium containing stories of cosmological significance and precession. I make the surprising thesis that even the ancients never understood their myths correctly – the average ancient saw them as cultic literature. The mystery of the epic trope is deeper than we imagined.

Today we may understand the stories of Gilgamesh, Hercules, Isis, Jesus, Mary, Mithras, Samson, Jason, and Moses as a secret code of star cosmologies. The impact of this discovery is still unrecorded in any previous theory of English poetry. Yet the way ahead is clear. It is no longer necessary to seek the archeology of the Bible or the Old Testament. They were all sacred stories – *and fully true and actual*. Full stop. Only rarely are any events in the Bible historical events – and *still* they are only actualities on the astral plane. Why? Because, in Story Theory, human ideation on the astral plane is *real*. It is physical matter that is an illusion. The reader, at this point, will see the necessity for a new language of reality – and a new theory of poetry.

Modern linguistics cannot contain this radical perspective. Only a story is *real* in the astral plane. This perspective honors a new precedence of life. Stars are the real inhabitants of the universe – not the momentary manifestation of human bodies. Humans are star information. There is still a large construction to make until this view is clear.

It is no longer necessary to account for the power of any particular Bible story or myth through archeology. It is only necessary to establish the foundations, in Story Theory, of how the human mind operates. There is a certain cosmological framework. When our minds are consulted with the information of the stars, this information has ideational power to form our civilization and increase the human opportunity for more time, more space, and more personality. This central insight is expanded upon in *Chandos Ring*.

This book has discovered that consciousness is at war and that all forms of speech are prophecy. Each is a separate book of discussion. More alert, this book has taken some pains to focus on one subject: the quality of human information. I have marshaled evidence to illustrate that all human information is transmitted by means of a linguistically patterned translation of ideation. By this criterion, we have discovered that modern information is an agency of linguistic, idiomatic faith – as any human age is exactly an age of linguistic faith. We have discovered that consciousness, as all languages mimicking consciousness, exists as hermetically sealed, self-referent points on a grid of ideation. This is an advance in philosophy.

Thus, we discover that modernism cannot accuse or reform itself – modernism will only replicate the linguistics that has been constructed to verify the *necessity* of modernism. Any *sealed* linguistic structure is a kind of madness. There is no way out. A hegemonic linguistic edifice can only be eradicated with a superior idiom. We do not intend to modify modernism. It will collapse under the weight of its own unresolvable contradictions. There will be a crisis first.

Only such a structure as Story Theory, that does not promise to be of any ideological formation, can attack the virus of ideological modernism. Story Theory pretends only to illustrate how the human consciousness operates; humans make story and follow with their eyes the story they assert. There is no privileged ideology in Story Theory. Politics is of no interest to the writer. Politics is only another Proto-Story. As with the misprision of romantic love, politics is a crying game. Anyone whose heart beats rapidly for victory over Eros or politics will bitterly learn the idiom of bursting stars.

Chandos Ring begins with the new constellation of Aquarius. It will require the superstructure of a new perspective, a new message, and an alien idiom. And yes, there will be a large field of death. A crust of tears will dry on eyes. But it will be a form of death that contains information. After all, in the end, our poem must recover the information of death. Our poem argues for the nobility of *death* – as much as life. How could a myopic and arrogant modern age attempt to eradicate a full half of all human information – I mean, the information of a neglected death? The man that does not seek the full information of his death is not fully human.

Story Theory uses an alternate linguistics of future human life outside the nursery planet. *Chandos Ring* does not seek to erase the scientific insight. We want spaceships, not new idols that choke our free speech. We want to be free to outclass modernism.

It is the purpose of *Chandos Ring* to verify that the information of *modernism* is only a temporary construct of linguistics – that modernism can only be supported by a hermetically sealed, self-referent linguistic idiom. If modernism is thereby *temporary* and *unreliable* – then poetry alone can embed the long count of human information. Further, since all civilizations can be shown to undergo a poetic translation of life – then we may reassert the privileged linguistics of poetry as the reliable, eternal, and balanced source of human information. If all human information is poetic, then strong poets may be heard with the same attention and respect currently enjoyed by their brother poets – the scientists. Above all else, we have discovered that there cannot be strong poets until the schism between vernacular speakers and the secret linguistics of science is healed. We have aimed our device at this prospect.

We are in a good position to conclude our argument.

Are there facts of Being? Yes. They are embedded in consciousness. 1) Nothing exists outside of consciousness – and thus, everything within consciousness can be manipulated by the sentience of the conscious observer. 2) Consciousness contains an unknown source of bias. 3) Consciousness is still unfinished. 4) All forms of speech are prophecies (poetry). 5) When a human attempts to give an account of the purpose of human life, he transitions immediately to story. These are the arguments that verify that poetry contains superior information of the human condition.

To oppose these facts – even in the first syllables of a challenge – would only confirm each of them. First, in your challenge to me, you could only speak of things *within consciousness*. If they are within consciousness (including planets, stars, and men), they can be modified by the conscious observer. Second, you will immediately reveal that you contain a *bias in your argument*. Third, you prove that consciousness is still unfinished since you make *innovations of consciousness with every syllable you speak*. Fourthly, by your speech, you project your poem of future life. This is prophetic speech. Fifthly, show me your value of life – of justice, love, romance, equality, salvation, strength, courage, virtue – and I will show you the epic text from which your value of life originated. Every human civilization is structured with a narrative of value from the epic trope.

CHAPTER THIRTY-ONE

Where Is Your God? Where Is Your New Machine?

I conclude my thesis with a discussion of the gods. It is because of poor phraseology that we do not know god. It is less than useless to look for archeology of god. God is not a terrestrial phenomenon. Man is not a terrestrial creature. How do we identify gods in Western literature? The same way we identify men in epic literature – on the astral plane.

We know exactly how to define a god. Everything in a god's *speech* comes true. What, then, if a man performs the same protocol – what if everything in his mind comes into fruition? This is that human element that most resembles a god. The epic trope records these events. Crucial human events all begin with stories of victory over life and death. What else is there to the information of life? What is life if not a discovery of a value of victory? That is the epic trope.

It is not gods we lack; we lack a correct linguistic interrogative of the life source. What is science, after all, but an alternate interrogation of the origin of life? Of course – science has asked all the wrong questions – they have only made an interrogation of the material mirror of life. But they have proven the poetic necessity to innovate and alter the linguistic phraseology of the quest for life. I remind the reader again and again, every wondrous machine, every high technology, can always be traced back to a single interrogative phrase. Therefore, the origin of all things is a linguistic selection of voice. Everything ever made began with a poetic choice of interrogation. All new machines will originate from the seed of a newly selected linguistic phraseology. *This, finally, is the case for poetry as information.*

The concept of Story Theory (and thus, *Chandos Ring*) originates from a crisis of modern information. What if our lives verify evidence of a source of spiritual power – and yet learn (later) that the narrative of that spiritual power contains no terrestrial archeology? By any account, this is the crisis of information of the last century of Western men. There had to be a *Bible* that organized spiritual power into an effective form of ideation (proof) – even though the *Bible* itself could be shown to be only a series of remarkable consistent poetic texts. The protocol of epic phraseology was true – even if there never was a biology or archeology to prove that humans made any of the events listed in epic narrative! We have to understand, therefore, why epic narrative is still true. If the human mind is only a terrestrial organ, then yes, all human texts are worthless fictions. Yet any cultural human that reads these texts – the parables of Jesus, the Exodus out of Egypt, the death of Hector – knows instantly that they contain vital information of the human astral mind. This, finally, is my proven thesis. Epic texts can only be true if the human mind is operating on the astral coordinate.

There had to be a more exact way to account for the power embedded in sacred narratives, the ancient myths of gods, and the wide spectrum of the epic trope. Every Western civilization has lived by an epic narrative – whether of *Moses, David, Virgil, Homer, Dante, Matthew, Mark, Luke, John,* or *St Paul.* Each of these is a narrative of spiritual *exclusivity.* In each high civilization, there was a miraculous recovery of language – verifying the protocol of human singularity as story making – as poetry. There has been exactly no pattern of high civilization without a *narration* of spiritual *exclusivity.* Yet we simply have no terrestrial archeology of this structure – except the epic trope. This tells us that the human mind operates on the astral plane – not on the terrestrial. Story Theory is the missing link that confirms the assertion.

Modernism teaches that if there is no archeology, then there is no historical truth. That is to say that without a terrestrial fossil of verification, there is no basis for a *valid* and *operable* spiritual truth. If modernism cannot explain the source of spiritual power, if religious narratives are discredited by archeology – then there must be a missing link between the *information* of materialism and spirituality – a vital link that is still unexplained. I found that link. Story Theory explains how the mind works. Story Theory discovers that there truly is no terrestrial archeology for the human mind at all. Terrestrial, global, materialism cannot account for – or explain – the condition of self-consciousness of the human mind. Consequently, Story Theory discovers that the human mind does not operate on the terrestrial plane. The terrestrial mind – as organ – is an assumption made with incorrect evidence. Thus, it is less than useless to search for the terrestrial archeology of the human condition. We trace the organ of events portrayed in epic narrative to the astral plane.

My examination of the epic literature gave me this insight. Thus we should not look for the bones of gods; we should look for the origins and patterns of men embedded in all epic and mythic narrative. The patterns of the epic interrogative are eternal, reoccurring, and significant. Their interrogative constancy is of such a remarkable accuracy – across cultures, poets, and eons – that the narrative pattern cannot be happenstance or coincidence. This book asserts that the epic texts reveal the original location and purpose of the life source on the astral coordinate. Story

Theory narrates this new construct. *Chandos Ring* is the product of this new paradigm of human life. There will be beautiful new machines arising from this new structure of life.

Epic literature traces the genealogy of gods. Yet this is only a symbol of the search for the source and purpose of life. The answers of these questions are within our reach. The fossil of life is embedded in human story. Therefore, we don't need more archeologists; we need more poets. Western literature is a search for more life, more power. Every giant of literature is a hero precisely because he is able to perform the will of his mind. This is how a god performs. Our heroes of literature represent a search for gods. The last line of every poem is an assertion of poetic *seizure of consciousness*. The epic trope records the men who have managed to seize control of consciousness. They are human heroes and demi-gods. They did not die in their beds.

There is a lot of hand wringing over gods. It is not important whether or not there are actually gods. The question of gods is a *Red Herring*. The question of gods, in Story Theory, is only a human linguistic construct – an urge to enchantment. Only enchantment engenders devotion to a cult. We may state this problem in other terms. God is hidden because the mind of man is hidden in its origin. What is important is that humans still seek the evidence of ideational power. We must search and tease every symbol of life. We are the symbol eaters. The human gods function exactly as symbols of ideational power. So our focus is on this creature that is able to powerfully sustain ideational structure. The world, after all, is what we say it is. Our politics, our human rights, our justice, our love, our humanity – are what we say they are. Only the human makes an assertion of justice, or love, or humanity.

The world, thus, is a pure ideational structure. The operational field of all human ideation, properly understood, then, is the astral coordinate. The Earth is only tangentially included in the human concept of life because we have terraformed the Earth with our astral minds. The proof? Wherever men travel in the universe, they will terraform their environment – with the power of their mind – their mental organization of value. When a man arrives at an astral grid coordinate, he terraforms – no matter on *which* astral coordinate. Thus, the Earth is only tangentially involved in human life. No theory of poetry has made an accommodation of this vital human information.

Kosmoautikon, a new term of mastery, is able to freely self-create ideational reality at will. A *Kosmoautikon* can move between dimensional branes. He is a star-runner. A god is inferior in rank to a *Kosmoautikon*. Humans search power with deep emotion and intensive story. This is a correct act. We will never cease to seek power. Story is essentially our means to seek the source of human power. We have discovered the existence of a *Kosmoautikon* by story – not by science or photography.

So long as we accept idols, we make linguistic gods. It is to be remembered that any ideology – as Western liberal ideology – operates exactly like a belief system belonging to the cult of any god. Even secularists operate within a pattern of their own belief system. This applies to charismatic leaders, celebrities, criminals, and artists. To be a criminal is only to operate with a differing linguistic pattern of prestige than the rest of the population. Each person has his own linguistic mythic code.

Consciousness is a strange protocol. Why? Because, above all else, consciousness ensures there is *something*. All texts of literature, all languages, are a search for *something* – as opposed to *nothing*. This is what the materialist overlooks. There is *something* existing beyond the visible, mortal frame. Each reader may confirm this as time permits.

It is a victory for any poet if his poetry contains information. We have seen in this volume that epic poetry contains cosmological information, genetic information, charismatic information – information that confirms the still unknown bias of consciousness. We have shown that poetry contains reliable information of the cosmos that predates even human history. Poetry was the first to insist that our solar system is a binary system – that the stars emit pulsating ions containing information. Our epic myths contain the history and purpose of the sentient consciousness embedded in star constellations. Epic poetry, ancient and unchanging, is thus reliable. Either way I can proceed.

CHAPTER THIRTY-TWO

The Genesis of Chandos Ring

The Genesis of *Chandos Ring* is rage, peril, and idolatry. Again, a pattern appears. A soldier finds himself sheltering in the same alien camp, recognizing the same impassible terrain.

Chandos Ring is an epic story of a family dynasty in modern poetic speech. Nothing can be more isolated in ambition or more private in composition. The opportunity for miscalculation is generous. If there were not at least the supposition of a well-considered preparation, the race would not be wise. We all live by suppositions, I discover. In my contest, I am certain I have built a still incomplete skeleton with too many questions to answer. Let me assume that I have miscalculated. In the worse instance, there is a collapsed colossus of which even the rubble may make the passing spectator curious. If only the giant, alien feet of the colossus survive, it may still evoke a memory in the passer-by. So be it.

Why this book now? *Chandos Ring* appears at the high watermark of American influence in the world. Any culture that comes in contact with American popular culture is forever transformed. American music, cinema, fashion, technology, and political ideas instantaneously disintegrate the indigenous culture that makes contact with us. For good or ill, Western influence is unmistakable and unstoppable. Though we are now attacked on every front, still, Western linguistic codes are the future *world*. What is my evidence? China, India, Russia, Brazil, Japan, and Africa shamelessly replicate the modern elements of Western civilization. Modernism is essentially a civilization of global English. For how long?

Chandos Ring appears at the nexus of our unprecedented century of influence. Western linguistic hegemony has been verified by every global medium of modernism. Only Western poetry, so far, has failed to monument our unprecedented influence. I see no takers.

I rage against the crisis of modern poetry. Modern poetry has stumbled at the very moment that Western influence is at its absolute height. It stumbles just as we are challenged by foreign hatred. On one hand, I modify the language of the most hegemonic idiom ever achieved: modern English. Then, acrobatically, I swivel to critique the corrupted information of modernism. I must inexplicably sneer at the hand that has bred me: modernism. I have explained the reasons for this critique. Modernism contains corrupted information. Modernism denies its need for prophetic speech. It denies that all speech is prophetic. It embeds a linguistic contest in modern speech – a fatal schism between the linguistic adherents of contemporary secret languages and the vernacular-speaking human. The outcome is still not clear.

Our sense of self-consciousness is deep. A new epic text must consequently be deliberate – and not accidental. A new epic text must be a narrative of deliberate self-examination. We are beyond the point of waiting for accidental or charismatic arrivals of text. We have to self-consciously produce new innovations of linguistics. A successful innovation of original language is the only measurement of success. The result should not *only* amount to an *alternate* modernism. An assembly of new element was demanded. I sought a new form of *Our Mercury*. It had to be an alien idiom, unsourced in local waters – yet recognizable. This trace of DNA recognition could verify a fossil link to the original source of human consciousness. My labor was not positioned accessible to relative moderation. Yet moderation and restraint was the only way to arrive at the goal. The effort would necessitate deep engagement, but could not be built without detachment from the result.

The poet of an alternate vision of future Western men must contest against the arrogance of a troubled and aggressive modernism. We are all under the surveillant eye of an all-conquering, hegemonic, ideology. How to block out the megalith? First, I had to ride the beast to its limit. Then, after it carried me farther than any beast could voyage, I had to cut its throat.

This beast is the supreme vehicle of modernism – American English. Though it is currently disparaged, it is only correct to monument its achievement. To be modern, to even attempt to compete with the West, foreign powers must learn an industrial Western language. To perform genetics, for instance, even this small sector of Western specialty, China and India must speak Greek, Latin, and English. Example. The word *mitochondrion* comes from the Greek, μίτος or *mitos*, thread + χονδρίον or *chondrion*, granule. This is only one example of the language of modernity that has already been developed to maturity by the Western mind. *Mitochondria*, as all high discoveries of science, was unknown by the Chinese until we coined the term. The same, and unavoidable, threads of Western language are found in atomic theory, quantum mechanics, particle mechanics, physics, chemistry, aviation, rocketry, etc. The Galaxy has already been named with Greek, English, and Latin patterned script. I will defend that universe and not acknowledge any other as real. I have no choice. I am a linguistic creation.

It is a sub-thesis of these books that the architecture of a linguistic structure

– alone – leads to new discoveries of human consciousness. Every modern science that has matured has developed directly upon the basis of Western linguistic structures. Only a poem – and a philosophy – that unites all these achievements of influence is found lacking in modern Western hegemony.

Chandos Ring tests the thesis that language is the only *true* machine a civilization builds. It is the thesis of these books that linguistic idiom actually patterns ideation into specific forms of ideation – forms that would not otherwise be discovered if our particular language was not exactly coded as it is. A linguistic code is viral and particular. All our technology is a direct result of the flavor of our linguistic code. Perhaps this is a new discovery in human philosophy. This is an insight to be explored endlessly.

It is easy to convince poets that linguistics is the source of Being. It is easy to convince the religious that they live by linguistic codes, precepts, revelations, and poems. Prayer, faith, and belief are language-based forms of sentient perception of reality. Moderns are more stubborn. Moderns believe that their high science is separate from anything so fragile as a mere linguistic code. Yet in this book we have illustrated our thesis that the linguistic faiths of science and math are language-based forms of prophecy. A familiar theme by now.

But how to convince the materialist? Show him something new.

Human realities are *based* on human text. In a world of unproven phenomena, perception *operates* as evidence. Tests are our only evidence of human perception. My philosophy, embodied in Story Theory, attempts to *convince* secular materialists (scientists) that linguistics is *as* crucial to their structure of vision as linguistic prayer is vital to the monk in his cell. If, in Story Theory, there are no actual evidences, no facts, outside of consciousness, then science itself is based on human linguistic texts. As C.S. Lewis said, scientists *infer* there is empirical evidence of principles of the universe. This action is still a linguistic construct within a highly modifiable consciousness. In Story Theory there are no empirical facts. There is only power.

There is no technological or scientific advance – no engineering, no genetics, no physics, no cosmology, no computer, no lever, no machine – that is not directly connected to human linguistic bias. Every tool is a tool of idiom. Phenomena are linguistically transformed in the mind before they are transformed to images of value in the eye. Consequently, there could not be the appearance of a space faring civilization without a new form of linguistic literature – as text – to give structure to the new idiom.

This is why we construct a theory of poetry. Modernism has failed to give us reliable information. We seek a more reliable idiom for a space faring civilization. This is usually what we hope to construct with a separate genre of literature named science fiction. How could there be a new linguistic idiom if it did not have its own hermetically sealed self-referent points? Science fiction suits Story Theory well. Each attempt at new linguistics develops along separate channels of story-making. And what is the genre of science fiction if not a separate channel of linguistic innovation? Either way I can proceed.

I do not only say that science uses poetic terminology. More radically, I insist that the creations of all sciences – the actual theories, evidences, applications, and procedures of science – directly progress to their final constructions based on the code contained in Western linguistic patterns. This logic, carried to its ultimate expression illustrates that not only does the observer collapse the wave function of the photon into a particular location (as in quantum mechanics) – *but also that the entire visible universe does not exist until a human observes it and makes a sentient interpretation*. Every action in life illustrates that we modify reality to fit the conditions of life we seek. Even if we do not always succeed – the attempt is still made. This has deep implications about life in space and our innovative means of space travel. If Being consists of an infinite number of branes, then there must be a sentient creature that is able to move across these branes. The imaginative sentience of the strong poet is that creature.

Our future human condition waits upon our present linguistic treatment of life. Man's future is contained within consciousness – therefore our language code will modify the future of consciousness that we seek to realize. If we seek to colonize the Galaxy, then our consciousness will be structured to meet the conditions that we seek of that conquest. If we are ashamed to ensure the galaxies reflect our way of life, then we have already linguistically ensured our eradication. Our belief of science will radically modify. Science rises to its highest linguistic horror in *Chandos Ring*. Science, itself, soon enough, is encrusted with wounded moralities.

Story Theory corrects the misunderstanding of materialist civilization – and clearly presents the argument that poetry – as the evidence of our highest linguistic achievement – is central to any human progress. Science illustrates my thesis in so far as the highest concepts of modern physics are phrased in poetic terms – as String Theory, the Event Horizon, Black Holes, Big Bang, quarks, quantum mechanics, Higgs Boson, particle mechanics, etc. Each of these theoretical (and invisible) concepts is a form of poetry – not empirical products of materialistic science. The modern scientific world is an Age of Faith. In Story Theory, any age of man is an Age of Faith – since human life is poetically patterned, organized and believed.

To Match Consent to Our Manners

Chandos Ring reflects the same themes that America represents. America is the first nation to successfully attempt to become a space faring civilization (with the Apollo Moon mission). Likewise, it is not unusual that *Chandos Ring* tells a story of spacemen. America has represented the *future* for humans for over two centuries. *Chandos Ring* is a story of future civilization – not a past battle. America has been the primary market for the science fiction genre. The poem has a science fiction theme. America has been the home of the world's greatest technological and scientific advances for the last century of the modern era.

For the first time in the history of poetry, science is now a central actor in an ambitious poetic narrative. Unbelievably, astoundingly, inexplicably, science has been utterly ignored by modern poets. *Chandos Ring* finds a way to accept the narrative of science into the enchantment of the poet's work. No poet has managed to find a way to assimilate the scientific insight. This is especially incomprehensible since science is so evidently a form of the modern human poetic imagination.

American history represents the tension between luxury or justice, free capitalism or populist socialism, and between charismatic secular gods (humanistic natural magic) or fundamental religious tradition. Each of these elements is on display in *Chandos Ring*. The question is not why this poem now, the question is why has not a poem of this scope already appeared? The world is interested to see what poetic value our civilization may defend against all other forms of competitive linguistic achievement. American poetry has seldom attempted a movement to hegemonic expression of the poetic achievement – and chaos – of our civilization. This is an opportunity of freedom to create. I am astonished at the opportunity.

Chandos Ring meets my own requirements of a new theory of poetry in English. This is necessarily only a model of what may still be achieved. A modern idiom has been found promiscuous to adaptation to a new perspective of human life. A story of ancient and modern information is combined seamlessly in one narrative. The vernacular of the poem modifies incrementally, until at the end of *Chandos Ring*, Western man is discovered to speak a new idiom of life.

What are the requirements of a new theory of poetry? This book has examined each of the following requirements of an American literature able to sustain the epic trope. 1) Poetry must be able to tell a narrative of power. Lyric poetry, that does not make narratives, in consequence, has failed to sustain the prestige of the human singularity: that is, poetry. 2) Future poets must manipulate the vernacular with strength sufficient to outclass the *alternate* poem of hegemonic science to create a new human mind. 3) The human mind must be addressed as operating on the astral plane. This perspective necessarily privileges the information of relative cosmology – and corrects the faulted assertion of terrestrial causation. 4) The epic trope is recognized as the database of the permanent information of human life as a function of spiritual cosmology. All civilizations, all archetypes of the human mind are found in narratives and texts of the epic trope. 5) Consciousness is still unfinished, and thus, the poet can establish the condition of life he seeks for future human life. 6) The human mind is central as the supreme manipulator of consciousness. 7) All speech is prophecy.

These seven principles fulfill the requirements for a strong theory of poetry of future men. I would challenge any academic dilettante to remove a single requirement.

Chandos Ring is a product of unconstrained freedom. It is the most controversial large work of literature to ever be attempted by a Western poet. I had to supersede the tired and abused modern lyric form. True to my critique of poetry, the epic trope presents a monument, at times horrible, of the achievement of the Western idiom. Above all else, I had to explore what was possible to win from a lifetime of thought and searching. The race is still long and uncertain. Let no child, queen, or jester prevent my expansion. Let me pass.

This project is a construct of fictions, yet fictions perhaps within our reach. We set out with our souls newly opened, not only for the stories and pictures of another planet, but with the hunger gained from so much forsaking.

> We leave the Earth
> not wanting riches, not needing knowledge,
> but once to match consent to our manners,
> we set out, lifting the stakes that held our tents.
>   (*Chandos Ring*, Book one, Canto Nine.)

CHANDOS RING

List of Characters

Aaron	Leader of the American exodus from Earth. Mad.
Talon, in chains	Scientist from Earth/Io. Exchanged his human body for a lizard. Mad
Wakeda	Faithful companion of Aaron. Military Chief of staff.
Vargus	Second in Command. Delivers 300 Slavic girls from Eastern Europe.
Black Terry	Aaron's only living human son. Pretend cook. Prophet.
Jurate	Child wife of Aaron. Future mother of Kosmoautikon.
Antebbe	Astral being from Sirius System.
Cheda	Alien son of Aaron. First Homo Faustus.
Nehi Hussein Nampour	Democratic senator. Political officer. Trojan Horse.

Argument Book Three

IN MY ATOM IS ARK

Aaron nears completion of the Galactic moon-ship. Vargus has returned from his mission to manipulate the smaller moons of Metis and Thebes to impact into the large moon of Europa. The first collision with Metis burned off half of Europa's immense salt ocean. Metis, also guided into Europa, broke the crust of Europa and exposed the hot interior of the frozen planet.

Thebes's collision into Europa reforms the planet. The effect, as planned, is a further reduction of the salt oceans and an increase of temperature at the core of Europa. The result of these impacts is the formation of shifting, continent size tectonic plates. Subsequent volcanism spews mineral and gas into a nascent atmosphere. The heat of volcanic activity combined with a heavy cloud cover slowly raises the temperature of the planet to liquefy the remaining ocean ice. Talon's scientists have made a virus-driven compost that will exponentially reproduce basic biological fauna in the space of 10 years – on over a third of the planet. This fauna virus is dangerous but effective. Aaron's artificial greenhouse gases commence a long warming process. Within a few years there will be the first domes of habitation established on the Europa – which is twice its previous size and contains a gravity more suited to Aaron's new creatures – or men? If the scientists are mad, the specific structure of the madness is irrelevant. Europa is now raised in its elliptic further from Jupiter's rays and appears as a twin moon with Callisto – so near are the two moons now to each other.

Book Three contains a masque performed by the children of the crews. The entire Western world gathers in a large amphitheater to hear a story of the future success of their great project. But who wrote the play? Is it mere propaganda – or is it an actual prophecy of the future? Did Aaron write it or Antebbe – Cheda's new companion from Callisto? Antebbe is a creature speaking a strange new idiom. Like Aaron, she is a creature of immense natural charisma and the humans cower as she enters any room.

She assists Aaron in his experiments with the human skeleton – to make a higher advancement in the human body and mind. But was this reengineering already performed thousands of years before – when Homo sapiens were made from the "black footed ones"? The purpose now is to create a race of men able to survive in low gravity environments based on other forms of mineral – and not dependant only upon oxygen and carbon.

Finally, the 300 girls from several orphanages in Latvia, Estonia, Lithuania and Ukraine slowly begin to mix two by two with the crews. The men see these women at the performance of the play and are crazed with sexual interest. All insurgency is curbed – since Aaron has promised to release these women to the ship's population of desperate human men. Strangely, the young girls are creatures that have been reformed by Aaron's intensive reeducation. They speak perfect English and know English, French, and German poets by heart. They not only have an exotic and charismatic Slavic beauty, they are, eccentrically, willing to mate only with the men who support Aaron's visions.

This changes everything in RingWorld. The human issue of these unions forever changes the nature of Homo sapiens. They have a lighter skeleton, larger eyes and brains – and exhibit a powerful spiritual perception of second sight. *Homo faustus* is born – only the beginning of the story. The scene opens as Aaron conducts his eccentric medical operations. A new language is used to address the newly created genus – Homo *faustus*.

CHANDOS RING

Book Three

IN MY ATOM IS ARK

I must create a system or be enslaved by another man's; I will not reason or compare; my business is to create.

William Blake

The chief mission of all other races and peoples, large and small, is to perish in the revolutionary holocaust.

Karl Marx

I appeal to the chemists to discover a humane gas that will kill instantly and painlessly. In short, a gentlemanly gas — deadly by all means, but humane, not cruel.

George Bernard Shaw

America is therefore the land of the future, where, in the ages that lie before us, the burden of the world's history shall reveal itself.

G. W. F. Hegel

Chiasson's . . . vignettes can at times seem to verge on dithering, a sort of poetic fiddling while Rome burns... charting that peculiar but all-too-recognizable interval between hiding and being found...where we wait, on and on, simultaneously fearing and craving the arrival of a Virgil capable of explaining everything, once and for all.

NYRB (review of a typical modern poet.)

Even now in heaven there are angels carrying savage weapons.

St. Paul

CANTO ONE

When I Smoke the Bones of Western Men

1
i   *(Aaron addresses Homo faustus – supine on a table.)*
Aaron. When I smoke the bones of Western men
the bodies cough and shudder with cold.
Shivering, they ask for warmth.
                         I know –
your prior state was a hermetic chamber.
I have placed you on a humid tile. Yet
it is your new condition that chills you.

I perceive merit in your protest. The root
of sentience is fragile with bias. Who first
told you that you are human? It was spurious.
That was the prophecy of perilous men.
Until you have my idiom, you have no
dimension – no prescience. No symbols
cling on your brain.
Look. I have opened your valves.
Spread yourself promiscuous to inspection.

Ah, this is my intent. I see your lips move.
Do you already search with precognition?
Tell me where the itch of bias populates?
Do you stumble? I see your eyes still search. Why?
For what? It is not enough only to breath? No.
I know what you want.

You want to cup every sensation.
You want to terraform an astral coordinate.
You want to pray an altar of insatiable wishes.
You wish to discover unknowable gods.
I grant you this. Though it is useless –
it will only increase your frenzy.

The truth is less complex. All that is required of you
is that you read the symbols left for you
from an ancient idiom.

I am your storm.
I have traveled from Earth to enhance your
atom in this gravity. How will you still revise
the idiom of life? What story do you assemble
from fear of extinction?

Speak, and I will mark a page.

ii
A. Your mind is made attentive by my wish.
The seven waves of sentience now enter
the egg observed. I, as eighth ancestor,
form you with my observation. By this, you are
sentient to speak to all dimension. Yet, notice,
you cannot observe an object until you
have a symbol for it. That is why you
will forget these early moments. You
cannot see, or live, or cry, unless you eat
a symbol. Yes, all of you here are the symbol
eaters. Manically, that is not enough. I have
added an accumulation of dimension.
Now I lodge all space and time in your temples:
it is from a single word. Symbols are a mnemonic device,
a spider web on which you place all ideation.
You still do not know what this means? I see it.
How long will it take for you to find your sound?
It itches? It moves? It is intemperate with emotion?
Yes, I see it.
Already the bias of consciousness
takes the footing of your creature.
As long as you have breath, you will search this bias.
Again, it is a single word that divides incessantly.
Does sentience change the observed? I am certain.
To be a god is to itch across the sentient membrane.
Every word for god is only a symbol. There is no
corporeal structure. There is only a wind – a wave.
What is god, except a power you distinguish?
Every bias embeds a cry for seizure of element.
You will mistake this. You will attempt to mimic
the atomic form. You will cry after a combination
of lessoning, dying cells.
What exchange is biased in your assembly?
I was cautious. I made an estimate for spleen.
Is pleasure your highest contribution?
Reconsider your urge. I would take its crown.
Then what is alien to our rumor? Unlawful death?
Yes, there will be a small death.

A crust of tear will freeze on eyes.

2

i   *(Aaron begins to make stitches in the flesh.)*
A. What you don't know – what you don't suspect – is
your life, like your death, is a condition – not
a substance. I have embedded a small death. Because
your present form, your structure, your energy –
in this brane – because it is only an ark–– your death
contains information. How many tears will you subscribe
till you cry aloud that death emits structure and tincture?
Yes, the density of cries has an hour of expiration. A cry
belongs to story. It has a beginning, middle, and end.
It's only as complicated as that. Do not show alarm.
The life force is always guarded – in a place safe
from influence.
Death is small. So small that it may yet
temper with observation. Life, still unfinished, seeks
peril, divination, selfless risk. It has no safe harbor.
No northward passage. If you are prepared to burst – be certain
it is a short channel. Death is bravery, then. Love, germane
to death, likewise proves your courage. Henceforth, every
breath you suck leads to peril. You will accept this danger.
No. There is no sanctuary, not in character, not in restraint;
so you must burst, farming the phantoms you have
accumulated. The white walls may catch your liquid spleen.
    (Continues suturing a large wound.)
Against these specters, you may assemble speech.
Observe it closely – it reveals an urge to
enchantment. The patterns you make reveal
the intent of the god that sent you. For this purpose
you are also made – as god. What will you kill
with this temple?
Step into the world. Measure its shroud.
Gods do not fear to lose their form. Why? Form
arises in sentience, as a cloud forms a moment
in atmosphere – math, engineering, love – concise poetry –
each the conditional and selected progeny of linguistics.
As much as you will seek a height of idiom,
you must smother with electric wire and night pillows
the high poem of the stranger.

Observe. I shall now tell you your future. Each
of you can be replicated linguistically at will.
Since you will seek enchantment, I will allow
you to move across dimension. This is your treasure.
Yet here, in this place, your time is brief. O lovers,
your high requests cannot remain.

Draw near in the wind where they escape.

ii
A. If you have illicit cunning, do not be ashamed.
It is assumed.
　　(Wakeda appears with papers. Aaron waves him away.)
You are a condition in my mind. Therefore, resist
the urge to become a *thing* – as glass, jug, or feldspar.
Yes, I know you will forget. So how can you remember?
You will make every stratagem to become a *thing*.
　　(Black Terry appears outside the glass. Aaron waves him away.)
Sentience has a stagnant element. The ebullience of
sapien flesh is now inert. Give it another moment.
It must alter. I have eradicated the long and toothy
nerve of *other*. We must begin again our idiom.
So I have made you ruthless. I have killed *other* with
pleasure. You are born with the water carrier. Now
you must make a severe selection. The ebullient
element of Pisces is removed. The propaganda
of brotherhood no longer shall constrain you.
I have carefully shielded your atom from the
constellation of the home planet. Yes, you are
perfect in construction.
　　　　　　If my heart heightens its pulse,
I mark a page. I have found my weak element.
I back away. Let me once hear an astral voice. Pure.
A voice with no element of pre-positioned tincture –
no heavy earth.

You are now perfect in your generations.
Open your voice. I see you tremble.

Yes, there are others here. Look.
They are silent now. They are cold.
Ignore them; they cannot hurt you.
You will see that you are some altered.

My clothes are moist with sweat.

3

i   *(Moving to another creature, supine on a tile.)*
A. Your form is much improved. Like mine.
I was not pleased with the human skeleton.
It was smithied by a race of alien gravity.
Observe. I surprise nature with a lesser inclusion.

You will not miss the globular element of your
fire-burned ancestors. There are still traceable
genealogies of the Age of the Bull, the Ram, and the fish.
You will still seek sensual force and hardy laws.
In your remaining genes, I still prophesy
a smoke and rising steam of love remains.
Yet it is not primary. You are healed.
The Age of Aquarius signals your raging ballad.

Some search a prerogative of element. Every
specialist is taxonomic. I have advanced your
genetics to a higher idiom. Yet I intend
you are comely, proportioned to my taste.
Well formed and blood young, the overlaying
superfluity accumulates a sensual charge
and an urge to folly; your gray eyes summon
inspection with intent. Try to rise now. Before I kiss.
I hesitate to add a higher construction. Stop.
I fear to make a miscalculation.

I may have an urge to keep you with me. What
would be the outcome? Eros lessens gods and men.
Jupiter embeds an erotic charge. Checked with Saturn.
The giant, displaced, has revenged men with Eros.
I was a pilgrim on the stations of that cross: *Homo
sapiens*, I learned your language. You can read
symbols. But you fail at Eros. Eros cannot mature.
Cannot advance to new invention. You repeat
endlessly in the machine. What is Eros then?

Yes, I know. A prayer. A supplication for divine
sensation. But then you stop and retreat.

We had to remove your planet – and then
your bones.

ii

A. I see there are tears. No. You trouble me. Do not cry.
I shall finish you before you suffer. What shall
counter my wish to erase all other DNA? Love of life?
Nothing else? The danger of love, *as message,* is clear.
It attempts to pose, complete, as *all* of life. This is a mistake.
Love is one of many trials of substance. Observe.

Have you seen the night sky? A new constellation appears.
New cutthroats cry from their crib of stars. Love, now abused,
is the crumpled message of Pisces. A wounded morality.
The *water carrier,* purified, now floods the plains
of misbelief. A severe selection is telegraphed.
No longer may you only cry, *love, love, love.* Men have
murdered so that they may love after your spleen.
No more may you politic with the cry – *proliferation!*
You smothered life on Earth with human proliferation.
The water carrier enters. He has a new message.
Yet it will appear charismatic to you. Even hostile.
Was not the loving Christ feared and killed by the *Chief Priests*?
So now there is a new message that will appear alien.
There are those that will make counter philosophy. Why?
Because they see the final intent of life? No? Yes?
Tell me something I can use. You will feel a small
prick. Accept gently the front stepping opiate.

There. The Sirius pulse now signals motion in your
brain. Still unresolved, this is the source of your
atom. Yes . . . look . . . in your atom is now ark. Aquarius, rise.
You are now a living star. Do you feel the rush?
You are now like a man stung, searching
for the snake that bit him. If restraint convene
from eminence, speak, and I will listen.
    (Moves to a third creature.)
I see you . . . struggling there. Still moving to retrograde?
Yes, I know, *Homo sapiens* will die. After so many revivals
of high fornication, so many deceits of self-sweat,
what new idea has advanced? A new element of story?
Something yet unknown? Only proliferation?
    (Injects the faust gene mutation.)

No, I know the answer. Or your erotic state contains
a secret you may still reveal? If not, then what?
No more erotic answers? No more dilettante youth
to ennoble? No higher idiom to innovate?
Then have we arrived at our last station?

Exactly. So you see the origin of my work.

I Dreamed Last Night of Machines

4   *(Speaking to Wakeda – entering impatient with papers.)*
i
A. Show me no more machines made in China.
I have fondled these till they bleed. Some are
broken. They were made to cost. Nemesis
was greed in our market. A machine of our mind
should contain no sheath of foreign idiom to betray us.
Any idiom seeks to homogenize and pasteurize its host.
I have released a virus against this foreign element.
My aim is taxidermic. The Earth, my sampos mill.
I dreamed last night of machines. What new scythe
shall I place in new men? Any machine we do not watch
will eat the hair of our bellies as we sleep. When
young, I was a student of medicine. Then called to
war. I prefer war. I tossed the Earth in my satchel.
My enemies die a good death. A death with information.
Where now shall I war? They say I am enraged.
So that is the ruthless spider in my vein?
It is relief to speak to men without terrestrial
coordinates – no earth wound creeping in the brain.
So many wounded moralities. Endlessly repeating.
You are the first not to know the difference.
Seize now your sharp clarities! Choose your linguistic device
with care! You will have to bed with them for eons.
You will make human marriage seem kind and gentile.
I have some new patents. You will see many
original insights from Dr. Talon. They are altered.
He was mad, yet I have made some new attempts
of audacity. Everything made is soon broken.
Every invention is always used. If you once
learn to alter a man's genetics – you will alter
ruthlessly. To a man with a new tattoo,
every square of skin – an empty canvass. Till
so compressed with inks, the former man is discarded.
Then the monster remaining lives only for nostalgia.
Every new innovation amends the idiom. Amend mine.
I have reworked his equations with advantage. There is
a new gene. My assistants were troubled. Why?
Now they cannot be found. Silence is a sacred precinct.
I accept – the scope of *sapiens* is scaled to a point.

240

ii

A. I dreamed last night of machines. They acted
like men. I was surrounded. They took the form,
inexplicably, of torn and ragged sails . . . of passing
ghost ships. Again, I greet the astral position of my mind.
They were space pirates – dead of some insidious
self-injected plague. They spoke to me cationic.
To discover which of them were men, I had
to ask them to make a poem. They failed.
Quote me a poem, I said. Some of the machines
tried to pass the prose of Mr. Whitman as a poem.
I cured them of superficiality.
I seized their crown.
Sapiens, your skills are mediocre. I asked each child of Earth
to make a résumé of needs. I asked them to add desire.
The list of human faculties amassed end to end
produced a small postage stamp – of repetitions. Eat,
sleep, fornicate, hoard. Repeat. Add terror.
How stringent in construct all need and erotic
desire! How minimalist in moral division! Human rights
are singular in summary. They list them on a little square!
Earth has withered you of variable element. Your
language displays no further pretense. You have
deserted your words of high moral philosophy. Show me
your epic poem of audacity? No? No epic bone?
Empirical, I conclude men are diminished in scope.
Yet I do not exterminate. Your DNA already
contains the alphabets of new unmapped Galaxy.
Do you know how much data is secret in this genome?
So much still unleavened, pristine? Spiders on human eyes
still frozen; still two legs, silent, testing the air. I have found
all the alien genealogies. Every ghetto of back alley crib.
Every answer to every linguistic question already
folded and inscribed with gold letters. Here. Just here.
Watch. I activate a new region of the genome. There!
Silence! Yes, I am listening. Speak! An ancient genealogy
asserts antennae to all stations alert. I am present
at this creation. Let my eyes see this for all time.
In the year that ripens the sparrow and the hawk,
let this be the elephant memory of my heart!

(Waves away all documents. Wakeda leaves.)
Stop. I am vindicated.
I must carcass new my kiss.
Stand close. I crush
the brick-brack of this species.

5
i   *(Aaron now speaking only to himself.)*
A. There is no clarity without murder.
Death precisely fixes valuation.
Build me a spit of audacity.
I find no orthodoxy, no point to rest.
An incessant bias shakes in me. Once
perfected, innovation is placed behind a glass,
as spore and dust – a lever once that
moved the sun. What is a symbol – if not
a space to monument in sentience – sentient
selection? So I advance this idiom.
It is a small pause in sentience to measure
a further advance. I release the acid in your veins.
A machine has not this perfection. We have
projected a field to our wide beam. I made
a new man today. She cried. Will I fail
at the moment of your crisis? Perhaps.
You will try to smother me. I may never see.
She said, "Master?" Already, she fails.
So these are the men I can recognize. What is this
instinct we face? Peril, rumor, selfless risk – each
perfected by death, my saint.
O, if I paint upon your bone long legs of rocketry,
what cartography of creature could I seal as secret
cosmology – and future savants read the page?
And if I have seized this pretext, what other
spaceman, before me also, made my speech?
And if they are legions to my single spear?
The part unused
in your genome is map and text of worlds
won and lost. And other half – future rumor
of still unpaged and grizzly mode of life. Stepping through
the lexicon of your blood – I read and answer letters
anciently posted – and future texts of un-stepped peril.

I reply to Buddha by these works.
I cancel all Eastern men by my exercise.
When I smoke the bones of Western men,
I release the spiders on our eyes.

ii   *(Suddenly turning to kiss the new-made creature.)*
A. What else? Not enough? I know. I know. I know.

Certain. I do not tease my guilt. I do not privilege my guilt.
I merely observe it always sitting in the corner.
You alone will love me without prior statistics.
Look, it is so simple. Which hegemony do we confirm?
Our tongue – or the eternal idiom of the oppressed?
I look and see there is always the *oppressed*.
By whose fantasy should they be released?
Only to turn and oppress others – subsequent?

Who, once unshackled, will not *oppress* in turn?

Every high idiom builds a temple. How do we
know there is a temple? Because there is a sacrifice.
Why should I self-immolate? Guilty?
Who is not guilty? Who would not rule? If
I canceled my own sound, would they, the *other*,
not, in turn, intend to summit me to their idiom?
Exactly.
I form my enemy's temple already with my sound.
If I can fix him in dogma – if I can force him
to his text – then I have defeated him – since god
is still unfinished. And I will color between the lines.

What proof is there of my existence? We know exactly
how to detect it. I exist since I have modified *other*
with my linguistic equation. Thus, I promise
dominion of our sound. You may try to kill me.
That is an honest act. But do not ask me to praise
a stranger's voice. Do not beg me that I should love China.
They hate us *bitterly*. How could I even perform the act with
competence? This is the policy of a coward.
So many have died already for our code.
I ensure they die for theirs.

You will find my text close to your vernacular.
You are here to witness my high device.

Nothing now turns back the acid
entering your veins.

It is now sentient with precognition.
Look. Read this symbol of cosmology.
It coils a tale of alien spleen

intimate to the first cry of men.

Political Interlude: Are Spacemen Free?

6   *(Enter Senator Nehi Hussein Nampour.)*
i
A. I am ready to see Senator Nehi.
I have a promotion to offer him. Oh, you are here!

Hussein. Admiral, what is the air in this room? I can't breathe.
(Sniffs.) Methane? Sulfur? What happened here?
When do you restore the will of the Demos?

A. You mean, when do I allow you a chance
to swarm my projects? I will disappoint you.

H. Senator Rufus tried that. What have you done with him?
We all are wary of you now. We are watching you.

A. (To Replicant.) What happened to Senator Rufus? Speak.

R. He died of hypoxia. Gave his body to science.

H. Hypoxia?! You strangled him!

A Where did you come from? How did you get in my ships?
I did not detect you before. You are a Trojan Horse, Mr. Hussein.
I know you. Are you the one that insists upon a secular state –
only to establish Islam after the defeat of the Judeo-Christian
achievement? This is you then – yes? The Murmers . . .

H. Achievement? What *achievement*? Europe again?
You are out-numbered *white man*. Me? I was a stoker at the fire.
When you murdered Rufus, the party elected me
first political officer. I was a community essayist.

A. How are you in contact with Earth?
All the men there are dead. You speak to phantoms.

H. As Senator of the Demos, I am authorized.
Dead? Who is dead? I have . . . information.

A. Me too. I have new information of universe.
You are superseded. I have a device – no, a weapon –
of more reliable information. I eliminate the terrestrial.
That includes *you*. Would you like to see it?
It is moving in the next room.

Come this way. Just here.

ii   *(Hussein replies.)*
H. I will remain here. . . . It's true. You are mad.
You speak like a single, high priest? We are a secular nation.
It offends me. You are an ordinary human, no? Please
tell me if I mistake? They told me to *ask*!
Sir, we now have over three hundred new
civilians in these ships. Article 3.1. mandates
all civilian persons the right of self-determination.

A. I begin with philosophy – but always end with theology.
You have heard this? Article 3.1.2 mandates military control over
civilians attached to Theater of Operations
for the duration of authorized missions, etc.
Second, they are not citizens of our Empire, etc.
I will enforce our laws to the letter, etc.
We are an altered society. I see, you hate it.

H. Empire? Empire? We don't use that word – as you know!
As any tyrant, you are arrogant with *eccentricity*. And
I am being kind. You prefer the coin of life and death.

A. You will not tempt me. I know your
hidden prophet! There is an entire class
of you that proscribes speech. You only wish
to eradicate the West. Do you know my rage?

H. You confirm our suspicions. This journey in space
has taken your reason. You are utterly mad.

A. No. You hear the voice of free speech in Space.
You hear the sound of reliable truth. Strange to you.
I say only what all modern men have not dared
to speak – for fear of *their* government.
Modern men have been under surveillance
for three centuries. Freedom was moot
the first hour of total surveillance.
I seize the machine!

H. Madness! There is nothing higher than science and . . .
You are only a servant of the Demos.
You reach for galactic divinity…what is the word?
Kosmoautikon? You will die a psychopath.

A. I swear. By this new word you have already murdered millions. Not since the name of Caesar will so many die to possess it. Observe, fire stoker, how a single word contains so much murder.

7

H. Admiral, your mission was to establish
our nation at *Callisto Wolf.* You should
announce a date of the cessation of
operations in this Theater. I will ensure
the Slavic refugees apply to citizenship.

A. You will *just* ensure to wipe your own ass.
You will not speak to the foreign nationals.
They are now under . . . language training. Their
future shall be their choice. They may choose
among our men, or they may join as cadets.

This nation is not secure. Look out your
window, Nehi Hussein. The Ring scaffold is
not built. Carbon life is constrained to the
slight breath of these ships. There is a new
physics – viral at this depth of space. This is a crisis.
I suppose you see this? The portrayal of mission
success is the prerogative of the Supreme
Commander. Until Europa is reconfigured
for carbon life, enlarged for gravity,
my officers will lead this project.
There is no world till I fuse world.
There is no time till I braise time.

H. Madness! You think the creatures you make
will be any different than the humans
you have exterminated? If it has its own
mind, it will make its own choices. You
will force one of us to murder you!

A. Thank you. Your future is now assured.
(Aside.) Have you made a record?
    (Replicant appears from a concealed place.)
Replicant. Yes, admiral, we have made a record.
He has threatened to assassinate the leader.

A. Thank you. Now leave us. (Replicant leaves.)

H. Ah, you bastard… I see you have a plan.
How many more humans will you kill?

8   *(Hussein continues.)*
H. First, this is madness. This is not science!
You make rhymes. *(Slurring)* The *science* is
not proven. It is fantasy. Your lunar plan
could not be achieved in two thousand years.
A planet has never been reconstituted. You
are leading us to destruction. There is no living dirt.
Third, I am not under military authority.
I demand access to the other ships.

A. Science? Coal essayist? Science? You speak . . . as if . . . it is
an element of balanced acidity! An equal spoon
feeding! A soothing universal cream! No! There is
my science – or there is *your* science. Science
is a *linguistic* element! A selection! Clear?
It is a choice of linguistics – mine or yours?
There is no single science. First a human sells it,
then he injects it. Like a woman – first she is sold a line –
then injected. You wish to inject your idiom into me –
I only outrun your needles. No one will jump
ahead of me. Clear? Get it?

H. You are mad! Science is universal! Science is perfection.

A. No! Yours is a dead science . . .mine is alive!
It's alive! It's alive! It's alive! It's alive! (Hussein cowers, afraid.)
You lost control of the modern world one hundred
years ago. Your science no longer gave reliable
information. You know, I guess, the physics
is distorted at this remove from Earth?
You know this, yes? There are voices. Yes?
There are apparitions! New objects. *Bad* physics.
Democracy is the tool of the foreign element.
I alone am *born* on the Fourth of July!

H. You wish to become a god of murder!

A. No God! No God! (Slurring.) We are
at the rings of a giant because the demos
outlawed reference to god. What did you expect
with *this* innovation? You cannot now act as if you
still rule seven oceans. You have no Carriers left!

I cancel the cry of failed Western *sapiens*! You are alive
now only because I need your DNA.
I am mottled star! I am wonder!
This is what you *get* with *innovations. Inoculations*!
You get me!

    (Aaron, attempting to be calm.)
A. I will allow you access to the swimming
pool. And fifthly, in honor of your former
authority, I promote you to Warf Detective.
My cameras observe your honesty. No more bribes.
    (Hussein rises. Recovers composure.)
H. Admiral, you assume arbitrary rule here.
There is a name for this. Some of the men
are in radio contact with Earth. You have lied.
The Senate is not as silent as you mean to tell us.
The Demos questions your public statements.
They intend to rescind your original orders. What
is sacred? The United Nations is sacred. The
unity of men! We must be bonded in empathy!
The Demos is a priority over your experiments.

A. Which Demos? Be clear! That government of
foreign control? I know these men. The Demos that
destroyed everything it touched? That same body?
Whose science destroyed the Earth? Who made
the word *freedom* into an euphemism for total
surveillance of every citizen? That Demos? The Modern
Empire that poisoned each forest, each society it touched – with
advertisement, mutated grain, greed, commerce?
The same liberal Demos that subverted
all indigenous people? Japan, India, Russia,
Asia, China – Tibet! – these colonies
that became mere echoes of popular Western
fashion as they aped Western life styles?
We give the world an embedded pornography!
In *ten* generations, modernism gutted the Earth;
the competition for resources finished
both men and nations. Did you ever constrain
the populations of Earth? India? China? No – why?
Because they contained markets! You cowards!

So I did this for you. Now you still wish to proliferate?
Consciousness is selection. I select. *No god! No god!*
Does that word even have a *pulse* or *lexicon*?
I am mottled star. I am wonder. I break out.
I cure you of your illness. I remove your bones.

H. You are irrational… sick! Restore my people to our rightful
power. You cannot resist the political will of the UN.
There are more of us than your kind! We will swarm you.

A. Then I will strangle you all as one neck.

H. Will you make a record of this statement?

Speech Is Free Again in Space

9

H. Are you a socialist then, Admiral? You
are against our free markets, our advanced
sciences – our generous medicines – our rights!
Our respect of human rights?

A. Free? I see only slaves with their hands out.
Human rights? This is another euphemism
for the UN to seize and divide our material civilization.
No, I am against *you*. You respected human rights
so well we had to exterminate the billions seeking
our idiomatic rights – seizing our high idiom –
demanding everything we built? How could the Demos
deny refugees our own comforts – our pharmaceuticals?
How could linguistic modernism be denied to any human?

Then the wars began for water, food, and oil.
Democracy exterminates! The Greek Demos
extinguished itself in three generations!
Socialist? Does that still have a meaning?
How does that differ from meddling Demos?
I hate all forms of government. I am a strict
exceptionist. I have made a severe selection.
I am against the bias contained in your machines;
you have no scale of Galaxy in your brain. You lead
men that were never soldiers. What did you risk?
An election? A machine? What is a man?
To continue to solve another problem?
Then a problem. Then another problem?
Your idea of life is unconstrained proliferation.

I make a severe selection. At least it is honest.
I have an exact idea of who shall live.
I have incubated a race that will teach you shame.

H. And who will teach you shame? A billion
dead souls, crying for your shame? We will swarm you.

254

A. Yes, I have made an allowance for that.
Liberals don't believe in souls – so do not use the . . . the . . .
high scaffold of a construct you do not honor.
You make all minds small . . . till they are broken.
And then, like you, they talk as machines.
What use is the sound of *modern,* when a man must
stoop and genuflect his soul to be modern.
A. I am against the *kernel* of your information.
Your idioms no longer contain information.
It would be better that you eat humans,
since you only farm them – feed them
with doctored and defiled information.
I move ahead of your pattern. Look in the night sky!
I am cosmological. I am the water carrier.
I am mottled star! *(Screaming.)*

R. They tell me you use astrology in your work!
You are mad - certain! A battery of pharmaceuticals
must be found for you. Water carrier? What is *water carrier*?

A. The end of Pisces, *fool*! Yes, I have found the new
message. You are shocked at my freedom of speech?
Yes, I see it. My freedom sickens you?
You prove we speak separate languages.
Different sciences. Different genetics.
Yes, I see it. *I see it.* Do you? *Do you*?

How did democracy destroy a nation? For a vote
you promised each man a middle class life.
You lied. Ten Earths could not supply enough
wealth and resources. So we made war against
all other. Then the Demos used the war to get votes!
We used war to absolve our China debts!
It is *I* that redeemed these debts . . . in China blood.
No. Now I *seize* human consciousness. I will
make it *fit* the conditions I seek.

When I am dead. When Europa is terraformed.
When there are verdant pastures to poison,
green fields to exchange; when there is wealth
and cheating markets again. Medical journals
that reconstruct forgeries of information. Then
you can all fight it out and have your democratic
hypocrisy. It is your *information* that I reject.
It was *democracy* that eradicated life on Earth.
I am balm to the wounded universe. I take it back!

So – a greater work is within my reach! I could
accept every insult - till the *igig... touched* . . . our high idiom.
    (Now shaking)
Wakeda! Come to me.
(Enter Wakeda, concerned, seizing Hussein.)
Release him to his quarters.
    (Screaming – as Hussein is carried away.)
I am against your *information*!

10

i   *(Aaron speaking, now alone.)*
A. There will be lies told about these days.
They will say that our love failed, and thus,
our speech was second in kind: this new world,
faulted in foundation. Love? That is only Pisces
in retrograde. When did men love well? Once?
No, I am already an ancient speech. Our time is forecast.
Now it is a Western force. Fed on Dark Matter.
I could allow them all our goods, and wheat, and cattle.
I could not let them touch the idiom of my heart.

ii
A. I survive to make this text. An occulted art.
How else could I have arrived at. . . at
this cosmology – if my device might fail?
I know the answer. I am authorized to speak.
Every symbol reveals my mind on the *astral plane.*
I reject the terrestrial globe. I took away their planet –
and then their bones.

If, after, the Demos accuse me with my dead –
yes, they are mine. I accept each blackened relic.
Yet I have made a discovery. I have traced our genes
to a prior creation. Past *Homo sapiens.* I am ancient.

No man makes a weapon that he does not use.
No high language fails to pasteurize
the pathogens in the spectral body. Peace is a
propaganda to let the *other* infect our sound.

Death is likewise language. Loud, death makes a value
of cognizance. In this dimension it appears with a fright,
yet it is the small death of fish. Then I swim again.
So what is purposed by life? Only to breath
another day? No, surely it is coinage – a test
of value. What species can perform this with sentience?
Yet I am lashed with gourmands and list makers.

When the Earth was smoked, my language
escaped . . . clean. If you breathe at this grid
of space, then you have authority to breath.
There is no dice of chanced nightmares.
No one else tried. No one else came forward.

Aggression is weakness; brute force, an honesty.

I terminate all other operators.

CANTO TWO

Antebbe Says You Are One of These:
The Secret History of Planets

1   *(Aaron is handed a document.)*
A. What is this? A list of Kings? Planets?
From which ancient dynasty?
Oannes, the god dressed as a fish?
A fish? No – a man in a space suit – surely?

"Sippar, the city of the sun-god Shamash?"
Cheda, why does she give me these texts?
I read. Appollodorus of Athens. *Fragments
of Berossus?* I never read this account.
Is it spurious?
   (Aaron reads from a list.)
Aloros, reigned for 10 shars.
Alaparos, reigned for 3 shars.
Amelon, reigned for 13 shars.
Ammenon, reigned for 12 shars.
Megalrus, reigned for 18 shars,
Daonos, reigned for 10 shars.
Euedoreschus, reigned for 18 shars.
Amempsinos, reigned for 10 shars.
Obartes, reigned for 8 shars.
Xisuthros, reigned for 18 shars.
Senseless. How does this list concern me?

Cheda. Antebbe says you are one of these.

A. How does she know I am one of these?

C. Because she is one. She told me she improved
the genes of men from wild hominids – as you
improved my genetics to Homo *faustus*.

A. Where is she now? Why does she not appear?

C. She steps from creature to creature on Callisto.
When she finds any deformity, she cuts off the head,
before they are replicated. She says she is a star.

A. This is too much. No. Bring her to me.

C. She said she will come when you are ready.

Vargus Reports the Death of Metis *(Into Europa)*

2

i

Aaron. Vargus. Enter. I saw your work. Metis
impact into Europa. It was a near run thing.

Vargus. Eight Metaclites. Did you see the light?
Four more tries. Twelve. Metis let lose. She loosed
her braids to our elliptic. Our equation puzzled
behind our shields. The flash of suns as mirror.

A. Yes, I saw the record. Metis made a conflagration.
Our Murmers talked with her. Metis replied:
she saw no need to die her death. Her path
was ancient, etc. . . . and the summons
of the giant was still in her ear, etc. . . .
Small planets are petulant.
I heard it all before.
Like men on their scaffold who still cry
the fixed assembly of their electrons.

V. Sir? I don't follow.

A. The Murmers . . . our readers . . .
said to Metis that humans were the sentient mind
of this giant, Jupiter. The Murmers said that
Jupiter was junior to our solar system. That men
were more ancient. That it was good we are here.
Men were foretold. This was news to Metis.
Metis was uncertain. Jupiter watched.

V. I don't follow . . . I never believed – I admit –
if I did not see with my eyes. Did a man do this?
I am not sure the planet can take another such hit.
Or do I miscalculate?
I was not sure I could perform this.

A. What did *you* perform?

ii   *(Aaron continues distractedly.)*
A. The work is yet incomplete. Still unformed.
Be cautious. As we told the Arabs in the first war,
the camel's nose is only in the tent. Otherwise
they could not count our legions. Prepare
our crews for the next trial: move Thebes
into the core of Europa. Europa's temperature
is still too low. We need a magnetic, molten core.
We need orange spider legs rising. Complete
my Atlas legs. Lift a new planet to our ring
and with promethean fire strike a flame to
smoke the bones of Western men. *(With mock solemnity.)*

V. Sorry, sir. I don't follow.

A. Vargus, you are unaware of your position.
I have made you a god among damn builders,
an icon of reverse irrigators. Instead of planets
that have made men, now men perform
the first act of creation. What else can I give
you for fame? Is there still something?

V. Sir? I don't follow. I have prepared a few notes.

A. Show me. Yes. Let me read . . . *(Reads. Gives back text.)*
Yes, you may enter the ship theater. Speak generously
of the skill of your crews. I will not contradict
your agency. Ensure your crews are praised. *(Vargus leaves with text.)*

iii   *(Black Terry accosts Vargus leaving the room.)*
Terry. Great Vargus. A giant of pricksters! You honor our race, sir.

V. Ah . . .Terry? Thank you. Race? . . . which race?

T. Yes and yes. We await your speech. May I . . .see?
I'm on pins and needles! *(Reads text.)* Sir, you are
new here. This speech lacks the proper education freely
given to you. The ladies were told to expect a great speech –
they are *red* with hard application. Let me look again. *(Reads.)*
Yes, you are a rough, camp soldier, sir. May I suggest some altercations?

V. The composition was in haste. But they say you are a cook?

T. Alternate cook, sir. On reversible church holidays. I am
as *savory* as any cook. May I slightly correct your text?
We are *all* at school here. I see some estrangements.
Two subject/verb agreements. Multiple cogitations.
And three sentences ending in "of," "is," and "for."

Vargus Recounts to the Ships:
Did You See The Light

(Work continues on the text until the last moment. Unsure how the text was changed, Vargus recites the mock epic to the crews and girls assembled in the theater. Text kindly marked with appropriate breathing caesuras and accents.)

3

i

Vargus. I chased Metis timed across the home planet,
aligning her path parallel to our chase. Small
Metis – a giant stone, really – nickel, iron, iridium –
touched fire at Europa's middle ocean ice.

I seized Europa, silent running. Then Metis,
subverted from her circus into Europa bent,
sudden romanced a penetrating spear. Thirdly,
Metis thrust her egg into the core of Europa ice
till bright hell in dark vacuum cried furious maw.

Europa grimaced bright teeth
to her root of gums.
I saw white spray gust out
her mouth hoary snow,
like a great whale in winter
blows her lung.

The canopy of ice silvered on our ships, rim
frost on our shields melting as we touch. Stunned,
holding my breath as all men aboard. Then
a disk of obsidian ocean broke – blue flaked chisels
tinkling against our canopies, slivered nails
on our coffin lids; blinking eye fragments
of ice shattered glass blue with chill, radio
waves of phosphor in a vapor ring aurora –
something strange to eyes.

Did you see the light?

(Sporadic, embarrassed applause.)

ii   *(Vargus, emboldened, continues recitation.)*
V. The caldron planet still beaconed red
when to Thebes we set our course.

We changed our scheme of hunt. I landed
nine ships on Thebe's jagged monster's neck.
And formed a cone of engines. Slowly
the large comet moon raised its elliptic turn
to the calculated speed and trajectory.
We got away the last hour.
24 eggs left to hatch,
to open bright hell on Thebe's stony back.
Now we watch for the circle orbit perfected.
These treasure eyes of witness
unlike all other men of time.
This . . . new ancient birth of stars,
portrayed
in this approved recording.

> *(Sporadic polite applause, sarcastic comments
> from the crowd are overheard.)*

"Is this serious?"

"What is he talking about?"

"This is a joke, right?"

"The Admiral wrote this? Sure."

Riot in the Theater

4

i   *(Aaron calls out.)*
A. Wakeda! What is that noise?

Wakeda. A? The crew has seen the women.
B? Terry incites the crowd with his obscenities.
C? The dogs are barking at the . . . the females.
How much longer should we wait?
It is not safe for you to be present now!

A. Are the girls seated together in the center?
Let them all get a good look at each other.
Let the hook be set.

W. They have looked . . . long. . . hard enough.

ii   *(Meanwhile, Terry sneaks on stage. Then, with mock solemnity, speaks.)*
T. Attention please, pigs! Pigs! Rent boys! Lewd papillons!
Countrymen! LEND ME YOUR APPENDAGES!
Open . . . open your dribble caked mouths to my lips.
Soldiers, you know what love I hold towards you?
      (Gesturing with appendage. Laughter.)
How shall I express-s the juice I hold for you?
How to folliculate my true feeling into false words?
To speak as a dead man pumping moist? Behold!
I make you a masque of poetry in the wilderness!
      (Shout from the audience.)
Leader, give us one of your poems! No Earl Oxford crap!

T. Are you worthy, slave?! A scholar in the hall?
What is your toilet and breeding? In the bowl again?
I jiggle no aged poet's honey cord. Have you no ear?
I have made large water in composition! *From*
within my bowels idiomatic gestation descends!
It dumps down as the plump rain on pimpled cheeks!

(Others.) We are not *here* for you! Get off the stage!

T. Shall't listen? Shall't attend? I will wait for my silence.
My newest composition: *Egyptian days.*

(Others.) Pretend cook or pretend poet? What's the point?

Egyptian Days

5   *(Terry suddenly slashes his arm. Blood flows profusely.*
    Room is suddenly silent. Careful and solemn elocution.)

i

T. No alarm shall come to you by fire beacon, or signal.
You who are far from your homes will never see their homes.
I saw holy men and righteous burning. Tapers in a blackened sky.
And if scared men turn their necks, once having second thoughts,
no beacon reaches them on a rough and churning, charcoal sea.

Some, I know, sought knowledge and judgment first, but
the promise made to you is void – of works, riches, honor. Nothing
you have gained can be kept, nothing you have loosed shall remain loose;
nothing you have tethered from your cribs, shall stay tethered;
and no signal shall reach you from a further shore.

The cunning of books and lamps failed both man and priest.
No charts for propitious hours, no lists of fortunate years,
no Egyptian Days can forewarn you the going-out
and the coming-in. And though the sea is charcoal black,
no light, no fire set upon a hill, shall reach you.

Nothing I spend now will come back to me ten-fold;
when there was an hour for kindness, I was not kind;
when love was begged of me, I did not love.
Mouths stretched and dried on pepper stalks, my neck
will turn, human for homeward glances;

and though the sea is charcoal black,
no beacon will reach me,
no signal sent out from shore,
no fire upon a gentle hill.

   (A stunned silence.)

ii   *(Terry – with real tears – becomes angry.)*
T. Idiots! You spos'd to clap. There's no more t'it!
Did I take something from another place?
Not my own derivative? Not my own honey pot?
Any Oxenford? Any Golding's Ovid?
Any Walt Wit-less?
Any Yeast? No? Then, resolved.
Let us be separately distained.

   (Holding theatrical knife that squirts blood.)

T. A prop! A prop! So silent for blood then?
The gorge of silent and ancient memory? As *hits*?
I study for my upcoming thes-pez-ory.
See? The children scream and run.
Strange *press-age-ment*!
I see your mouth waters in silent
prefigure of taste and smell.
So often seen? Blood? Yes? – And a'licked?

6   *(Black Terry continues antics on stage.)*
T. My speech! . . . where was I? I. . . I. . . Yes!
Let me remember my lust towards my men
and my hand . . . mostly my hand. Silence!
I gift you pearls of great value. Ruby-lipped girls!
Fresh! I have primed the girls with my pump!
They are pneumatic, and after, balm-ed!
This proves my care for you!

(Others.) "What girls, Admiral? You keep them all to yourself!"

T. Q. What is a girl? Fags! So long *and-roger-us?*
A. Not like a man, a girl is a thing with a bottom.
B. *Not like a girl, a man's a bottom with a thing.*
And vice versa.

Not as nature? I begin again . . .let's see . . . girls!
After a taste of honeyed girl give them
back overstretched! If they eviscerate,
I have a small cream! They have fresh lobotomies,
wiser now, certain not to scream –
Now prophesy I with thrown flints . . .
      (Solemnly dramatic, cuts neck with fake knife, more blood.)
In three days there shall be . . . large death
in these ships. Few of you will survive; all
shall be altered. Some secretly.
Talon has entered our ship unaware!

(Shouts from crowd.) "In underwear?"

T. Yes! I have found underwear...male-lic-fic-ally marked!
There will not be further forced feeding in this ship till each
tire mark is found! There will be an immediate
inspection of bottoms . . . me first! *(Shows possibles.)*
I release a godly force . . . the *(Lets lose his wind.) force* . . . of my fable!

      (Wakeda enters with guards to seize and confine Terry.)

T. Wa-ho! . . . Stand aside! Now comes the chief fool!
(Terry hauled away shouting.)
I have been ill-cunt-strued! I demand the liberty
of a mothball! I am touched intimately! Snatch
and grip! Wait! Wait! I have a part to play – in... this... masque.
Ouch! Easy, boys! Oh! I am suspended with disbelief!
I am supine in my boat of sky. I escape!
      (Girls enter theater, then seated with much commotion.)

Cheda Commences Pilot Training

7   *(Meanwhile in Aaron's ship.)*
Aaron. Come with me, Cheda. This is Major Marsh.
He was my pilot in Estonia. You will go with him.
Do not release him, Major, until he has perfected
his skill. You will find that Cheda has a touch.

Marsh. How long do I have with the young officer?

A. As long as it takes. You will find that the syllabus
goes fast. He has memorized FM-100.
Remember, he needs to pre-breath methane;
he can support 30% Oxygen for 7 hours.
Any more is a fire hazard.
The *Sterling Type* is an intermediate ship.
Are you prepared, my son? Where is Antebbe?

Cheda. I am ready.
She is at Callisto. She has killed some of us.
She walks from cave to cave with a knife of light.
A beam. A light. She selects those who may live.
They beg for life and she smiles. Calls them slaves.
She gives you this letter.
She had some trouble with your language.
I transcribed it in your tongue. . . It's. . .

A. A letter? Where did she get our language?

C. I worked with her on our tongue. She asked
why we used the word *god*. She said there
was no admiral, animal, or mineral to fit the term *god*.
What we named as *god*, her people knew
as *Kosmoautikon*. As far as I could understand,
Kosmoautikon was a . . . I suppose, a spaceman
moving between the crib of suns with a device
used to slay Bulls. He was called ... *Mit-ras*

A. Mithras! Why *Mithras*!

C. Perhaps . . .You know the man . . .*Mit-ras*?
They dine together on . . . on the *Table of Destinies*.
She would tell me no more. She let me live. She said
I was perfect in my generation.

A. Kosmoautikon? Again, that term!
When can I see her?

Antebbe Letter

8

i   *(Aaron reads letter.)*
A. "Choose from my smiles your sentence.
Take the joy I should extinguish.
Extinguish me and stoke my brain.

Tear my arms, I cannot hold you.
Crush my hands, I cannot touch you.
I eat desire. I swallow distaste.

What object do you seek no gift,
love by winning shall be won,
plastic prize or approbation?

Cloak my delight, avert my eyes,
even innocents must suffer.
I pity us no gifts.

But you, silent, lifting a bowl from shadows,
stun my ears. I can hear you.
Strike my eyes. I can see you.

Taste me and make, in me, taste."

ii
A. Cheda, she wrote this? Or you?
I see you borrow from our German poet.
A slight improvement of inflection . . .
Where is she now?

She is still our friend? There is hope.

Do you know Sumerian script?
Cunic runes?
Strange gods?
No?
Nor I, for all my book.

9   *(Aaron continues to speak to Cheda.)*

A. Cheda, the list of kings you gave me. I must talk to her.
I have lost sleep with this damned list. My early study is blemished.
The Greeks misled me. The Romans were copyists.
I failed to learn the early Sumerian Epic form. As far
as I can read, the Semitic Jews were *later* Sumerians? Look,
the Jews seem to have lifted the Sumerian epics whole.
Like others, I have dismissed them as impossible myth.
I violated my own rule of finding secret patterns in text.
There were far older . . . and stronger poets. Yet these are not gods!
Surely they are cosmic symbols. What are symbols if not
the world replicated? Yet what world? What pattern?
Why temples? Why thrones? Why texts? What alien mind?
I have been attacked for my astrology. Yet how else could
early men live as aged to make exact observations?
The twelve houses were given to us from DNA of other planets.
I can accept this. I accept the first alphabet, as like.
It proves plausibly the sentience of genetics! What else?
Is my own text affirmed? I would accept that bias.
Yet, what else is hidden? I am an idiot.
I need to know more. I am a beginner. Listen now.
Tell her to stop her killing until she speaks to me.
If what she insists is true, then I have something to say.
Can she be constrained? That is my message.

C. Master, she told me to ask you.
Is the Ark full? Is the Ark ready?

A. The Ark? Is this why she came?

C. She said by your code she found you.
She said our arrival was tracked.
We set off the trip wires fixed at Mars.

A. My code? I summoned her . . . by my . . . ?

C. No living prophet speaks . . . as strange as you.
She said. There is no stricter code. Who else
makes this run? None but you.
She said to tell you – Speak again.
"Executioner," she said, "do not stop to speak."

10   *(Cheda leaves. Jurate enters, comes to his side. Aaron speaks to her.)*
A. Jealous voices accuse me. And you?

No, I am amazed – not *you*. *Who* are you? – As me?
To give our seed ceaseless voice . . . to sound
in all dimension? That compassion was absent?
That we did not extend our hand to all other?

Yet my accusers are on their knees. I saw they
were prepared for self-extermination. I cut the
boil. No one may contradict my evidence. China?
To let a giant prevail was certain immolation.

I looked. I did not see my accusers in battle.
So, we who made these wars of selection,
testify and report. Weeds choke life. If I
am a weed, then prevail over me. I assent.

I see there is silence at my challenge.

I note defects in my constructs.
Not will to *decision*. Not will to
audacity. I am eccentric.
I have made an allowance for psychosis.

Yet if we choose between our own folly
and arrogance, or the folly
and arrogance of the stranger,
I choose our own high madness.

With my clods of living dirt, I am well-arraigned.
Yet I look, and see no one willing to make
my sprint; who else would play my card –
of *single*, one-way rocketry?

Accuse me with your brave, tall sound. Then,
already countered, you would praise me
by similar idiom, which, except for me,
you have not moved to innovation,

nor any prophetic sound unchain
my fist of text.

CANTO THREE

In the Theater: A Mask for Children

(Enter director of chorus.)

1

A. Les gosses sont-ils prêts?

"Monsieur, ils sont les vrais anges!!
Ils ont passé deux mois à répéter.
Oh, vous devez absollument entendre
les inflexions des petits garçons !

Oh, je suis sur des charbons ardents!"

(Aaron replies.)

A. Bon, j'attends avec l`impatience. Mais, fais attention
aux garçons – d'accord? Après, ressemblons-nous.
On fête la naissance d`un Nouveau Monde.
Du passé faisons table rase.

How many times have we hatched a world?
When has man broke and increased
a home planet? . . . and made a record of it?
Let us probe this device.

(Terry, reading script, calls out from confinement.)

T. Are you the person paying for this??
This is your idea of a play? Some of these lines
are double construed.

A. I am the one. The risk is mine.
It is a minor sketch. *(Aaron not recognizing the masked voice.)*
Who speaks?

T. Not sure it makes any sense . . .
You think they understand . . .
it's the end of their world?
The end of everything they have . . .?
Is it not more than children can portray?

2

i

A. Who are the players?

Director of chorus. Jaimy as *Flash*, pilot in command,
American Commander of ships.

Simon as *Lt. Spark*, US Marine,
American Guard of Talon.

Phillip as *Talon*, in chains,
Mad scientist from Earth/Io.

Tisha as *Lillith*, abducted Earth girl,
Original Murmer.

Jurate as *Antebbe*, Queen of gods.
Charismatic being from Sirius System.

Tanya as the moonlet, *Thebe.*
Second moon to crash into Europa.

Terry as *Dedalus.*
Counselor to Antebbe.

The other children perform as Chorus.

A. I like the list.
Is the chorus not too young?

    (Terry calls out.)
T. They will do very well. They are the only ones
that can't observe our madness!

A. Is Terry confined?
Release him. He cannot hurt us.

Prologue of Galactic Play

3

i   *(Spoken by youngest child –stepping forward.)*
Small planets, comets, sentient spheres
step to our stage as men of little years.

Small children change with me the house of time.
Hear childish pilgrims future mirrors mime.
     (Forgets line…then begins again.)
Tired eyes, steal a gentle dreamer's sleep:
imagine manners present times may keep.
     (Another child comes forward to speak.)
The room is dark. Girls' flute and cellos tune.
Tipsy men, guard your hearts before they wound.

Shaky lights project in dark a dusty beam.
A smoke from mouths, caked red-lipped cream.
     (Another child comes forward to speak.)
Standard stones
transformed to tempting treasures,
broken stars
redeemed with marbled measures:

what was wished in eyes and then made kind,
what was seen at night but lost on waking,

what walked by day and then moved on;
it must be sharp – not seconds, thirds –

no sleight of hand space age ray gun,
no weaving closed on inner cupboards

tease who may reach or keep its cellars
the string in ear to other houses shelters

lips as sheath beneath all lids.

ii
"Silence! Silence in the theater!
Take those dogs out!
Silence those bitches!"
     (Crewmember comments.)
"Look it's Terry – he's free already?"

Act One: Rocket Men

4   *(Enter Thebe as dying moon. A child in planet costume.)*
Thebe. There is something… there…standing in the dark?
You. Come a little into the light. . . Stop.
Just there. Who are you? Oh . . . I see . . . you are gods.

Flash. No. We are men . . . once from Earth.

T. Men? No, I think I know you. Your planet
is white with new ice. *Sapiens or faustus?*

F. The *terrestrial* mind is silenced. We are *astral.*

T. Faustus, then. New death. Yes, I know you.
You fly madly like a moth around Callisto. You
kick up a dust. Where is small Metis? She is gone.
You took her? Then yes, you make a little death.
So you are gods – then. I always show the same face.

F. We are rocket men. We sent Metis into Europa's
core. See how the fragments of ice remain… circling?
Europa was here. She now moves close as twin to Callisto.

T. I see the ice. I saw the flash into Europa.
Yes. She makes a little fire. She is farther now.

F. We raised her above the giant's rays.
The rays make men ill. Now . . . you must enter Europa:
Europa is still too close to Jupiter. Still too small.
Too cold. Too oceanic. Too eccentric.

T. But what are these weapons? I see them.
Behind you, lifting rootless from the ground.
Who are you? Who shall praise your gods
if you come bearing such weapons?

F. Before the Deluge of Earth, a demi-god led us,
saying: "Men of the West, tear down your house!
Build fleets of ships! Give up possessions. Seek new life!
Aboard the ship take the seed of all that lives!"
And so we have come to meet our fate with you.

T. And what do you find at Jupiter? Gold? Red drink?

F. As on Earth. We consume everything.

5

F. Be wise. Make a good death. Your time was short.
You were already descending into Jupiter.
Jupiter would kill you. Go with us. You will live
again as human bones and blood on large Europa.

T. I do not want. I do not like. I am ancient in this path.
I move by greater force. Are *faustus* so dangerous?

F. We are the sentient part of stars.
We are the mind of god. We are the only new
world becoming. Besides us, there is no sentience.

T. O small god, you talk so much. What is your force?

F. We have the fire of suns in our hands. Self-
consciousness is our god. We have your mother: *Megaclite.*

T. Where? Show me you hands? No. They are dirty.
No. Since nothing you have shown us is equal
to the representations you have made, leave.

F. It is time. Children of men wait in somatic
prescience to be born. Breath waits.
Take our hands. Your mother touches you.

T. No. I always show the same face . . .Tell me.
How did you join the congregation of the gods
in your quest for life? What part of you is god?

F. On account of my forefather, who joined
the assembly of the gods, I have come; about
death and life I am pleased to speak with you.
I am not the first. You are already our text.

T. No. You are reckless. The way you seek is hard.
Rocket men guard the moon's gateways;
their terror is spectral, their glance is death.
Their glaring beam sweeps the comet stones;
They watch over Shamash as the gods
ascend and descend from Orion, Cygnus.

F. Good. We have come for them as well.
Show us the face of these demi-gods.
We will meet them with our text of letters.
We shall make a good death.

T. Yes . . . I see. You wish to die as gods!

Act Two: Talon In Chains

6   *(Flash transports the prisoner Talon.)*
Talon. I know forensics.

Lt. Spark. So? You know forensics.

T. You are a black man.

Lt. S. You are a dead man. Want to trade?

T. I can heal you.

Lt. S. Heal yourself . . .heal what?

T. You have an impending cancer.

Lt. S. You have a date with a rope.

T. I can dissolve the rope.

Lt. S. Shut your hole. *(Kicks.)*

Flash. Silence. We approach.

Lt. S. Why were we told to meet here? This far out?
Why transfer Talon to this ship? 'Hundred years
we search for this killer. I don't like this.
He has confederates that have protected him this
long. Hid this lizard-man in caves. I don't like it.

F. I am vigilant. I have confirmed the transmissions.
They have our IFF codes. Changed daily.
Only our ships in this grid. His ships are taken.

   (A giant ship begins to appear – as large as a moon.)

Lt. S. See what I'm talkin' 'bout?! What d'a hell is d'hat?
Weapons on, sir! Gate is armed. Report, stations!

F. Wait! It has an American flag!
I have seen images of this ship!
. . . How can this be?

7

T. Merde!! Now we're kettled!

Lt. S. What the . . .?! What is that?! This is wrong.
It's . . . It's a giant! Crazy . . . giant . . . It's a seed?

F. Scanner confirms it is a galaxy ship. . .twelve decks.
Fission power source. Lead core. Nickel, iron, lead surface.

Lt. S. A. . . giant . . . sweet . . .gum seed!
Crossed spires as spikes . . .with . . . look!
It even has a withered stem! How far away is it still?

F. 59 kilometers. Sweet gum? Sweet gum?
How do you know about seeds? I know this class of ship.
There has not been a ship built like that since men
lived above Callisto. This is the ship that Talon abducted
after he killed my grandfather.

Lt. S. It's all made of lead, crossed spires… and spikes.
Man! I do not like this.

T. This is a Womb-ship. Escape now. That is not a human ship.
Do not let that . . . *thing* . . . get on board. She will eat us.

Lt. S. Shut your hole. *(Kicks.)*

T. You are fools. Too late. You are in their ore-bolt! Idiots!

F. The controls are not responding. Check override.

Lt. S. Check, sir. Autopilot disengaged. You have control now.

F. They still do not respond. Check power source. Circuit breakers!

Lt. S. Breakers are in. Look! The controls are moving!
I told you, I don't like this! Look at the escort crafts!
I see their faces. Are those pilots . . . human?

F. Transmission received from this other ship:
"Welcome Commander. Your ship is under our control.
Accept the escort crafts. They will not harm you.
We confirm the transfer of our prisoner."

Lt. S. "Their" prisoner?

T. They will blister me now with hot pincers!

Act Three, Scene One: First Encounter

8   *(Door of the ship opens slowly.)*
Lillith. Hello? Your door is open! Hello?
Come down from your ship! Where are they?
O come down, you long-boned dogs! What do you do there?
I will not eat you. Bizness? I am very small.
Look here! "W. A. S. H. . ." These are funny guys!
What a stink is in this ship!
(Aside) What is the name of the pilot-man?
"Flash"? How divine! Monsieur Flash – oh!
Come down! Coucou! Couscous! Cocoa!

(Aside.) Perhaps they speak only French? Coucou!
Pourquoi tu te caches? Tu m`étonnes.
Coucou! Je peux te voir, en fait! I see you there!
Je m`éclate. Il faut que tu parles un peu.
Perhaps they speak Latvian?
    (Capt. Flash appears.)
F. You speak English then?

L. Yes, a lot! We are Americans. What else
should we speak? Did you see the flag?

F. Americans? But we are Americans!

L. Yes! They are everywhere!
This is our Galaxy. In fact – note – you are
in the Galaxy. *(Aside)* They are testing me!
A'hungered? A'thirst?

F. We need to know your identity?
What is this ship? Why are we here?

L. So earnest! I am Lillith. You are Flash.
"One is crawfish; one is crawdad."
This is the first galactic ship. These *(pointing.)* are our possibles.
We have watched you for 60 years. *(Outlining number with finger.)*
Your wars of . . . *"THE DEMOS"*. *(Making phonetic sign.)*
A big *to-do* here! You seemed to be set on exterminating
yourselves. Only *faustus* survives ... Now we can talk
with you. . . with you . . . wait. What is this . . .?
(Aside) Lady . . . *he* is in your line!
    (Reading from ancient memory.)
"As I look upon thee, Utnapishtim,
thou art not different at all,
even as though I am thou."

9

L. You are not *Flash*. That's only a familiar name.
You are . . . Cameron . . . by birth. Yet there is more...
(to herself) Lady, you did not tell me . . . he is germane.
(to Flash) Jurate was your grandmother?

F. Yes. How do you know this? I know you.
Where are you from? What is your purpose?

L. (Aside) Yes lady, this one is yours!
Sir. *(Bowing.)* I am from Earth . . . I was the first Earth . . . man.
Then I was strangled when they *botched* the first
human. He had wings and two heads!
A sponge, a cake, and a lyre. Ta da!

F. How did you have control of our ship?
Our codes change daily.

L. Oh! You don't need those guns here, cowboys.
They don't even work. See click, click, click.

Lt. S. Now we're for it! We might as well be
legs up – exposed to their power –
these *players* have us under complete control.

F. Silence! Until we know their purpose, you will be calm.
We have a prisoner. He is dangerous.

L. Oh! Him! Another big *to-do* here! A gemological drama!
No . . . gynecological? Gene-e-co-log-i-cal? Its genes, anyway.
We already have him. He sleeps until he improves his manners.
(Mock saluting) Job well done, Commander.

F. Who? What? Where do you take us?

L. It's dinner time, cowboys.
You've got a date with a lady.
The Kosmoautikon speaks to *you* also.

F. Dinner? Kosmoautikon?

L. Gilgamesh. Don't you remember?
What is your quest?

Act Three, Scene Two

10

Dedalus. Come close to me. Let me touch you.
I see you are well formed. You are taller now. *(Examining him.)*
The bones are now mended to accept this gravity.
Your heart valves are increased. Your eyes are familiar.
(Attempts to strike. Flash grasps wrist before striking.) Yes.
You have the sight. Your ancestors were from the first generation.

Flash. I am third generation *faustus.* Who are you?
You are designer of this vessel? Are we in danger?

D. Yes. . . I am the designer of this vessel. *(Smiling.)*
It was built before your time. How is your mind formed?
Have you been trained? I gave your family a . . . code.
It is a sound no machine could decipher.
*"Ein Gott vermags. Wie aber, sag mir, soll
ein mann ihm folgen durch die schmale leire?"*
Yes?. . .Do you know the rest?

*F. "Sein sinn ist Zwiespalt. An der Kreuzung zweier
Herzwege steht kein Temple für Apoll."*

D. Good. I know your line well. An ancient race.
A man in trouble. Why is your state in chaos?
You lurch from crisis to crisis. What shall you do?

F. I am a man in trouble? What shall I do?
Every year a new party is formed. We have
no consistent policy. Murder replaces votes.

D. Of course it has. Then you will exterminate each other.
(Voice: "Seize the state with charismatic force!")
Yes. There must be a new political ideation.

F. I am not a politician. *("Seize the state.")* What is that voice?

D. It's in your blood. You must be the new KA.
("*You must seize the state.*")
I cannot intercede. We dine with the . . . the sun-runner of
this Galaxy. She is only here a few hours.

F. Sun-runner...? KA? Galaxy? Which Galaxy?

D. Exactly! Sentience along the . . . *(Waves hand.)* . . . wave.
. . . "Für ein Gott ein leichtes."

CANTO FOUR

Act Four: Goddess

1
i   *(A spectra appears. Antebbe, as star-runner speaks.)*
Antebbe. Draw me no longer electron.
Summon me no more to screens. Stand
in separate chambers. The flash of sight
instructs on contact. My eye selects you as legion.

At Argos star, the quantity of forms compress
to single luminance. At germane stars,
sentience expands to the construct of gravity.
Here, gravity is weak. Light expands to view.

Sound escapes, troubling all calm waters.

We move from sun to sun in quadrant.
The pulse emitting waves search sentience
for the charge of sentience. Who is this creature?
Does he know? Is he initiate?

No, I see
the figure of his mind is still unfinished.
Does he know his fate?

ii

ANT. I saw there is a message just stifled at the
throat. Speak. I am Ninmah. I am Nin.ti.
I am An.Tu. Prepare him. Must I touch their genes?
The creatures whose names you uttered,
their names have come down to us:
Anunnaki, Atra-Hasis. Western men. Bind on them
the image of our line. Prince Gilgamesh?

They came from Earth? Where is their gold?
No, they do not remain silent.
Now I see them on the stars. What is their intent?
To people the vast deserts of stars?

No! Their brains are a map of stars.
Who will tell them? Where are their scribes?

What chance do they have? Who will reveal the
secret of this creature's dark flashing rune?
They must extinguish every love.
I know the secret. They seek star rune . . . not love.

F. I am sorry. What does she say?
She is so tall. Is she . . .? Human?

D. It's a new language. *Try* to listen.

F. The sound may contain rich digressions . . .
But I must study the idiom.

D. *"When the gods as men speak . . ."*
At her star, Sirius, gravity is strong.
Sentient form is reduced to light.
You have atomic form – as accident –
since gravity is weak in this sun.
She speaks of ancient cosmology.
What word would you use name her?
What do you say she is?

She says we are all beginners.

2

i   *(Antebbe continues to speak.)*

ANT. There is a creature to consume the alien fruit.
I know the sound they make. We have to bury the
lovely skeletons lest the bodies return to claim
their star – and all our sound then cease.

I hear. They trade broken charms for stories. Their
love fails perfectly. Then men demand new worlds.
From cries, from language of lament, universe
and sentient stars pretend to speak. Then speak!

Yet when you speak only death is selected? That
is the constellation of water. The *Water Carrier* selects.
Do men know the message? A new ruler?
I see few men in this dimension. Where are they?

Is there still sharp North? Declining West?
The East still juts a spear as point? Then draw
a circle round. Bring me legs. Attach them.
Let me see this man who makes new world.

Do men know yet that there is no Earth as mind?
There is no terrestrial mind - as Earth –
there is only the ideal astral plane. As me.
A coordinate of consciousness. Two lines as circle.

F. Is she talking to me? I am unsure what she wants.

D. Simple.
She wants your eyes.

ii   *(Antebbe continues.)*
ANT. They made a bible? Shamans in this dimension?
How many? Two, three? No more? Insensible poems.
A faith as large as mustard seed that moved a
mountain? I read. When did they use this epic structure?

Not once? – Yet they demand new world?

Who told them our art? Did they find? Hang all
their prophets except *one.* Can he be found?
You sir? A sweet prophet? Yes. I know you.
Let this one leave. Do not kill him.

We have to see what value he may make.
The form you mime, prophet, is the only form
I do not yet know. I do not create; I become.
Make me. I am still unformed in this dimension.

I have seven waves.
The observer, as eight, makes an octave.
You have mistaken this for a world complete?
We had to remove their planet –
and then their bones.

F. I am sorry. What should I do? What does she say?

D. She does not judge you. You have something she wants.
She is constrained by your language. She has other . . . speech.
The patterns of *faustus* are still strange to her.
You will live.
This is her message.

F. Why . . . am I judged? I don't . . . wait, where is Lt. Spark?

L. Ah, yes! At last! Dinner is served!

D. (Aside.) Remember this.
You have something she wants.

3

i

F. And Talon? Where is Talon?

D. He wished to live forever! Yet all
we could promise him was long duration.

L. So! . . . and this is the good part! –
we placed him on a wet table – sliced in dishes –
arranged thus in division:
His liver on a glass dish. Still connected.
His lungs bathed in a warm liquid.
His brain tepid, chilled in a skillet.
His bowels teeming with gorging spiders.
His eyes still bobbing beneath a steady drip.

F. And the rest?

L. Let's eat!

ii   *(Antebbe departs.)*
ANT. Time will reveal everything.
We shall build a skeleton,
and upon these naked bones
I hang sinews of stranger flesh.

There is a creature to consume the alien fruit.
Speak until there's only sound of your star!
Do they understand how life is structured?
I am still unformed . . .

F. I am sorry. I am not hungry.

D. Here, take a cracker of paradise.
My child, eat from the *Tree of Life*.

Act Five: Return to Ship

4   *(Flash collects Lt. Spark and returns to ship.)*
F. Where have you been? It's late.
We have to get out of here.

Lt. S. I don't know. A pretty girl. I was sick.
I was taken to a room. There was . . . a table
with organs placed in . . . . in dishes of liquid.
I was given an exam. I slept, I think.

F. An exam? Let's get out of here.
Are you ok? Have you any incisions?

Lt. S. Two tiny pricks. Nothing.
I feel good. Euphoric. Hungry.

F. Then you have been drugged. Your genes are altered.

Lt. S. Where did you go? What did you see?

F. I am not sure. Nothing I can speak of.

Lt. S. I think I saw Talon. He was...

F. Yes, I know. Don't speak of this. We are released.
We shall never see these . . . people again.
Get in the ship. Wait! What is . . .?

Lt. S. Damn! It's Talon. He is alive! Still
in chains where we left him. He was here all along!
Good, I thought it was our skin!

F. That is not Talon. I know the message . . .
This is now the charge we deliver to the state.
This is our fish . . . in a wrapper.

Lt. S. Fish? What's *fish*? *(Turning to Talon, now silent.)*
So silent now? *(Kick.)* Can you talk? No?
What did they do to you? Cut your tongue out?

T. I always show the same face.

FINIS

Postscript: In Bridal Chain
Now Mounts Her Church

5   *(Play over. Actor playing Lillith comes forward.)*
Lillith. Let us now praise all liberal men.
First, to the Demos we owe our song.
They gave us the crafts, the soldiers, cause
for large war, the survival of the rich,
the wonderful fission weapons, our gifts
to the dead, now row on row.

What beauty can surpass the freedoms of
democratic counselors? What wisdom excels the
people's choice of liberal hippocratic leaders?

Enough! We may not even live to see the future!
Change with me this scene of broken speech –
enclosed behind curtains . . . still spectered beings of sound.
Men of this ship have made a new thing! *I have a list!*
We have answered justice, avoided luxury, kept our
integrity of free movement – survived outside of
Earth. Now we assemble a greater ark of text.

Our nation has reconstructed a planet of
future Life. Item. Metis has entered Europa
with Promethean fire. Item. Thebe, next,
in bridal chain now mounts her church.
Europa's nuptial bed of broken ice reformed,
warmed with lava vapors, aromatic with
nitrogen clouds, which, at times, will part,
revealing smoking peaks of steam, rising
land, tectonic lakes of orange agate. New-made
minds configure voids new-made. Certain buoyant
continent to men sucking past eggshell holes
final, lessening, strangled, panicked breath.

My saints! Recover us! Be certain of our labors!
Will you be teachers to these children? *(Noise.)*

Now players – fold your tents. Raise your eyes from sleep.
In the desert dunes of space all teeming cries
slant to silence, release the stakes that hold your tents.
Depart. Men, so angled, so tightened at the joints,
breath, circling, *expands,*
moving like an ancient torn sail,
a wind-borne ship in god,
now cupped as cataract, now blown by *sands.*
  (Curtain. Only girls applause manically.
  Men, still observing girls, ignore play.)

Nehi Hussein Nampour to His Feet

6   *(Hussein rising to his feet in darkness)*
H. This is propaganda! This is a dark and
troubled vision! Our children are corrupted
by this mime of trash. The state is horribly
denounced! We are insulted by this text!
We demand freedom of the Demos! The
Earth is a fixed globe! Not an ideal plane!
There are no gods. There is only science!

(Unknown voice.) "Take him. Kill him! Silence him."

H. We are led by a tyrant. He will kill us all!
He experiments with human bodies!
Talon has contacted us! He arrives!
We must kill this tyrant!
Allah is great. Allah is great!

    (Vargus enters.)
V. Return the females to their ships!
Guards, circle the Admiral!
Aaron, stay down!
Talon is here? Did you know this?

(Aaron replies.) Yes. The clockwork is set.
Bring the senator to my room. I suspected his hidden secret.
His *Demos* heart hardens at the sight! Let him
once detect a charismatic apparition.
I shall loose Allah in his heart.

Let him see Antebbe with his own eyes!

Roll Call of Armies

7   *(Crews immediately are silenced and Aaron commands in loud voice.)*
Aaron. Silence! Soldiers, on your feet!
Commander! Call the Armies! ...*A-TENT-TION!*
Sound off! Have your commanders... *RE-PORT!*

(Vargus replies.)
V. The Armies are here!
Soldiers of the Army of Estonia! Brigades *RE-PORT!*
How many died? Who remains?

(Veterans respond.)
Millions died. Only we remain.

A. Army of Estonia, pass. You shall make a new nation!
Soldiers of Theater Moscow! *RE-PORT!*
How many died? Who remains?

Millions died. Only we remain.

A. Army of Moscow, you shall make a new nation!
Soldiers of Theater Kiev! *RE-PORT!*
How many died? Who remains?

Millions. Only we remain.

A. Army of China! Are you present!

(Long pause. Aaron comes forward.)
We are present! We survived!

(Terry suddenly interjects.)
How many died? Who remains?

(Aaron replies finally.)
A. No one remains! Avert your eyes!
Silence! Silence! Only Silence remains!
From this silence I make a Galaxy
. . . perfect in its generations!

Aaron Speaks to His Nation

8
A. Take your seats! *(Waits for silence.)*

No leader should live longer
than the love he holds of his people.
    (Some chuckling.)
If he was hard,
then there were hardships to survive.
If he was severe,
there were severity of dangers.
If he denied the comforts of home planets,
there was no longer a planet of home.

He should sacrifice all goods for the
nation's mission. He should prefigure his
vision to verify the needs of his men – even
before the need arises. I have seen your need!

I saw that men at Callisto, Europa,
one day would need the hand of kind women
to make a home. I allotted scarce resource
of my mind and power to the need of men.
I have trained wives to take your language
and made them ready to accept with composure
your laws. The rest you must do – and nature!
    (Cheers!)
I declare to the Armies – each girl present
is now to be released to share the duties of
crews. *(Wild cheers!)* When you build new ships,
they shall build new ships next to you. In
a short time, each will be coupled with a man
of knowledge, experience, and moral strength.
None shall be held back. None shall be concealed.
    (More cheers!)
Usually it is enough if a leader finds a way to
complete his mission. I have added to my care
your future contentment in my plan. I have not
only found a new world – I will give you this
world complete – and the hope still of a home.
I do not preview only your labor at our station,
but kind women and children for our nation!
    (Cheers!)

298

9

A. How have I left the state for your good?
No enemy might now prevent us – only our
own greed and shame might prevent us.
My work is exacting. It is uncharacterized.
The work you complete
is the work which no other group of men
have ever attempted. Yet no work, no
matter how glorious, is of value if the
workers themselves obtain not the fruits.
Therefore, I ask Vargus to delegate from your
number elected sergeants to view from within
my ship the education, the civility, the charm of the
females – here – soon to be released to your own ships.
(Mad Cheers!) Yes! These chosen sergeants will verify
the numbers and the correct times. Already
your genetic codes have made possible new
life on Callisto. And these shall also extend
our pattern of human language to other
atmospheres – that our own limits of mortality
cannot bridge by nature. You have already
seen the record – as we formed this new race.
The military mission is not complete.
When Europa is finally calm, when enough
ships are built to support human life,
then, when I am enfolded in my nature,
there will be a choice of citizens for their
leaders. I do not preview the details now,
I will not legislate for you, since these will be laws
made by your own choice when my mission
is complete. The final point. There should be
no difference of goods, luxury, justice, or wealth
between the care the state now gives to soldiers
and the care it should give under a future leadership.
So we already share the total wealth of possible world.
There is no further wealth to be horded or hidden
from you. You make everything, and you take
everything. Nothing remains of justice or luxury
to give you – except my love and care. These girls
expect your strength of mind – do not fail them!
    (Cheers! – no further speech possible.)

10 *(Jurate grabbing Wakeda, cries out.)*
J. Wakeda, watch him.
Aaron plans his own death.

W. What? Child?! What do you know?
If he seeks death, it will not be the first time.
I am tired of saving his life.
He no longer values . . .

   (Terry appears from behind, speaks)

T. The sun does not rise on morning dew.
There is no pleasure of forest scent.
There are no animals. No variety of specie.
There is no living dirt. He lives now
only to give the Galaxy some living dirt.
Any child can perform as well. Look at these
girls! He knows we no longer need him.

W. If we lose him, which of us should lead?
You Terry?

T. Simple.
There will be another massacre.
Massacre upon massacre – until we find a
tottering balance. Then we start the extinctions
again with perfected joy.

   (Vargus overhearing, alarmed, speaks.)
V. Let the women be mated to the soldiers.
This is no time for political discussions.

W. Typical, commander!
Which do you choose for yourself?

V. A score!

W. Exactly! *(Aside)*
I smelled your scent before.

CANTO FIVE

Marriage Minus Jupiter

1
i   *(Aaron officiating throughout.)*
A. Bring the two to be joined.
Are you the candidates for approval? . . . *Silence!* (*Dogs barking.*)
State your names.
(Aside) . . . *Take the dogs out!*

"Tatiana, father." *(Aside)* No, child... call me Admiral here.

"Captain Falkan, Admiral."

A. Falkan? . . . yes, well . . .
These . . . children . . . ah . . . These souls
do not come lightly to my authority.
They make at Jupiter an eccentric ritual. There
is nothing more human than the question and the reply –
what value do we place on life? What respect do we show?
Our love of another is both *the* question and *the* reply.
Only the high sentience of men poses a question . . . and a reply.
We have spectral minds – not animal minds. Animals are terrestrial.
We live in space because our minds are active on the astral plane.
We prove our reply of life by reaching beyond our animal.
A spectral mind is of no value to the animal. It is an abundance
that has no earth fossil. Thus, our minds are star maps. Maps of
questions and replies – to the source of life. We accept the challenge.

I have examined in private their compatibility.
Their charts are prosperous. I have severely
charted the nearness of ascendants.

I ask them – no, I ask you all – *is there a power
greater than your private will?* (Aside)
Now . . .respond, children. As rehearsed.

"Yes. We perceive there is a power
greater than our private will.
The Spectral Empire that protects us
has a right to our care."

Come forward, then. Let this be the form.

ii

A. I approve your intent.
But I will say aloud what captains and lovers
are shamed to speak. Eros is promiscuous.
Erotic secrecy contains a social worm. Eros is
an urge to hide – as a coward hides. Eros may heal,
but more often it harms. Why?
We accept our own appetites. So does the coward.
We approve our own pleasures. So Does the child.
Yet every coil of pleasure has a weak bias.
Pleasure seeks its own good before the good of another.
So we feel disgust to witness appetite in other men.
Why? Because we know that promiscuous men
are cowards when hardship blocks his pleasure.
So let me speak as captain of this nation:
We cannot find the source of gravity;
yet we feel gravity.
We cannot find the source of contentment;
yet we feel contentment.
We cannot find the source of love;
yet we feel love.
What is this? This equals faith.
Thus . . . yes . . . children . . . we admit to faith in men.
A strange admission at Jupiter – but certain.
So what is man? A courage of faith, surely.
And his love? A proof of courage. (*Dogs barking again.*)
Why? Because . . . because . . . Man is not a fixed star.
Love is not a fixed planet. Thereby . . . sentience
is a condition – not a place. Men are a condition.
Love is a condition – made and kept as texts of faith.
Love alters with manners, with appetite,
with sudden hardship. Love is peril and challenge, then.
What does this all mean? Only this: You must guard the
condition of love. Love, as life, is a value to be proven –
and not only consumed. Love learns sacrifice.
Love is not a *thing* – as man is not a *thing*.
Emotion – real, felt – is a condition embedded
in sentience. Both appear to us as charismatic totem.
From miracle we seek to secure the gifts of miracle.
So there is honor and justice in your faithful speech.
Come forward. (*"They are already forward, Sire."*)

2

A. Silence! I will wait for silence! . . . *Silence the bitches!*
Come forward, then. *(Aside) . . . Who let the dogs out?*
Ah-hem! . . . I stand legal guardian for this girl. (*Others: Look it's Terry!*)
I give her away. Who harms her tests my authority.
Any questions? You recall the responses?
Let us proceed. I will pose the question . . . and you answer. Yes?

A. If there was honor and consent before union,
should there still be honor and consent with vows?
    (Couple recites.)
"In this union there is honor. Let it be proven."

A. If there was faith before union,
should there still be faith confirmed with vows?

"In this vow there is faith. Let it be proven."

A. If assembled in the elements there was love before union,
should love be honored in the fixed temple of two bodies?

"We alone see the elements of love in our bodies.
Let it be proven."

A. If assembled in the rudiments of respect there was restraint,
may restraint convene from appetite?

"Our appetite is satisfied with the gift of our two bodies.
Let it be proven."

A. I give you then my protection. Let it be as you ask.
Do you have the rings?

(Tatiana interjects.) "*Rings? Asbestos or bitumen?*"

A. Iron. Ancient Earth. Only iron. Let it be the sign of our first home.
The Earth is iron. This is the meaning: as rings of iron rust,
let faith outlive decay. When these rings fall away – and you still love –
you are then elect. I saw that gold only mocks a human bond.
I saw that gold was astral – nothing human at all. Iron.

(Terry appears from behind, speaking.)
T. You mean it mocks my *Roger dodger*! What man here may ever outgrow his prick! A spicy hunter of strange. Churlishly comported. What is marriage? *Terrestrial* surely? Who is my mother? Where is she? In Hell a'lick'd? Smoked and burp'd behind a Diner? What is bitumen, master? A black maw-engulfing ring of hell fire? What is marriage? A meal for'dained to putrefy?

A. Wakeda! Who let Terry in!? He will *not* be married today!

3   *(Aaron speaks to Vargus.)*
A. Vargus, release this text to the crews:
   (Terry comes forward again.)
T. Master, I will do it!

A. Not now Terry. Leave!
   (Voices aside.)
"Why does he suffer this fool to speak?"

   (Vargus reading text to crew.)
V. Confined to ships and danger,
the Commander will not license fornication.
Lust is promiscuous. Lust is cunning.
Lust is not single and seeks diversity.
I do not license unintended consequences.
It endangers ships in action, safety, training;
it threatens secure crews and a stable life.
   (Terry again interjects.)
T. Of course you have had your fill, then?
   (Vargus, now angry, continues to read.)
V. Those who come to marriage show a courage.
Forfeiting promiscuity, they have matured
to a new sense of life. What is the result?
They have discovered a new order of mind.
So let there be no mock of legal union.
Social union is a promise of high structure . . .
respect for life – our order of life.
Newly formed,
the human race is marginal and few.
We constrain the unseen force of gravity.
Let us constrain the force of Eros. *(End of Memo.)*

A. (To all.) Resolve, then, with me.
Bind with red silk ribbon the hands and arms
of these two spectral pilgrims. The cloth may freely
be torn away – or freely, they may be kept chaste
and clinging. Bring the bag of iron rings.
Engraved is my sign. Guard them.
There will never be a circle of iron
as like.

V. (Aside.) What brings about this conversion? Policy?
(Then aloud.) Who is next to be joined?

4   (Aaron questions Wakeda)
A. Wakeda, how many wait in line?

W. Out of your mind? Today? Twenty.
Tomorrow. Twenty.

A. Let Vargus and the other commanders officiate.
Follow my exact form. I have given it some care.

W. Are you serious? This is not possible.
I have already proposed this. There is a storm of tears
on this subject. They want their *"Dear father."*

A. Absurd. I cannot read every ceremony. Call the Army
Commanders. Call Vargus. He must learn this office.

W. Why? Are you sure he is fit to fill your place?

A. What if he is? What is wrong with you?

W. Just like that. You are surrounded by . . .

A. Of course I am. So I allow you to talk to me
as my own family. Yet, do not cross a limit
of your understanding. There is another reason.
I need Vargus to perform my own marriage.

W. I saw this – are you losing your mind?
Never did a fruit-eater invent such a construct
– merely to foreswear all fruits.
(Enter Terry and dogs.)
T. Is father worn out from triple sweet-meats?
No more hands in the cookie jar?

A. Terry! Did *you* let the dogs out again?

T. Why, the dogs have no right to be married? This
is a specie–o-logical slur – sir! Animals have rights here. Have
they not mouths to eat, lips to bark – and butts to fill?
They wish to be married as well – before you go!

    (Wakeda replies, suddenly concerned.)
W. Father? ... how *father*? Before you go?
Go Where? Go Where?

5

A. Vargus performs my own ceremony.
Should I remain . . . promiscuous . . . if I
require others to make . . . a bond?

W. You! Marry? Who? . . .What?
No! Not that girl! Are you mad?
You are in a diabetic fog. No other explanation.

A. Silence! *(Aside)* There are things you don't know
about that girl. She is not what she seems to be.

W. She is a danger to men and boys . . . an unknown mystery.

A. No, she is just a girl, Wakeda. I have
a human line. Not a new idea – I guess.

W. A human line? What does *that* mean?

A. Wakeda, she is so constructed . . .so pieced together
that I know she was sent. If I resisted her, another
form of her would come. Item. She is with child.
She would not leave me in peace. You don't
know this girl as I do. She is . . . selected. She selects.
I cannot . . . I cannot lead these men and not follow the
bonds I impose on our community.
I renounce all others . . . this day.
I cannot explain it. My force is blunted
on all the flesh that has passed my coil.
I have discovered that there is more virtue
in surrender to a girl than command of
a list of successive ships, plans . . . problems.
Someday you'll see my meaning. Call Vargus.

W. I don't like this. There is a spell on you.
You seem to renounce . . . our work.

A. Really? Do you know my work? She will
continue my work as no other. She contains . . .
my work. She has *gravitas.* Show me another?
She has taken a Murmers' initiation.
And you will protect her. As you love me . . .
Promise me . . . *Now! Now!*

Girl Diaries *(Sung by Terry)*

6   *(Jurata appears behind Terry. Terry plays instrument.)*
i
There is no censure in her year,
not in her choice, or the hurt of players;
they beckoned wildly for their play,
she put on shadow for their drowning,
they wore a salt of waters.

Bones settle to the bottom from ideas
a single summer in your flesh, raise
flat rock above your waters flashing;
put away all vaulted rhyme,
my single ransom showing through your dress.

There is no knowledge for my word,
not on my blood or the colder season;
cake hard porphyry from Prometheus' blood,
raise red soil on words in girl diaries,
lightly call them to my play.

My ear a treasure house to keep their sound.

But if my words falter and hold no city,
fail to please the eye's tall kingdom,
put away my brain, my ships, my trains and towns.
I will go; but stay again. A single strike
of spider ore, the sparkled studs above

girls' flashing waters.

ii   *(Aaron, listening, moves to her, then speaks)*
A. Any Ovid, Terry? Any Golding? No?
If I could only have robotic arms!
And a single great robotic appendage!
I myself would people this planet
and so ample – except that proliferation
secretly assumes the immolation of men.
With over abundance there is no need
for further enchantment. So I fix *my* Apollo
at the crossroads of *my* need. I slay.
If I could only be sure that my work
has reached a limit of my own cunning.
Then I could walk away content.
What is the consequence of extinctions?
Appraised, I discover no concern, no lost intent . . .
I have to proscribe a measure of spleen . . .
Have you not observed . . . after extinctions,
life continues exactly as before . . . how?
Thus our minds are not terrestrial, not globular.
Life is an astral pattern we accept. Beauty, a pattern we accept.
Contentment, a pattern we accept. Justice, a pattern we accept.
Minus planet, minus globe, the mind terraforms.
Thus the mind is astral – not fixed to molten earths.
What new pattern did I release in living dirt? Do all
bodies circle our Black Hole at the same speed? I observe,
as eighth ancestor, the seven waves of being in the egg.
What further minus in dimension can I alter?

   (Terry suddenly interjects.)
T. Have you heard the news, father?
They have found a dead frog in *CPT Tandy's* ship.
There is a riot. No one has ever seen a frog.
It told them it was a cat. They were not sure.

A. Bring me this specimen, Terry.
This better not be another *device* of yours!

T. The whiskers or the tail?

Interlude *(Some Girls Refuse to Marry)*

7

W. There is a delegation of officers to see you.
Subject: *"Item. They can't get girls to marry."*

A. I already heard of this. My girls are . . . improved.
Send the men this list of poems. No . . . ask them
the name of the girl in question. No . . . Do not show the list!
Look . . . next to each girl's name I have listed a poem.
Have the men memorize the poem . . . of each, separately, I mean!
I mean . . .Do not show the entire list. Let that remain a secret.
I have . . . each poem an incantation. Let them work.
Then after, if they still have trouble . . .
Only then . . . will I intervene. No . . . not before.
Yet I do wish they would close with nature… quickly.
Keep me informed. How many girls have we released?

W. 210. And I *have no idea* what you just said before.

A. What I said? Does it matter? The Replicant will tell you. . . .
I must work with the rest. Some are delicate.
Some are damaged from their youth. They had
poor handlers in Estonia . . . Abandoned. Some are hard to . . .
some are touched. But who of us is not touched?
I'm accused to be mad. Am I mad, Wakeda? . . .
Again . . . yes . . . I made a note here . . . in my hand.
Wakeda, have this female brought to me.
This one is . . . somewhat special.
She is somewhat dangerous.

W. Aaron, don't even try. Full stop.

A. Ah, you haven't seen the plate that you refuse.
Be wise, my friend. I do you no harm.
You will see if I have shown a care for you.
Consider, dear friend. What else could I give you of me?

W. Aaron . . . no . . .

Letter to Jurate

8   *(Terry sings behind as Aaron writes)*
i
What secret do you hide where others touch,
what part of me do you grant at all hours,
how much am I the flower in your flesh?

What could I give or take without your gift,
how much of you is given when I touch,
or hands that touched before how much?

Away from me, what hands can touch,
who enters now with arms or hands,
what space in you is still untouched?

Cry up tensions teased from flesh,
guard for me nothing that can't be kept,
give to me nothing except what I take,

compress meaning with your effort,
feed me hungry, refuse me sleep to wake.

ii   *(Terry again confronts Aaron about his plans.)*
T. Sodomy aforethought! Or coming after-wards?
That is, from behind? I see you there. . . resolving.

A. Not now Terry. *(Enter Jurate, standing behind silent.)*

T. I see what you do. What will you do with Black Terry?
Does he go with you? Hard for a cook to follow – no?
You think *that girl* will keep me? I cannot talk with her.
She does not like Terry. *(They eye each other – Terry drops to knees.)*
Oh father, please . . . please.

A. Stop. She will care for you as I care, Terry.
Besides, I am here. I gave you the sight of
prophecy – as purposed. She will honor it.

T. You think any of these humans will ever let us live?
Each of them will turn on me when you are gone.
You don't think they will toss every pot and pan you perfectly
balanced – still spinning on stick? You are greater fool, then.

A. I have made sure of her. She will care for you all.

T. Let Black Terry kill them, after you are gone!
    (Suddenly pulling Terry violently by the collar.)
A. Child, you are not even *black*. Why do you pretend to be *black*?

T. Because . . . because. . . I see your race lets them sport as
children – and you pardon to correct them. I watch.
If not a black'n, father, then tell me what I am?
How did you make me? *(Sobbing uncontrollably.)*

A. As marginally human. As an angel – minus.
I made you to cry – like this, child – to prophesy, to die.
What else of the angel's hierarchies do you desire?

T. What if it is not enough? To prophesy? To die?

A. Child! This is the very *thing*. You do not see it?
You chase after stars minus element. So long as you
cry *Not enough!. . . Not enough!* – you prove my
choice. How else could you ascend to gift? Except
you are free to move across dimension with
thirst. . . with hunger? Now . . . *curse* the satisfied mind!
You are higher than gods who cannot seek, or cry, or find.
This is how I made you. Gods beg for a moment of your chance.
Master this one thing in you. Master something – anything.
In that sky of mastery there will sun enough. What is eternity? –
only another text of life. So live. Burn brightly. You are in the room.
I make of you a man *today*. Tell *(Waiving hand.)* . . . what you saw here.
I let you walk among us . . . as god walked in his garden at noonday.
Now shine *brightly* . . . beloved prince. Your time *arrives*.
    (Releases him. Speaks to Jurata with manic passion.)
You! You will honor his life . . . with your life!
Agree to this now! Kneel!
    (Jurata, Kneeling, afraid.)
J. I will honor his life . . . with my life.

9

A. Now . . . composed . . . as friends . . . here . . . woman and child,
let us move to the bow of the new ship.
      (Terry and Jurate follow. Shapes now moving in the living soil.)
The air in this room is tepid. The worms escape their pods.
This way, child. Yes, both. I want you to see Thebes' final life.
A little death of fish. – Let this room and ship be filled with dirt.
I want to see mounds and mounds of living dirt. Then send
the ship entire with my . . . the ship entire . . into Europa.
The Committee of *Living Dirt* proscribed
a sever limitation of temperatures. We must
contaminate the surface with an exact dose
of excrement. I suggested certain members
of the Committee. No? . . .Then let it be me!

      (Terry, aside.)
T. So that was what was in the box!
It was marked, *"Terra Preta. Amazon basin?"*
I jiggled in it a thousand times!

      (Aaron rolls his eyes.)
A. So, let eerie science now rule our committee.
We have counted every weapon in our inventory.
Thebes will not so easily rise to our projected
trajectory. By trial of Metis, our calculations are fixed . . .
      (Others speak.)
"No! Then we must build more. We are exposed."

A. Yes. Of course, of course, build more weapons.
My concern now is . . . taxidermic. I am
opposed with the scale of the physics. The
masses are too large for my first calculus.
My concern is to ignite a heating fission. One
that does not scorch Europa; one that does not
break the planet; one that does not make a fire.
None of us are certain of Europa. It is obdurate. Alien.
I want a rising steam.
Stand back! *(Throwing a canister of liquid.)* I release
this vial, timed, after we depart, the doors forever
sealed, there is contained a monster virus of
mitochondria . . . that . . . itself will make Genesis.
Go . . . dark bugs, carpet your talons into Europa.

What I want is bone, jade, and feldspar.
What I want is a living steam, a moving dirt.
Trade my own bones for a little scrap of green moss.

T. Oh, father, let me be mossy!
    (Aaron continues.)
A. Because the water in the pond of Bethesda
is stirring . . . I don't know if I can be carried
down by you men fast enough to touch the healing
waters. What is a Captain that does not make proof?
Every Captain should fall to pattern. It's a proof of life.
Why do you all furrow your brows? Are you so unread
in our poems? Are modern men unfit to be bold?
I change your speech. There is no other code of
torment matched to my hope of torment. Where
to place my scabs, my crusted lips of sores?
Let Europa live! I need to be redeemed.
I killed the planet of blue and green.

    (Terry moves up on the mound of dirt, releasing vapors.)
T. Father, tell us why you destroyed the Earth?
I know . . . I know . . . but they will not believe my report.

    (Startled by the challenge, Aaron pauses.)
T. You said to me, "Because . . . I looked one day. And I saw . . .
I saw ... an old man's *shoe* had no glamour on Earth.
Only youth . . . only youth had a voice with this race."

A. Yes, child. I said this.

T. I see. I see. Yes, this is clear . . . this is clear.
Replicant! Did you get that?
All this *rocketry* . . . for an old man's shoe?

A. No. Because . . . our idiom was in danger of
cycling back into oblivion. I, well . . . *(smiling)*

T. All this . . .*murder* . . . for a school . . . of poetry?

A. Certain. Show me any text. I will show a murder.
Text is murder . . . Who writes a book, kills.
That is *you*, Terry. What is your poem?

T. On what crust of tear
did all other mistake our text?
If we stay, we pick the bones of men?
If we leave, we pick the bones . . .*That's it then*?

A. Let it be said for all time –
"*because an old man's shoe had no worth*
on *that* planet." I have said it . . . a last time.
Can we proceed . . . child? Vargus, begin!

Film of the Death of Thebes

10

i

A. Good? . . . Then . . . Now . . . We watch
as Vargus ignites suns with robotic arms.
Let us see the one-time spectacle.
Play the report. Darken the room!

(Crackling radio signal, exaggerated voice of emotion)
V. The caldron planet still beaconed red
when to small Thebes we set our course.
We fixed our spears of pursing azimuth.
We landed nine ships; we ran our engines.
Placing Megaclites inside eight of her cavities.
The fuse all lit, we began to spin the oblong moon
and moved, as a twisting bullet turns
with aimed trajectory – and force. Slowly
the moon of Thebes raised its elliptic to the
calculated speed and arc. So slow, so slow, we burned our Titans.
We got a way the last hour. 24 eggs left to hatch
to open bright hell on her stony back.

The canopies of fission, hydrogen and
retroactive ions seal a counterforce.
Scientists on edge, mere blacksmiths at their fires,
wet with sweat, faces lit by heat and forge, made exact
the course of calculation, chewing on sticks,
adjusting only once with three more emitting fires
placed behind our shields of counter-ion pulse.

ii   *(Terry cries out.)*
T. But will the candle light?
Why so much sweat for a frozen glob of snot?
I slurp a chipped daiquiri – with more use to men!
Father, you said we want a star – not a pea.
This is policy . . . sure?

A. We will get our star. Now silence!

iii   *(Sputtering film continues.)*
V. When Thebes hit middle ocean,
maw spewing Europa,
already crossed with spider orange obsidian fires,
seized the giant cargo moon
as boiling lead accepts a spoon
dropped in caldron leaden soup,
and sealed again the liquid surface. A counter
explosion closed our eyes against sun-bright flash.

(Aaron aloud.) I like this part! Watch!

V. We saw large chalice of molten moon
bulge with abscess, a dome of liquid glass
escaped the orange scaffold honeycomb
mixed with life-forming lava.
We held our breaths and watched as
magma emitting hot iron mountains
rose to our position. Then as sudden slowed,
as if to observe our monster acts,
and collapsed again into the caldron
new-made giant. We moved
to look away our escape – but our eyes now
fixed . . . as pillared salt: What would happen next?

We did not stay, since the hot
heat-barking globular ingots
critical to our ships circuits, already snapping
from the pulse emitting ray. Three ships
disabled – now in tow. We withdrew, stumbling from
the scene of still-elemental maw,
still-brewing barking tongues, bullets of molten glass
counter-sealed robotic arms with blackened casts
of layered sprue – snapping down like branches caked
with rings of ice. Nothing left to crush, recast, or break.
Our talon gripping fusion spires – once erect,
now descending, setting fire to the small rain.
The giant egg of caldron moon replete and throbbing –
now deep in incubation. She is now a living giant.
    (Lights come on.)
This is the report. What are your questions?

CANTO SIX

Apocrypha: Antebbe Formed an Image of Anu in Her Heart

1   *(Aaron questions Antebbe. She reveals his lineage.)*
i
A. I knew the moon was hollow. I kept the secret. How did I . . . ?
The question is germane.
How do I know a charismatic force?
Come forward. I know you are a god.

   (Cheda follows behind Antebbe, making a wall of steam
   from a hose, out of which the form of Antebbe appears.)

I have studied the language of gods.
From what I learn of gods, I see
they bring new forms of death. Or do you make
sound as gatekeeper? To be a god –
must there be rituals of sacrifice?
This is your message? You are a god of death?

   (Antebbe quotes an ancient poem.)
ANT. "As I look upon thee, Utnapishtim,
thou art not different at all,
even as though I am thou...
I see you are formed with my bone."

A. What text do you read? You call me brother?
In you – what distinction remains of sentient
consumption? What machine is made in you
of heart? How do gods speak? How may they eat?
And if saints – how do you make a saint work?
Your sentence is metered. Is this a strategy
of temptation? When you speak, in so far as
I understand, does your understanding mock me?
Is poetry your true voice? Do I self-speak?
Is *modernism* the last idiom of men? Or is *silence*
our last wisdom? What is the answer you can make?
Stop. I already know your answer. Death,
why are you called by so many names?

318

A Wheelchair of Gold

2   *(Antebbe replies.)*
A. I alone have loved you. Kosmoautikon.
You entered suns. I came this way by weak suns.

What are gods, my brother? When you make
a sound, you form a small god in your breath.
The rest of us have spectral consciousness.
There was a lumination at Sirius. Great need.

In Babylon I was Ishtar, twin of Shamash.
Before, I was Inanna. And you – Utu. I formed an
image of Anu in my heart. So men became sentient.
You have done this work with me, Aaron.
You are my brother. We make space and time from speech.
We are multiple in dimensions. There are many.

We made these men first as slaves,
then again, to make them in our image.
Now, a final time, you advance their code
a further innovation. How much longer – human?
No. We cannot remain. The planet is passing.

Seize the spaceport – here! The terrestrial
form of god is the highest structure of speech they
seek: In the end, the word *god* has no
meaning. It is only a text of power you seek.
You mistake this. Make a spaceport here.
An astral portal. Past all cells of blood.

What is my proof? I will tell you. If a man
finds a god – what would humans report?
A sound. A rumor of sound. Only this.
Only the *sound* of the god in the ear!
Not Her talon hands. Not Her emitting fire.
No. They would engrave in gold letters
the words of the god. They would hang our letter,
scripted on an enameled gold disc – from their
temple wall. One sentence. A golden rune.
A page. A poem. Placed in a golden chest. A golden chair.
See? So god is a text. A language. A wind.

Men draw near in the wind
where gods escape. As text.
     (Terry, hiding, cries out, then runs away.)
T. Father, do not leave us.
She is a daemon. Leave now!
     (Antebbe hisses, then continues.)
ANT. What else would these men make with a god?
Could there be any other means of sentient
encounter with deity in this dimension? No.
So do you see, do you finally see? Nothing else
is possible to these but a rumor of god – a text.

You gave them our sentient code. Then
everything becomes a god their eye may idol.
Every human speaking to gods
made a tablet of sentence, a text of stone,
a ladder of tears, a wound as charted rune –
placed this tablet on a *wheelchair of gold.*

Tell me when this was not performed
exactly as I have told you? Not exactly?
Yes? You see my message? Their ark is a sentence.
Their godhead is only a ladder of runes. Numbers.
I give you back the *Tablet of Destinies.*
You must change your form to fix the margins.
They are here . . . at my hand. You see them?

     (Aaron marvels at stones – and speaks.)
A. Strange emitting structure! What new element?
No. I fear to touch. By your oracle, then, Antebbe,
all my tear, all my blood, all my lust – only text.
What are these spectral monsters rising from
the tile of beams . . . the pulsating table . . .?

ANT. Yes. Finally you see. Finally you ask.
The *Tablet of Destinies.* I have hid it for you.
Draw near into the emitting beam.
Closer. Closer. Now closer!

There. You are fixed! Now rest.
The time is fulfilled!

3   *(Antebbe continues)*
i
ANT. In this wheel-house there is a ladder –
only a ladder you can make of life.
Eight octaves. Seven waves of life – altered to fit
the conditions of the eighth ancestor. To fit his mind.
Nothing else you can make of life.
To love ineptly, to break, to bleed,
to live with fault, to kill the arrogant,
to die with clarity from a concealed fault.
In your dreams you have seen this text.
My voices have searched your dreams.
Can you recall the message?

But when you return from this house, you must
give us your report: We are the watchers. Sung
in the *Tablet of Destinies.* Your death has information.
What did you see? What was in your dream?
You are made of voices. They return to their source.
From selected sound you rule all circled maths.
Multiple, the circle is perfect – you test the paths.
Hexarch! Astrologer! Caster of bones!

ii   *(Antebbe enters trance.)*
ANT. Where are the fragrant trees of cedar?
What have men done with their Earth?
Are they really so much like us then?

Why did you run so far?
Who told you were human?
I have nothing to say to these.

They repeat themselves. The list-makers.
The same wish. The same taste. The same cries.
The same itch of pain. The same sweet.

I kill them again. Do not delay the ark.
What does this tell you?
What else do you need to know?

4   *(Aaron, halting, speaks.)*
i
A. I have remembered and remembered.
That's a thing a man can do . . .

I read an epic poem. That was Earth. I shivered.
I thought that, as men, we were already gods.
I believed the sound of my own voice.
It was enough for me then . . . to be a man.
I did not know yet – it is impossible to be a man.
That state of man is a terrestrial impossibility.
When young, confused, I thought men were as gods.
Fragrant sentience encouraged my misdeeds.
I shivered because I saw no other gods – but me –
my sound was my only house of Being.
I did not know the deep ancestry of blood.

   (Antebbe rejoins.)
ANT. You are not blood; you are a cloud that forms.
God is not a thing. God is a condition that forms.
I am a cloud formed in this gravity.

We cannot remain, Aaron. Cross the page of DNA.
Spit-out the tar-cave . . . In your atom is ark.

ii

A. What you intend is my death? I see
death can be strange – as other. Its moment seems
eternal as men prefigure unknown qualms.
Arching comets make men supplicant for
every still-suspected fear. I feel this challenge now.

How can I let these men go?
I have brought them so far. I removed their planet.
I destroyed their terrestrial element.

There is not one that can take
the levers of this machine.
I cannot let them extinguish in space.

ANT. You and Talon give them every cunning,
every device. We have embedded
our cosmology in this narrative. A new planet is
formed. Leave them. We must watch.
Aaron, give me back your terrestrial mind!

A. I cannot leave Cheda.
I cannot leave the Murmers.
I cannot leave the girls I have formed.
Did you see how they learn their poems?

C. Lady! He cannot leave!

ANT. No. Give me back your brain of stars.
I fear what they will make. I must find them all.
I prefer to kill them all. Kill them.
Let Cheda live. He is mine.

A. It is hard . . . to inflate my own scaffold.

5   *(Antebbe, angry, finishes the argument.)*
ANT. You have already said too much! They cannot
share your mind. They fear strange information.
They keep lists. If they could see our work, we would
be exterminated. They would murder you. You act
as a god. Yet look, no man could suffer a god
in this generation. What is god – but a seizure of
consciousness? This new race you will secure with us.
If they stay, they will be hunted by men.
The methane planets are far to the center.
The women . . . Let the men have them.
Is your ship ready? I want this ship. Prepare
your ship. Build a ship. I give you one day yet.
I see your men have made your ship strong.
It is good. You have heard our signal.

A. Antebbe, one day? No! I need an eon.
Europa is still unstable.
Thebes must make a fire at her core.
I must cool the planet with weird moss.

ANT. No. These generations will never see land;
they will be nomads until they are dead.
Some will try to return to Earth. You have said it.
You still can watch. You will not let them extinguish.
Kill the rest! Grind them!

A. You make no sense. I am newly married.
I have promised. There is a human child.

ANT. The child she has must be born near Jupiter.
He will be kept fortunate and separate. There is a new codex.
The political leader must be kept separate from the ruled.
The mother? I know her. She is mine. She knows what
she must do. She will kill them. Her idiom of cunning is perfected.
I have made her in her heart. I have made Tiamat in her heart.
Earth still lives at the end of her long legs.
She is my flesh.
She loves you.

A. So I cannot leave. Let me die with them.

6 *(Antebbe makes a final plea.)*
ANT. Yes, die of them. Not with them.
No. Be wise. Time will reveal everything.
You have built a new skeleton, and upon
these lighter bones I hang sinews of stranger
flesh. These men you have advanced
must now contaminate with our bias.
I did not come to preach, Aaron.
I came to restore the supremacy. Finish
your work. You cannot protect them anymore.
I prefer they die on our spider ants.
Release the spiders on their eyes.
Ants tease to perfection the honor of slaves:
A high idiom of our need. A noble sign of life.
The human? It is not life you seek . . . it is measure.
Life is organized not to rule with biology.
Life is the path to be selected *out* of biology.
As they die, we can hear the sound they make.
There are more worlds of selection. This is the
salvation of breath. There is always more selection.
Life must not proliferate beyond selection.
Life is not a revolving prayer wheel. We search the highest idiom.
Consciousness counts by fingers. Death enrages all value.
Life is selection. Life is never promiscuous – so Earth offends me.
We come to burn. Show me the two seeds in your hand!
Let these two seeds build their world.
They would not have left Earth
if you did not lead them away from Earth
Singe all carbon. We depart.
Each hour you stay with them,
they lose their own chance of virtue.
We left them in the last eon.
Let them have their new eon,
new text, new language.
You have already formed new genes.
They eat of the Tree of Life.
Now Talon performs his mythic code.
He must come to slay you.

Cheda, tell your master what will happen.

7   *(Cheda answers.)*
CHE. Master, you must show all men *faustus* . . .
You must activate the *Tandem* gene. I have asked her
to use my body. She refused me.

A. So I must be killed, Antebbe?

ANT. There will be a courage. Yes.
Think, Aaron! One perfect moment.
A moment, a man. Then a moment, Utu, my twin.
Prove the theorem! Perfect this syllable!
What is asked of you, my love? It is only
a further application of sentience.
Seize motion across conception.

A. And if I cannot? If my heart second-beats?
Can I do more than I have asked other men to do?
Let me see! I did not think my challenge
would return to me – as soon, as soon.
I recognize the message. I may still see it! A moment.
I recognize the signature of this fear.
I know it! I greet it – as astral! Front stepping . . .
It is mine. It is ancient to my rumor.

What other miracle can I perform here?
If I stay, do I solve another problem?
Make another speech, break another planet,
deepen my carnal diversion, break more moons,
experiment with codes of farmed genetics,
eat, eat, eat, eat . . . or step ahead of all human cunning?
It is unending terror.

I have a choice? Choice allows the weak
a brief heritage of courage. I am weak. Let a
weak man make a world with breathtaking choice.
A little dish of death. A bravery then. But can I be sure?

ANT. Yes. You always have had a choice.
It is long delayed.
Move closer.
Come close again. Just here.
Closer.

A. Then let me enter the opiate . . .

Return Journey

8   *(Terry sings in another room as Aaron cries.)*
T. For those who meet on the China Road,
who trails from hands the earth of their cribs?
Each grain effaced by feet,
memories cleaned by steps.

What life do we share underground,
if we meet and kiss and return alone?
Pack down the dust of trails
cleaned and kept by prints.

How should we cup our steps as the savant steps
death's green trimmed maze? And how shall we live then
still eating the life
that fills our mouth?

When are we clean as lover's breath is clean,
or what shall we take before we can give?
By mouth and by word
we will live and be clean.

As on instruments of the pear wood tree,
some shall play us before we're done,
who run onto our hot tear,
as hot oil down a wire.

And how shall two pass into our strength,
or tease from flesh our myth and story?
Rehearsed and named,
remembered by fires.

9   *(Wakeda and Vargus, concealed, attempt to make sense of events.)*
Vargus. Wakeda!

Wakeda. What? Who is that? . . . Vargus?

V. Did you see that?

W. What did you see?

V. I saw a giant pass me. She did not even look
at us! As if she never saw me!

W. I saw it.

V. What was that . . . *thing*?
She is with . . . *Cheda*? I don't like him.
He makes a face – like he knows something.
He never blinks. He looks straight through me.

W. Yes. She is with him.

V. She has the codes? I don't like it.
They are connected? She is from Callisto?
Yesterday I heard that *fool* Terry call to Aaron –
as *father*. Is that possible? Who else is *his* kin?

W. I heard it. She does not use codes. She
moves with Cheda. She goes from cave to cave,
cutting off heads. We are next. Terry is *bi-polar*.
A name as good as any for fool.
He hides his medication. He is on a *high* today.
Yesterday he was *low*. He eats jello with his fingers.

V. Is that what they now call *fools*!

W. It takes days for him to calm down.
Not like you at all. Any more questions?

V. What is your problem?

W. Terry is the *only* person that could keep Aaron
with us. *This* is the quality of a fool – and you? . . . And me?

Two by Two: Farewell of Girls to Aaron

10 *(Aaron speaks.)*
A. Diminish from time my assiduous station.
Release from consent my sentient sound.
Secede from restraint new flesh and seed.
Go, two by two. Take no longer years

to build my moral. You are priests of my sound.

No longer stationed on my cross, repeat me
no longer rhymes from other worlds. Echo
me no sound of high terrestrial idiom. Now, single filed,
surprise me with a strike of syllable.

Now you shall function on my election. Released.

What are these? Tears? No. You are now elect.
The men will love you elect, care for you elect – they will
give you more time, they are more worthy of your affection.
Your father watches over you. No harm will singe

the small hair of your perfected skin.

You are not yet citizens. Though I have made you
certain to our gene, you must be joined with law
to our aeronauts. Then, I myself will come to decree
your union with cheerful rite. You contain a secret rune.

Your regenerative cells are some altered.

You will give dying sapiens new life.
I know I may trust you. I have placed in you
a certain fondness for my person. It is reciprocated.
And you are forever elected to our line.

Go, two by two. Enter this elevator.

When you appear to men, you will move as gods –
move in the same space as gods –
eternal founders of this nation.
I give as dowry each a galaxy, your sons
each a ship of devil cunning, a mark of high idiom.

Teach new flesh your sharpened tongue.
Preach . . . wide dominion of this gene.

CANTO SEVEN

In Our Atom Is Ark

1   *(Aaron speaks.)*
A. As you pass near me, Antebbe, I feel
a sense of you. The small hairs follow
as bending wheat on my arm. If you are not a god,
then, I am sure, you move in the same space as god.
When I search the quality of men,
I list the named quantities of deity.
So far I can proceed. Then they make a stop.
They repeat themselves. In you, I detect
a further urge to enchantment.
Yet when I turn to face the forms of deity,
when I search the evidence and compass
of god – all I find are conditional spaces
made from a moment's structure. A pattern
of idiom. You are a structure of language?

   (Antebbe replies with anger.)
ANT. You forget yourself. You speak like a beginner.
You mind is terrestrial – as bent! Come around – before
the conditions change of observation. Yes.
Many names. Many loves. Many atoms. Many arks.
Enough talk. Language is slanted cosmology.
All the myths of world are cosmology. Every speech
belongs to us. Every word may be traced back to a star spine.
Call me sister. Call me Ishtar. Call me spouse.
We are joined in our atom as ark. The count of the
electron tells our entire history. Our family –
nakedly spelled in the atomic structure.
Place your hand on the wall next to mine.
Yes! Just like this! Watch! Watch!
Now, brother, what do you see?
The moisture of the wall dries where you touch!

I see you are formed with my bone!

2

i   *(Aaron and Antebbe continue as Cheda and Terry observe.)*
ANT. Tear down a house, build a ship!
Take the seed of life. In our atom is ark.

A. Why do you repeat a speech?
Why do you read to me?
Cheda, what text does she quote?

Cheda. Master, I have taught her the new texts.
This is the only poem she knows of Earth.
She said she learned it five millennia ago.

A. Five millennia?

ii   *(Terry face down, on his knees)*
T. Oh master, let me build a temple for you
and . . . one for Antebbe. I must go with you.

A. Terry, not now. It's dangerous for you to be here.
Leave. Have you understood a single thing?
How long are you only spectator?
Cheda, take him away.

T. No. Wait! O let me watch the high tea of gods!
I am sick to make the sound of fool.
Heal me, goddess, of my tree in ear!
I am surrounded by terrestrials.
I prophesy with my tool! I throw my atom!

(Antebbe hisses loudly; Cheda takes Terry as she strikes.)

3   *(Antebbe enters a trance.)*
ANT. I see these creatures die as moths,
their faces frozen with fixed eyes.
Fatherhood taken away by the wind that dries.

Anu to Earth the words was speaking,
Earth to Anu the words pronounced,
Ishum, executioner, scorched their bodies.
Seven sun bright fires. Ishum it was.

Ishum, I see you. We warn Abraham
before the cities of the plain.
We silenced the races of misbelief.

There are too many cities. Let all burn.

Terry. No. There are no more cities.

ANT. Misbelief is formed in the planets.
The mind of the world is turned from axis.
Burn the misbegotten!

Go – with me.
You have promised you will live forever.
You have said it.
     (Antebbe awakes.)
Talon, bring the knife!
Do not let men touch the device.
They cannot perform the rite.
Do not touch the sting.

     (Sudden metallic sound in adjoining room, then screaming.)

A. Talon?
. . . He is here?

4   *(Antebbe speaks.)*
ANT. Enlil made you. Nisaba bore you.
Wide understanding perfected for you;
wisdom he gave you; writing she gave you,
now lasting life we give to you.

Anu is formed. Live seamless!
From the passing planet we sent you.
Place memory in you. Now! Look here.
At my finger. And here, again, look!

A. What new world is this, Cheda?
I see! I see! I see! O, I see!

ANT. Open the sight-way in your eye!
     (Jurate enters screaming.)
Leave now. Prepare a ship. Cheda,
take the new creatures with us. Ten I allow.
Ten pilots I allow. Ten servants I allow.
The rest are deformed. I have killed them.
Wife, you must not see this! Leave!
Cheda, take her away. You, Aaron!
Hurry, my brother, before the conditions
change of our appearance. There is a moment,
like a steam that goes up.
The star nears in position.
We are bound, as breath,
to condition forming in sentience.
We are star bones.

I may not be able to summon you again.
Time is short, my brother. Already,
you have delayed too long.

The planet is passing.

5   *(Antebbe speaks.)*
ANT. Many times we erase *sapiens*. Cunning!
They were numbered as ants.
We gave them ears to star spines
so they would erase all other sound.

They gathered again and chanted repetitions.

Now, by fire, we let them burn. By ice, we seize
them. All we counted was a few that answer
the antennae of our signals. The value of life?
What did they do with our waves of life?
The harvest was small. Somber death music,
a score of epic poems. Ten perfect lines.
This alone the selected harvest of sentience!

Few answer. Few reply with sentience.
We must observe selection.
What do they prove when they have their wish?
They touch their children. They touch themselves.

They self-destruct. When they have wealth,
they are miserable. Their children are desperate.
When they are poor, they learn to love.
When they are satisfied, they learn to hate.

The little life we let them have, they grip,
without a further urge to enchantment.
They do not advance without our intercession.

I see so few heroes in your ships.
Their sentience follows narrow channels.
I see only lust and vacancy.

Kill them all. Let others fill the vacuum.

A. What you say, Antebbe, contains no mercy.
I harvested my years to bring them here.
Let them live. They are so few now.

6 *(Antebbe speaks.)*

ANT. No? Yes? Sentience has a severe mercy.
So what race would you choose? Which fat lip?
Which misbegotten cow eye? Your sentence?
Which god to keep? The tribal god of B'nei
Yisrael? I know him. He has no arms.
We did not let him in our ship.
His legs did not move. In my atom there is ark.

Watch. I go from creature to creature.
I cut and dismember the eccentric bones.
I decapitate the female with two heads.
Some have grown wings and I end their
creeping dance. I do not come to heal.
I come to kill. That is my sweet poem.
Life? It comes again. Let their forms scatter
as small rain on my cheek.

Life? The test has failed.
Harvest angry corn.

A. This speech is proscribed by democratic laws.

ANT. What is this word, "democratic"? A new cloak
for every sin? All things are allowed for this word?
Nothing higher? You lie. Murder is your highest art.
Do not self-destruct . . . for an eccentricity of speech.

What else is sentience? But to select and to judge?
What is judgment, but selection?
What is law, but selection?
What is mercy, but selection?
What is language, but selection?
What is truth, but selection?
What are human bodies, but selection?
What is atom, but selection?
What is ark, but selection?

Selection is the language *we* make. Opposed?
Proliferation – a failure of narrative.
You have burned away the dross of
these miserable beings. They sought only wealth.

O executioner,
you are beautiful in our eyes.

The Human Element Is Described
As a Figure of Salt

7   *(Aaron speaks.)*
A. What brought me the dreams I have seen?
Were these your angels, Antebbe?

ANT. No. You are a salt boy
going down to the ocean.
How could you taste the salt of ocean?

A. How did I chase bitterly the structure of gods?

ANT. You are a salt figure swimming in a salt sea.
How could you taste salt?

A. Why could I not sink under the guilt of my murders?

ANT. You were a salt man – wet in the salt ocean.
How could you escape the lick of your own taste?

Try to see. You are a salt figure. All as salt,
your guilt was only a language you made.
Your crust of tear as salt. The water, salt.
The kiss, salt. The flesh, salt. The blood, salt.
Your death, salt.
How much of salt makes distinction across salt?

O salt god, come out of your salt-green ocean!
Your heart is full!

Antebbe Recounts the Secret History of Cosmology Embedded in All Myth

8

i   *(Antebbe gives her final argument.)*
ANT. Do not mistake your heart for terrestrial things.

Do not mistake your salt for other salt!
We have domain of this galaxy. There are many.
Life is still unformed. All atoms are Replicants.
In Sirius gravity there is no proliferation.

There is no sanctuary in sentience.
Judgment does not accept all opinion.
I summon your eyes to make a choice.
When did you believe true gods?
They are already placed in your mind – as map.

There are no gods of salvation.
There are only gods of bursting paths.
The body is not a temple, it is a line of code
that trace a line of bursting.

The stars burst. Love bursts.
Wish bursts. Sound bursts.
With sentience they must all burst.
Let me taste your salt.

Aaron. I read your message. I must burst.

ii *(Vargus speaking to Wakeda. Both hiding with weapons.)*
V. Do you understand any of this?

W. I cannot make out a single sentence
of meaning. Of what are they speaking?

V. They are both mad. There is no meaning.

   (Terry, bandaging his wounds, speaks to them.)
T. Then you are both fools. Tree stumps.
What use are you anyway? Are you *both* apes?

This means that *Sapiens must die.*

iii *(Antebbe continues to speak.)*
ANT. The crisis of this race
is the failure to read DNA as cosmology.
As information.

I read. "Leaving his cave in Crete,

great Zeus reached the mainland. Killed his
father, Cronus." What is this? A star text.
Alien Jupiter entered this solar sun,
displacing the giant Saturn from his place.

Where is a tool to measure? Only a text remains?
Not once did their savants read cosmology.

Again, in stone, I read.
Still found inscribed in desert places – I read.
The hieroglyphic of god, Amen: "*That which weaves waves
into particles – in a place hidden from interference.*"

We already gave them the lexicon of Kosmoautikon.
Ignored.

Is Your Heart Full?

iv

ANT. Again, I read.
There were eight ancestor gods in Egypt.
Seven waves enter the egg. Amen – as eighth – observes.
Eight ancestors circle the Amen particle. As photons.
We already gave the source of phantom particle.
Seven waves flow in the second world.
Eleven waves enter the egg in the triple world.
Amen – observing – as eight, then as twelve.
You have not seen this number yet?
Yet you know it.
Eight are the ancestors of Egypt, Sumer. Second world.
Eight, the octaves of oracle and music. Then, the third world:
Twelve, the Western gods. Twelve, the tribes of Jews.
Twelve, the followers of the prophet.
Twelve, the knights of Arthur, Beowulf.
Twelve, the constellations. Twelve, the labors of Hercules.
Twelve, the roads to the third world.
I am Sirius – forth world. Again, I read.
In the first clay tablet, the first sapien writing,
previously inscribed. The planet, the genealogy,
the intent of the giants. Gilgamesh made a
complaint. The spaceport was breached.
Eighty-thousand tablets – proclaiming.
Each a syllable of star information.
Repeated, again and again.
Your machines are linguistic Boy Scouts,
hollow, self-echo-formed joints – as broken fonts.
Bad physics. Bad stargazers! They froze their lives
to look for a prize! A prize. A plastic prize!
Poisoned Earth for a certificate of participation.
Never once did they read the message
of the twelve star constellations.
Every story, every hero, every myth – contained.
Cosmology as only one test: Is your heart full?
I see that you have heard.
I see that your heart is full.

Antebbe Has Aaron See His Face

9

ANT. We take some seeds in our hand.
Then burn and burn and burn.
What are the seeds you select?
I see you have seeds in your hands!

  (Aaron falls to his knees.)

Aaron. I remember now the rebels!
The smell in my nose! I see it again!
They took three hundred women of Earth!
And now I? What part am I in this rebellion?

I will remember . . . I see . . . the first language of stars!
Open the way. I will take the road.
I see the constellation of my birth.
Replete with its plan of symmetry.
  (Aaron recites an ancient poem.)
"*Stern forward Argo by the Great Dog's tail*
is drawn . . ."

I am the storm.
I am wonder.
I am raging star.

Aaron Plans His Succession

10 *(Speaking to his staff.)*
Aaron. Sit. Record this session.
If assassinated, or by any means of death,
this will be the crisis listed in 3.3.1. The death of
a Commander in Theater is superseded by
the Army Commander, you Vargus, or, lastly,
the Chief of Staff, you Wakeda.
You are the only two I trust. The men are . . . competent . . . etc.
The nature of my ships . . . their design, etc. Of course.
Yes. I see. I see. Where was I . . . ?

Wakeda. Aaron! *Enter the world again*! There will be chaos.
None of us knows how to perform your work.
The scientists are corrupt – they have been bribed.
The creatures of Callisto are beyond our competence.

A. Exactly. So now. . . so now . . . we must measure the depths.
Is the mind terrestrial or astral? Is this your question? Yes.
Who has measured the depth of star messages? Who has
seen the full consequence of $4 + 4 = 8$? It is unending terror.
Vargus, you will use this terror to complete *Mission Thebes*.
These are the cargos of chemicals to be released
on Europa. To cool the crust at her margins, etc.
We still must release *Our Mercury* into the living
belly, etc. An enduring moss. Wakeda, you will
finish the integration of the women to the crew, etc.
You both have a function. If I am killed,
you must protect my work. This is sufficient . . .
If the women have not completed their
training, you must let the Murmurs finish
their work. I have . . . I have . . . . accelerated
my contribution. Each must mate with the crews as soon
as possible, etc. Let nature mount a sharp attack, etc.
Some ships may be lost, never reduce the
building program, etc. The women, the girls,
you will find, etc. This is my list. It is complete.
Am I clear? Questions? Vargus? Wakeda? Are you here?

W. Aaron! What *is Our Mercury?* You make no sense.
Why? Where do you go? You stay here!

CANTO EIGHT

INTERLUDE: Aaron's Elegy

1   (*Aaron speaks throughout to Jurate.*)
i
A. Though your thighs are parted, the raising twist
of your lips consent. They receive an equal greeting.
I have remembered and remembered. Teach me

forgetting where the long limbs end.
Where we lay the lashing tongues
lick the wet root,

and a strong urge to forget
compliments the pleasure we desire.

ii
If we must have satisfactions in other worlds,
and not only a memory of dark matter,
let it be just one day of mastery,
desire's wish, lover's touch, child's trust.

And though already we gain and fall
from spells woven in other worlds,
we will sleep and eat in winters
more cunningly held in store.

Fix My Sleep at That Beam

2

(Testing the theory that time is altered when we move at the speed of light. The poet (Aaron) proposes an experiment where a camera fixes on a light beam moving at the speed of light, thus freezing lovers in static Erotic embrace. The lovers thereby escape the decay of Eros and death itself. Yet the poet is cautious; he has made allowance for the integrity of the human emotional element. Aaron is speaking.)

i
A. If two

arrest a path of light embalmed
my flash-encrusted breath – but fixed,
as captive play resides in camera,

then fix my sleep at that beam
all-speeding from glow emitting north,
my eye abreast a lover's shard of light.

There, delayed, with highest long-limbed rocketry,
preserve us fresh as child, still moist and humid
spouse. Our fevered bones releasing light:

our willing jointure braised a narrow optic sun,
where crimson-cheeked escapers sooth appeased
mortal-timed regression; two spheres of breath

scouting past uncharted black-holed death.

ii
Yet, if

annulled of human pulse, no single-singed,
no carbon stitch survive – then faithless the device,
no proof of human mass within,

then speak, returning shades stone-gray at dawn:
leaching blood, broad element of high embracers –
turn – your prints have left a trace.

Tell. If limbs of time and love hold hands;
if consciousness a condition and not a place:
if desire amends to lead – cry, cry, cry

where any brittle fraction part the lip, the valves
and sluices washed with spoil. I know, I know, I know.
Emotion spent, once dry of marrow,

no material photon of elemental stew,
no years retrieved from couple's wintered thaw,
no reproductive kiss escape

Eros' black-holed maw.

iii

So,

resolved, as saints, by lovers' fortunes' cast,

esoteric math retains no lovers' mass.
Science collide its lost photon; laughing poets
compress all kiss. New-prized inflection alters

ideation – as linguistic pulse – visual charged
ions double-loaded with component,
all thought extinguished: song, alone, cries

octaves outside of proofs. I learn. I learn. I learn.
Mnemonic, let desire a moment cup its life.
Let the learned poet delight the breath.

I strike.
My second sweat condense the juice loving bark,
my text of human warmth on ageing cheek;
my new-braise tongue all first tongues seek,

my song recovered ark my numbered kiss close-fit –
my moving hand on walls, my prophetic king,
my fire-blistered rune, now charred and altered,

now smoke and rising steam.

Attack Beyond Mars

3
i
When I find the living words, there will be
nothing left of a life you could recognize,
not by the measures of your youth and your
second youth. But your third will be hungry.

All that modern men can do is live as youth,
not once blessed with youth's fixed, proud piercing.
Every youth is lost and bartered for an insect's
chewing lodgment in the tongue. So its measure.

Escaping, to the stars, Jurate,
all our errors are described
with the same marvelous characters,
unaware of our days away from station.

We may not pass through the eye of the needle. But
if we attack beyond Mars, surely we should find
high idioms of our mind. If we can gain mastery
and still live, let us set this course. Our bounty
shall be all that we may imagine.

We set out with our souls newly opened, not only
for the stories and pictures of another star, but
with the hunger gained from so much forsaking.

We shall need the light of the moon
in our brains for this
and leaves of beaten gold in our heart.

ii
What did the young give us in our youth?
It is hard to recall their gifts.
What they give they keep and spend again. Shirts,
mother of pearl, confidences – our bodies,
the common market that we traded.

In our youth, we leave on boats for open seas;
older, we raise our heads,
passing under bridges that lead to other lives.

I became a prophet when I was killed in Kyoto.
What is Homo *Sapiens*? Eternal soldier. At war with time
to rage my sound. So many died when I sang.
I will never return to Earth. We still
have to find a way out of this Sun.

My mind is the only New World. Show me,
prefigured, my spider-stung scalar lattice.
Let me remember correctly the sound
of locust eating in my ears. Let me alter the genes
allowing us to swim in every gravity and sun.

iii
I called up to high towers.
I cried down from wind-blown, empty scaffolds.
I called out to men that build beams,
to the smelters at their forge.

They said from their shelters they were cold.
They had already entered below Earth.
They said they no longer had hearts of steel.
They said, shivering, they wished me well

on other worlds.

No! I cried a sudden arc.
I took a carbon shield,
I breathed an iron lung
above a dying sky.

By force of raging tears,
ten-fold moons I demon sank
on Europa's footless ice
to a shoeless ocean floor.

I did the hardest thing.
I carried fire to the ice.
I sparked with flints
the atom in my ark.

4

i

I know. You believe in the one great god. If you
find him, never tell me his name. But tell me
the intent of this god. If he has a language,
I prophesy he is a god of genealogy. If he has a song,
then I am sure there is a pattern of justice. For
what is music or gentle poetry – if not justice?
Since all you can make with language is a further
innovation, I know this god is *still* unformed.

Opposed. If they may never see their greatest hope,
let it be true what you say, a poet will show
us something fresh and new. If they fail, they are
paid in earth, rebated to every human antiquity
with freshly moistened mouths.

ii
Since I have everything known to tell, my poem
may prefigure an advanced form of mind. No hatred to the
enemy, no contempt for the victim. Do you remember
these syllables from your childish books? If my strange
and "other" rune sounds broad, or jars, my saint, you still
may make margin for this sound. If your heart is full,
you will hear the echo of the bell before it rings.

I remember,
in my first youth, only you had something
to give. Your form briefly followed
the linguistic pattern of desire. That is your strength
as a woman. In those days, you share the same space
as god. I remember how a god moves in his
garden at noon day. Again, a linguistic pattern of desire.
Yet if a poet ever finds his voice,
it is because nothing is left of his life
but gifts.

Who will measure the tension
weighted in the tool?
The few straight lines
made from the little teeth of the bit?
An eddy and a mesmera of discontents,
a moistened pressing from lips.

All you ever wanted was my story,
and, after, the small heat of my body.
Now that you have everything,
what is your report? If your heart is full,
it will contain cosmology. Assess the cast of bone.
When my boy's bones are lightened,
and you, and him, and misbelief increase,
I shall exist only as language in this dimension.

Draw near in the wind where I escape.

5

You want to renew your body? O high misbelief,
is that the only problem you have? How many
units of time shall I add to your biology?
How many years will you still keep hunger?
Could you ever say "enough – enough?"

O dying *sapiens*,
I hear you complain when you are hot or cold.
I see you grieve for want of amusement.
Could you ever say "enough – enough?"
Let me show you this cunning step.
Until we burst we have no voice.

You say that it lies with me to share with you
the inner mystery of knowledge? But you know
already. Every genre of tear and joy gives
information. Consider how sweet it is
that your greatest toil is to choose between
the information of science or poetry. You
will fail – since both are linguistic shards. Both
ruthlessly seek enchantment of bones. Every form
of speech contains fossil traces. A code is embedded.
Then what will you choose for your avocation?
After the trial of your own experience, what
is your report? There is a map of my mind.
Yes, I know. My death contains information.
Only later will the hidden scaffolding appear.

How should you interpret it
if I tell you secrecy is the most essential
quality of this mystery? Close counsel,
introspection, the word not said. Yes,
there is a time for silence. Silence is large.

I've addressed these issues,
wondering at the same time
how to interpret their significance
in both our lives. Yes,

you must live on without me.
But I shall give you a greater child.

This child will have a bloodline of high stars.
Protect this code. No man can
over-teem his blood.

If you fail,
then try to retrace your steps.

6

i

If now no music down wires,
make a builder's face
that has no house to keep a count of sandbox loss,
no short-haired eyes to see our store-bought hate,

all for the sake of one word behind firewalls,
not studded, not set in stones,
no twist or gleam in idea kingdoms,
an essential ore untouched, full powered; yet

by the same cunning they reach to unseen things,
I have the craft of gods to ring through us
ringing out in them.
I am the water carrier. Seven waves
of being enter the egg. I, as eighth ancestor, make
the observation that forms the universe you name.

There is no more complexity to the work of a god.

ii

For the poet there is always the same difficulty:

to which woman shall we carry the news,
summing in a sentence the constellation
now arrived? Does she have god's secret –
that there was just one thing worth having?

O Gilgamesh, Jason, Moses, David, Jesse,
for a thousand years you sought magic,
the jewels of our head,
the sudden smile of poems –

no eyes upon all losses.

iii

No poet should survive the last insight
of his long poem. If he survives,
then something has gone wrong.

Everything I have to say is still unfinished.

I am racing ahead of god's arms
unless he lay over me.

7

i

You ask me to recognize that there has always been
a goal to your investigations. I acknowledge this.
I believe I have shared with you the same quest
and the same ambition. Yet all you can use of life
is pleasure? Caution. Another man, a-hungered
would take its crown.

In the last sentence of your letter,
you despair of a solution to your inquiry. You feared
that I would reject you for your small age? Child,
do you so little know men? I think not. Then
what would you make of my uncanny answer?

You regret the loss of faith for the great Yahweh
of your youth – did you think it was something so small
that it could be lost in Jerusalem? Yet what if he was still
so small that he was ashamed to show himself?
                                        Yes, I am certain
there is a star close to you. You both move in the same
spaces. Yet if god appeared to you now, all he
would give you is a rune. And you would forget.

He would only tell you that his heart – though full –
is still unfinished – and that explains
an ancient absence.

Of his sound,
you would only make on knees
a chiseled-syllable tablet of words.
A gold lettered script set in a gold wheel chair.
And then you would forget.

So what is god then? A poet's text.
What then is the value of enchantment?

A device of god.

ii
It may be that you have fallen among thieves
and someone wise has kept your faith safe for you.

Maybe it was always too large for this little voice
you could just now this moment bear up on hands.

I can tell you he will claim you for his pleasure
where you have hidden your wetness.

We should step into the night sky signaling faith
till we fall upon it again
where the gods have kept it for us.

Until then, learn selection with your sentience.
The only language gods hear is singular.
Is your heart full? It is a single shout,
a single cry.

Even if for three lives
you play on terra cotta instruments,
by the fourth,
you will be the priestess of their cult.

If you have been certain once and had to give up
your certainty, inwardly, let this be your sign.

We all shall be pieced together as broken chants.
Serve me until I release you.

In return, I give you the secret of my genome.
It is the tar cave of our sound.
It is the my atom is ark.

8

i

Already, what you have admitted is much.

I share

your confession. It is not salvation you ask for; it is
more space and personality.
You are honest to admit this.

If once,
you had to choose between god and life,
what final choice would you make? Yes, I know your
answer. You would choose life every time.
This discovery now surprises you? Yes, I see it.
What does this tell you about gods? Therefore,
show caution with your idol. Yet the goal
you have set for yourself is attainable.

These are heavy burdens,
knowing at the same time
no greater work has been within our reach.

Through a labor of dreams,
I seek a more lasting accomplishment.

ii

Insofar as you can,
do not replace your youth with middle-age.
Surely, that's another youth.

Hold yourself ready for the moment beyond which
your thoughts and your desires must be confined to
secret communications. In the hour of betrayal,
you will recognize it, and it will be everything to you.

In the years that ripen the sparrow and the hawk,
let them be the elephant's memory of your heart.

Tell our son the things I did.
No information is lost in the Black Hole.
And since sentience is still unfinished,
I know

my human spleen is still not empty.

9

i

If you were hungry in those days, you will hear shouts.
This was the roof of the mouth before another day,
and when this shout is lost, we must all build camps
to hoard a more hungry hour.

Call down to the clenched teeth
that await our fall
how without hope we must raise a yell,
lift all blocks to shouting, already stone
with our own pity, shame, or terror,

how with a pauper's purse of cotton lint,
a hair shave of old memory,
we stumble, lift, or carry
to the world's edge

our own red sun rising.

ii

You will hear many things of my last days.
Many wise men will bewail the loss of Earth.
These are the speeches of backward-looking men.
I had to find a new speech for a new form of life.
I had to position the human mind again on the
astral plane. The Earth blocked this message.
The mind is an astral coordinate – not terrestrial.
I took away your planet – and then your bones.
A space fairing voice of altered new string. This
new human will make beautiful new machines.
Yet, at first, it will sting. It will offend.

Till then, let only fools and children speak;
Terry will tell you what truth looks like
when you least know what is true.
He has still a trial to make of life.
Let my son learn to love him.
Wakeda will protect you until the child
comes into his voice.

Teach him my book. It is all I have as gift.
It is an eddy of discontents.

Cross out all the rage you find.

FINAL INCANTATION

10

i

If our lives are reversed, let it also
be an exchange of vitalities. Sleep.

"If by some cunning I have thrown my clay
self-made by one degree of separation,
myself once for all time find and place,

this same voice my own still ours by such need
for want in us to know the nail god keeps
so by a stranger's reach and word our script

our form by threads just once
god's eyes and face."

ii

Now wake.
When my incantations are deconstructed
the sky will fall. Your bone will be lighter then.
In those days, it will be clear who I was.

Until then, continue to mistake the end of the world.
Until then, I consent where stars consent,
nothing lost along the path
where we listen, trust, and talk;
repeat the charm prepared against this hour,

leave the ground transformed where I walk.

iii
In the triple world, we meet and converge,
whether we know or do not know,
whether we are willing or do not will,
once touched and once gathered, always flood.

We need no single terrestrial element.
Where a man wanders with his star,
he forms aloft his tent,
his astral mind, he terraforms
all beggarly, hungry, parched spacescape.

If your heart is full – enter.
I make the same protocol.
I enter the consciousness I have prefigured –

naked, except for desire,
and a little purse
of images.

CANTO NINE

Leave Behind All Moisture

1
i   *(Music sounds. Aaron speaks in his dream.)*
A. What were the voices?
What were the voices I heard singing?
Just now. There. I hear you!
I marvel at the sound.

(Voice of black men.)
"We were the men that lived in Africa. We are
the black-headed ones. Workers the gods made."

A. Who are you? How did you come to this place?

"I am of the Dogon people. I was in Egypt.
We are the first men that spoke to alien races.
We are the first that learned the star cosmologies.
We are the first that met the eight ancestor gods.
We have kept the star lists. You are foreign to Earth.
Your DNA is a new alien race. The Earth is brown."

A. How are white men different than you?
A color of skin does not subtract virtue.
We fought wars over this controversy.

"You spoke a more ancient tongue. Your mind has
no Earth-fossil. You were sent from the rebel
clans of the Dog Star. You encode a new structure.
Akhenaten was alien ancestor. You have the same face.
I saw his face. A horror! Gone now, they are mixed with us.
You expelled us from Egypt. Then you built monuments
of your power using new magic. *Baalbek, Giza, Rome.* Now
angered and raging, your kind came to destroy the Earth –
with your all-hating mitochondria. I followed the killers until
the road narrows and ends. There, I found your kind."

A. Then you have seen legions. No. No! This is insipid talk.
I oppose you. I have read your code.
I expel you again.

ii
"You have an advanced cancer.
You have not asked its name?"

A. No. If I accept its name, I accept its logic.

"This is wise, alien. *Kosmoautikon*,
you did not learn this from men.
How shall you meet this challenge?"

A. Clear. This is human. When did the King of Jews
ask the name of an affliction? Not once.
These events all have the same meaning.

"Jesse? Human? What part? Tell me?
You know, of course, the origin of this trial?"

A. Yes. I explore a hypothesis. You prefigure my death.
But I refuse the ark of human logic.
In my astral mind is ark.

"Is it still within your power? Your response?"

A. I claim my own pattern of mind. The ark
you attempt to place in my mind – would kill me.

"Good, *Gilgamesh*. Alien scythe! Rise.
You may join the fraternity of gods."

    (*Aaron awakes in sweat. Speaks aloud.*)

A. In my journal, I have marked before
how the dreams of men contain equal parts
past and future acts. And so, oddities combine.
Yet now I repeat my own repetitions. I am mad?
Do the waters shake in Bethesda pool?!
Where are the friends to carry me down?

There are no more futures to my misprision.
All my futures then are present
and all foresight narrowed to a point.
I write my last page.

An uneven excellence of prefigure.

The Same Voice Returns Again

2 *(Again, Aaron sleeps. Black voices speak.)*
"Like all the men here, we were murdered. You know
us and you hated us. You chased us out of the Nile valley.
We pleasured the light-skinned Pharaohs on our knees.
You can still see the colored papyruses. You are the executioner.
You were sent. We can see the sign above your head.
You had a choice. It was the voice you heard."

A. *As a dream – there is no sense. You come now to accuse me?*

"There is a clear message. I come to release you."

A. *Release me from what?*

"From guilt in this dimension, from the misprision
of your consciousness. The astral mind contains a string
to charismatic bias. If you release it, you can be free.
Can we even speak? I am not sure.
Who has taught you these secrets, my saint?
A man occurs from nothing we can verify.
Only a sound of bias. The universe is to a man
as a shout that goes up. Immediately, as an insect lights
from my arm, you make a selection. (*Insect burrows out of his skin.*)
The visible spectrum was not contained –
before – in anything – except the sound you make.
You are a creation entirely contained in your own mind.
Did you suspect? All other men – all worlds, all passions,
all sorrows – are only a construct of your mind."

A. Suspect what? What is your identity? You
are a god then? Outside of consciousness?

"Fool! When has there ever been a black god?!
Show me one *thing* outside of consciousness!
Fool. You brought all this with your mind!
You are a condition in consciousness – not a *thing*."

A. All players, all acts, contained my own rehearsal?
Each act of life – exclusive to my self-reference?

"Your cosmology is biased – thus formed for *you* alone.
Your language has become a self-genetics – entire."

A. I do not understand. This is a great discovery - then?
Repeat. You make no sense.

3
"Again. The human mystery is like a man
that is sent to kill. You are an assassin.
It may be Earth, or it may be not Earth.
It may be a planet, a comet – a broken shard of ice.
It may be a spool of thread you lost. You don't know the man
you are to kill. You don't know the time you must kill.
And in that hologram you made from words,
it is certain that you find the world *you seem* to move in.
You will shiver in recognition. The world you *experience*
is a codex. A mirage of value. There are no separate actors.
Your soul is invisible to you, since *all* souls are only
shards of your *single* entity. To *kill* was always,
from the beginning, your *world soul*, and the world entire
made for your day of killing. Each person, each event - text.
You may think that you chose the place to kill, the person
to kill, or the time to kill. *All of life* is only your mind. As if,
the entire universe you found in a bottle. Again, it is your mind.
Strangers, events, are only elements of a world self-made
for your own reference. It is only a photon collapsing
on your choice – your codex – of sentience.
You found death in bottle. You found it in a photo.
You found it on a rusted metal sign in that country,
that you must hunt and kill tattooed bones. The bones
were waiting for you. And if you manage to kill,
you prove – there is no love – there is no hate.
There is only a focus of bias in consciousness.
Do you understand the message?"

A. What message? Your information is degraded.
It is late. I must sleep. Who sent you? Terry?
Are you Terry's other component? I will deny you!

"Exactly! Only *you* can say no. That is a god!
You prove in one breath my entire message.
No other creature can make the sign – *yes or no.*
All other players must follow the pattern you
choose. All others are mimes. This is a world
made by your *mind* – to fit the conditions of your *mind*."

A. I do not understand. You make no sense. What do you want?

4
"Again . . . the human is like a angel made
to explore the emotion of love – like fitting a shoe.
You don't know where you are to love;
It may be Earth, or it may be not Earth.
It may be on a comet, or on a broken shard of ice.
It may be a spool of thread you have lost.
You don't know whom you are to love.
You don't know the time you must love.
You may find it on a head of hair,
or on a rusted sign to that country,
there, you certainly find the person you must love.
When you locate this love, and name it,
you must lose it straight away. Then you learn
precisely the bias contained in love. Its gravity
is only a bias. Nothing else is there. Not love, not loss.
You feel pain – yet you have lost nothing separate
from yourself. Every lover you meet – yourself.
Every lover you lose –yourself. Your recovery –
yourself. It will try to kill you every time.
You may think that you chose the place to love,
the person to love, or the time to love. But
to you, these things were not there before –
not before the bias of your linguistic pulse. A codex.
Thus – *do you catch it yet?* – the universe
does not exist until you form it. *Say it once!*
Is it actually there? Is there a distinction
between sound – or the sight of the sound?
Speak. Your race is Kosmoautikon!
Only death can set you in motion."
    (Aaron cries out, still asleep.)
A. *This word again! I do not know . . . !*
The answer is no, there is no universe until
I name it. Every snowflake is already placed in my mind.
I know this already. All that was meant for me
is to make selection. What is your intent?
I do not understand. It is late. You are an agent
of my own dissolution? Myself, I accuse then?
I have summoned you, then – by your explanations?

    (Apparition suddenly cuts its own neck. Aaron, screams.)
A. *Wakeda!*

5   *(Aaron, startled at the blood, recoils in sleep.)*
"Look at me, *Kosmoautikon*! Alien to Earth!
Alien to brown-skinned Earth! This is all
I ever learned from you – death! Now, I always
show the same face. Your life, a bias. Your
long sought death, a bias. If you die now,
will it contain information? What information will
you construct with death? All gods are contained
in the sound of this bias. Can you read signs?"

A. I cannot read signs. I know nothing!
Leave me in peace. Who are you? You bleed!
How am I tested? How is it that you still can speak?

"I am the first Homo sapiens. I see they are dead.
None of the men in your ships are like us. Why?
If you know what happened to my daughters,
I would be silent. I would listen."

A. No. I do not know your family! I did not kill them!
What happened to you? I see you are deformed.

"No they are here now – with you.
I hear them talking now. Look. Here. *(Pointing)*
I am not deformed – we are the black-footed ones,
made by the gods to dig in the mines.
Now you have killed us all. When you speak, you kill.
Now . . . I will show you your death."

A. No! I don't know your family.
I did not kill them. Do not show me my death!
I will not be killed by slaves! I deny you.

"Good, you have learned to say it. What does the
truth feel like? Yet you so easily have killed us.
Release your codex! After the manner of gods,
I must kill you now. Open yourself,
promiscuous for transformation."

(Other voices.) "Cut him now!"

   (Aaron fully awakes in sweat.)
A. Merde! My own language accuses me!
Why do I accuse myself with slaves?
I did not make them! We freed them . . . surely?
Yet – with sudden emotion – I am light in my heart.
I trace the fossil of my spleen! In my atom is ark!

Ahead of Heavy Frosts

6 (*Finally awake, Aaron begins feverishly to scratch a final poem.*)

From the two bellies of the whale, from
lines on salted crusts the skins I took,
saw already the towers I could build.

Raised up two faces and a steam on glass,
two tilted panes on jests of borrowed blood,
watchers on beekeeper towers saw signs

on the first day of trips, on every journey made,
lumbering winter nights the road through guts,
the heavy wheels that smooth the paving stones,

carefully cut a coat to fit the blanket of my crib,
stiffened my body some to take its weight.
For wishes lost,

my door made thinner by a door,
for lovers won on sleeping beds,
my gate lengthened by a gate,

who come and go till gladder hands release
a lightness touching lids on painted brows
fixed on brief intents planted stolen glances,

by the ease of loving that we choose this love,
trails of losses tracing prints to each a god
ahead of heavy frosts reaching up to eyes.

   (*Scratching stops.*)

7   (*Next day, speaking to Wakeda. Aaron visibly weak and tired.*)
i
A. I am tired of problems. I want to be a boy again.
I agreed that there be a committee of *high morals.*
In committee, their only conclusion was: there must be another
committee – of *low morals. I turn away from rationalists.*
Another committee meets today to decide the future of algae,
moss, and yellow flowers. Another meeting is planned for the worms
moving through organic dirt. I lose interest. How can I survive an
assemblage of slow drips? And they hope to love with competence?

ii   (*Enter Terry as pretend cook. Aaron, smiling, speaks to him.*)
A. Love is a condition – not a thing, Terry. Love is blurred
to the sight of eyes. And our eyes see only ourselves as youth.
Love forms as a question – we fit the answer patterned to our need.
Love, then, is an answer to loss of courage, as scratching to itches.

T. Yes, Love *is* scratchy! Certain, it is wet. It is mossy. As a rag is mossy.
     (*Pausing to consider the boy's speech, Aaron continues.*)
A. Men seek language that will answer their need,
provide their need, solve harms embedded in their need.
Eros, as hate, is observation of *other.* We make a severe
selection of life – idiom, child, death, spouse – yet Eros, naked,
is an urge to youth. Till the aged, insulted with this *text,* cannot love.

T. I know many I would scratch out. That big lady, for example.
I see that love makes hate . . . So do we hate also little fish?

A. No! I speak of love – as the language-makers know love.

T. And they are all wet? I prefer the dry terrestrial land of gods!

A. Terry, what are you *saying?* What do you know of love?
Who let you out of your room? Sleep, now, child.

T. I made love to the fishwife! I smoked her with my tongue.

A. Out!
     (*Sudden tears.*)
T. But I came to save you! Leave now, father! Please!
     (*Antebbe hisses and cuts his ear. Terry cowers and runs.*)
A large eccentric lady has mitered me! I am crowned!

Carried To The Waters of Bethesda

8 (*Final scene with Antebbe.*)
ANT. What is this? It moves on the wall.
   (*Aaron replies.*)
A. That is moist blood. You cut him. No! Look! It is a
hand that writes. I see letters appear. . .
The walls are wet with drops. I read . . .
   (*Amazed at wetness, Antebbe rejoins.*)
ANT. I see *wet* then. How strange is *wet* rune.

A. Yes. I see now. When you pass, the moisture
suddenly dries as spit on a fire.
What does it mean? What is the source of this physics?

ANT. Physics? *Physics?* What is physics, Cheda?
   (*Cheda follows her holding a hose emitting a*
   steam wherein the form of the specter appears.)
ANT. Are tears physics? No, tears cancel physics.
See, it dries. Observe. I make an alternate claim
of physics. There is nothing more terrible than *wet*.
I must take some thought to learn it. *Wet!*
   (*A sentence forms on the wet wall.*)
What is the word that is written? Read!
"Seize . . . the Space-port."

ANT. We come. We come. Enough!
Let me now watch your . . .
Now listen to my words, Aaron. Follow my hand.
Just here. Again here. (*Pointing*)

A. Watch? Watch my . . .? Watch? Wa. . . .

ANT. Stand back!
He loses his voice. The blood empties from his eyes.
If you still can brother?. . . Again, here.
Yes, look here. See? Follow the vision.
A light appears on your eyes.
Tell me what you see? Here . Just here.
O Aaron, why are your eyes now wet?

We will carry you to the stirring waters.

9

ANT. Aaron. Sleep. Do not speak.
Silence is large. Take silence with both hands.
You repeat again. Find new sentence.
You said everything you have come to say!
You are only stumbling. Jump to new structure.
You have nothing else to say? Then sleep.
      (*Aaron, disoriented, unable to rise to his feet.*)
A. But . . . how can I sleep? My heart is full.

ANT. Silence is large. Grasp the device of silence.
Accept the front stepping opiate. Turn away.

A. Yet I have a sudden fear. I resist . . . Something . . .
Something moves towards me.

ANT. Follow the object. You will see. You can accept it.
There is no other way. . . Enter composed.
You have learned this language. Enter composed.
Now turn away. Watch what I show you.

A. I can't. My heart double beats.
Who will write my text?

ANT. You have already made margin and text . . .
Let the poets find you. Your voice wins eternal youth.
No man may ever erase your soul.
Your voice already is swimming.

A. I cannot . . . speak. I am drained of . . .

ANT. Now turn away.
This way. Just here. Turn away.
O salt boy . . . Now. Go down to the ocean.
There. (*Antebbe touches him for the first time.*)
Receive gently . . . the front stepping opiate.

10

i

A. I cannot . . . can . . . not . . . see. But there! I see it.
I know this thing I see. I know it. What maw
reversing pulse? It moves, expanding. Flashing . . . white,
blue, black, red pulsed dimension! A twisted hair-lined surface!
A single strand pulled from within, along
its length – back on itself. I am slicing – yet whole.

ANT. You are wet . . . so violent wet, child. Let me catch you.
Yet . . .yet? . . .yet? . . . You cannot speak? No more speech?
     (*Faintly*)
A. No. No. I am . . . *shriv* . . . in this form.

ANT. Yes. Leave your body here, child. Sleep. Now, Talon!
Step out of your mask. Cut him. Cut him! (Antebbe *screams.*) Aahhh!!
     (*Talon appears behind a mask of Wakeda*
     and cuts Aaron deeply. His body drops.)
Blood on the walls! Show the *Kosmoautikon* of Anu!
Go out this way, my spouse, my brother. Come.

ii   *(Antebbe backs away slowly, crying in orgasmic awe.)*
ANT. Aahhh! Aahhh! Aahhh! It was performed well!
(Long pause, Antebbe looks around slowly.) You! Seize the ship.
I must look one last time . . . at this strange world.
The walls have drops of illness. Slaves. Gourmands.
There is an illness here of grinding stomachs. It has no charm.
It is horrible. Show me one of these I should keep?
I look. You? You? Dark electrons. Who are these
lumps of bones? *Sapiens*? *(Hisses)* What do *you* look at *slave*?
Kill these black dogs. Talon, bring the ship.
I let you keep your trinkets. Fool! Spread his blood and spleen
on walls. Bandage him in sheets. Show his dead body
to the crews. Let blood drip from the doors.

Talon. Look! He still breaths!

ANT. A second voice! Yes, he has the mind of . . .! Let him speak to his wife.
No, do not kill her. She will stab at you. She is mine!
She has no fear! Show them your terrible weapon. Take the ark!

Talon. But they need this ship! Cheda, tell her.

ANT. Silence! *(To Jurate.)* A single moment, wife! Then,
place him in the round ark. Bring my tools of life!
No more sound. No more dry. Cheda – *you know what to do.*
Let me look at this . . . human . . . horror . . . dimension
– last *time*! Last *horror*! *(Form of Antebbe disappears.)*

CANTO TEN

Silence! Bring Me the Tools of Life!

1 (*Blinded, Aaron whispers final words to his wife. Lips never move.*)
A. As I step into my sound, I find myself intact.
Recognized. I accept the prefigured rune.
My heart is still full. In my atom is ark.
I seize motion across conception.
I see that every death is a prayer,
in case the door is closed . . . to my falling house.
How could I sing if I could not fall? When has
there once been perfect communication ear to ear?
What is justice – but a pattern we accept?

My arc follows a path of justice; it is not even,
yet it is deeply etched . . . I see it there . . . as twin.
It is not human margined. I see a twin . . .
The bias placed in choice finds patterns,
my mitochondria is twinned with pattern,
and what is pattern but a coupled symbol,
and what is symbol but a movable math,
and what is math but a secret language,
and what is language except a figure I distinguish
of justice? What is justice except a model I accept –
or each kiss of love? Except a prefigure of loss?
So I find perpetuity in loss and forms exchange.
My form is the intention I make. I follow the path
of this intention. Look! The seams of this house
are so slanted – nothing else in this element escapes.

And my life, my force, as sure as any instrument,
soon a worn and winding road – I see it there!
A trail. Press down the dust of trails. . .
. . . a weightless twist of twine.

There. . . Jurate! Look! I make large dimension.
. . . I see my sound still intact . . . as luminescence,
nor any slight dismemberment
of my echoing rune . . . .

(*Aaron's corpse turns into a mummy of uncanny antiquity.
Jurate suddenly hisses and strikes anyone that approaches.*)

2

i　　(*Vargus, before, cowering – suddenly speaks.*)
Vargus. He is gone! His blood, his breath – stops.
Wakeda, freeze the robotic arms!
Talon escapes with our ships.
No! He takes just one ship. Look.
All our locks are sealed!
Talon has changed our codes!

ii　　(*In another ship, Antebbe speaks to Talon. Aaron's dogs barking.*)

ANT. Silence the teeth! What are these monsters?
Fools! Silence! Get these barking slaves out of my sight!
Bring me the tools of life.
Let me touch his mouth!

Talon. He does not respond.
I have cut him too deep!

ANT. Silence! Rule the horror of eyes!
Watch you mind! It is the eyes that make you a slave.
Why did my father select you for our kind?

T. Because I saved his life in Nippur!
I am the maker. I keep the forge and bellows.

ANT. Silence! Fool! He should have killed you!
You are deformed! Igigi scum!
Sapiens . . . must die!

T. But I am not . . .!

(*She swings at him. She hisses. Talon cowers.*)

Some Girls Refuse to Mate

3

Slavic girl. Do not leer at us. Stay away from us. Die.
No, I don't like. Go, leave . . .go die some place.
It is forbidden to speak. Don't look at us.
Where are your masters? Do not touch!
Ukrainians do not touch. You are disgusting.

Crew member. So how do we know you – if we cannot talk?
Are there better men? We are the best.
We are pilots.

Sg. Pilots of what? Tubs? And your manners? Clean your lips.
Have you seen how the master makes his dress?
What is wrong with *these guys*? Cut your hair!
Bring us crackers of paradise!
What are these shoes you wear?
    (*First crewmember, disgusted.*)
Cm1. Ok. Ok then. Today, there is more arriving.
I want to see what comes next through that door.
How to even make a choice?
Let the Chiefs take these . . . cunts.
Bitches!
    (*Second crew member, interjects.*)
Cm2. What? Are you too refined for us then? *Cunts.*
We'll wait for the others. (*Aside*) Did you see *those two*
in the theater?! Can you believe that? Where did that
come from? So young . . . so still . . . unformed.

(*To each other.*) We shall wait then.
What are these crackers of paradise?
Where do we find this food?
What's wrong with our shoes?
What is that? Listen! What is that screaming?
    (*Officer enters breathless.*)
Talon has killed the Admiral.
He escaped with the new ship!

Vargus Gathers the Females in Lithuania

4

i   (*A memo from Vargus found on Aaron's desk. Vargus speaking.*)
We took the list you sent us. Such strange names.
Imastu. Klaipeda. Antoshka. Grasi. These
were the orphanages we found with difficulty.
They remembered you. We collected the girls.

We read the names. The girls came forward,
tentative – yet expectant. They were prepared.
Each with a little bag. What did they have
in their minds? My skin was black as night.

Each had a gold wire around their neck.
It was sign you placed on each child.
Some cried. I remember, they wore outsized
white ribbons. They held little travel bags.

The bags had a logo from a long-defunct airline.

I never saw the eyes turn down from snow,
from low small breasted mountains to a
stranger's face – what smoke I made at the mouth:
sirens all broken empire's hear.

The women you paid to teach English did well.
We spoke hurriedly to some of them. Others begged
us to take them too. But I had no places in the ships.
They offered me every form of nature. I ate deeply.

It was three years since you were there. Then

three years till they reached the rings of Jupiter.
All at school with English. Math. Astrology.
What was your advice in this work?
It is eccentric. What is your secret plan?

I hope you know what you do.
All so young. So . . .

5

i

Others begged us to take them. Women came
forward from the towns. I talked to them.
I told them things they never heard before.
I had to explain, no, the other American's were

not so black. This was their chief concern.

I told my story, the list of my ancestors,
omitting no adornment and some shame,
the day I must leave and the name of my home
unpronounced to their ears but catching at my

words their whole wish. "*I go to great Cyclops.*"

And it was enough for their heart's poverty,
enough for a mother who bartered a long-held
virginity, stowage for every maiden
voyage and promised me to treasure it,

turning forever their daughters small feet
down to my ship

and sudden loss at sea.

Put away your gods for a time, all your
long held virginities, and ride a cunning
tongue so many roads up and down in me,
one day new marriage beds,
some lost at sea.

ii

Are these the ones I brought?
They are so . . . so . . . mature. Tall.
More than I remembered.
What did you do with these girls?

A Voice from Imastu Orphanage

6   (*A voice appears. The dead director of the orphanage.*)
I know you, Admiral. You look the same still.
Your ships came east in the first war. Such slaughter!
We heard from Tallinn your helicopters arrive.
I feared for the older girls. I was the House Director.

The boys ran to your machines. They wanted
then to be American pilots – like in the films.
I was the only one that spoke your language.
I screamed. You touched my neck. I remember this.

You said you would adopt some of these girls. So many?
I was ashamed at your purpose. I though the worst.
Yet, how could I know you were not like the others?
They were so young. Far too young.

You placed your hand over the heads of each child.
"This one," you said. Then again, "This one."
How deep were the soundings you took? Why such care?
Surely you could have taken flesh from any nation?

No. You had a far-learned plan. For a thousand
eons your people worked this precision of gene.
Your gods concealed us behind the Iron Curtain.
Stalin, you said, was of your alien breed. You said their
genes had to be perfected for your service. Why?

You gave each elected child a gold necklace.
Later, the dishonest tried to touch it, but it burnt
their hands. How did you perform that magic?
You gave me gold to be sure of me. I was faithful.

We were so poor. You said another would come
to take the girls when the time was perfected.
None of us thought you would ever come back.
It was a horrible war. The Russians came – again. The boys died.

One day a man named Vargus arrived. Why so black?
He had the keys to each of the bracelets. His men
placed a plastic band on the wrist of each girl. Before
the bombs fell, they entered your machines.

What deep, far-range cunning you have!
Let me see them now. I know what you did.
I know what you placed in their bodies!

Can the Truth Be So Hard to Speak?

7

i   *(A loose manuscript left on Aaron's desk – marked "FIRST DRAFT.")*
The Earth is a nursery planet. Fixed in
consciousness. A soft fish mouth where it is wet,
curved entering below the curled bone.
Is there more to human than youth?

I passed the fields of grazing animals.
They did not look. They did not answer me.
They could not help my sentient condition.
I asked, *What is the use of Earth?*

I passed by the Churches where the people sleep.
They did not look. They did not answer me.
They never used the magic in their texts. Not once.
I asked, *What is the use of Earth?* It is a Dark Age.

I saw an old man's shoe. It had no value.
I saw the old men as they fell into their graves.
No one cried. No one kept their far-learned scripts.
Only the young, outside, chanting, could sing.

And the young said, "If by some evil we die,
and we might rise again, we would only move
again to fornicate, to place our tongues
up each the other's alimentary fold." *(Line scratched out in manuscript.)*

They would not ask for the new poems of men
written since their demise. And then I knew –
despite the picture of the pale-skinned girl
pouring fresh white milk from the jug
in window sunlight.

I knew then. Sapiens must die.

I passed by the cities of men.
They did not look to see me;
they could not answer me.
They had no power in lost rituals.

What is the use of more men? Each Galaxy
contains a protected nursery planet.
Earth is the smallest of these hidden planets.
A soft fish mouth where it is wet,

curved, entering below the curled bone.

ii
I walked past the machines.
They did not move unless I first moved a lever.
What is the use of more machines?

So I called out to the gods passing
from the waters to the stars: "This race was
mute, their cries are mute. They self-lick."

"*Kill them all*," the passing gods replied.
"*Erase them – they are made by increase.*"
"*Release the methane beneath the seas.*"

"Give us new minds of our likeness
and new codes before they defame
the quantity of our first measure."
Can truth be so hard to speak?

Homo sapiens must die.
Slay the schooling fish of Pisces.
Observe rising now the Water Carrier!

Anu heard my summons.
By Anu's word was I sent.
I made an image of Anu in my heart.

Where a Tailor Made a Seam

8

i   (*Jurate recites on old poem, refusing to leave the body of Aaron.*)
"A thousand years of you might be easy
and a great work, but by then we would see
with God's eyes, hair, skin, teeth run along a
line, stuck with lint – no more conjure sap

past the stitch to my head, wave me on;
my spice empire may not always rise on
your breath and my only crown my body
templed with your hands, two last thin priests

crying warmth over a cold black pearl
in a bed of sleep without space enough or time;
my wish no body of heat but by some other
priest his book more space and time,

where the soul becomes a point
and works itself."

ii
"But lighter brides, who take this church, clasp these
hands, sweet and foul so nearly placed, both an
hour priestly blind – till one, the gates,
valves, sluices, stand up dry, exposed,

stuck in its rant. Send out code from my bone,
hammer and anvil, though there is no space,
no peace, no mercy, this faith is still good;
crown my finger with your taste, make it run

where a tailor made a seam. Then if you
carry war to the China Sea, I can still hold
your guns, keep the wheel in your terrible
ship, take all your good with all your sin,

where love becomes a point
and proves itself."

To the Senate *(Aaron's Last Testament sent to Earth)*

9

i

Words and letters have no treasure – lovers
judge their touch and kiss alone are rich. All
things that lovers take in lover's eyes are rare;
they esteem the articles of civil deeds.

We are not strangers of other time,
of questions posed and put aside;
we gather what we own from other days,
the trial and body of our wish.

If the human dead were collected, what feast would they
summon? To enter red-cheeked, juice imbibing,
the carnal act? A soft fish mouth where it is wet,
curved entering below the curled bone.

Therefore, I sentence Earth to irrelevance.
Myself, am sentenced as proof, parallel to your fate.

I know I have not the weight I wish to carry,
nothing I have now I will have long,
what I got or summoned with a penny play,
what I touched or tasted to my eye.

Large, our work is done and already paid;
we reckoned all our loves on minor lists,
they held our bones but never looked,
they closed the flesh that fell away.

It's not their worth how they are rich,
they are wise who have no words that
lovers judge that every word is rich
that falls and sits silent on lover's lips.

ii
O my new-made saints,
when the sun hits your eyes through your window,
you will still see the Venus star emitting Eros
near its conjunction with distant Earth -
now a frozen moon on your fiery skin.

No, I do not know
how long we will still be nomads.
Learn to die well – that is a great victory.

The Tablet of Destinies...Commences

10

i   (*Jurate rises with blood on her dress.*)

Jurate. This is not . . . *Over*! (*Stomping.*) Fools! You witness nothing!
Wakeda! Look at me! He is gone. Gone. (*Marks him with blood.*)
I have to trust you! Change the codes of his ship.
Let no outside eye enter his ship. Look! Their eyes
already turn to his hatch! (*Shaking him.*) I am talking to *you*!
You recall my husband's last command to you?
You gave your promise to protect his line!

Wakeda. His line? His . . ? And so? Did I see this . . . this madness?
Why? Are you in danger?

J. Yes! We have only minutes. Bring the Senator to me.

W. Hussein? That thing . . . *Antebbe* . . . killed him.

J. That is what you know. He has new prosthetics.
Hussein is in cell 54. We saved his life.
Aaron sewed back his limbs.

W. How do you know this?

J. Fool! Learn this – once *for all time* . . . I know everything!
How do I know to carry the child of a god?

W. A god? A fool? Yes, a fool . . . and you?
. . . More gods? No . . . I see. You are a child.
You are in shock. You are only . . . sad . . .

ii

J. Silence! Bring me Hussein. I give you the 95 secrets. Only. . . we
must keep the codes of the Megaclites. This is our security.
There are *Tablets of Destinies*. You know *nothing* of *these*.
We must give Hussein what he proposes. Enough rope.
There is a . . . a *supremacy*. The Demos is my danger.
It needs to kill . . . us. I allow his Demos once . . .
then never again. It must lose all its promise. I – you and I –
will help him to restore the Demos. Also . . . I will need
the royalty of . . . three ships. He cannot bargain from his
position. We must remain separate . . .with Megaclites.

W. You will allow? Royalty? . . .of ships? Who are *you*?
Your voice is different. How do you change your voice?
You are a little mad? I can't think. The Demos in power?
By a fool? You cut him up and then sew him
together *again*? Aaron told us . . .told me . . .
democracy would lead to extinction and wars. . . again.
Democracy. . . to reverse his work? Are you mad?
What next statement follows? You are in distress. I do nothing.

J. You did not open your body! You did not mix blood
with Aaron. I have knowledge of blood destinies.
Of maps . . . without end! Do you wish that Vargus
were now our ruler? You want Vargus to take charge
of our *genetics*?

(*A pause.*) Ah, yes . . .there it is . . .
I see it turns in you. The stink of revulsion! The *core genome*!
Trust me. We need time and peace. Let them have what
they *think* they want – so we can destroy both in one action!
This child is the only ruler of Galaxy.

W. Ruler of Galaxy. . .? But . . .it's a child! No . . .
it's not even a child. . . yet! Let me take you to see the . . .

J. He is part god, part Murmer. I am a Murmer.
Bring me Hussein. Stay close to me.
Bring your wife. Serve me.
She already serves me. She also is a. . . !
(*Touching herself.*) Protect the right of this *Kosmoautikon*
in my body!

W. Kosmoautikon? Who are *you*!? That voice . . .?

[*There begins a solemn funeral procession as the mummy is ritually moved to the new Galaxy ship. Music instruments from the Sirius constellation, never before heard by human ears, sounds, freezing all humans in a trance.*

Final scene. Two ships slowly part. One, Aaron's laboratory ship, now full of moving dirt, descends towards Europa. A second ship, massive, moves away from Callisto to the outer galaxies.

The remaining sapiens are left in several ships. Riots begin].